HAPPY FOR THE CHILD

Happy for the Child

a novel by

Robin Jenkins

"*Home was home then,*
happy for the child."

R. L. STEVENSON

London

JOHN LEHMANN

FIRST PUBLISHED IN 1953
BY JOHN LEHMANN LTD
25 GILBERT STREET, LONDON W.1
MADE AND PRINTED IN GREAT BRITAIN
BY PURNELL AND SONS LTD
PAULTON (SOMERSET) AND LONDON
SET IN 11 PT. BELL 1 PT. LEADED

To My Children

Chapter One

PAGES 256 and 257 were missing. Shocked, the boy slowly and in fear became aware that the book in his hands was merely a destructible contrivance of gum and paper, and that in spite of it round him in the little kitchen crowded the familiar baleful furniture. The tall forests dwindled to the oilclothed table with the mended leg, the blue seas faded into the grey linoleum, and the voices of macaws and adventurers became the gabble of women outside hanging up washed towels and shirts and babies' napkins in the sooty sunshine.

For a minute or two, after the spell was broken and he had made the necessary shivering adjustment, he still could not put the book down but pressed it against his jersey and kissed its grimy edge.

In the grate the fire was almost out, and he had been warned by his mother to keep it well stoked for his sister coming home from work. Sneering at the low-paid unambitiousness of that work, and at Mary's pride in it, he tenderly placed the book under a cushion, picked up the shovel from the hearth, and went into the dark scullery where the coal-cellar was. Mice lurked there, and he was afraid of them. As he clanged on the stone floor with the shovel he realised clearly the contrast between this timidity and the tremendous daring of Amyas Leigh in the book; and in the shadows he smiled in self-contempt.

When he had stoked the fire and pokered a little flame into it, he lifted the clock lying on its face on the mantelpiece and saw that soon his mother with the wonderful purchases would be home, and he ought therefore to be setting the table for tea. Instead, dissembling his excitement, he went calmly to a little oaken biscuit barrel on top of a chest of drawers, and before

7

opening it gazed at the tiny reflection of his face in the gleaming brass adornment. Smiling, looking thoughtful, he recalled what he had overheard one of his teachers say to another: that young John Stirling had the most thoughtful eyes she had ever seen in a child of twelve. The other teacher had agreed.

Amidst his reflection he saw his parents' initials inscribed on the brass so fancifully they were difficult to decipher. Still admiring his reflection, still savouring the teachers' praise, and still dissembling his excitement, he considered his mother's pride in this biscuit barrel. It was the only wedding present of any value left in the house; the rest long ago had been sold or else pawned and never redeemed. It would have been too, despite its sacredness to her because of her dead husband's memory, had the man in the shop not insulted her with his miserable offer. She had brought it home again, and had stood here, where John himself was now standing, hardly any taller than he, and had set it proudly and indignantly in its accustomed place, only to burst a minute later into a long sore oblivious weeping.

Before opening the barrel, prolonging the delightful delay, the boy turned and gazed at his father's portrait on the wall. His father was smiling, as apparently he always had been, smiling and careless; his motto had been, the roses will grow again. He wore a soldier's cap with two crossed machine guns as its badge. He had been only thirty-one when he had died, less than a year after his discharge from the army. A pension had been claimed but refused, and the parish had had to bring up John and his sister Mary. John had been only two then: he was not to blame.

Nevertheless as he opened the barrel and took out the letter, he glanced about him with guilty frightened resentment at the besieging poverty. Some day for revenge he would live in a large house with its name in gold letters on glass above the front door; it would have a garden coloured with flowers, and would be full of dear furniture. He himself would be dressed in expensive clothes, not a darned jersey and patched shorts.

8

He remembered his mother would be in soon with the parcels, and smiled.

Eagerly then he read the letter, though he could have recited it by heart like a poem. It was addressed to his mother.

"Dear Madam,

"I am very glad to be able to inform you that as a result of the bursary examination held in June of this year in Muirton Academy, your son, John Stirling, has been successful in gaining one of the bursaries, entitling him to a three years' course at that school, with an additional two years should his progress warrant it. Free books will be supplied; stationery, however, will not.

"If you intend your son to make use of this bursary, will you please communicate with me immediately. The session starts at the Academy on the 1st September. Where possible, it is expected that pupils will wear the school colours."

It was signed by the Director of Education.

The boy's smile remained, but a curious sneer mingled with it as he remembered the writing of the important reply. There had been a typical quarrel. His mother, whose handwriting was coarse and stupid, could not be allowed to write it. If she did the Director of Education and perhaps the Rector of the Academy would be sure to despise any scholar whose parent was so plainly uneducated. Mary was a beautiful writer; indeed, writing had been the only thing she'd been good at at school, and it had got her her job as office-girl. But she had been jealous of John's good luck, and had pretended first that she didn't know what to write, and then that it would be dishonest if she wrote it, for she wasn't his parent. In the quarrel she had as usual been pale but very cool. John had wept and yelled. Their mother had sat on the sofa, hiding her face in her hands, moaning that he would not succeed, he would fail as everything connected with her had failed, God was against her though she did not know why, having worked hard and honestly all her days. Her hands covering her face certainly

9

had proved her claim to have worked hard: they were raw and hacked and swollen. She was a charwoman, and how to keep this hidden was going to be the greatest difficulty when John went to his new school.

The reply, however, had been written, and in a week's time he would set out for the Academy. That very afternoon his mother, on her way back from her work, was to buy his new clothes: Academy blazer, cap, stockings and tie. He had not gone out to play football or explore along the burn, although the sun was shining. He wished to be in when she arrived; he wished to untie the string himself, pull aside the brown paper, and be the first to see the blue and green splendours.

He had set the table and was again absorbed in *Westward Ho!* when his mother returned. He did not rush into the lobby to meet her.

She came in carrying the parcels; but by the way she threw them down on the sofa and then rushed past him to poker the fire furiously, he knew something was wrong.

"Surely you knew Mary would be in in half an hour?" she cried.

"I put on a fire," he muttered.

"Aye, but you must hae waited till it was nearly out. Is reading all there is to do in the world?"

Timidly, obsequiously, he smiled at her, after another apprehensive glance at those parcels. "I've got to read a lot, mither, if I want to do well in English. That's what Mr. Richards said."

"Mr. Richards!" She repeated the old headmaster's name with contempt. Yet as she rattled the ribs of the grate with the poker, she remembered how he had told her, dabbing his desk with his forefinger to make every word solemn, that her son John was far and away the most brilliant pupil he had ever known in all his long career.

"Fine for him to talk," she muttered. "Likely he has a servant to his hoose, who'll be putting on a fire while he's reading."

"I set the table," he said.

10

She screamed at him. "Do you want me to fall on my knees and thank you for that? Hae I not been on my knees all morning and afternoon? Am I not on my knees mair than any priest, day in, day oot? I'm tired and worn oot, so I am, and I'm not coming hame here to be tormented by ingratitude."

He knew now for certain the parcels were the cause of her anger; he looked at them in terror, forgetting to be sly.

She did not look at the parcels, but still with her old grey coat on rushed into the scullery to fill the kettle. "You might hae had this filled," she said, returning, and in the same aggressive tone added, "Can you not open them? Am I expected to do everything for you?"

Slowly he put down the book, hating it even, and went across to the sofa. There were two parcels, the large one no doubt containing the suit. He began to fumble at the knots in the string.

She took off her coat, put on an apron, and began to fry herring for the tea.

"Use the scissors," she said peevishly, her back to him.

"Where are they?"

"Where do you think?" she cried. "Look for them. God kens, if you're smart at lessons, you're useless at everything else."

He ignored the insult. The scissors were not on their usual nail.

"Mary must have had them," he muttered.

"Oh, blame Mary. It's little wonder she complains that she always gets the blame in this house. Take a knife, can you not? If you hae brains, for God's sake use them."

From the table he picked up a knife.

"Maybe it would be better," he muttered, "if I didn't go to Muirton."

"Maybe it would."

He shot her a terrified glance. "I'll not go then."

"Please yourself." As she spoke she looked at him, read the misery and weakness in his face, and to smother her sympathy and love rattled the frying-pan and turned over the herring.

11

"It'll be a hard road, mind that," she said. "You'll need all your brains; but you'll need mair than brains. That's something you forget. You'll need spunk. You gie in too easily, like your faither."

With the knife in his hand and the string still uncut, he turned and gazed at his father's picture.

"He was a sodger," said his mother, "and he was wounded himself, and he saw many men killed on the battlefields of France. But I've seen him in this hoose sitting on that same sofa, greeting because he gave in too easily. He kent his weakness; he had his ain method of trying to forget it."

He knew she was referring to his father's habit of getting drunk.

"Go on, cut the string," she said.

As he sawed through the string he suddenly paused. It had occurred to him in a flash of hope that his mother's bad temper might be caused by her sore back, which had troubled her for years.

"Is your back sore?" he whispered.

"Aye, and my heart too. Is the string made of wire that you should be so long in cutting it?"

He continued sawing at the string. If under this brown paper he found blazer, stockings, cap and tie, what had caused all this bitterness? Why had his mother, in spite of her sore back, not come home happily, eager herself to cut the string and get him to try on the new clothes? Still seeking a reason, he thought that perhaps they had been even dearer than she had anticipated.

"Were they very dear?" he asked.

"Too dear."

The smell of the fried herring was strong in the kitchen now. He liked fried herring, and if only under this brown paper which he was now about to unfold were revealed the blue and green garments he had prayed for, he would enjoy his tea tonight more than he had ever enjoyed any tea before. As the saliva came involuntarily into his mouth, so did tears come into his eyes.

"I don't want any herring," he muttered.

12

"Please yourself. It's either that, or bread and margarine."

"I don't want anything."

He opened first one parcel, then the other. Both contained disappointments. There was a suit, but not in the Academy colours; there were stockings, cap, and tie all right, but as they matched the suit they too were traitors. He knew now it was not the ache in his mother's back which had caused her to scream and be nasty to him. The letter demanded that he should wear the school colours. She had promised to buy them and she had broken her promise.

"These are no use," he said quietly, with a sigh.

She had been watching him anxiously in the hope that, with a little bravery, a little understanding, he would after a minute's forgivable disappointment, shrug his shoulders, laugh, and then blithely try on the new clothes, which though not what he had wanted and she had promised were nevertheless better than any he had ever worn before. Now when he said so quietly they were of no use she knew he was going to give way to his weakness and torture himself and her. He was so sensitive it was like a disease. Often she felt it would have been better for her, and for him too, if he had been like one of her neighbours' sons, not particularly clever but plain and cheerful, eager to escape from school and go to work in pit or steelwork.

In spite of her sore back, of her irresistible contempt for his cowardice, and of her fear the herring might burn, she made an effort to coax him to be sensible. She went over and put her arm round his neck.

"I ken they're not what you looked for," she said, in tears. "The Academy things were far too dear, son. I just couldn't afford them. They were mair than double these."

"These are cheap."

She could not help being indignant. "Cheap!" she cried. "Are you aware that I had to work for a whole fortnight, and hard work too, to earn what these cost?"

He said nothing, but he was reflecting that her work was very poorly paid; as it must have been, for it was low mean work, washing and scrubbing. How could he explain to her that

13

her work, of which she was at times so stupidly proud, would be his greatest worry at Muirton if ever he went there? If he agreed to wear these cheap clothes, it would be like carrying a notice on his chest stating he was only a scrubber-woman's son.

She controlled her temper, forced love to subdue contempt. Her tears flowed unchecked, undried, unvalued. "Listen son. Don't make yourself miserable. Look at it sensibly. Right enough there'll be dozens at the Academy who will wear better clothes than you. I'd be silly to deny it. There'll be doctors' sons, lawyers' sons, teachers' sons, publicans' sons, all paying fees. But remember this, John, none of them will be superior to you in what matters most. You'll hae better brains than the most of them, and you'll hae the pride of knowing that it's through your ain efforts you're at such a fine school, getting such a fine education."

She paused, hoping though not expecting that he would contradict her and say it wasn't just his efforts but hers too. He remained silent and she picked up the jacket.

"Try it on anyway," she coaxed. "When you see it on you'll change your mind; you'll look well in it."

He wrenched himself out of her clasp. "What are you arguing for?" he muttered. "It says in the letter, doesn't it, that I'm supposed to wear the school colours?

"It says, wherever possible," she pointed out meekly. "For us it's just not possible. There are sure to be other poor boys there. You'll not be the only one. Many of them will not wear blazers. I've seen Dr. Linton's boy going to school withoot a blazer."

"He's got one though."

"He doesn't always wear it."

"If everybody knows you've got one," he sneered, "it's easy not to wear it. They'll know I've got none."

"What about it if they do?"

"There's just this about it, if I don't have the Academy colours I don't go to the Academy."

"Then you don't go; that's all," she said simply, and sinking down on the sofa hid her face in the jacket.

He heard her harsh sobs and heard the herring crackle in the pan. As he turned to go out of the house he regretted the damage her weeping might do to the jacket, and also his having to forgo his tea or at least to postpone it. Later when he came in, as he would for all his vows of never returning, his herring would be cold; and his mother for spite, and Mary for fun, would refuse to reheat it for him. A consolation was that the suit, cap and stockings, were better than he had admitted; with his new shirt and shoes they would look well enough.

As he slammed the door shut, he felt in his heart a great timid fondness and pity for his mother; but he would not all the same go back and comfort her by saying he was sorry and by praising the clothes. He could not, for she represented for him all the deprivations and denials of his life. Young though he was, he knew she hated being that representative; but he still could not forgive her.

15

Chapter Two

As he raced down the road towards the fields away from the buildings, he tried to pretend he was an outlaw, innocent and persecuted, escaping on his swift and beautiful horse. As always with him, the truth persisted in his mind, mocking the pretence: himself a coward, fleeing uselessly from his cowardice, in sand-shoes thin and torn, with his mother behind him in the house weeping in misery although a smile from him would have made her happy and proud.

There were palings to keep people from falling in the darkness down into the burn. He stopped beside them, glancing round cunningly as a murderer might outside his victim's house. Complaints had been made to the police that boys were wilfully destroying these palings, which were wooden and could be made into bats or boats or swords. There was one half-broken, hanging by a single staple; one wrench would pull it off.

As he put his hands on the rough wood he gasped in an ecstasy of terror and guilt. Then a flock of pigeons clapped over his head. Although he knew to whom they belonged—old Tam Rollins the miner, so stooped his back made a landing-stage for them—yet they seemed to him sent from God. Gaping after them, whimpering, his hands still on the paling, he thought of their being hurled out of one of those high white clouds to warn him.

Years ago there had been in the house, hanging in front of his bed, a large gilt-framed portrait of Burns with long side-locks, white cravat, and strangely smiling eyes. Light from a street lamp outside or from the moon had lit up this face, which never slept; and John, after his prayers, waking to whimper for a drink of water or because of some terrifying dream, had imagined it was God gazing down at him without speech, without curiosity, without pity. Always now when he thought of God he saw Burns' moonlit face.

He expected, as he struggled with the paling, that at the moment it came loose something divine and dreadful would happen, the birds would return swift and sudden, a rat from the burn below would creep up through the long grass and show its teeth, a voice would shout down from the sky.

It was this last expectation that happened. The staple flew out, the paling was free in his terrified hands, and the voice fell. Not a deep thunderous voice such as God might usually have, but an old wife's peevish squeal, just as awful.

"Oh, you imp you, you deil, you vagabond you," she squealed. "It's the police I'll set on you, Sam Gourlay. I ken weel who you are, you rogue, you damager. Wha was it fired the squib in my keyhole, hey? It's the jail you'll end up in; you'll be hangit yet, you'll see. Aye, run; but I ken weel wha you are. Do you want folk, auld folk, to coup ower there and break their poor auld brittle necks? You would like that weel; that would be a great joke for you. It's a murderer you are, Sam Gourlay. Wha killed Mrs. Tamson's auld cat Teenie and flung him up on the tely wires whaur he hung and stunk for days? Come back and tell me that, if you daur."

Stirling stopped gasping behind the tall railway sleepers where she could no longer see him. Here too on the railway line was a forbidden place; a few yards away was a notice in blue enamel with black stone-bruises threatening trespassers with a five-pound fine. He crouched low therefore amid the long grass, safe behind the thick fence, and grinned.

Old Mrs. Cowie, so smelly in her long black shiny skirts and with her jaws yellow and hairy, would be certain to tell the police; she was always clyping to them. Twice she had called him Sam Gourlay. She was nearly blind and she hated Gourlay. Everybody hated him, especially those with good eyesight who saw all the wickedness he did. Nobody would believe Gourlay if he swore he hadn't been near the palings that afternoon.

17

Crouched there, with small startlements from bees and butterflies and tiny hopping insects, Stirling kept grinning as he compared his lot with Gourlay's.

Gourlay was a dunce thrashed every day by his teachers for stupidity or insolence. Gourlay would grow up to be a criminal as Mrs. Cowie had prophesied like an old witch. Gourlay's mother was a huge cruel desperate woman who hammered and starved him. His father, small, sleekit, idle, wore the same dirty green muffler always and, jouking down as if it was a joke, picked fag-ends off the street. His sister Jeanie, a specky white-faced pimply girl with teeth missing and with great red blotchy hands like docken leaves, worked in the laundry. Gourlay had already been at court several times, for stealing, for doing damage, for setting squibs off in the street; it was said he was on his last chance, next time he would be sent to a reformatory. Although more than a year older he had once been in John's class, but had been kept back. Stirling's grin developed as he remembered how Gourlay had read a word at a time so painfully that the teacher always in disgust had roared to him to sit down, such reading was atrocious, an infant in the penny-buff could do better. The class laughed, but Gourlay sat down with a sneer of defiance for the teacher, and a threat for those who were laughing. Sometimes the teacher in a rage rushed up the passage, dragged him out, and leathered his bare legs with the belt, yelling it wasn't for his abominable reading but for his insufferable insolence. Gourlay never had cried.

Still wishing to enjoy the sweetness of sinning, with no danger of being found out, Stirling crept up the bank, darted across the rusty lines, and scrambled down the other bank where he was hidden from the road but was watched by Farmer Gilchrist's wheat with its millions of golden eyes.

His own eyes averted, he stumbled along beside the fence, hating his own feet when they kicked against a concealed can and made a noise. Once he almost screamed in fright when some tangled grass caught him like a snare, so that for a moment he could not move. He began to whimper he was a fool skulking there when he could have been safe at home,

18

seeing his new clothes laid carefully on the sofa, and enjoying the herring. He remembered what he had read once about herring, that of all the fish in the sea they had the most enemies: seals ate them, and sharks, and the great diving gannets. Shaking his head, he denied they had more enemies than he himself had: all the blazered boys and girls at Muirton Academy who would jeer at him and despise him if ever they discovered his mother was a charwoman; and all those others, like Gourlay and his own sister Mary, who would be delighted if he failed and had to leave the Academy in disgrace in spite of his brilliance.

He halted beside some bramble bushes. The berries were still hard and green. He plucked one and nibbled at it, hoping its bitter juice was poisonous and later that night, when the moon was shining, they would find him dead there, pale-faced, but smiling in forgiveness of them all.

He acted that sad death, sinking down first on one knee and then on the other, taking care to avoid the sticky cuckoo-spits in the grass. Then he began to pant, "Oh mither, oh mither," and rolled carefully on to his side. He saw the blue sky above Drumsagart bing, and noticed how much greener were the wheat-stalks near their foot. Next moment he was on his back, eyes shut, limbs stiff, dead; but the moment after he was alive again, dementedly so, trying with wild arms to save his life from the big persistent wasp that had come buzzing over his face. Wasps' stings were really poisonous: the wound swelled up, a blue line crept to the heart, and then death came, with no resurrection possible even if a million wasps, as many as there were blades of grass or ears of wheat, hovered however angrily over the corpse's face.

Soon the wasp flew away, but death remained there beside the bramble bushes for the wide-eyed boy. He was remembering, with sweat on his brow, the time when Mrs. McCrorie whose son Davie had died, had insisted on taking John up to see him in his little white coffin. He had been six years old. She had seized him by the hand, weeping and saying that he had been her poor wee boy's best friend and must come and see him and give him a farewell kiss. Too shy to protest, he had been lifted up over the corpse that smelled like candles, and had had his face shoved against the dead boy's so that his nose, wet from agitation and from being held almost upside down, had left a smear across the icy brow. Mrs. McCrorie with her apron had wiped it off very tenderly. When Davie had been alive she had often wiped his nose with her apron, but never as tenderly as that; she had often scolded him, for his poor health had made both of them fretful. John had unconsciously noticed the difference between all those former wipings and this final one, and now by the bramble bushes recollecting it he partly understood. Since then Mrs. McCrorie had had two more children; one of them, called Bruce, was very bow-legged.

Sighing, and disturbed by a worry vaguer but far more deep than his fear of ridicule and failure at the Academy, Stirling left the bramble bushes and hurried along towards the bridge where he would be able to regain the road and return safely home. The wheat field gave way to his old elementary school, separated from the railway by a high stone wall. Sometimes balls were kicked over and never found. He looked for them as he crept along, but saw none. Instead he saw rusty gaping tins, a green glittering beetle, broken bottles, a frog, a bird with a yellow head, hundreds of cuckoo-spits, several jenny-long-legs, and an old red bicycle tyre.

Sam Gourlay, who harried birds' nests and blew up frogs with straws, once had come down Drumsagart brae on a bicycle with no brakes. To avoid a bus he had charged on to the pavement into a pram. The baby hadn't been hurt much though it had been spilled out; but Gourlay had been knocked unconscious with his skull split. The mother had rushed out of the shop screaming, snatched up her baby, and then madly had started to kick Gourlay's face as it lay on the pavement mixed up with the bicycle and the pram. She had had to be dragged away. Afterwards Stirling had overheard some women whisper what a pity she hadn't been allowed to finish her kicking.

Arriving at the bridge, Stirling was so eager to set foot again on sanctioned ground that he did not look along the road before he dropped from the wall. It was an easy drop, and he was an expert dropper. He fell on his toes and let his knees give, taking care not to crack his teeth on them as he had seen clumsy droppers do. In a second he was upright again, flicking the tell-tale wisps of grass from his jersey and stockings. Then he felt absolved, free to smile and race home and there enjoy his tea and admire his new clothes. But as his fists were raised to his sides and he was about to send himself off on that fleet and happy race, he saw approaching, about a hundred yards away, the police-sergeant who was called Bawface. In a whining panic Stirling turned and fled in the opposite direction to home.

He ran headlong past the school, along the road that led to the Episcopal church whose Sunday school he attended, and did not falter until his breath failed and a stitch stabbed his side. Even then he hurried as fast as the pain let him. There was a roundabout way home across Drumsagart bing, but some fields would have to be trespassed through, and the bing was a high and lonely place. Maybe it would be better to wait on the wall outside the church hidden by the hawthorns which grew thickly there. The way to the police-station was by another road, and when the sergeant was gone he could creep from under the trees, praying to get home safe.

When he turned the corner at the church two boys were standing at a fence by the hay field. To his terror he saw they were Gourlay and his pal Charlie Dean.

He slunk into the shelter of the hawthorns. At first Gourlay and Dean did not notice him, being too intent on what they were doing at that fence-stob. He heard Gourlay's sudden wild vibrant laughter; Mr. Armstrong had once said, bellowing with laughter himself, that Gourlay laughing was like the sound of a wild animal trapped in a steel snare.

He wondered what they were doing, and what they would do to him if they saw him. Gourlay had once chased him nearly a mile to take off his trousers and throw them on top of a lamp-post. But if he stayed there under the hawthorns the sergeant might come or Mr. Fotheringham the minister; and if he went back towards the bridge now he might meet the sergeant who had stopped to talk to somebody. He did not know what to do, where to go. A bird flew out of the bushes above his head and he envied it its free and joyous wings; it could fly as far away as Africa if it wished.

It was Charlie Dean who caught sight of him. He looked up from what they were examining at the post, and by accident glimpsed Stirling's pale face amid the green thorned branches. Instantly he elbowed Gourlay who stared along. Stirling could imagine the bared teeth, the furrowed scarred brow, the reckless green eyes, and the jumping freckles.

"Come and see this, Stirling," shouted Gourlay. "Here's something you never seen in your life before."

Stirling did not move; yet he felt fatally curious; that something in Gourlay's voice, that fierce devil-may-care eagerness, fascinated him as it did always.

"Come on, Stirling," cried Gourlay again. "This is worth seeing. I'm not just kidding you. You're one that likes to learn, aren't you? Here's something worth learning."

Still Stirling did not move. He saw Dean turn with typical swaggering contemptuousness and speak to Gourlay, who listened as likely as not with his left eye shut.

"Are you frightened I'm going to hit you, Stirling?" he shouted. "I'm not going to hit you. I'm just going to show you something."

Dean laughed and spoke again.

"I'm not going to take off your breeks," shouted Gourlay. "There's something on the fence here that's interesting." He was obviously proud of the word for he repeated it. "It's awful interesting, Stirling. You could write a good composition aboot it."

Stirling was always winning praise for his compositions. Slowly then he came out into the sunshine and walked towards them. After all, why should he be afraid? It was true he could write good compositions; at all subjects he was clever; and in a week's time he would be at Muirton Academy, as far out of Gourlay's reach as if he had flown to Africa with the bird in the tree. Yet as he drew nearer and saw Dean's crimson tie hanging down like a long tongue, he remembered his new suit and again lost faith in it. Would they at Muirton really sneer at its cheapness? Dean was always well-dressed; even his present suit, though neglected and rumpled, was plainly of better material than Stirling's. He was an orphan and lived with his aunt and uncle. They gave him plenty of pocket money and hoped he would grow up clever and good, able to get a job beside his uncle in the cashier's office in the steelwork. But at school he had been lazy and a dunce, and his chief crony had been Gourlay. His aunt, a lady with a gentle voice, had begged him in tears to keep away from Gourlay; his uncle had thrashed him with the same intention. But Dean, who often did not seem to like Gourlay much, kept faithful to him. He did not seem to care what happened to himself in the world, whether he succeeded or failed, whether he pleased his aunt or broke her heart. He seldom was cruel himself, but was fond of urging Gourlay to be cruel.

Gourlay of course was dressed in dirty jersey with holes in it showing his filthy shirt beneath; and there were even holes in his shorts. He wore no stockings on his thin bony legs, and his toes stuck out of his sandshoes. But Gourlay never worried about his clothes.

Stirling saw in a glance what they were doing. Part of that sport he had played at himself once: with a stalk of grass poking earwigs out of crannies in old fence posts. The part he had not played at caused him to shudder just as it was causing Gourlay to grin in comradely glee. As each earwig came out, Gourlay had seized it, with iron-fingered audacity, and set it on top of the fence rail where he had impaled it with a pin that Dean had nonchalantly handed to him from his jacket lapel. Stirling counted fifteen earwigs there, each one with a gleaming pin through it. They all wriggled in a strangely similar way, lifting up their heads and tails in a sort of dance, and seeming to utter cries of pain too remote to be heard.

Gourlay stuck his face close to Stirling's; his breath smelled of apples.

23

"See them?" he cried. "Like a lot of wee Christs."

"I said that," sneered Dean, his slant eyes almost closed.

Gourlay generously admitted the claim. "That's right, Charlie," he cried. "But it was me had the idea. Wasn't it?"

"I had the pins," said Dean, showing he still had more in his lapel.

Suddenly Gourlay seized Stirling, but not in anger or menace; friendliness rather, in simple enthusiasm to have him share this joy.

"You stick one, Stirling," he cried. "It's easy. You hear a wee crunch when the pin goes through. Go on, try it. Charlie will lend you a pin. Willn't you, Charlie?"

"You've got a hope," sneered Dean, with the pin already in his hand to offer, "thinking wee mammy's pet would ever lift an earwig. Do you no ken she still uses pins to tie up his nappies?"

Gourlay, baffled for a moment, glared at Stirling; and into his face crept the familiar defensive cunning. His left eye closed and the left side of his mouth opened and twitched upwards. He plucked at his top lip with forefinger and thumb; he did it deliberately as if there was a tiny scab there he wished to pick off.

Fascinated, Stirling remembered those fingers had so recently been touching earwigs.

"That's right," said Gourlay, quietly, "Aye, that's right. Mammy's pet. I never thought of that. You're just a coward, Stirling. You're frightened to lift an earwig."

Unexpectedly Stirling rebelled; not only against Gourlay, but against all his other enemies.

"It's cruel," he muttered.

Laughing, Dean glanced up at the stone cross white with birds' droppings on the church high above the trees.

"He goes to Sunday school," he said, and made as if with the pin he would transfix Stirling like a sixteenth earwig.

Gourlay's slow brain did not grasp the inference; he grinned as he strove to understand.

24

"Cruel?" he repeated, turning back to Stirling.

"Sure Sam," said Dean impatiently." Surely you know they teach you at Sunday school to be kind to animals."

"I know that," retorted Gourlay. "Everybody knows that. But earwigs are not animals. I'm sure it says nothing in the Bible about being kind to earwigs." He turned again to Stirling, still without viciousness as if he was anxious to learn the truth. "Do they teach you in your Sunday school, Stirling, to be kind to *earwigs*?" His amused incredulity made his pronunciation of the name almost a squeal. "Does the teacher say: Be kind to earwigs? Just like that, name and all? Is it in the big Bible or the wee hymn-book?' He went on more eagerly and more confidently for Dean was laughing as if these witticisms amused him. "Come on, Stirling. Say the earwig commandment for us."

"Thou shalt not commit adultery," quoted Dean. "Do you know what adultery means, Stirling?"

Gourlay grinned. "I ken," he said. "Oh, I ken that. I've seen dogs at it. I've seen them have to be separated by pails of water. And I've watched auld Gilchrist's bull."

Dean jeered at that enthusiastic ignorance. "So you've seen dogs at it, Sam?"

"Sure. Hundreds of times. And sparrows."

"And what about your ain sister Jeanie and yon pape Donoghue? Have you seen them? I have."

Gourlay was instantly savage. Dean jumped back, smiling, to avoid the expected blow. Stirling too recoiled, as Gourlay cursed and clenched his fists. An earwig in panic ran along the collar of Gourlay's jersey near his ear.

"Look, Sam," warned Stirling, pointing, "there's an earwig on your collar. It'll try to get into your ear."

Gourlay made no attempt to knock it off or even to squint down at it. He stood panting, his teeth showing, his green eyes glinting.

Dean leant forward. "It is an earwig, Sam," he said, appeasingly. "You'd better not let it get into your ear. It'll burrow into your brain."

There was a moment's silence, broken by Gourlay's snorts.

"I've heard that too," murmured Stirling. "They can kill a person by burrowing into his brain."

Gourlay exploded into a characteristic rage. He whirled his fists about and yelled without any meaning. Then in frenzy he began to feel for the insect on his collar. Finding it, he thrust it into his ear, no doubt maiming it with his violence.

"Do you think I care if it burrows into my brain?" he cried. "Do you think I'm frightened of earwigs? I'm frightened of nothing. Let it burrow, let it burrow."

Stirling, horrified and feeling his own ears itching, detected on Dean's lips a secret smile of contempt. But openly Charlie still tried appeasement.

"The trouble with you is, Sam," he said banteringly, "you can't take a joke. I was just joking about your Jeanie."

The muscles in Gourlay's face grew contorted, whether because of the tickling caused by the earwig or by his fury against Dean, Stirling could not tell.

The earwig desperately reappeared, overbalanced, toppled from ear on to jersey, and from there to the ground.

Dean stepped forward, still wary of those wild fists, and crushed it under his boot.

"That's another one less," he said, laughing.

"You saw them in the public park on the seat under the white cherry tree," said Gourlay. "And he's not a pape."

"I don't care what he is, Sam. He used to be one. I told you I was just joking. Stirling will tell you I was just joking. Sure I was joking, Stirling?"

Stirling discreetly nodded.

"I'll kill him," snarled Gourlay, looking far away towards his sister's lover.

"Are they not going to be married?" asked Dean. "It's all right if they're going to be married."

"I'll kill him," repeated Gourlay, "or I'll kill her."

"Better not do that, Sam," chuckled Dean, with a wink at Stirling. "She's handy for slipping you a tanner for the pictures."

"She can keep her tanners."

"But if she stops giving them to you, who will you get them from? Not your mither, or your faither."

"I'd take them just as I took the apples."

"What if you're caught? Remember what the man in the court said last time? Next time it's the reformatory."

"Do you think I care?"

Dean, who had a comfortable home with a bedroom to himself and an aunt who never denied him sixpence for the pictures, lifted up the end of his red tie and smiled at it as if, thought Stirling, its colour was caused by blood and it reminded him of the reformatory.

"They'd leather you with the cat-o-nine-tails," he murmured, with smiling relish. "They'd strip you naked to do it."

"I'd never let them," cried Gourlay.

"How could you stop them? There would be six of them, six big hefty cops; more than six if they were needed; fifty they could be, all with their jackets off and their sleeves rolled up. They would hold you down on the table while you got the cat. You could never stop them. If a doctor says you're strong enough, you get lashed till you faint."

"I'd not faint," said Gourlay. "And when they loosed me, do you ken what I would do?"

Dean sneered at the braggart. "Greet," he said. "You'd greet."

"No, I'd not greet. I never greet. Have you ever seen me greet? Have you, Stirling? You've seen big Armstrong give me a dozen as hard as he could draw; and did I greet? Go on, tell Charlie if I gret."

Stirling shook his head; it was true, Gourlay had not wept though the thrashing had been so severe as to make some of the spectators weep.

"Do you see, Charlie?" cried Gourlay. "I never greet. Remember when the barb wire stuck in my leg and ripped it; rusty wire it was too, and you couldn't see my leg for rusty blood. Did I greet then?"

"All right, all right," admitted Dean. "You don't greet.

27

But the cat will be worse than big Armstrong's belt, and worse than rusty barb wire."

Gourlay shook his head. "I'll tell you what I would do when they loosed me. I'd catch the cop's hand with the cat in it, and I would bite it down to the bone till it crunched like the pins crunched through the earwigs." He giggled shrilly in his great excitement. "They'd never make me let go my bite. I'd be like a bull-dog. If they flung boiling water on me I'd not let go." He saw that Dean was waiting to destroy all these claims with a sarcasm. "I'll prove it to you," he cried. "I'll prove it to you that nobody can hurt me and get away with it. Would you like to see me prove it, Charlie?"

"Sure. Go ahead and prove it." Again Dean risked a wink at Stirling.

"Right. Who belongs to those haystacks?"

"Auld Gilchrist."

"That's right. He got me fined five shillings for stealing three eggs, didn't he, though I never stole them, just found them? Do you want to see me get my own back? Just watch me. You watch too, Stirling, and you'll see how I get my own back."

They watched as he climbed eagerly and clumsily over the fence, and rushed to the nearest rick.

"What's he going to do?" whispered Stirling.

"Pee against the wind," smiled Dean. "Get his own back. You heard him."

Very calmly Dean began to pluck his pins out of the fence, letting the earwigs drop without a glance at them. He kept staring at Gourlay who, yelling unintelligibly, was clawing his way to the top of the hayrick.

"You're good at mental arithmetic, Stirling," said Dean. "Three eggs for five bob. How much was that each?"

"One and eightpence."

"That's right. One and eightpence each. Do you ken how much they are in the shops? Tuppence. I tell you, he's mad. Look at him getting his revenge. It's the asylum he'll end up in, no the reformatory at all."

It seemed a likely enough prophecy in spite of its disloyalty. On top of the rick Gourlay had first leapt up and down, beating his chest with his fists and uttering peculiar howls, as if he was Tarzan. Now he was tearing the hay up in handfuls and scattering it; most of it fell back down on him.

"He's doing damage," muttered Stirling anxiously.

"What do you say, Stirling?" suggested Dean. "Should we slink away and leave him to it?"

"I think we should, Charlie."

Dean glanced at him. "If the cops came round the corner yonder," he said, "and caught us here, we'd get share of the blame. Do you know that?"

"We're doing nothing."

"That's right. We're doing nothing. We're innocent. But it makes no difference if you are innocent. Cops like to catch as many as they can. It gets them promotion. We'd get fined a pound each, maybe more. Your mother could never afford to pay that, Stirling."

"No."

"But it wouldn't be the fine that would be the worst part of it for you. The court's up at Muirton where the Academy is. They'd hear about it. You'd be expelled. I mean they wouldn't want jailbirds at their posh school."

"No. I'm going hame."

Gourlay was shouting to them to come and help him; it was great fun, he cried.

"Great fun!" sneered Dean. "A wean three years old would call that great fun. Listen to him sneezing with the hay up his nose."

But it was a triumphant sneezing, as the rick was now in ruins.

"If I was a cow," shouted Gourlay, "this would be a great feast." He pretended he was a cow, using his arms as horns, mooing, and snatching up mouthfuls of hay.

"Mad," grinned Dean. "Do you ken what I've seen him do? I've seen him take a dummy-teat from a wean in a pram and suck it. What did he do that for?"

"I'm going hame," said Stirling again.

29

"No, no," smiled Dean, who had him by the jersey. "It's not polite to run away when a person's talking to you. There was no jam on this dummy-teat. Snotters, more likely. And the wean bawled like murder. And there was Gourlay with the teat in his mouth enjoying it. Was that not mad?"

An angry distant bellow interrupted them.

Dean let Stirling go. "Auld Gilchrist," he cried. "Run for it. Across the fields up to the bing. You'll get nabbed along the road. Just take a look at Gourlay."

But Stirling's terror allowed him no leisure to look at Gourlay jigging with glee on the strewn hay, or at the old farmer stumbling in fury towards them. Whimpering his innocence, he was compelled to scramble after Dean over the fence, across the hayfield, away towards the desolation of the bing.

They went racing past Gourlay.

"What's the hurry for?" he asked, shrill and cool.

Dean could not help laughing at that audacity, but he raced on, jumping across a ditch and vaulting another fence into a corn field. He lingered a moment to peep over the swaying golden heads to see, not Stirling swithering in anguish at the field's edge, but Gourlay still tantalisingly among the hay and the farmer with stick brandished charging nearer.

"He'll see him from that distance," he muttered. "Though he is half-blind he'll recognise him." Then he himself crept rapidly through the corn.

Stirling followed, taking his anguish with him. He knew that now he was no longer innocent, but was doing damage as expensive as Gourlay's. To keep it as little as possible, he tried to follow in Dean's tracks; but he knew that in court this extenuation would be laughed at.

Midway through the corn, far now from the fatal hayrick, Dean turned round and stood up, a poppy in his hand. It was as red as his tie. He held it at his nose, as if enjoying its fragrance. Its petals fell off, one by one, clinging to his jacket and white shirt like huge blobs of blood. He saw Gourlay had at last left the hayfield and now was dancing after them through the corn without any attempt to hide or avoid damage.

30

When Gourlay noticed them halted he turned himself and looked back to where amidst the scattered hay the old farmer was stopped, puffing and wiping his face with a large white hankie that looked like a flag of surrender. Gourlay tore up a stalk of corn; it was as long as a rifle and he aimed it like one, the ears tickling his cheek as he squinted along its green and golden length. As he pulled the imaginary trigger the old man sat down suddenly. The coincidence delighted Gourlay, who pulled the trigger again and again, paying no heed to the white flag that kept fluttering. When he proceeded on his way he bent the stalk and stuck it through his hair, as if it was a Redskin's feather. Seeing some poppies he plucked them, but their petals dropped off before he could decorate himself with them.

Soon at his reckless pace he made up on the creeping Stirling.

"Do you ken what I've been thinking, Stirling?" he asked. "You're going to be a teacher, aren't you?"

Stirling could not answer for terror. Already corn and sparrows conspired to hinder him; corn thrust out twisted stalks to trip him, sparrows stealing in dozens made him glance aside. Now Gourlay was joining these hinderers, and he was the most persistent.

"I said, are you meaning to be a teacher?" he repeated, in indignation. "Are you deaf?" Still getting no answer he reached forward and grabbed the tail of Stirling's jersey.

Stirling wailed, "Let me go, please let me go."

"Do you think I'm auld Gilchrist?" cried Gourlay, disgusted. "I just asked you a question. It's not good manners to kid you didn't hear. I asked you if it was a teacher you were going to be."

"Yes, Sam."

"I mean, you've not changed your mind?"

"No, Sam. Oh please crouch down."

Gourlay was standing upright, his head above the corn. "Do you think," he asked, in loud scorn, "auld Gilchrist can see me from this distance? He's as blind as a bat. Besides, he's dead. I shot him. He's lying yonder in the hay with six bullets in him."

31

So panic-stricken was he, Stirling gaped up half believing this tale of murder.

"Lying yonder in the hay," repeated Gourlay, with a grin.

"He'll go for the police, Sam. He'll be sure to go for the police."

"How the hell can he go for the cops if he's dead? But he's as blind as a bat. Have you ever noticed his een? They're like milk, with wee yellow specks in them. He's too stuck-up to wear specks. You'll be needing specks, Stirling, if you read a lot of books. It's reading that wears out your een. He'd never recognise me from that distance. If he says it was me he's an auld liar because he could never recognise me from that distance. Next time he meets me he'd better not bend over me and say, 'What price are eggs the day?' I'll ask him what price is hay."

"But if you do that, Sam, he'll know it was you."

Gourlay grimaced as he considered that remark; soon he nodded as he saw its wisdom. "That's right," he admitted cunningly. "You're the clever one all right, Stirling."

"Please let me go, Sam. Please let us get to the bing beside Charlie."

"In a minute. There's something I meant to say to you, but you've made me forget what it was with your girning. You'll wait there till I remember."

"Crouch down then, please."

Gourlay suddenly bobbed down on hands and knees. He hopped like a frog, and then lay flat on his belly nibbling at the stalks.

"I'm remembering," he said. "Just keep quiet, and let me remember." He grinned and looked about him. "I like it here. It's cool and green like at the bottom of the baths. Can you swim, Stirling?"

Eyes closed in prayer, Stirling shook his head.

"I can do nearly half a length," boasted Gourlay. "I'd be a good bit better if I could get more practice." He tried to swim there, stretching out his arms and kicking his legs. "It's like swimming under the water," he gasped. "It's hard under the water, Stirling. It costs tuppence a half-hour, and then there's another tuppence for the bus fares. I need more practice all the same." For a few moments he was silent, scowling at this necessity of practice. "I would like to be good enough to win a life-saver's medal," he said, and added in the next breath, "I remember now what I was going to ask you, Stirling. I was going to ask you if you knew that to become a teacher you'll hae to be cruel."

Stirling for a moment opened his eyes. "Cruel?"

"Cruel. What you said sticking pins into earwigs was." He crept very close to Stirling and spoke in a confidential almost comradely tone. "Giving ten of the belt is worse than sticking a pin into an earwig. If it was ten pins, it would be the same. Will you give anybody ten of the belt when you're a teacher?"

Inwardly Stirling answered, Yes, anybody like you.

"There's no need for that," went on Gourlay, still with the same seriousness. "My faither says one lick of the belt's enough. Mind you," and he began to grin, "one would be like a tickle just." He tickled Stirling's face with some corn. "Just a wee tickle."

Next minute Gourlay leaped to his feet, hooting, and began with great kangaroo loups to make for the bing. He was now disgusted with this yellow vital corn that belonged to old Gilchrist. He wanted to join his friend Charlie at the derelict pit, where everything was grass-grown, rusty, abandoned, and ownerless. Sometimes Gourlay went there alone and wandered amidst the ruins, knocking down some more bricks from a wall already dilapidated, or smashing with a length of twisted rail a slab of concrete discovered miraculously intact under grass and nettles.

Stirling followed in desperate anxiety not to be left alone. At first he had thought from Gourlay's sudden jump and hoot that the old farmer or the police were upon them, and he had burst out crying. He wept as he came through the corn into the deserted pithead. For him other ghosts than that of nemesis haunted there. Years ago, during a coal-strike, Mary and he had come creeping to this bing to search it for bits of coal to put into a bag Mary carried. Other people had been there picking, for coal was scarce because of the strike. Two policemen had appeared, blowing their whistles. Mary had stood where she was high up on the bing, the wind blowing her hair. He had tugged her skirt, screaming to her to run or they would be caught and put into prison. She had not run, and when the policemen, going from picker to picker with their notebooks, came to her and asked her her name and address, she had given them so clearly and defiantly people had laughed; even the policemen had grinned. Afterwards when the policemen had gone a fuss had been made of Mary because of her courage; but John, weeping, had just wanted to go home. She had refused to go until the bag was full. While waiting, he had time to endow with malevolent life every roofless shed, every contorted bit of corrugated iron, every rubble heap; but most terrifying of these monsters had been a great red lion of ash that crouched, bigger than a house, with its paws stretched out in front.

Dean was waiting, perched on one of those immense paws. He did not know it was the paw of a lion; like Gourlay he thought it was just a hillock of hard red ash.

"Don't tell me," he shouted down, "that you've brought mammy's pet with you."

Immediately Gourlay sprang round and waved his fist. "Don't follow me, Stirling," he cried. "You're a mammy's pet. Look, you're greeting. Your face is all black where you've been rubbing it."

"I bet you he's messed his breeks," cried down Dean.

Gourlay pretended to smell that mess; he held his nose. "That's right, Charlie. Oh, away home, Stirling, and get your mammy to wipe you."

"I'll tell you something, Sam," cried Dean.

"Whit, Charlie?"

"Do you ken what Stirling there is going to be?"

"Do you mean a teacher?"

"No, I don't mean a teacher. Something worse even than that."

34

"I don't ken what's worse than that," laughed Gourlay, shaking his head.

"A traitor, Sam, a traitor."

"A traitor? Ho, ho, ho." But Gourlay's laughter though loud enough was obviously forced; he did not quite see the joke.

"The first cop he sees, Sam, he'll blurt out that it was you and me that knocked down the hay and then trampled on the corn. He'll not be able to help it just as he couldn't help messing himself."

Gourlay understood; at once he advanced on Stirling to deal out punishment for that treachery.

"You'll be a traitor, Stirling," he cried. "You'll give us away to the cops. I'm going to smash your mouth so that it'll be too swollen for you to speak."

Stirling retreated. "If I told the police, Sam," he pleaded, "I'd be giving myself away. Do you think I would give myself away?"

This seemed sensible to Gourlay; he turned and shouted up at Dean, "He'd be giving himself away, Charlie."

"I know that," said Dean coolly. "I said he'll not be able to help it. He wouldn't hae messed his breeks if he could hae helped it."

Gourlay was again convinced. "You'll not be able to help it, Stirling," he said. "You'll just blurt it out, as Charlie says."

Dean shouted down some more cool advice. "Maybe it would be safer, Sam, if he never left here."

"Never left here?" Gourlay again didn't understand.

"Sure. It would be easy in a place like this. Not many folk ever come here. If he was buried here they'd never find his corpse."

Gourlay, enlightened, rubbed his hands in glee.

"Should we murder him?" he cried.

"Is that not how they put traitors out of the way in the pictures?"

Gourlay nodded and lifted in his two hands a large boulder; he raised it high and advanced on Stirling. "I'll smash out your brains," he cried.

Stirling scurrying backwards knew Dean was joking, but was not sure Gourlay understood that. In Gourlay's green eyes murder gloated. He kept shouting he would smash out Stirling's brains.

Then Stirling in his backward flight fell. Gourlay was above him with the boulder raised. Weeping, he seized Gourlay's legs and begged him not to kill him.

Gourlay glanced round for a likely grave. "Over there among the nettles," he shouted. "That's where we'd bury you. Nobody would ever dig among the nettles."

"Don't, Sam, please don't," moaned Stirling.

Gourlay threw the boulder; he threw it over Stirling's head and it crashed against another on the ground, breaking into pieces. Raging, Gourlay rushed across to the nettles and pulled up handfuls; then he rushed back to where Stirling still knelt, head covered with hands.

"You mammy's pet," yelled Gourlay. "You traitor." And with nettles he rubbed Stirling's neck.

Stirling screamed, and Gourlay waving his fiery hand through the air to cool it, raced back to climb up on to the ash beside Dean.

From that height they watched Stirling on his knees creep across to dockens to soothe his neck with them. Then as they jeered and hooted and threw lumps of ash at him he rose to his feet and crept away from the great red lion and all the other monsters there, with one hand out to placate them; his other hand of course held the dockens to his neck.

Chapter Three

———————⊙≈≈≈≈≈≈≈≈≈≈≈≈⊙———————

THE OLD farmer grunted as he strode up to the row of men on
the dyke. His big sunburnt fist tightened on his stick, as if he
was minded to swipe them all off like a string of corbies, so
that they would drop squawking into the gully below where
the rats would gnaw them and find them no titbit. Gourlay's
father sat amongst them, hands in pockets, green muffler
round his neck, long grey hair straggling down under his
cap, neb pecking at the air as a corbie's pecked at a dead
sheep for maggots. No doubt Gourlay was finding maggots
there in plenty, maggots of filth, of sloth, of spite, of envy, of
blasphemy. From their laughter and their pale crazy colliers'
faces it was plain all of them were enjoying belly-fuls of such
maggots.

Small wonder, thought the farmer, young Gourlay was so
vicious, brutal, and destructive. A healthy bull and a good cow
produced, with the Lord's blessing, a sound calf. At the bulling
from which the boy had sprung the Lord wisely had stayed
away. It scunnered the strong-stomached farmer even to
imagine it: this decrepit humorous long-haired bauchle on the
dyke, and yon creeshy stinking foul-mouthed furious bitch
whose udders, he was sure, were ingrained with dirt and
nippled with scabs. In a bug-ridden bed in a scummy kitchen it
would have taken place. Aye, no wonder sweet Christ had
kept away; and no wonder the offspring, the fruit, the harvest,
had been rotten. All over the country such was the human
fruit now being produced. It was a miracle the soil itself, and
the sunshine, remained clean and fertile, able to yield good
tatties and good corn and good turnips. Clawing at his long
grey beard, John Knox in heaven must still be demanding some
rights for Scotland.

He stopped squarely in front of them. Their shy nods and smiles he crushed with his bold contempt.

"I'd like to have a word with you, Gourlay," he said, "if you can spare the time."

Gourlay snickered, showing the gaps in his teeth. He pulled one hand out of its pocket and with what he seemed to think was a lordly or a king's manner looked at the back of his wrist as if a gold watch with diamonds sparkled there, instead of a greasy frayed sleeve and thin rings of aged dirt.

"Why of course, farmer," he cried. "I believe I can spare you a minute or two."

His cronies laughed; Gilchrist laughed too, but differently. He had not missed the weaselly anxiety keeking out from amidst the grand play-acting.

"Of course, Gourlay," he said, "if you're sitting up there solving the world's problems it would be a disgrace to disturb you."

Gourlay, stiff with long sitting on the hard stone, had to turn over on to his stomach to drop down the couple of feet to the pavement. While hanging there, back to the farmer, he spat neatly down into the burn below, and then winkingly peeped round.

"Did you not hear?" he asked. "I found that solution long ago."

"I never heard."

Gourlay still lay there on his stomach, his legs dangling. Great holes in his socks were revealed, and also the yellowish dirtiness of his heels. The seat of his trousers was slack and shiny.

The farmer who liked big strong generous backsides in horses and men had to restrain an impulse to thrash those thin mean buttocks with his stick.

"All that's wrong with the world," said Gourlay, with another tidy spit, "is that a certain appointment's no been kept."

Gilchrist guffawed. "Hae you been sitting there for all these years then, waiting for somebody?"

38

Gourlay dropped and turned round. Especially beside the burly well-fed farmer he was a small shilpit man. With a ridiculous fastidiousness not altogether assumed he dusted his suit although it was so filthy and worn that the farmer would have hesitated putting it on a tattie-bogle.

"You're right, farmer," said Gourlay, glancing up with gap-toothed craftiness. "I've been waiting for somebody. We've all been waiting."

"Me as weel?"

"Aye, you as weel. I should say, especially you, farmer."

"Oh. Is this somebody from the cattle market maybe?"

Gourlay smiled and shook his head. "I couldn't say as to that, farmer. It could be from the cattle market. Why not? There's no kenning where from. It's never been stated in as mony words."

The farmer, not understanding, lost pleasure in the jest. "I've no time to waste havering with you, Gourlay," he said.

"Why not from the cattle market?" repeated Gourlay. "There were kye in it at the beginning. Do you not mind, farmer, of the manger?"

Gilchrist gripped his stick fiercely. "I'll listen to nae blasphemy."

"Blasphemy?" said Gourlay, with raised brows. "There's no blasphemy. Was the appointment not made?"

"Not with the likes of you."

"In the past, farmer, appointments were kept with lepers, and penniless widows, and whores."

"You should have a chance then, Gourlay."

"Just what I said, farmer. But to tell you the truth my patience, and my arse, are numb waiting."

"You'll be pleased to hear then I'm here with news of another appointment, one you'll not be kept waiting long for. It'll be with a man in a wee wig and a red robe."

"A red robe?" repeated Gourlay. "Would you be meaning Santa Claus?" But it was obvious he understood and was inwardly dismayed.

The men on the dyke understood too.

"It looks like you've bought mair eggs, Jimmy," said one.

"At a quid each this time," added another.

"See how the cost of living rises," sniggered Gourlay, as he moved away with the farmer.

When they were out of earshot of the dyke he asked, with a small plaintive virulence that amused the powerful farmer, "Well, what in the name of God is it this time? Has he frightened your prize coo into laying a calf withoot a tail?"

Gilchrist laughed, but did not speak. They were passing over some peaver-beds chalked on the pavement, and the girl whose turn it was to hop paused to let them pass. The farmer walked past with sturdy gentleness, but Gourlay suddenly upped on one leg and with his foot nudged the peaver into another square. The girls squealed at him, more in affection though than annoyance, as even Gilchrist noticed. He noticed too a furtive sadness in the grey weaselly face.

"You're auld for the peaver," he said.

"I used to be a champion at it when I was younger."

"I thought it was a lassie's game. I thought a boy would be found deid rather than be seen playing peaver."

"I was found deid hundreds of times," said Gourlay bitterly.

"Well, if it wasn't your prize coo he frightened, what was it?"

"You seem sure it was your laddie."

"No surer than you. I hope you've got sound proof."

"Sound enough for the sheriff."

"Don't think I hae an unqualified admiration for the impartiality of the law."

"You think the sheriff would be biased in my favour?"

"You're a man of property. The laws were made hundreds of years ago to protect the owners of property. Men were transported for life for stealing a loaf of bread."

"You'll be better at the history than me," laughed the farmer. "You've got the leisure for study. But are you not a man of property yourself?"

Gourlay turned out his trouser pockets. "This ooze is mine," he said, picking off atoms of dirty fluff.

"And the trousers of course," added the farmer.

40

"I'm allowed them for decency's sake," snarled Gourlay. "The law's got a queer notion of decency. If I starve to death, it'll not interfere; but if I pawn my trousers to buy a loaf, and then walk the streets with my bare backside, the law will arrest me for indecency."

Gilchrist chuckled. "When I said you were a man of property I wasn't thinking of your breeks. It was something else; it was your son, as a matter of fact."

"You had a son yourself."

The farmer ignored that; his own son had been killed in the war. "This afternoon," he said, "in front of my very een he wantonly pulled one of my hayricks to pieces; and then, to soften the blow, he went dancing through my corn."

Gourlay was silent.

"You're his faither," said Gilchrist. "It's up to you."

"Christ, what do you want me to do?"

The farmer jerked up his stick significantly.

"That's been tried," muttered Gourlay. "Little else than that. Sticks twice that thickness hae been broken over his back. Maybe a hatchet would be mair effective. Should I use a hatchet, farmer?"

"Weel, you could try the blunt end, to start with."

"Murder; you're egging me on to murder. What's the law's penalty for that? Has it never occurred to you, elder, he's just a child."

"In years."

"You're a farmer."

"As weel as an elder."

"Aye, as weel as an elder. But you're a farmer, and you ken how things grow. Hothouses force plants, don't they? Poverty's a hothouse, farmer. It breeds crime. Surely you've read that."

"There's no compulsion on anybody to live in a hothouse."

"You mean, it's our ain fault we're oot of work, and poor, and hungry, and dressed in rags?"

"This is a free country, Gourlay."

"Christ help you, farmer. If it's true there is a hell for punishment, then Christ help you. You accused me of blasphemy. What

41

you've just said is blasphemy ten thousand times worse than mine."

"That may be," grunted Gilchrist. "But we'll not bother looking so far ahead."

"Jingling round with the wee red-plush bag once a week's hardly enough, farmer," warned Gourlay, shaking his head. "I'm serious, mind you. It used to be, in the pit, lying on my belly, in the half-dark, with small room to move, I had visions of what might be at the end of time."

They had now reached the closemouth through which Gourlay lived. Gilchrist halted just outside, preferring the sunshine to the obscene chalk scribbles and the cats' piss and the children's messes.

"The ancestral halls," grinned Gourlay, with a shake of his head.

"Now, Gourlay, is this affair to be settled oot of court?"

"Best that way, farmer, surely."

"Will I get my compensation that way?"

"How much?" and again Gourlay turned out his trouser pockets.

"Five pounds," said the farmer coolly.

"It was hay, wasn't it? I mean, it couldn't hae been a pile of diamonds he scattered?"

"There was the corn too."

Gourlay fingered his nose. "Should it not hae been cut?" he asked. "It's ripe for cutting."

Gilchrist could not help laughing at the impertinence. "Are you setting up to be a farmer?"

Gourlay was feeling through all his pockets for a fag, although he knew there was none to find. He put his fingers to his lips; it was as if he was blowing little kisses.

"I could hae been a versatile man," he muttered. "I always was one for thinking. That's been my tragedy."

"Mine at the moment's a ruined hayrick. Maybe you would like to come doon and build it up again."

Gourlay flapped the linings of his trouser pockets. "Like the tongues of dead men," he muttered; "eloquent enough."

"I'll see your guid wife and get her verdict."

"You ken she'll use force, brutal force?"

"I'm thinking it might be weel applied."

"It's a fine Christian endeavour to set a mither on to savage her ain son."

"You make a great use of the word, Gourlay."

"Christian?"

"Aye."

"How can I avoid it, farmer? We're all products of a Christian civilisation, aren't we?"

Again the farmer couldn't help laughing. He stared down at the maggoty grey-haired rubbish that claimed to be a product of Christian civilisation.

"Your boy too, you mean?" he asked, and laughed again.

Gourlay with an archbishop's gesture pushed the jeer aside. "I once read something a big religious man said. He was an archbishop, dressed in all his robes. He said that in everything we did we should be acting as Christians; not only in forgiving them that had done us harm, though that was important of course, but in tying our laces even, in stirring our tea, in ploughing our fields. He said that in everything we did there should be an attitude of mind learned from Christ. What do you say to that, farmer?"

"I say," grunted the farmer, sneering at the withered ridiculously eager face staring up at him, "that there's a great guff of cats' piss from your close there."

Gourlay looked disconcerted by this coarse irrelevancy. He shook his head and began another hopeless search of his pockets. He stared down at the spittled pavement.

"Is this your lassie coming?" asked Gilchrist.

Gourlay with shame and yet with a kind of love squinted towards the approaching girl. "Aye, that's Jeanie. She's a Christian."

"I've never noticed her at kirk."

"She doesn't go; but if being kind, and loyal, and helpful, and free from spite, makes you a Christian, then she's one."

Sceptically the farmer gazed at the young skinny girl. She

43

seemed to him little different from the rest of the keelies that worked in the laundry: women who swore filthily and made foul signs and were capable, in their vicious quarrels, of clawing the knickers off each other in the public street. Gourlay's Jeanie looked a typical specimen; only her specs saved her, for they gave her, perched low on her nose as they were, an appearance of glaikit softness. Likely her kindness that her father bragged about was just a soft-headed inability to prevent herself from being imposed on by her bloodsucking family. Like her father she had skimpy buttocks, and her breasts were hardly any bigger than his. The farmer shook his head as she approached: too often he had found that thin scraggy cows gave a poor yield of milk; this one's supply of the milk of human kindness was not likely to be ample.

Nevertheless she had the decency to look ashamed, and she was coming home tired from work.

"What is it, faither?" she asked. "It's not Sam in trouble again?"

Gourlay sullenly nodded.

Jeanie sighed, and with one of her raw red hands pressed her pimply brow. Fresh air, thought the farmer, and plenty of good solid food, might improve her looks. He had to admit she seemed genuinely concerned about her brother.

"Is it damage that can be paid for?" she asked.

"Everything in this bloody world can be paid for," muttered her father. "All you need's money."

"That's a hard doctrine, lass," said Gilchrist.

"What did he damage?"

"Och, he just chewed a hayrick to bits and then, by way of celebration, danced through my corn."

"Will ten shillings do?"

Gourlay laughed, but so far as the farmer could see, it was without meaning.

"Have you got ten shillings then to spare for your brother's sake?" asked Gilchrist.

She nodded; her large hands kept clutching her coat.

"You wouldn't take her money, farmer," said her father.

44

"She's saving up to get married. It seems there's not enough martyrs; she wants to create mair."

Queer martyrs she'd suckle, thought Gilchrist, with those breasts the size of crab-apples.

"Jeanie's got faith," said her father. "She thinks if she got Sammy into another environment she might save him. She dreams of getting married and setting up somewhere in a cottage by the sea with white and red roses climbing the walls. There she'd save Sammy. That's her dream, farmer. What will the reality be? A single-end up some close with an outside lavatory to serve eight or nine families. There'll be nae room for her ain weans, if she has any. And of course, farmer, the fellow she wants to marry is just a man like you and me; he's no saint; he thinks it would be asking too much of him to take Sammy in."

"Faither, please don't talk about that; it's my business," said Jeanie.

Before her father could reply, while he had his toothless mouth open to reply with love and wisdom, his wife joined them. In spite of her bulk Mrs. Gourlay had padded flat-footed down the close, unnoticed.

She surveyed them all, laughing. She sounded, thought the farmer, like a cow with a turnip stuck in its throat. But the similitude was unfair to cows, which were peaceful creatures; she looked more like a pregnant she-bear, hungry, with toothache.

"Chatting aboot the crops?" she asked.

"Guid-evening, Mrs. Gourlay," laughed the farmer. "Aye, just that, chatting aboot the crops."

Roughly she pulled Jeanie aside so that the full force of her glower fell on the old farmer.

"You'll hae eggs to sell?" she suggested.

"I always hae," he said, "at a fair price."

She snarled out a shocking oath; he had never heard worse, not even from drunken ploughmen.

Her husband was again feeling through his pockets; he sniggered when he found no fag.

"Mither, please," whispered Jeanie. "It can be settled withoot unpleasantness."

"I think so," agreed Gilchrist, for the girl's sake.

Mrs. Gourlay spat out another oath, as vicious and horrible. She had a wart on her brow. It was said she ripped it off in her fiendish rages. Certainly she would look ferocious with the blood streaming down that thick stupid face. It was said too she had rages of lust. No wonder in that case her man looked as if he had long ago had all virility mauled and crushed out of him.

"Swearing," said the farmer calmly, "will not restore my rick. I see there's a policeman arrived at the corner."

They looked along, and saw he was speaking the truth. A policeman was standing at the corner near the dyke where the men had been sitting. They were now off, dusting their trousers: sitting on the dyke was illegal. The policeman, a youth nineteen years old, had looked away in shame as the old men had given up their seat.

"The majesty and the might of the law," sneered Gourlay.

"They got off gey smart," commented the farmer with satisfaction.

"Wha would think," asked Gourlay softly, "wars are being hatched, folk in millions are being left to starve, and financiers are planning how to steal huge fortunes?"

The farmer didn't understand, but he was enjoying the woman's snarling bafflement. Obviously she didn't relish this threat of the policeman.

"There's no need for the police," whispered Jeanie. "Will you take the ten shillings please, and go?"

"Ten bob?" howled Mrs. Gourlay. "Who offered ten bob? Was it you?"

The question was to her husband, who giggled bitterly. "Am I Croesus?" he asked.

The farmer misunderstood. "Mair blasphemy?" he sneered, and regretted that, being an elder and sure of salvation he would not be present when this louse crackled in the flames of hell.

46

Gourlay retired puzzled: he had no scruple about blasphemy, but could see none in what he had said.

"I said I would pay the ten shillings, mither," said Jeanie. "Sammy spoiled one of the farmer's haystacks."

"Just a rick, lass; a stack's a different thing. If it'd had been a stack, there would have been no talk of quietening it with fifty half-notes, let alone one."

"If your hay had been piled as high as the building here," said Mrs. Gourlay, "I still wouldn't gie you a ha'penny. If you hae money to hand away, Jeanie, I could tell you somebody much mair in need of it than this auld money-bags."

The farmer laughed, quite merrily: he enjoyed his miser's reputation; with more than eight thousand pounds in the bank he had no need to worry about the envy of paupers.

"If it wasn't for the lassie here," he said, "I wouldn't even discuss terms of settlement with you, woman."

"Don't woman me."

"No, maybe I shouldn't."

"Look your fill, farmer." She made it easy for him to do it, by thrusting herself out at him. "It's all here, farmer, mair woman than you could ever cope with, even in your prime. Maybe you'd like to carry your investigation further in private?"

He grued visibly; even his stick would be defiled touching her.

"No thanks, Mrs.," he grunted.

Jeanie was chewing at her knuckles in horror. Her father felt for his fag.

It was Gourlay who noticed Sam at the corner. The discovery was consolation for the failure to find the fag.

"Enter the villain," he jeered, with a jab of his thumb.

They all stared along. Mrs. Gourlay held out her massive arms.

"Fetch him, Jeanie," she said. "I'd like to ask him a question or two. I'm warning you, farmer, I'm going to take his word."

"Is he not famous as a liar, too?"

"Truth can be got," she said, wriggling her fingers like snakes.

Jeanie began to sob.

47

"It depends on what you call the truth," said the farmer.

"That's a philosophical quest," remarked Gourlay, but nobody heeded.

"Fetch him, Jeanie," ordered her mother, "and the rest of you in here." She lugged her husband into the close, but the farmer struck her hand away; he went in by himself.

"If he suspects," said Mrs. Gourlay, "he'll stay oot till after midnight, and at that time, farmer, I'm in no mood for hammering; it's something far different I'm slavering for then."

"I don't want you to hit him," said Jeanie.

"Not me," grinned her mother. "I'll take him to my bosom; it's fine and soft there."

"If I may put in a word," murmured Gourlay. "They'll hae warned him along there that the farmer's been. Better tell him the farmer's gone, Jeanie, and that it's all right for him to come hame."

"That would be a lie," said Jeanie.

"Tell him the truth then. Say the farmer's here thirsting for blood and money, and your mither's got her sleeves rolled up and her nails sharpened."

"If I get him to come, mither," begged Jeanie, "will you not touch him?"

"I'll stroke his cheeks," promised her mother. "You forget, Jeanie, he lay under my heart for nine months; I suckled him at these breasts. I could show you the mark where he bit me once."

"I'll try to get him to come," sighed Jeanie, and went off on the hateful duty.

From the closemouth they watched her.

Then her father, remembering, tapped the farmer on the chest; or rather tried to, for his friendly finger was knocked away.

"You're under a misapprehension, farmer," said Gourlay. "I said Croesus, no Jesus. You thought I said Jesus?"

The farmer was contemptuously silent.

"I said Croesus. He lived thousands of years ago. He was so rich, his name's used to describe any very wealthy man."

"While you're having such a friendly chat," said his wife, "bum him for a job at the harvest."

"Farming's hard honest work," said Gilchrist. "Do you want your man killed?"

"I could be a tattie-bogle," suggested Gourlay bitterly. "Christ, is it forgotten I worked in the pits for twenty-seven years?"

"Don't give us past history," jeered his wife.

"All history's past. Napoleon, for all his conquests, is in the grave. The twelve disciples are dust. Is it my fault I'm idle? The pit was shut doon, wasn't it?

"There are other pits."

"Where? In Poland do you mean, or the Ruhr in Germany? Name them in the vicinity."

"Shut your gob. You were born lazy, Jimmy. Do you mind what my mither used to say when I was courting you?"

"She was a coarse auld bitch." He hesitated then, because he detested conjugal squabbles in a stranger's presence; it was always in the presence of another man, especially a big powerful man like the farmer, that his wife started them. Nevertheless Gourlay felt he ought not to let pass unrebuked that public insult to his young and hopeful manhood.

"She was prejudiced against me from the first," he muttered. "Just because I was of a serious nature; because I had pamphlets in my pockets."

His wife guffawed and ogled the farmer lecherously.

"She was the true auld prophet though," she cried. "Ken what she said, farmer? She warned me he would be a poor performer; she warned me I'd go to sleep often biting my fingers; she warned me I'd never find satisfaction where a woman needs it most if she's to stay sweet. That's why I soured. Was I always like this, Gourlay? Cast your mind back, and then tell the farmer if I always was like this."

He cast his mind back, though it was a martyr's journey. She had been slim once, with breasts like fruit, soft and fragrant and never cloying; now, if fruit, they were like rotten melons. He had strolled with her then along green country lanes, his arm easily and deliciously round her waist, his lips on hers in a green abandon. He had whispered poetry to her, and she had

49

been proud. God, he thought, awakening there at the close-mouth, was it possible those same hedges this summer were still green and lovely, did those bees and butterflies still sip from the wild flowers? Should they not all be putrid and withered now, in keeping with other things? Had they escaped the curse?

Cackling, she watched his face as he returned from the past; she shoved out her lips as if to give him a kiss.

"You used to call me your Helen of Troy," she cried. "Do you mind that?"

"I mind that, Nelly," he sighed.

"Do you ken wha she was?" she asked the farmer.

Curtly he shook his head.

"She was a whore that ran away with another man," she explained, "and started a shindy that went on for ten years. That was a long time for the bottles to be flying and the razors to be slashing."

"Are you not leaving out the poetry?" asked her husband, with anguished smile.

She drew back from him, deeply disgusted. "Christ, aye," she muttered. "Poetry. I forgot the poetry."

The farmer, sick of that nonsense, was relieved to see Jeanie approaching with her brother. "They're coming," he said. Aye, they were coming like any innocent brother and sister. The girl had her arm round the boy's neck. It could have been affection, but it was more likely a precaution against his bolting.

"See, he's got the nerve to laugh," snarled Mrs. Gourlay. "If he's in a laughing mood, I'll tickle him," and she held out the ticklers, her large fat greedy fists.

"You promised Jeanie you wouldn't hurt him," said her husband.

"I promised you once I'd cherish you, Gourlay."

"But this is no joke, Nelly. There's a trust between those twa. Don't break it. It's the best thing left in our lives, Nelly."

"Trust?" grinned his wife, holding her fist under his nose. "There's no satisfaction in breaking a trust. It's bones I'll break."

50

It was an ordeal for Jeanie to go up to the men at the dyke, not only because she knew they made jokes about her unloveliness, but also because Geordie Lucas was amongst them. Before she had met Tom Donoghue she had walked out with Lucas, and had let him coax her into doing things she had known were wrong. He was a loudmouth and a boaster, and she was afraid he might tell Tom. Every night she prayed Tom never got to know, and all the time she was praying she knew she must before they married tell him.

Quietly, because of the policeman's presence, they had all been chaffing Sam about the farmer's visit. As usual, he did not understand most of it. By the time he saw one joke, another two had been cracked. But what puzzled him most was their hostility. He always thought that the men should like him, admire him, praise him for his fearlessness; after all he did things they themselves were afraid to do. Yet they badgered him with these jokes, and sometimes even the older men threatened to kick him if he didn't clear off. Had he been a whiner, a mammy's pet, a coward, like Stirling, he would have understood it.

Therefore he was secretly relieved when Jeanie came for him. She halted a little distance away and called.

"Sammy, tea's ready," she called, and waved.

"Ask her if auld Gilchrist is haeing tea with you," said Geordie Lucas.

"Auld Gilchrist should hae specs," sneered Sam.

"Oh, he can get a loan of Jeanie's," said Lucas.

Sam laughed. "If she takes them off," he said, "she can see nothing."

Lucas whistled a few gay bars. "She doesn't need to take them off," he added. "Does she go to bed with them on, I wonder?"

"You should know," cried one of his cronies.

An elderly man objected. "That's enough of such talk. As for you," this was to Sam, "can you not see your sister's waiting for you?"

"I can see," answered Sam coolly. He knew the younger men

51

liked to tease old Muldoon; and he knew too that Muldoon's daughter Nancy who wasn't married had had a baby that called Muldoon grandfather. That kind of baby was a bastard.

"Nane of your impudence," cried Muldoon angrily. "You ought to be damned well ashamed of yourself, getting your family into trouble. Your sister there is worth a hundred of you."

Lucas murmured something at which his cronies yelled with laughter.

"What was that you said, Lucas?" asked Muldoon suspiciously.

"I just said Jeanie would be grand at boiling shirts in the laundry," said Lucas, and again he whistled his gay love tune.

"Sammy," called Jeanie, waving.

"Will I not do instead, Jeanie?" cried Lucas, pointing to himself. Somehow he made the gesture obscene.

She tried to ignore him, but blushed. There came into her mind too the recollection, sharp as thorns, that beside the place where the act had been committed pink wild roses were growing. As long as she lived roses, and everything beautiful, would fill her with guilt unless she told Tom and he forgave her. Now even the love and loyalty she felt towards her young brother were contaminated.

At last he came slouching over to her.

"Are you going to the pictures, Sam?" shouted Dean.

Sam halted. "It depends," he shouted back, and took a hand out of his pocket to jerk it in Jeanie's direction.

"All right then, outside Tony's at seven," cried Dean. "I'll not wait if you're not there."

"I think I'll be there," said Gourlay coolly, and putting his hand back into his pocket swaggered up to Jeanie.

The men talked about them as they met.

"That's a good lassie," said Muldoon. "She's a damned sight too good for him. He's the kind that will spit her kindness back at her."

"She's certainly more of a mither to him," said another elderly man, "than his ain mither is."

52

"Jeanie a mither?" asked Lucas, in a simple surprise. "I doubt you're mistaken, Erchie. Her breasts are the size of peas." Others laughed, and he was indignant as if he thought they were accusing him of exaggeration. "Peas," he repeated, and showed their size on the tip of his forefinger.

"Well, you should know, Geordie," said one.

"Does this fellow Donoghue from Ralston know about you and her, Geordie?" asked another.

"No."

"And I don't think you'll be the one to tell him," snapped Muldoon.

"Why not?" smiled Lucas.

"Because I've heard he's pretty useful with these," and Muldoon held up his fists.

"Is that so, Pat?" smiled Lucas. "Well, nobody can say he's useful with this," and he tapped his temple.

"He's like a wee ape," said one. "His arms nearly trail on the street."

"Just his arms, Bill?" asked Lucas, with that innocence which his friends found so amusing.

They banged one another in their mirth. One even took off old Muldoon's bonnet and tickled his bald scalp. They were sobered by someone remarking that Rosy Cheeks, as they called the young policeman, had stopped to talk to Jeanie and young Gourlay.

He was still at the stage where he hated public officiousness more than he loved promotion. Often he blushed and was more polite than became his uniform. For instance now, before speaking to Jeanie who after all was just a laundry-girl, he touched his helmet; and he tried to give Sam the smile a nineteen-year-old youth should give to a boy of thirteen.

"I don't want to alarm you, miss," he said, "but I've just had a complaint about your brother here."

"About the hay?" asked Jeanie, alarmed.

"Hay? No, it wasn't about hay." He examined the boy's clothing and saw wisps of hay all over it. "It wasn't about hay," he repeated. "It was about the palings down by the burn You were seen breaking one this afternoon."

A rush of indignant innocence into Sam's throat almost choked him; he gaped and gasped and could not speak. "Palings?" he managed to say at last. "I was never near any palings this afternoon."

"Likely not," said the policeman, plainly thinking him a liar. "But I'd advise you not to do it again. Good-evening, miss." Touching his helmet he walked away.

Tortured by inability to express his indignation, Gourlay glared after him and ground his teeth. "The bastard," he gasped, "the big bastard."

"Sam, that's terrible language," cried Jeanie. "He was just warning you. It was nice of him. You shouldn't have touched the palings."

Sam turned on her. "I never touched any palings," he yelled. He raised his fist as if to strike the disbelief from her face. "I tell you, I never touched any palings."

"All right, don't shout."

"I never touched any palings." This time it was a particularly loud and aggressive shout.

"All right, I said. Be quiet. Everybody's listening."

"Do you think I care who's listening? I tell you I never touched any palings."

She tried to put her arm round him. "I believe you, Sam."

He punched her arm viciously away. "Do you think I care whether you believe me or not? I touched no palings."

The pain of the blow on her arm made her wince, but she would not even rub it because people were watching.

"We'd better go and get our tea," she murmured, "if you've to be outside Tony's at seven."

He consented to walk on. "I've no money."

"I'll give you sixpence."

"Sixpence!" He spat with scorn.

"It'll get you into the fourpenny seats, and the other tuppence will do for your bus fares."

"Am I to get no sweeties to eat? When you go with

54

Donoghue, he buys you boxes of chocolates with ribbons round them."

She smiled, and nodded. It was she herself who had told Sam about Donoghue's generosity; she had had to boast about it to someone.

"All right," she said. "I'll give you another tuppence for sweeties."

Mollified, he began to chew the sweets in anticipation. "I'll buy chewing-nuts," he said. "You get a lot of them for tuppence. Maybe I'll buy hazelnut chocolate."

Again she tried to put her arm round him; this time after a scowl he allowed her.

"Sammy, did you make a mess of Farmer Gilchrist's hay?" she asked quietly.

Still chewing those imaginary sweets he shook his head.

"Was it not you?" Her tone was hopeful in spite of the hay on his jersey.

He shook his head again. "It was Stirling," he said.

"Stirling? You mean John Stirling, that lives in Burnbank Place?"

He nodded.

"But he's a quiet wee boy; he wouldn't do a thing like that."

"I saw him."

"Did you, Sam?" There was no sarcasm in her voice, just wonder and regret. As she picked the hay off him she made it like little caresses. Last time she had mentioned to Tom about taking Sammy to live with them, he had not been so angrily opposed. He had just, kissing her ear, whispered she was trying to be an angel without wings. She smiled there in the street as she remembered. Some angel, she had whispered back: an angel with specs. Tom had kissed her specs then, dimming them so that she couldn't see and had to take them off and wipe them with his hanky.

Sam suddenly stopped.

"Has auld Gilchrist gone?" he asked.

She hesitated. The lie told then would betray not only Sammy, but also her happy memories of Tom. Yet it had to be

55

told. If she were to tell him the farmer was still there, Sammy would run away; but when he came back punishment crueller than ever would be waiting fo him.

"Yes," she murmured, "he's gone."

"You don't seem very sure."

"I was thinking, Sammy."

"About auld Gilchrist and his hay?"

She smiled and shook her head.

"I ken who you were thinking about."

"Likely you do," she whispered, "for I think about him most of the time."

They walked on again towards the close.

"I don't like Donoghue," he said. "He's mean."

"Oh, that's not true, Sammy," she cried. "He's very generous. In fact," laughing proudly, "he's too generous."

"He never slips me a tanner," said Sam dourly. "Other chaps slip tanners to their tart's brothers."

"He's shy; and in any case, Sammy, please don't call me his tart."

"Well, what are you?"

Smiling, she looked at her engagement finger; nobody else would have seen a ring on it, but she did.

"I'm his lass," she whispered.

"Tart's the same thing."

"No, Sammy, it isn't. Tart's not a respectable word. You shouldn't use it about any girl."

He grinned. "Could I use it about Nancy Muldoon?" he asked. "She had a wean and she wasn't married. The men say she was a whure; that's the same as a tart, isn't it? Geordie Lucas said every lassie over twelve's a tart. He should ken, for he's had lots." His grin broadened as he remembered she had been among Lucas's conquests. "You used to go with Geordie. You should have stuck with him. I like him better than Donoghue."

She could not answer; it was a relief therefore, a dreadful relief, that they were now at the closemouth.

Only their father was to be seen there.

"What was Rosy Cheeks saying to you?" asked Mr. Gourlay anxiously.

"He said I broke a paling, and I never was near it."

"Innocent, eh?"

His son nodded, grinning. He did not like his father, but he was not afraid of him.

"What's for tea?" he asked brazenly.

"How would roasted hay suit you? Or maybe a dish of trampled corn?"

Laughing, Sam pushed past his father and sauntered down the close. His mother and the farmer were waiting in a recess. She lunged out and caught him by the hair. The door of the house was open, ready. She dragged him in as if to a cave or den.

"Mither, mither," cried Jeanie, weeping. "For God's sake. You'll kill him."

"I'll have a damned good try anyway," roared her mother.

Before he disappeared into the house Sam in spite of the agony managed to turn his head and glare in hatred at his sister.

"This is your fault," he cried. "You said it was all right. You said he was gone. You wait. I'll get you for this."

"I couldn't help it, I couldn't help it," sobbed Jeanie, pressing her face against the clammy chalked wall.

The farmer stood watching her. He had not accepted Mrs. Gourlay's invitation to follow her into the torture-chamber and watch justice being done. Mr. Gourlay stood at the closemouth, still searching for the fag.

The farmer put his hand on Jeanie's shoulder. He pitied her, not because she had been forced into betraying her brother, but because here she was home from a long day at work, and no good dinner was ready for her.

"Don't greet, lass," he muttered.

Her father came creeping up to them. "Don't greet," he repeated. "Is she to laugh then, and do a dance of triumph? Will I tell you, elder, why I don't believe in hell? Because I'm convinced it's beyond the ingenuity of even the Almighty to think up worse punishments than these. We breathe and we're in hell. Listen."

They heard Jeanie's sobbing, a bus on the street outside, and in the house thuds and screams from the thudder.

"So greet on, Jeanie. Likely all your tears are doing is making a mess of your specs; but they might, for all we ken, be washing away our sins."

"Shut your mouth," growled the farmer. "Is the lassie not suffering enough without you snivelling your blasphemies at her? I'll away for a breath of wholesome air. Tell your guidwife I'll make no charge. It's for the lassie's sake."

"What about the boy's?" asked Gourlay.

"Oh him," cried the farmer as he strode out of the close, "he's getting what he deserves."

Gourlay stood staring after him, as if in thought. Then he, or rather his fingers, seemed to waken up.

"I wish to God," he muttered, "I had a fag."

Chapter Four

On the morning Stirling was to go to the Academy for the first time he got out of bed before his mother came to knock on the door, and walking bare-footed across the empty carpetless room gazed out, pale, intense, and self-contained, at the early sunshine as at the coming to pass of an anticipated miracle. Last night on his knees on the hard floor he had prayed for good weather, and now this morning the sun shone more beautifully than it had done for several days; yesterday for instance there had been hours of rain. Yet not by a whisper, nor even by a silent movement of his lips, did he reveal gratitude for the prayer answered, or wonder that the prayer could be answered. He stood gazing out, in a deep sinister enchantment; his hand rested on the curtains so lightly that though these shivered it was because of the window open at the top.

Today he went to the Academy, and he had no raincoat.

He had been standing by the window for about five minutes when his mother knocked.

"Are you wakened, John?" she called.

He recognised the excitement in her knuckles and voice, but did not respond to it by so much as a smile.

"Yes," he answered, "I'm up."

She suspected his strange calmness; for a moment on the other side of the door she was calm herself, not examining her suspicion, but dreading it. Then she opened the door.

She laughed when she saw him at the window. Both of them knew there was some falseness in her laughter.

"See, it's going to be a braw day," she said. "It's going to be warm. Even if you had a raincoat, you wouldn't be putting it on."

He shook his head.

"Are you all right, son?" she asked. "You're not feeling ill?"

"I'm all right."

She stood by the door, holding on to the handle, playing with it, turning it this way then that, as if she was the child.

"Don't worry," she murmured. "You'll get on fine."

He looked at her and she could see no meaning in the look. It frightened her; she told herself she would rather he wept or sulked, for in that case she would understand him, be in his company, be able however feebly to reassure him. Now he seemed very far away. Sometimes she warned herself that the better educated he became the further he must travel from her; but that remoteness, however sad and hard to bear, was easily understood. This one by the window mystified her.

"I promised you I'd get you a raincoat," she murmured, "and I will. It maybe won't be new, but you know I wouldn't get one that would make a fool of you. It's a blessing it's going to be a good day. Mary's up. You can come ben as soon as you're dressed. You've plenty of time. That's Mary singing. See what the bright weather does to her."

As his mother held the door open wide, he listened to his sister singing.

"It's a silly song," said his mother laughing. "One of the latest. I've got a good hot breakfast for you your first morning: porridge, and fried slice sausage."

"Are there rolls?" he asked, and somehow the ordinary question did not bring him any nearer to her; perhaps because she had to answer no.

"I'm afraid there are no rolls," she murmured. "I know you like your slice sausage inside a roll." She tried to laugh. "I'm fond of that myself, so you must have inherited the notion. Maybe we'll be able to afford them one or two days next week."

"They're as cheap as bread."

"Oh no, that's not the case. If they were as cheap as bread do you think I wouldn't prefer them? They're a good bit dearer. They're classed as a luxury; for us anyway."

"It makes no difference."

"That's right. Bread's just as nourishing. It's called the staff of life, isn't it?"

"I meant, I'm not hungry."

"No, I ken. You'll be too excited." Yet if he was excited it was such a deep excitement she could see no sign of it. "Still, you'll have to eat as good a breakfast as you can. You'll be away all day, remember. Now just get dressed. There's plenty of time, but come through as quick as you can."

As he dressed in his new clothes, not even their contact, nor their undeniable presentableness, lured him out of his rapt oppressed mood. Before leaving the room he stood by the window again and gazed out at the miraculous sunshine.

He had washed thoroughly the night before, and now needed only to wipe his face with a wet cloth.

Mary peeped into the scullery. "My goodness," she cried, "just a cat's lick, and you going among the élite!" It was a word she had heard used in the office recently, with the same sneer of envious sarcasm as she used it now.

"Come and take your breakfast, Mary," said her mother, "and don't be stupid. He had a good wash last night."

Mary sat down at the table. "No porridge," she said. "You know fine they bring me out in heat spots."

"It's funny that," sighed her mother. "They never affect John and me in that way."

"I've got fair skin," said Mary complacently.

"So you have," agreed her mother proudly. "You always had, even as a baby."

Mary never liked to be reminded that she once had been a baby. "And I don't like slice sausage very much," she said crossly.

"I'm sure I do my best," complained her mother. "You would think I purposely got what didn't suit you; I get what we can afford."

"All right, all right," cried Mary, holding up her hands in impudent surrender. "No lectures, please. Give me the sausage. But I'll soon be having as many spots as Jeanie Gourlay."

61

Her mother dished out the sausage, paying no heed to the sniffs of distaste with which they were received.

"Right enough," she said smugly, "poor Jeanie's not turned out very braw. She was much nicer when she was a wee lassie."

John slipped into his place.

Mary frowned with elegant disgust at a piece of sausage on the points of her fork.

"What are you so sad about?" she asked irritably.

"Leave him alone," snapped her mother. "He's not sad. Why should he be sad? He's excited. Would you expect him not to be on his first day?"

Mary admired her own cool pink prettiness in the small twinkle of her knife.

"I wouldn't say he looked excited," she said. "I'd say he was in a trance. Wake up," she cried, rattling her knife against her plate. "Wake up."

"Don't be silly, Mary," smiled their mother. "And I hope you're watching the clock."

"How can I do that?" snapped Mary. "If you'd buy a decent one, I could watch it."

Wearily her mother went to the mantelpiece and lifted the clock from its face. "It's five past," she muttered.

"Are you sure? That thing's never right."

"I'm making allowance for that. It's five past. You'll need to hurry."

"Do you want me to take indigestion as well as spots? And what are you smirking at?"

The question was to her brother, who certainly had not smirked; indeed he had not been listening to the conversation.

Mary looked across at him, sneered, nibbled at sausage, hesitated between each nibble, was obviously tempted, and as usual succumbed.

She laughed pleasantly, to lighten the sin.

"You look quite the little gentleman," she said. "One of the élite already. Of course, if it rains it'll be a pity. I don't just mean because everybody will stare at you without a raincoat. I mean it'll be like Cinderella at the party; when the clock struck twelve all her fine clothes turned to rags, you remember. It'll not be the clock striking twelve with you of course; it'll be the rain. You see, cheap materials shrink very quickly."

As she spoke she watched her brother closely, loving and pitying him. As if deaf and blind, he went on supping his porridge; his face though was as white as the milk. The milk in his spoon shivered in a little storm.

"It might not rain," she murmured.

Her mother had her hand pressed hard against her mouth. She knew that to deny Mary's accusation of cheapness or to reprove her for it would simply be to give it emphasis.

"For God's sake," she whispered.

Mary glanced out at the sunshine. "It's sometimes not a good sign when it's bright too early," she said. "Clouds come later and then there's rain. They come out of the Atlantic Ocean."

"If there's a God in heaven," muttered her mother, "it'll not rain."

Mary jumped up, daintily wiping her lips with her handkerchief. "I'm afraid, mother, if there is a God in heaven, he'll have more to bother him than how John gets on at school." She went over to a mirror and put on her neat blue coat and hat; she was very particular as to how her hat sat on her head; certain curls had to escape from under it, at the front and the back. She looked very sweet and charming. "Nobody today believes in God really. Some people say they do, but it's just lies."

"Mary, you shouldn't say things like that."

"Why not? Will God push me under a bus for spite? Miss Craife believes in God; she says she does, and she goes to church every Sunday; she's a member of the choir and of all sorts of church societies; and she's a bitch."

"Still, I hope you don't forget to show her proper respect."

Miss Craife was Mary's superior in the office.

"Don't worry, mother. I'm a good hypocrite." She gave an example of her hypocrisy. " 'Thank you very much, Miss Craife; it's very good of you.' Bitch."

63

"A hypocrite's not a nice thing to be, Mary."

"So they say, mother; but it's necessary. Cheerio."

At the door she turned and blew her mother the paltriest kiss. She glanced at John. "Good luck," she said, meaning to say no more, but words came into her mind and she would not resist them. "You'll need it," she added. "If it rains, you'll need it." Then with one of her prettiest smiles she was gone.

Mrs. Stirling busied herself lifting the sausage from the pan on to John's plate.

"Don't heed what Mary said," she muttered. "She's as keen as I am that you do well."

For the first time he smiled; it was a very faint smile, yet she knew it expressed his opinion that Mary was so diseased with envy that she hoped he failed.

"She's not really jealous," she went on. "It's just that she's not very happy in her office. I think this Miss Craife isn't very nice to her at times."

Again he smiled faintly.

"And I'm sure it's not altogether Mary's fault," snapped his mother, nettled. "She's got a lot to suffer from that upstart. I only hope if you meet with a snob who's nasty to you that you'll face up to him with the same spirit as your sister."

His smile faded, and she knew she had said too much; but she was not willing to revoke it and thus be disloyal to Mary and to herself.

"Mind I've warned you," she said. "You will have to stick up for yourself."

He got up from the table.

"You've not finished your sausage."

"I don't want it."

"Well, if you choose to fall out with your food just because— oh John son, I'm sorry, I shouldn't have spoken to you like that, not this morning." Shyly she made to embrace him, but he avoided her. She stood then with her rejected hands clasped in front of her, in a praying attitude, and watched him as he brushed his hair, put jotters and lunch-piece into his case, and examined his pencils to see if they were sharp.

"I'll be going," he murmured. "You'll not be in when I come back?"

"No, I'm afraid not."

"Have I to light the fire?"

"It would be a help, son. I'll have the potatoes all ready peeled, and you could put them on about quarter past five if I'm not back by then."

"Maybe I'll have home lessons."

"Surely not your first day?"

He was over at the door and would not look at her.

"Tomorrow'll not be my first day," he said. "Will I have all this to do then too?"

Still with her hands clasped, she tried to laugh.

"All this?" she repeated. "It'll not take you five minutes."

"You'll want me to set the table too."

She burst into anger and snatched her hands apart.

"Isn't it terrible of me that I should want you to set the table for me?" she cried. "Look at James Brown and Walter Donaldson. It's not tables they set. One delivers milk and rolls, and the other newspapers. They're not older than you either. Mr. Machrie the newsagent asked me just the other day if I didn't want the job for you. I said no, it wouldn't be fair seeing the distance you've got to travel to school and the home lessons you'd be expected to do. I could see from his face he thought I was being too lenient with you. And now you're hinting that I'm trying to overburden you with work just because I'm expecting you to set the table and look after the fire. What do you think I'll be doing? Do you think I'll be sitting at my ease in luxury? I'll be down on my knees scrubbing; I'll be feeling such a pain in my back I could scream; I'll——" but it was no use going on, the door quietly shut, and he was away. Weeping she rushed through to the room and was in time to see him pass the window. She knocked on it and called his name in love, but he walked on without heeding. As she hid her face in the curtains, weeping sorely, it was in the midst of her hurt and disappointment and foreboding, a consolation that in his new clothes passing the window he had looked indistinguishable from the sons of gentlemen: at the Academy he would not be disgraced.

At the bus-stop, while he was enjoying a sad self-pity at his mother's unfairness to him, he was accosted by Sam Gourlay. The latter came out of the Co-operative store swinging a basketful of groceries, and saw Stirling standing there at the bus-stop. Eagerly he raced up to him. A roll jumped out of the basket. He picked it up, rubbed it against his jersey, and threw it in again.

He stood winking at Stirling. His face was still bruised and swollen from the leathering his mother had given him last week.

"Hello," he said.

"Hello," whispered Stirling.

"Is this you away to the Academy?"

Stirling nodded and looked to see if a bus was coming.

"You're a great toff," said Gourlay, in sincere admiration. "They'll never ken you there. They'll think your faither's got bags of money. And you've got no faither, Stirling." Gourlay laughed at that peculiar joke. "They'll never guess your mither scrubs floors. Will you tell them that?"

Stirling did not answer.

"I mean," Gourlay went on, "somebody might ask you what your faither does. Of course you can say he's dead. Will they all be toffs there? Better not say anything about your mither scrubbing floors if they're all toffs. They'd snigger, so they would, Stirling. Me, I'd knock their teeth down their throats; but you, you'd just blush and look away, Stirling. That would make them snigger all the more. I don't like toffs." He took from the basket the roll that had fallen on the pavement and offered it to Stirling. "Here's a roll for your dinner-piece. You can bite the dirty bits off."

"No thanks, Sam. I've got a dinner-piece."

"Is it in your case?" Gourlay went down on one knee and stroked the smooth side of the case. "It's a beauty," he said. "You don't want the roll then?"

"No thanks, Sam."

66

"What's in your dinner-piece? Is it salmon? That's what I like best. I wish I got it oftener. What is it you've got?"

"Banana."

"Oh, that's all right. I like banana. But I prefer salmon. It's a good long ride in the bus to Muirton."

Stirling nodded and again looked along the road.

Gourlay was now sitting on the basket, nibbling at the dirty roll.

"How would you like it, Stirling," he asked, "if me and Charlie Dean was to walk to Muirton and shout to you through the gates? How would you like that?"

Stirling tried to smile. "It's over six miles."

"Oh, I ken that. I've been in Muirton. I hung on the back of a lorry once and it took me to Muirton. I'd to walk half the way back. But we could bus it. Charlie's always got plenty of money. And look what I've got." He put his hand into his trouser pocket and brought it out clenched. "This isn't a ha'penny," he warned, with a grin. Then he unclenched his hand; in his palm lay a threepenny. He squinted down at it with a peculiarly cunning satisfaction. It was an instalment of Jeanie's penance for betraying him. She thought she was buying his forgiveness; but he was not going to forgive her, he was waiting for the right time to take his revenge.

Stirling too gazed at the coin. He had begged his mother for threepence over and above his bus fares, not to spend but just to give him confidence. She had said she could not afford it.

Gourlay put the coin back into his pocket.

"We'll stand at the gates and shout to you," he said. "All the toffs will get a shock."

"But you're still at school yourself, Sam."

"I'll plunk it."

"You'll just get into trouble, and it would be a silly way to waste your money."

"I could hang on the back of a lorry, though the last time it gave me a sore stomach."

Then at last a bus swung round the corner.

67

Gourlay leaped up and rushed into the roadway, holding up his hand.

It stopped, and Stirling saw two boys with Academy caps staring out in amusement.

"There you are, Stirling," shrieked Gourlay in glee. "I stopped it for you."

Blushing, Stirling climbed on board.

For about twenty yards Gourlay raced after the bus, shouting, "Look for me at the gates."

Without finding it funny Stirling saw that a small dog at Gourlay's neglected basket was up on its hind legs with its head among the groceries. He saw Gourlay galloping back to chase it.

Stirling chose a seat at the back of the bus. From it he could study his Academy schoolmates without their knowing it. Already, passing them on his way to his seat, he had noticed that not only their clothes were better than his but their cases too, which were of real leather whereas his was of painted pasteboard.

They spoke loudly and confidently, boasting about their holidays: one had been in the Hebrides, the other at Bournemouth in England. Obviously they did not have to be careful not to say 'naw' instead of 'no' or 'wouldnae' instead of 'wouldn't'; they could utter any nonsense fearlessly, knowing they were safe from mockery. At the Academy there would be hundreds like them, all speaking properly, all boasting about their holidays. John himself had not been away from home indeed he had never in all his life seen the sea, far less, as the taller of the two in front was bragging, watched seals swimming in it with heads like comical old men. If he was challenged as to where he had spent his holidays, he would say Rothesay. In the house was a postcard sent by a neighbour who had been a day's trip there, and John had studied the coloured picture so long and yearningly that everything in it had become alive and familiar, the people putting, the bright flowers, the glimpse of the sea, and even a small white dog that seemed to have no owner.

For a while, as the bus sped through country districts where the stops were lonely and no more Academy pupils came on, he had leisure to consider Gourlay's mad threat of appearing at the Academy gates. If he did appear there, it would of course mean the finish of everything; not only would he be wearing his dirty jersey and shouting swears like Christ and bastard, but he would be sure to yell that Stirling's mother scrubbed floors. If he in his stupidity forgot to yell that, Dean would remind him. Like a monkey climbing the bars of its cage, Gourlay would cling to the gates, with his swollen face keeking over the top. A blazered crowd would gather. They would be amused by his antics and puzzled by his yells. Who was this Stirling, they would ask. What did he mean crying that Stirling's mother scrubbed floors? Did anybody know Stirling? And one would say there was a Stirling in his class, a John Stirling, and right enough he didn't have a blazer or any of the school colours, so it was quite likely his mother was poor enough to have to scrub floors. Then they would all want Stirling pointed out to them.

But Stirling, shivering, did not believe Gourlay would come; he often made threats and forgot them. His sandshoes were so thin-soled that before he had walked one mile let alone six his feet would burn with blisters, burn and fester, bleed and limp and leave blood-prints in the white dust on the pavement. Besides, at his school the teachers all knew him, they would guard him always as warders guarded a dangerous convict: the gates would be locked, and there were spikes on the high walls. If Gourlay made a race and leapt up on to the wall, a spike might pierce his belly; he would lie there, shrieking, his head and legs twitching in agony, like a giant earwig. But suppose he did climb over the wall safely, and suppose he managed to jump on to the back of a Muirton lorry, there were many policemen in the intervening villages who would be sure to catch sight of him and whistle to the lorry to stop. And as for using his three-pence on bus-fares, Stirling could not see Gourlay tamely and respectably enter the bus, hand over his money to the conductress, and then sit holding his ticket all the way to Muirton.

No, it did not seem likely Gourlay would ever arrive at the Academy gates.

Perhaps Stirling was able to overcome this worry about Gourlay because his other immediate worry, his having no raincoat, had been dispelled as soon as he noticed that the two with the leather cases and the correct voices had none.

If it rained later in the day, these two would make a joke of their having no coats; they might balance their cases on their heads, like horizontal umbrellas. Stirling could follow their example: not to the extent perhaps of capering, but at least he could smile up at the clouds with a little shake of his head, as if the weather had played him a dirty trick by thus enticing him out in the sunny morning without his coat and then scattering rain on him in the cloudy afternoon. If he smiled skilfully enough, nobody would suspect that he had not been deceived at all, that he was coatless in the rain simply because he did not yet possess a raincoat. As for the damage being done to his suit, while he was thus smiling, the anguish over that could be postponed till he reached home.

Now the bus was approaching the town of Muirton. It became crowded with Academy pupils, all of them, except one, with raincoats on or over their arms. The exception was a fair-haired boy with a large head, a large nose, and small eyes. More ridiculous than his appearance even was his dress: jacket and trousers didn't match, and on his left arm there was a big conspicuous black stain of tar or ink or oil. Stirling felt how poignantly he must be wishing the stain was on the inside of his sleeve where it could be concealed by keeping the arm still, close to his side. Though he came on with several others, nobody in the happy babble spoke to him; and it was no wonder, for besides having no coat and no cap and this dirty jacket, he had also no case. All he had was a jotter stuffed into his pocket.

While Stirling was cautiously congratulating himself on having found somebody far poorer than himself, somebody on whom all the sneers might be exhausted, he saw that the two others whom he had thought to be without coats

70

were now dragging down· from the rack dark-blue trench
coats which must have been crushed in there to be out of
the way.

He had no time to assess the effect of this strange treachery.
The bus stopped, the Academy pupils, boys and girls, jumped
out eagerly; and he himself, coatless and minus some other
protection neither visible nor definable, stood alone on the
pavement amidst a throng of merry pink faces and proud blue
and green caps that surged down an avenue shaded by tall
quiet trees.

The other coatless boy was standing beside him on the
pavement, gloomily pulling up his stockings.

"Weel," he said to Stirling as if they had known each other
for years, "I suppose there's naething else for it."

He spoke as coarsely as Gourlay did; he made no effort to
achieve an Academy politeness.

"The holidays are ower," he said, frowning and grinning at
the same time. "Weel, will we go?"

Stirling was dismayed. He wanted sympathy and company,
but not from this badly-dressed, coarse-tongued, wild-haired
fool. Still, he could not wait there conspicuously. He began to
walk down the avenue as if he was alone.

The other boy walked beside him; he did not seem to notice
he wasn't welcome.

"My name's Tull," he said, "Robert Tull. You spell it
T—u—l—l. You're new here, aren't you?"

Stirling had to nod. He had noticed that when Tull announced
his name, shouting it as if it were famous, some Academy girls
glanced over and started to giggle. Tull too seemed to have
noticed them, for he turned round, gave them a good stare, and
then forgot them.

"Do you know what I think?" he asked. "I think I'm not
going to like it at the Academy. Too many snobs."

Embarrassed, Stirling looked away at the tops of the iron
railings; shaped like fleur-de-lys they were. He was sure this
ignorant blethering Tull would not know what fleur-de-lys
were.

"I never wanted to come," said Tull. "It was my dad made me. Weel, he didn't exactly *make* me, if you see what I mean. I mean," and here he laughed loudly, with scorn, "he didn't threaten to leather me with his stick if I wouldn't come." Again he laughed and again bent down to pull up his stockings. He had to run to make up on Stirling again. "You see, my dad's a cripple."

"A cripple?" In spite of his vow not to speak, Stirling could not help repeating the sinister broken word.

"Aye. It was an accident in the steelwork did it, before I was born. He's got a bath-chair; you ken, the thing on wheels that you push. I push it. I like to push it. I like to push it better than onything else."

Stirling thought how queer that this stupid blurter, worse even than Gourlay, should have passed the bursary examination. It had been easy, but surely not as easy as that.

"I like my dad," said Tull proudly. "He and I have long talks together. Do you ken what he wants me to be? A doctor! He said it's the greatest thing in the world to discover a new cure. Have you ever heard of Pasteur?"

"I think so."

"He was a Frenchman. My dad told me all aboot him. He would like me to be a Pasteur; but dash it, I'll never pass the Academy exams even, never mind become famous. I'll try my best. I promised my dad I would try my best. Do you ken this, when the letter came saying I'd won a place, my dad had tears in his een?"

What's wonderful about that? thought Stirling. My mother often cries.

"Of course they were tears of joy; that's why I would like to do weel in the exams, but I'll never manage it. I'm not very clever, you know. Mr. Eaglesham, my qualifying teacher, was angry when I said I wanted to sit the bursary exam. He said I had nae right to; he said I'd gie him and the school a showing up. My dad had to gie me a letter to the heidmaister. What's your name?"

The suddenness of the question prevented Stirling from

72

equivocating. He had not wished to let Tull know his name, for that was the first step towards friendship, and he did not want Tull as a friend.

"John Stirling," he muttered.

"Stirling. That's the name of a toon. There's a castle there. Are you clever?"

"I think so. My teacher said so."

"Eaglesham never said I was. Even when I told him I'd passed, do you ken whit he said? He said from now on he'd believe in miracles; he asked me if all the ithers had fallen asleep at their desks. Sarcastic, you see. Did you win a bursary or do you pay fees?"

"A bursary." It should have been a proud statement, yet Stirling thought how happier if he had been able to say he paid fees. It would have meant, well, to begin with, a superiority over Tull, and a raincoat, and a mother who didn't scrub floors, a house with a garden, an Academy blazer and cap.

"I thought that," remarked Tull. "I thought you weren't a feepayer."

Stirling did not dare to ask his reason.

"Eaglesham was right enough all the same," grinned Tull. "I must have scraped past by the skin of my teeth. My dad coached me for weeks. What are you going to be, Stirling? That's to say, if you manage to pass all the exams."

And if I manage, thought Stirling, to keep my mother's work a secret, if I get a coat before the winter comes, if Gourlay keeps away from the gates.

"A teacher," he murmured.

"Ugh no!" cried Tull. "Not a teacher surely? That's the last thing in the world I'd want to be."

"They get good pay."

"My dad says money's not the maist important thing."

Quickly Stirling asked, "What does he say is?"

Tull laughed. "I don't know. It's a long answer. I'd like to be a bus-driver."

"But you don't have to pass exams to be a bus-driver. You don't even need to go to the Academy."

73

"That's right. But you need a good nerve to go in and out of the traffic." He demonstrated he had that good nerve by taking in his eager hands the wheel of a bus and steering it round sharp hairpin bends. "Do you think double-deckers are harder to drive than single-deckers?" he asked. "You've to be careful going under bridges when you're driving a double-decker. I'll admit it's not a very comfortable job in hot weather. But teachers are always getting daft answers to their questions. If you get a daft answer when you're a teacher, will you cover your face with your hands like this, see, and say 'Good God'? That's what Eaglesham used to say. A boy whose dad's in the Brethren brought a note once. Would you use the strap?"

Stirling remembered Gourlay's accusation of cruelty.

"I don't know," he muttered.

"My dad says the strap should be abolished. You should hae seen Eaglesham using it. He made his eyes go all skelly and he kept plucking at his whiskers though he had nane, and with his knees bent like this he slunk over to his desk, looking all round as if he was a burglar going to break open a safe."

Tull acted as he spoke, heeding neither his companion's embarrassment nor the giggles of some girls walking behind. As he resumed his normal pace, after a quick apparently extra pull at his stockings, he gave the girls a cheery grin of dismissal. It sent them off into shriller shrieks.

"That was how Eaglesham walked," he said, "and when he got the strap oot, you should hae seen the way he stroked it and called it names like 'Black Beauty' and 'Sweet Redeemer' and 'The Good Fairy at the Christening.' He used to tell us stories to explain what the names meant. It was all right for the rest of the class, they could sit back and enjoy the stories, but what aboot them on the floor, spitting on their palms? It wasn't all right for them."

"Were you one of them on the floor often?"

Tull grinned. "Aye, that's right. How did you guess? I think I got the strap on an average four times a day."

"Sometimes," said Stirling, in recrimination, "bus-drivers run over people and kill them."

74

"Sure. But it's the people's own fault, nine times oot of ten. They don't look where they're going. Have you ever seen an accident?"

"No." He thought of Gourlay's with the bike on Drumsagart brae; he wished he had seen it; he wished it had been fatal.

"I've seen one," said Tull. "Of course it's nothing to boast aboot. It was just a dog though, a big Airedale. A lorry run over it, a lorry not a bus. It was all squashed with its puddens hanging oot, and bluid gushed like a wee red spring from its mouth." Again his hands were busy conjuring up the gruesome sight. "A man said to pull it into the side in case something else ran over it; he meant it would make a bigger mess of the street. Do you ken who pulled it into the side?"

"You."

"That's right, me. Everybody else was scared. I caught it by the tail. Its tail was as stiff as this," and he stuck out his forefinger, rigid as he could make it. "Funny, that."

Stirling explained the mystery. "It was dead," he said.

Tull nodded. "That was it. It was as dead as a door nail. Door nails are stiff. Do you read a lot of books?"

"Yes."

"So does my dad. You can understand that; being a cripple, there's little else he can do. I fetch his books from the library. They allow him two extra tickets. He gets four books out at a time. Do you ken his record? Sixteen books in the one week. That's a lot of reading."

It occurred to Stirling as Tull boasted about his father that he hadn't once mentioned his mother. Perhaps she was dead. To ask might form a bond between them, especially if the answer, however cheerful, was yes, she was dead. Therefore he took care not to ask, nor did Tull as he chattered all the way to the school gate volunteer one word about his mother.

Luckily, going through the gates, up past the lawns with the bronze chrysanthemums and the high white flag-pole, Stirling managed to escape. Tull bent to pull up his stockings. A big boy whose path he blocked plucked the jotter from his pocket and tossed it over blue-and-green capped heads to another big

75

boy, who instead of catching it in his hands booted it, so that pages burst loose and fluttered down on to the paved avenue and smooth grass. Grinning, and tugging at his hair in some kind of cheerful threat, Tull jumped about picking up the jotter and then all the torn pages. Everybody laughed, except Stirling who slipped away under the arch into the playground to find amidst the hundreds of boys a lonely corner.

He waited under a large tree close to a wall; it was a place deep in shadow. At first he kept holding his case, but after a few minutes risked setting it down on the ground beside him.

Some big boys, in the fifth or sixth year, in long trousers and with deep men's voices, strolled by. One noticed him there, pale, apprehensive, apparently at bay. "Cheer up, sonny," he cried. "Don't worry. Your mother's praying for you." All of them laughed and moved away among the shadows of the trees.

The boy who had shouted the facetious consolation had already forgotten it; but Stirling for years would never forget the remark from the good-humoured hairy mouth. What made it permanent, like a slash with a knife, was of course its terrible truthfulness. His mother at that moment would be praying for him; but he found no solace or encouragement in that distant kneeling. It seemed to him in his fear that if a stranger could guess this about her so easily, at the very first glance, there was no chance at all of her being a charwoman remaining unknown after a day or two, with these hundreds of guessers. He did not then feel lonely: all these boys in sight, some chatting, some running, some playing football, none of them paying him any attention, were suddenly close to him in a dreadful inextricable relationship; they were about to know his secret. Soon they would be discussing it everywhere, here under the trees, by the flagpole, in the classrooms, on the stairs, in the corridors, in the lavatories even. Perhaps one of them might on a lavatory window draw a woman on her knees with a pail beside her and in capital letters the description 'Stirling's mother.'

Even in the teachers' staffroom it would be mentioned.

76

He saw Tull again, and shrank close to the tree to hide. But Tull was not alone. About half a dozen boys were with him, all about his own age, and all better dressed. He seemed to be telling them a story, for his hands were waving about and once he walked in a circle on his toes like a ballet dancer. He looked ridiculous, but two of those who were listening tried to imitate him, and next minute all of them in that little group were prancing round on their toes, screeching with laughter. Where Tull stood, out in the midst of the playground, the sun shone brightly and mercilessly, so that the stain on his sleeve even from that distance was clearly seen.

Stirling sneered, but really he envied Tull his merriment, not because it made him popular but because it made him impregnable. If anybody scoffed at him for having no coat and no case, or for having a father who was a cripple, he would just laugh and merely by flourishing his hands make, without knowing it, the scoffer feel foolish and ashamed. Stirling knew it; he knew that merriment was the armour to put on. If he was merry he could not possibly feel ashamed; and if he was not ashamed either of his coatlessness or of his mother's work, he would be invincible, even if the whole blazered blue-capped school, boys, girls, and teachers, flung at him spears of ridicule or slashed at him with swords of spite. He would be like the Black Knight in the tournament in *Ivanhoe*; he would be the champion of the lists, the conqueror applauded at the end.

But it was not possible to be merry simply by wishing to be. Rehearsing, he smiled, even laughed; but smile and laughter were too voluntary to last. Within a minute he was sad-eyed again. The fifth year boy passing would have thought he was still feeling strange and homesick; he would never have guessed that the small boy at the tree with the case at his feet was reconciling himself to the impossibility of merriment and the inevitability therefore of suffering.

Soon the janitor appeared in the playground ringing a hand-bell. It was a summons for them all to go into the school hall. As Stirling went he remembered how long ago lepers had been given bells to warn people to keep out of their way. Playing a game, he tried at first to avoid touching anybody, and gasped when a boy in a friendly fashion put a hand on his shoulder. "Have you got a boil or something?" asked the boy, laughing.

"Sorry," and he hurried on. In the hall itself of course it was impossible to keep from touching. He had to struggle desperately to reach the front where the first year boys were told to assemble.

Tull noticed him there, and shoved in beside him.

"Who're you pushing?" grunted the boy ousted.

"Plenty of room, fatty," chuckled Tull, and those who heard chuckled too in spite of the solemnity of the occasion with the Rector expected soon. They chuckled because the boy was fat and because Tull's tone had been so good-natured. Indeed even the fat boy had to smile.

"Where did you get to?" whispered Tull to Stirling.

"No where."

"I looked for you. Did you see them kicking at my jotter. Yon two play for the school's first team. Last year it won the shield. One of them's the goalie."

A tall lugubrious teacher at the end of their row cried, in a voice rumbling with professional menace, "No talking there."

"He's a maths. teacher," whispered Tull, out of the corner of his mouth. "Stinker they call him. That's not his right name. It's because he's a stinking teacher; belts you for six and six are nine."

"I said, no talking!" shouted Stinker, majestically affronted.

"See what I mean?" said Tull. "Stinker. What did I tell you?"

Other teachers were silencing the rest of the school. At the other end of the hall the girls were assembled in similar rows. A space had been left in the middle for the Rector to walk to his dais under a stained glass window depicting a man with greenish hair and a pink book under his purple oxter.

Upstairs, looking over the railings down into the hall, yawned rows of other teachers, all wearing black gowns. They stared down regretting the past holidays rather than welcoming the new session: more pleasant the memories of Skye or

Scarborough or Paris than the prospects of everyday scholars bungling irregular verbs or crawling, line by annotated line, through Shakespeare. Stirling, glancing up, thought them in their black-winged gowns magicians able to perform marvels. They, if they noticed him at all, passed him over as one of hundreds to be stuffed, more or less forcibly, with stale but certificated knowledge.

At last the Rector came scooting from his study down the aisle. He knew he had been keeping the school waiting, and to atone almost jumped up on to his dais. Upstairs, some of his male subordinates, covetous of his promotion and contemptuous of his authority, were disgusted as they watched him thus make a mockery of his position and profession in front of those too whose chief duty and purpose was to show respect. They did not think him worthy of his position or of his salary, which was nearly double their own. He was a classics scholar and already, on this first forenoon of the session, had announced with delight that during the holidays he had succeeded in translating into tolerable English verse one of Pindar's most intricate odes. He had not been aware of the grotesque obsoleteness of that achievement, and had received the ambiguous congratulations as innocently and proudly as a child. It was of course a common opinion he was in his dotage.

Carrying his Bible, and wearing a smile out of the New Testament, as one science master observed, the old man hopped up on to the dais and beamed upon his subjects. In one of the very least of these the proper adoration was diminished by relief. Stirling found he was not overawed by the little man with the white winged collar and the long meek wrinkled face, one side of which was crimson from the window above and the other green; his white thin hair had a yellow sheen. Somehow it was impossible to believe that this mild voice, now mumbling from the Bible, could ever bellow threats about caps or stockings.

After the reading the Rector made a few incoherent remarks of welcome and exhortation. After the first sentence he became inaudible to everybody except those in the first two rows, with

79

the result that the rest grew restive and talkative and had to be subdued by prowling teachers handicapped in their threats by the need for respectful silence. Then, after havering about the sacredness of education and the crying need for more of it in the world, the Rector fled, hurrying as if, grunted one teacher upstairs, old Pindar was waiting for him in his room. Another teacher, a classics man, suggested perhaps it was Sappho who was waiting. On the way to the staffroom for a last fag he explained who Sappho was and what her favourite pastime had been. Then they closed the staffroom door and shut out, for a minute or two more, the remorseless tramp of the classes coming up the stairs for their first dose of learning and culture.

The first year pupils were told to remain in the hall. The deputy headmaster, who had been reading out instructions to the rest of the school, stepped down and after a few minutes was succeeded by a lady with a bosom ambitious but sternly restricted and a mouth small from years of inculcating silence. When she had the novitiates quiet by her standards, which precluded even the creaking of inquisitive necks, she gazed down at them, fiercely solemn as a priestess. In her hand arrogantly ringless she held a list of their names.

"Look, please," she cried, and as if part of a ritual pointed oracularly to the wall at one end of the hall and then, before they had time to know what it was they had looked at, with a great curve of her finger over their heads to the corresponding wall at the other end. She had pointed to the gold-lettered dux-boards.

She allowed them half a minute's gaping reverence, with her finger all the time far outstretched, stiff as the tail of Tull's dead dog. Stirling it was who saw that resemblance, but not in irony.

"You all know what those names and dates mean?" she cried. "Every one of those boys and girls was new here at one time just like yourselves today. It may be," and here she looked coldly pessimistic, without meaning to, "it may be that by your side at the moment is standing a future dux, whose name one day will be on one of those boards in golden letters."

"Some hopes," chuckled Tull into Stirling's ear; but Stirling didn't hear.

Miss Naismith looked at them all. She always thought children whom she didn't know looked stupid; it was a prejudice she could never overcome. Here they gaped up at her, like little imbeciles almost, and yet she knew, for years of teaching had taught her this humility, that amongst them were indeed in immaturity better intelligences than her own. It was not invariably the case of course, for she in her day had won her diplomas too; but it was often true.

"Nobody, however clever," she said, almost with a sneer, "however talented, can hope to be dux without diligence. Diligence means hard work. Diligence."

"Bus drivers just sit and turn a wheel," chuckled Tull.

She noticed him, and pointed a finger inspired in its indignation.

"You, boy," she cried.

Expertly Tull looked about him for the culprit. He winked at the blushing Stirling.

"I mean you, sir, with the wild hair."

Though he gave it a cheerful tug, Tull did not seem to think his own hair was referred to; obligingly he kept trying to find the culprit for her.

"I mean you with the stockings at your feet," she cried.

He glanced down at his stockings; then he looked cheerfully up at her.

"Do you mean me, miss?" he asked, pointing at himself in a mixture of incredulity, astonishment, and humour.

"At last. Yes, I did mean you. Pull up your stockings at once, boy." She waited till he had done so. "Did you have the impertinence to speak whilst I was addressing the company of your schoolmates?"

He nodded.

"Where you come from, sir, a nod may have been considered a sufficient response when a teacher asked you a question; here, I may warn you, it is regarded as the worst of insolence. What is your name?"

81

"Robert Tull, miss."

"And may I ask what school has the proud honour, Mr. Tull, of claiming you as its product?"

"Do you mean, miss, what school did I come from?"

She made no answer, but bristled an affirmative.

"Lettrickhill Public School," he said.

She nodded; she had suspected so; it was a school in a squalid district. She knew she could relent. Ignorance, not wilfulness, was to blame. Nevertheless improvement had to begin.

"It's not considered sporting," she said, in relaxed tone, "to bring disgrace on one's old school. I'm sure you're very proud of Lettrickhill school."

That was a statement, but Tull chose to take it as a question.

"No, miss," he said, cheerfully and clearly.

She paused, with a frown: safer not to rush into anger, justified though this seemed; here might be one of those morasses in which inexperienced teachers foundered. If challenged the boy might give some apparently substantial reason for not being proud of his old school, antiquated insanitary buildings for instance, or even an unfair teacher. Better in the meantime, she decided, to remain on the edge; later, when she got to know Tull, she could explore further. Besides there were other points of attack.

"Did you comb your hair this morning?" she asked.

"Yes, miss."

"It does not look like it. I believe I have seen a hedgehog look more trim."

Some girls giggled and Miss Naismith smiled: humour in a school was dangerous, like dynamite; too much of it could blow discipline sky-high. A judicious little though could be used to slip without loss of dignity out of an awkward situation such as this presented by Tull.

"You and I, Robert," she said, "will no doubt have much to say to each other as the session advances."

Glancing down the lists in her hand she saw he was put down for 1E, the lowest class in the first year. Obviously he was no fee-payer; in the bursary examination he must have been near the bottom.

"I shall now read out the names of all those who will form class 1A. This of course is expected to be the best class; but for the sake of those who are not in it, let me inform you that often after the first examination some from 1A have to be relegated whilst pupils from 1B or even 1C are promoted in their place. The names are in alphabetical order. When your name is read out, please stand over there by the notice board. I shall tell you when to go upstairs to room 38, where your register teacher, Mr. Arbuckle, will give you what further instructions are necessary."

She read out the names with ringing solemnity, girls first. One by one, appropriately awed, the smiling élite crept away from the anxious mediocrity and gathered at the notice-board. There they gave one another thrilling smiles of approval, with a dash of rivalry in them.

Miss Naismith was reading out the names of the boys.

"Henderson, Ronald," she called, and paused.

Henderson had his hand up and was slinking happily over to he elect.

"One moment, please," she cried.

He turned, terrified, thinking she had made a mistake and ie had after all to go into 1B or 1C. He was a long thin teethy oy with a row of silver-tipped pens and pencils shining like nore teeth in his blazer pocket.

Miss Naismith nodded her head. He looked the typical tudent, a likely dux; he had been second in the bursary exam.

"All right, Henderson," she said. "You may join the others."

Wagging his head and showing his teeth in relief, Henderson urried across.

"Look at the long hair," muttered Tull, daringly. "I bet ou he's a swot."

But Stirling was too intent on listening to the reading of the ames.

"It looks as if you're for 1B," said Tull. "That's better, 1A, l swots you know; snobs and swots."

"Stirling, John," she called, even as Tull was whispering.

Stirling hurried away, but not quickly enough to prevent Tull from patting him on the shoulder.

Miss Naismith saw the gesture, and after momentary reflection liked it. She could not understand how the two boys knew each other: Tull came from Lettrickhill school, Stirling from Drumsagart, places miles apart. It must surely have been a disinterested token of admiration. She felt thrilled, and unconsciously stroked her great wasted bosom.

What gave the incident greater significance was that Stirling had been first in the examination, a good ten marks ahead of Henderson. Mr. Malvern who had marked the bursary essays for years had told her this boy Stirling's had been the best he had ever encountered, Robin Dailly's at the same age not excepted. She glanced at the dux-board where Dailly's name shone, for ever glorious: at Glasgow University he had taken first class honours in English Literature and later had repeated the achievement at Oxford. Now he held an important post in the Civil Service in London. Perhaps this small black-haired boy, so shyly holding the cheap case, was to be another Dailly, perhaps even a Robert Louis Stevenson or a Walter Scott. For Miss Naismith was not like other teachers who forgot that those soaring geniuses had once been small boys at school.

Stirling's name was the last in 1A. She went on to read out the names of those for 1B. She read these with more zest, her voice a little brighter. This was her resolve every year, never to reveal by her intonation that these names belonged to the less gifted. When she came to the bottommost class 1E, she would even squeeze affection into her articulation; for she regarded it as her duty, as teacher and Christian, to have the greatest patience with the most provoking and the warmest love for the least lovable. . . .

By the notice-board, marching upstairs, and sitting in room 38, Stirling kept on the calm fringes of conversations stormy through zeal, curiosity, boastfulness, envy, irrelevance, and delight. As they sat waiting for Mr. Arbuckle to arrive, some of them gathered round Henderson, eager to dim the shine of conceit that Miss Naismith's glance and their own wonder had surrounded him with. He had no desire to be dimmed, and kept flashing his teeth and indicating the silver tips of his armoury of pens and pencils, with stutters of assertion. He fingered his pens and pencils, thought Stirling, just as D'Artagnan fingered the hilt of his rapier: he would fight them all together in a duel of ink and paper and examination questions, and leave them stained with ink and conquered at their desks, just as D'Artagnan had left his enemies bleeding on palace stairs, in country inns, in highroads, in woods in the shadow of trees. Henderson, though, with his prominent teeth, thick lips, long hair, and skinny neck, was not nearly handsome enough to be an invincible hero. Besides he boasted too much: yet, smiling, Stirling remembered how D'Artagnan had loved to boast.

A boy called Stewart, plump, bland, smooth-cheeked, was the cool inquisitor.

"How do you know," he asked, "you were best in the bursary exam.? If you know, tell us."

"Aye, how d'you know?" jeered another, red-headed, kilted, called McGregor. "I sat the exam. I passed. But I don't know my marks. I don't know them because I wasn't told them. My father's a teacher and he said they wouldn't tell anybody his marks. So how do you know?"

Henderson brushed back his long hair, breathing earnestly. "They mark the papers," he said. "They're bound to know everybody's marks."

"I know that," cried McGregor, taking out of his sporran a paper aeroplane another boy, bored by the conversation, had slipped into it. "But what I said was, they don't tell anybody his marks. Did they tell you yours?" He launched the aeroplane across the room.

"That's the question," said Stewart, nodding. "Did they tell you your marks?"

Henderson keeked up through his hair at the ceiling. "You're admitting there are marks then?" he asked.

"We've all admitted that," cried McGregor, impatiently.

"There are bound to be marks," said another boy in anxiety.

"All right then," said Henderson, with a sudden smile. "If somebody 'phoned up and asked, he might be told the marks."

"Against the rules," said McGregor.

"If you've got influence," grinned Henderson, "you can break the rules. That's what my dad says."

There was a general nodding; all their fathers said that.

"Who 'phoned?" asked Stewart.

"Aye, tell us that," jeered McGregor. "Was it your dad?"

Henderson shook his head. "Ask Charlie there," he said suddenly.

Charlie, who had not yet spoken, scowled. He was an old schoolmate of Henderson's, but felt no loyalty to him. At the first opportunity he meant to desert and join these new allies. All his schooldays week in week out he had suffered the predominance of Henderson. Charlie had often been second, never first.

"Come on, Charlie," urged Henderson, "tell them who 'phoned."

Charlie appealed to Stewart.

"Well, who was it?" asked Stewart calmly, like one wishing the truth even if it destroyed his argument.

"Old Middleton," muttered Charlie.

"And who's old Middleton when he's at home?" asked McGregor, again picking the aeroplane out of his sporran.

"Tell them, Charlie," grinned Henderson.

"Our elementary headmaster," muttered Charlie, and added as a triumphant afterthought, "But he never said what the marks were."

Henderson's cross-examiners expressed their delight, McGregor by again launching the aeroplane across the room, Stewart by drawing a circle on his desk with plump forefinger.

"A lot of fuss about marks," grumbled a boy who hadn't sat the examination. "I'd rather play for the school cricket team than be the dux."

They ignored this philistine.

"We're waiting," said Stewart to Henderson.

"I'm waiting too," he said.

"We're all waiting," added another facetiously, "waiting till Arbuckle comes."

"Did Middleton say what your marks were?" asked Stewart.

"I never said he did," claimed Henderson. "He didn't need to say what the exact marks were. Charlie will tell you what he said."

"I forget," snapped Charlie. "Do you think I remember everything? All I was caring about was whether I had passed."

"Did he not say one of us had done exceptionally well?" asked Henderson.

Charlie nodded sharply.

"All right," admitted McGregor. "But it could have been Charlie he meant."

Henderson quietly laughed; he plucked out a silver pencil and tapped his teeth with it.

Charlie blushed and shook his head.

"Charlie's never beaten me in an exam.," whispered Henderson. "Never."

"Well, I certainly hope," said McGregor, "somebody beats you here."

"Who's going to do it?" asked Henderson.

Each, carefully setting his own claim aside, looked round at all the others and saw no likely champion. They looked at Stirling but shook their heads and passed on.

"Maybe one of the girls will beat you," suggested one, who found to his discomfiture he had offended them all.

They glared across at the girls.

A boy who, like Stirling, had been content to listen and smile, now spoke.

"My name's Rodgers," he said.

"Is that so?" asked McGregor, mimicking Rodgers's rather English voice.

Rodgers joined in the laughter.

"I just wanted to say," he went on, speaking in the same too refined voice, "that we all didn't sit the bursary exam. Some of us who didn't might be better scholars than Henderson."

"Might," grinned Henderson.

Rodgers looked at Stirling. "Did you sit the exam.?" he asked.

Blushing, Stirling nodded.

"Did you?" This time Rodgers asked the boy who had preferred cricket.

"No. I'm a fee-payer," he answered. "But count me out. I can pass, but that's all."

McGregor still hadn't forgiven Rodgers his accent.

"Are you trying to make out," he demanded, "that the bursary winners aren't better than the fee-payers?"

"Better at what?"

"At everything!" This of course was Highland exaggeration. Stewart with Highland canniness came to the rescue.

"No, he means at lessons," he said. "You see, Rodgers, there was nothing to keep anybody from sitting the bursary exam."

"I thought there was a sort of means test. I mean, if your father wasn't working or something like that."

"Who told you that?"

"I don't think anybody told me," laughed Rodgers. "I just thought it myself. I mean, my father's the managing director of Muirton Foundry. Sometimes he brings me to school in our Daimler. We have a chauffeur even. I mean, it would be silly my sitting for a bursary. The fees are only a trifle really."

"Really," jeered McGregor, desperate to show his animosity but not sure how. "I mean, aren't you a bit conceited?"

"No, I don't think so." Rodgers laughed. "I suppose I'm just lucky that's all. That's what I'm told anyway."

"Well, I'm telling you you're conceited," persisted McGregor, with a scowl. "My father's a schoolteacher. Do you think our fathers are all beggars just because yours has a Daimler?"

"My father's a foreman electrician," said Henderson. "He's not poor. Last Christmas he bought me a full set of the Children's Encyclopedia: it cost ten pound. Charlie's father's got a grocer's shop."

"I've got a bike," said Charlie, "a Raleigh."

They all claimed wealthy possessions and prosperous fathers. Stirling pretended to be looking in his case for something. Nobody asked him, but he noticed Rodgers smiling at him. Then all arguments had to cease when Mr. Arbuckle the register teacher came in. Another teacher was with him, a tall stooped white-haired man who peeped mysteriously from side to side with private little smiles, and had one of the wings of his black gown twisted round his arm. He was Mr. Malvern, the head English teacher, and he had persisted in coming along to introduce himself to class 1A, which represented in a scholastic sense the fertile ground of the parable. Mr. Malvern, unlike Miss Naismith, thought that in a world of prodigious and aboriginal folly it was a wise man's duty to despise and thwart fools, even embryo ones seated at desks and full-fledged ones wearing black gowns. He did not have a high opinion of most of his colleagues; they thought him a crafty buffoon.

He stood in front of the class. Mr. Arbuckle, like a discreet subordinate, lounged in a corner, with his hands in his pockets: he had time to waste this first morning and if old Malvern wished to perform, good enough. Mr. Arbuckle's August pay was in his pocket, September's would come along at the end of the term. Good enough then, let the old buffoon perform; it would make an amusing story for the staffroom.

Mr. Malvern performed. His favourite role when reading Shakespeare with the fifth was Macbeth; often irresponsibles guffawed at the way he murdered Duncan. But this morning without a text he acted Hamlet.

He pulled up his black robe to cover his face as far as the eyes, and from behind that mask surveyed the pink-faced unfinished conundrums, the eager little bundles of good and evil and indifference, the lispers of bad poetry, the groaners when Shakespeare was announced as the subject for the afternoon. He looked at them all and sought a meaning.

At first they were respectfully puzzled; then the respect went out of the puzzlement; then amusement came in; and at last puzzlement went, leaving only amusement. They thought he was acting daft for their entertainment, and boisterously they showed themselves entertained. Banging their desks, whistling, yelling, they gave a better imitation of Shakespearean groundlings than he was giving of Hamlet. Alarmed, he tried to silence them, but his gesture and shout were too dramatic, they seemed like a continuation of his game, and increased the hubbub.

Mr. Arbuckle stood silent in his corner, determined not to interfere. If Malvern lost control let Malvern regain it; he got his one hundred and seventy five pounds responsibility payment, didn't he? But all the same for his own future use Mr. Arbuckle took notes; he noticed who among the boys were the most obstreperous. Later if belting one of these for a misdemeanour the strokes could be made that bit fiercer, as partial payment for this scene.

To regain control Mr. Malvern had to stop being Hamlet. Instead he became James Spenser Malvern, principal English master of Muirton Academy, lover of literature, scorner of fatuous or despotic rules, despiser of the world and its cheap foolish gods.

"Good-morning, boys and girls," he said.

"Good-morning, sir," they roared back.

"Quieter, please. My name is Mr. Malvern. I am the principal teacher of English in this establishment of learning. (In his corner Mr. Arbuckle thought: why can't the bugger say school?) Let me welcome you here in the name of Burns (groans) Shakespeare (louder groans) and Robert Louis Stevenson (loudest groans)." The sacred names spoken Mr. Malvern could now be sardonic. "You will prosper here," he went on, "provided you remember three things. I shall tell you what these are. First, never, getting up or getting down, rattle your chairs. Second, never in monkeyish ambition scale the providers of arboreal shade in the playground. Third, and most important of all, when Boccaccio with the golden barrow and its silver freezer blows his trump at the gates, do not, if you love your palms easy and comfortable, scale those gates as if they were the gates of Troy or Carthage and buy the iniquitous wafers, either of the sponge or nougat variety, or most heinous of all chocolate boats with their cool white cargoes."

He was not surprised when he saw them uncomprehending. Brought up on the dogs' biscuits of bare monosyllabic language, how could they be expected to appreciate his little confection, flavoured and ornamented with satire, classical allusion, and even a pinch of poetry? What was it Shakespeare had said: caviare to the general? Mr. Malvern could not blame the children for the limitedness of their literary palates; he knew honours graduates whose only diet was dogs' biscuits.

"Hands up those who understood what I was saying?" he cried.

A few obsequious hands rose up uncertainly.

"Hands up those who didn't."

Proudly, with emphatic snaps of fingers, up shot the majority of hands.

Mr. Malvern laughed. "I thought so. I am not surprised. We creep before we walk; and most of us never learn to run. Mr. Arbuckle, would you be so kind as to read to them the same instructions in officialese."

"Certainly." Privately Mr. Arbuckle damned his superior for a daft old bastard; publicly he grinned as if delighted to join in the fun. He took the leaflet from his pocket and began to read out, perfunctorily, with his other hand in his pocket. "Instructions to pupils. Pupils must be quiet and orderly in class, especially when entering or leaving classrooms. Pupils must on no account interfere with the trees in the playground, either by climbing them or by defacing them in any way. Pupils must not during school hours leave the playground for any purpose whatever without permission."

Mr. Malvern held up his hand to interrupt. "The four words 'for any purpose whatever' are underlined. Is that not so, Mr. Arbuckle?"

Mr. Arbuckle nodded; he saw no sense in reading out these instructions, since every pupil would be given a leaflet containing them. It was merely an opportunity for Malvern to show off.

"The most criminal purpose in leaving the playground," said Mr. Malvern, with a glance towards the door, "is to buy wafers."

That was almost true. The Rector, though in Mr. Malvern's view an amiable man in most things and a genuine scholar, had taken a ridiculous umbrage against the buying and selling of pokey-hats and wafers at his school's gate. From the vast beach of modern vulgarity he had picked up this pebble to fulminate against. Nor did he seem to be aware, in spite of Mr. Malvern's coughs and shrugs and ocular hints, that his own insistence on school uniforms was a far more enormous sin against the holy spirit than a child's slinking out for a tuppenny wafer. He maintained, smiling gently, that wearing the school colours showed in a child a pride and loyalty most desirable. No, no, no, Mr. Malvern counter-claimed, wearing the prophet's agonised grin, it showed only a hideous uniformity, a surrender of individuality, a sacrifice of that variety in human life which had so fascinated and inspired Shakespeare. Now in the elementary schools children were strapped for putting antennae on their g's or tails on their y's.

Then Mr. Malvern remembered his chief reason for coming along to meet this class.

"Will John Stirling stand?" he asked, so sternly that most of the class, and Stirling himself, thought he was going to be accused of buying a wafer or intending to buy one.

"So you're John Stirling?"

"Yes, sir."

Mr. Malvern was disappointed. It was not the boy's fault of course. It was simply the descent from the poetic imagination to the plain reality. He shook his head sadly but bravely: this disappointment, or disillusionment rather, just had to be endured, it was in the nature of things, a fly in the universal ointment. No, it was not the boy's fault that he was ordinary, and lacked the dreamed-of enhalo'd grandeur. Probably even Shakespeare himself, met in the common flesh, would have disappointed.

"So you're John Stirling?" he repeated, shaking his head.

The gesture frightened Stirling more. "Yes, sir," he said faintly.

The rest of the class considered that shake of the head a bad sign. Perhaps one or two of the girls were sorry for Stirling; but all others, boys and girls, were too interested in finding out his transgression to bother about sympathy. Henderson particularly enjoyed the suspense.

"I shouldn't be saying this," said Mr. Malvern. "In fact I'm breaking a rule to say it; but intelligent people know there are times when rules ought to be broken."

Here Henderson turned and gave all his baiters a revengeful jeer.

"This is such a time," went on Mr. Malvern. "I'm breaking a rule to congratulate you, Stirling, on the essay you wrote in the bursary examination. It was an extraordinary performance." And so it had been, with its perceptiveness, its vivid and accurate detail, its beautifully balanced sentences: Mr. Malvern had wondered if on the same subject "A Day in the Open" he could have done better himself.

Henderson's baiters were trying to get him to turn round so that they could give him his jeer back with interest. He would not turn round.

"An excellent essay," said Mr. Malvern. "Do you not agree, Mr. Arbuckle?"

Mr. Arbuckle did. The essay had already been handed round the staffroom. If it had not been written under examination conditions, he would not have believed a child of twelve had written it. Indeed, he was still a little sceptical, especially as Stirling looked a quiet undistinguished little chap.

"Of course," said Mr. Malvern, "I know why Stirling here is able to write such a good essay. I know, and yet this is the first time I've ever set eyes on him. I know all right. It's because he has read lots of good books. Is that not so, Stirling?"

"Yes, sir. I think so."

"Now we'll see," said Mr. Malvern to the class. "We'll see what books Stirling has read. Let's begin with *Kidnapped*. Have you read *Kidnapped*, Stirling?"

"Yes, sir."

"Naturally." Mr. Malvern thought *Kidnapped* the perfect novel: those who preferred *Madame Bovary* were deluded. "Naturally. Who wrote it?"

"Robert Louis Stevenson."

"Right, so he did." Mr. Malvern made flourishes with an invisible rapier; he stabbed to death three boys in the front seats. "Who was the bonny fechter?" he cried.

Christ, thought Arbuckle.

"Alan Breck, sir," murmured Stirling.

A girl with fair plaits tied by crimson ribbons went off into a fit of giggles; trying to stop she made her face as red as her ribbons.

"Alan Breck it was," cried Mr. Malvern. "The siege of the roundhouse. Do you remember it? Who will ever forget it?" And he fired off two pistols at the class, seriously wounding the crimson ribboned giggler. "Read good books," he cried. "That's the secret. Read good books, and maybe some day you'll write them." He ended with a little laugh of wistful bitterness. Once he had written a good book, after the style of *Kidnapped* too, and had submitted it to fifty-three publishers. Though it yellowed in a drawer now, tied with the original green tape, he still thought it superior to most of the psychological trash daily vomited from the printing presses.

It was the moment for exit; the moment after would be anti-climax. With a wave of his hand he rushed out, his gown flowing behind; as he went out of the door he repeated his little poignant snigger.

For a minute or two Mr. Arbuckle broodingly let the class babble.

Most of them stared at Stirling who sank down into his seat, pale and trembling.

The giggler dried her eyes.

"I've read *Kidnapped*," muttered Henderson. "I've got it in the house."

"Who's going to be dux now?" asked McGregor.

"Essays aren't very important," said Henderson. "You just get twenty marks for an essay. Maths are the most important; you get a hundred marks for maths. I'm best at maths. Ask Charlie."

"How do you know Stirling there isn't as good at maths as he is at essays?"

Henderson scowled at Stirling. He shook his head and fingered his pens fiercely. He could not believe so small, quiet, and nervous a boy, without a single pen in his breast pocket, could ever beat him.

"I've read *Kidnapped*," he muttered, and resolved when he got home that night to read it again.

Mr. Arbuckle stopped brooding. He walked to his desk.

"Silence," he said.

The babble continued.

"Silence," he roared.

There was silence, except in the faraway corner where one boy still babbled.

"You there," bellowed Mr. Arbuckle. "Get up."

The culprit stood up.

"Name?"

"Robertson, sir."

"Deaf, Robertson?"

"No, sir."

"Merely disobedient, Robertson?"

Poor Robertson thought no answer was possible; Mr. Arbuckle differed.

"Disobedient, Robertson?" he repeated, in a voice that made some of the girls gasp.

Robertson hung his head. "Yes, sir."

Mr. Arbuckle with his fist banged the top of his desk.

"In here," he said, very softly, "there is a cure for deafness and for disobedience; indeed, for all complaints scholars suffer from; even stupidity. Is there anyone here who suffers from any such complaint? If so, let him come and be cured." He waited but no one came. "Ah, so this is a perfectly healthy class. Good. Sit down, Robertson. Now I am going to put up on the board your time-table for the session. Work has commenced; fun has ceased. You will take an accurate copy of your time-table, and you will keep that copy. You will not talk." He saw an eager-tongued girl likely to talk, and pointed towards her. "What is it you are not to do?"

"Talk, sir."

"Exactly. Talk in a classroom is sabotage."

He was proud of that definition, which expressed in his opinion the fundamental truth about teaching. He said it again. "Talk in a classroom is sabotage." It occurred to him some of them might not know the meaning of sabotage; but at that very early stage of the session he shrank from the complicated labour of explaining.

He turned to the board, with chalk raised. An instant later, without having touched the board with the chalk, he spun round to catch the saboteurs with their hands, so to speak, on the fuses. There seemed to be none. True, there was some noise, but hardly subversive: cases and bags were being opened, jotters brought out. Nevertheless it was noise.

"Silence," he cried.

As he turned to the board again he could not help grinning with pride in his shrewd understanding of his craft. The secret was to scare them into silence from the very beginning; jest, smile, be lax, even speak kindly, and the result would be unrestorable pandemonium to the end of the session, as there was always in Malvern's room. Mr. Arbuckle was a father, and had therefore a natural fondness for children; but it was also a law of nature that children in a classroom could be disciplined only by unrelenting severity. Those who said otherwise were theorists or incompetents.

He took a pride in his neat blackboard work, using a ruler to draw the large rectangle and to divide it into its forty compartments, each one representing a period. He used different colours of chalk for the different subjects, red for Maths, blue for English, and so on.

"Keep it neat," he remarked to the class, without turning his head.

It was far from occurring to him that for many of the pupils behind him those were magic words he was writing with the coloured chalks. If he had noticed the trembling of Stirling's fingers, or the biting of Henderson's lips, he would have thought these healthy signs of discipline like a vaccine doing its work against the germs of disrespect and cockiness.

96

History had two compartments.

"I'll be taking you for History," he said.

He frowned as he went on writing. He ought to have taken them for English too. Old Malvern wasn't so glaikit when it came to distributing the classes; he always took for himself the cream, leaving to others the sour dregs. Anybody could teach an A class. With the Ds and Es on the other hand it was slave, sweat, bawl, belt, all the time; and in the end of course poor results and no credit. In Mr. Arbuckle's time-table for that term there were far too many Ds and Es.

He turned round. "Did anybody speak?" he growled.

He had heard nobody, but a girl with startled eyes behind horn-rimmed spectacles put up her hand, timidly but honestly.

"I asked for the loan of a rubber, sir," she whispered.

He stared at her; he had a daughter aged seven; she too wore spectacles. It had been a disappointment. Magdalene, his wife, had wept.

"A rubber?" he repeated.

"Yes, sir. I put Science in the wrong square."

Science. He hadn't wept himself, but he had felt bitter about medical science's prompt and inept prescription of glasses. Sheila had had beautiful long-lashed blue eyes, frequently admired. As he gazed glumly at the little girl in front of him, a warm human feeling for her welled up in him. It was an irrelevancy there, and he turned back to the board.

"Be more careful," he said. "It's ridiculous to need a rubber the very first minute you start to write. In any case if you need a rubber, or anything else, you know the rule. Put your hand up. Don't talk."

"Please, sir, I had my hand up. You didn't notice because your back was turned."

"You should have waited till I turned round." Then he realised he was committing a fault as serious as Malvern's clowning: he was arguing reasonably with a pupil. Once that started, it would never end; education would become a farce. Even in the licence and privacy of home such argument was unprofitable: often he had to tell Sheila to shut up.

"Get on with it now," he snapped. "Don't waste time in talking."

They were let out for a long playtime. This pleased them all except Stirling, who was afraid Gourlay might appear at the gate. Going downstairs, Rodgers, the managing director's son, who was his marching partner, asked him eagerly if he ever played a game called headers. Stirling, who had played it often and indeed was proficient at it, nodded. "Good," whispered Rodgers, conspiratorially showing a small red ball he had in his pocket. "We'll have a game in the playground."

As soon as they were outside Rodgers seized his arm and hurried him towards a quiet corner far from the gate.

"We don't want that blow Henderson bothering us," said Rodgers. "All he'd want to talk about would be lessons. He'll never play at games. I bet he's never even heard of headers. Where will we have the goals?"

Running in his eagerness, to Stirling's surprise, Rodgers went to the wall, made a mark with his heel, and from it paced six steps, where he made another mark. "That'll do for one goal," he said. "What did you think of Arbuckle? Fanny Arbuckle they call him; I don't know why. I'm glad we're not getting him for English. Malvern's a scream, isn't he? We'll make the other goal with our caps." From the wall he strode about a dozen steps, hesitated as if he thought the distance rather ambitious, and came back a couple. "Here should do," he said, and as if it was a bit of paper round a sweetie flung his cap on to the ground and kicked it into place.

Reluctantly Stirling set his cap down the necessary six paces away. Luckily the earth was dry and what dirt came off it on to his cap could be brushed off. But what if in his reckless springs to save the ball from going through his goal, Rodgers trampled on the cap with his heavy brown shoes? He might break the skip which was made of cardboard.

"I'll take these goals," he suggested, standing between the caps.

"All right," agreed Rodgers. "We'll change at half-time. That's the rule, isn't it?"

98

Stirling had to nod.

"What will we make half-time?" asked Rodgers. "Six?"

"Yes." With two good players it might take a long time for one of them to score six. In that case the bell might ring before it was Rodgers's turn to guard the goal marked by the caps.

Some of their classmates had by this time seen them and had come up to watch.

McGregor was there. "Play the winner," he challenged.

Rodgers was leaping in his keenness to begin. "I don't mind," he cried. "Are you willing, Stirling?"

Stirling nodded, but inwardly made the condition that McGregor, who didn't seem to have a cap, would all the same have to provide his own goal-mark.

"Do you know what Henderson was saying?" cried McGregor. "He was saying you must have copied your essay out of a book."

"Rubbish!" cried Rodgers.

"That's what I told him."

"Well, let's forget Henderson," said Rodgers.

"Suits me. When's half-time?"

"Six."

In headers a player throws up the ball, and as it comes down strikes it with the side of his head towards his opponent's goal. A good player does not throw it high, he depends on the jerk of his head to give speed and direction. A poor player throws the ball so high he isn't sure of hitting it with his head. Therefore he catches it in his hand or tries to, and throws it up again, still much too high for certainty. He may do this half a dozen times. When he finally does attempt to head it, he does so with his neck stiff; the ball, instead of being propelled merely falls on his skull and stots wherever luck takes it.

Girls and cissies headed in that stiff lucky way. It was with astonishment that Stirling, ready to jump to save the thunderbolt he expected, saw Rodgers begin this silly game of throwing the ball a great height, and after five throws let it bounce on his outstretched head. Instead of having to leap to prevent the ball from flying past him, Stirling had to race away from his goal altogether to retrieve it.

"Poor shot!" cried Rodgers, laughing. He seemed unaware that it was a poor shot because he was a poor player. He fidgeted on tiptoes, hands upraised, ready to save.

A little throw in the air, a quick brief jerk of his head, and Stirling had the ball easily past Rodgers' arms. It was the first goal.

"Fine shot!" cried Rodgers. "I nearly saved it though. Look, it grazed the tips of my fingers. I knew the side you were going to put it to. I jumped too late."

In spite of his enthusiasm his second attempt was as feeble as the first, but he still remained enthusiastic. That puzzled Stirling who was never keen if he was not expert. Later he learned that Rodgers, an only child living in a large house within a large garden, had been accustomed to play with a small cousin, a girl three years younger, whom he could always beat easily.

Stirling himself had played with dozens of boys, in the school playground at Drumsagart, round backcourts, on quoiting greens, on bits of waste ground, in grass parks, on the streets. Once in a school tournament he had reached the semi-final, having in the first round defeated Gourlay who played no better than Rodgers did.

Although being overwhelmingly beaten Rodgers kept laughing and jumping about and promising that his next shot would be like a rocket, sure to whizz past Stirling's guard; but of course it turned out to be the same embarrassing foozle as before.

Soon, far too soon, Stirling had scored six goals to make it half-time. They had to change places.

"My goodness, Stirling, you're a great player," said Rodgers, as they passed. "Isn't he, McGregor?"

"I'll beat him," said McGregor, who had been boasting to the boy beside him that he could beat them both together; to support his boast he had pointed out Rodgers would be more of a hindrance than a help.

100

Stirling had to leave the goal marked by the caps. He consoled himself by deciding to keep sending the ball towards that side where Rodgers's cap was.

Before the second half started a boy strolled up licking a wafer.

"Where'd you get that?" asked somebody.

"From a Tally at the gate."

"But you're not supposed to buy from him during school hours!"

The licker laughed. "Who're you kidding? There's a crowd round the gate. You put your tuppence through the bars and the Tally hands you your wafer."

"Did you say tuppence? Don't tell us that's a tuppenny one?"

"Sure. This is high-class ice-cream. He's got chocolate boats; they're fourpence."

"I tell you what, Stirling," cried Rodgers. "After the game we'll go and buy chocolate boats. We'll need them to cool us down."

"I thought I was to play the winner?" demanded McGregor.

"That's right," agreed Stirling. He hadn't broken sweat during the headers, but Rodgers's proposal fairly brought it out on him. If he spent fourpence on a chocolate boat he would have to walk home. In his agitation he let the ball trickle out of his hands.

Rodgers in glee claimed a goal. He even picked up a cap and banged it down on the ground; it was Stirling's cap.

"Goal!" shouted Rodgers. "Oh, I must claim a goal."

"Some goal," said McGregor.

"Yes, it was a goal," murmured Stirling. He had hoped to crush Rodgers by twelve goals to nothing, but now at the chocolate-boat threat thought he could prolong the game by letting Rodgers score two or three goals.

The plan was successful, for Rodgers after scoring another two became so keen that he seemed to forget all about the chocolate-boat.

Then Tull arrived holding up a penny.

"Here's a proposition," he said. "Who'll go half shares with me in a wafer. That Tally at the gate's got no penny wafers. Did you ever hear of a Tally with a barrow that didn't sell penny wafers? Weel, there's one at the gate. And his tuppenny wafers are the size of penny ones. Who'll put a penny to this one, and go half shares?"

Even the players stopped to look at him.

"I've only got a penny," he said, quite unashamed.

Rodgers took from his trousers pocket a handful of coins, among them at least one half-crown. There seemed no purpose in the action. But if its purpose had been to humiliate Tull it would have failed.

"Some folk are millionaires," he said. "What about you, Stirling? You're no millionaire. Have you got a penny to spare? We'll get a neutral to halve it."

"I'll halve it for you," volunteered McGregor, "if I get a lick."

"Off whose half?" asked Tull.

"Off the whole wafer: a long lick right from one end to the other without lifting my tongue."

"I've seen tongues," said Tull, "as good as spades at shovelling ice-cream."

McGregor showed his tongue.

Somebody pointed out Tull still had to find a partner, as Stirling had refused.

"Stirling and I are going to buy chocolate-boats," said Rodgers.

"One each?" asked Tull.

"Of course."

"Millionaires. They're fourpence each."

Rodgers laughed and winked at Stirling. "We know that."

"They're worth tuppence," said Tull, "but they cost fourpence. If I had anither threepence all the same I'd buy one."

"Do you get a penny a day?" sneered somebody. "If that's your allowance, save up your pennies. It'll only take you four days to have enough for a chocolate-boat."

102

"You're not bad at the counting," said Tull pleasantly. "But I don't get a penny a day. This is supposed to be my bus fare hame."

"Do you not get an allowance?" asked Rodgers.

"I get threepence on Saturday."

The rest, with Stirling joining in, burst out laughing.

"I get sixpence a day," giggled one boy, small and round-faced. "My father said he'd give me sixpence a day when I came to the Academy."

"Your faither?" asked Tull.

"Yes, my father."

"Sixpence a day?"

"Yes, sixpence a day."

"What about Saturdays?"

"Oh, half a crown on Saturdays," cried the giggler. "At least."

"Sixpence a day," smiled Tull. "Anybody could say that. Seeing's believing."

With little miserly hee-hees, the boy collected the six pennies from his pockets. He thrust them under Tull's nose.

"See!" he cried.

With an unexpected tap on the underside of the gloating fingers Tull sent the pennies flying. He bent and picked one up, but did not return it to its blubbering owner. He held it in his fist and grinned invulnerably at them all.

Some, thinking he meant to keep his booty, were embarrassed. Some were amused. One or two were horrified by the outrageous injustice. Others remained impartial, alert, and apprehensive.

The owner of the penny wept and demanded it. He kept sobbing it was his, his father had given it to him, he would tell the Rector if he didn't get it back.

"Don't be a bully," said Rodgers scornfully.

Tull turned and looked at Stirling, as if at an ally; but Stirling felt humiliated.

"Do you ken what my faither says?" asked Tull.

They grinned at the commonness of his speech, his saying

103

'ken' and 'faither', but one, dour and with his attention unrelentingly on the main issue, asked what it was Tull's father said.

"He says that if one man's got mair than anither man it's just the same as if he'd stolen from him."

"More what?" It was a truculent question.

"More money, more possessions."

"And where did your father read that?" This was an aggressive sneer.

"In lots of books," replied Tull, blithely. "In the Bible for one."

"It never says that in the Bible." The boy who cried out this denial did so with great confidence: in his last school he had won a prize for scriptural knowledge.

"It does," said Tull.

"Are you saying," he was asked, "that every time we pass a beggar with a tinnie we steal pennies out of it?"

"Everybody should have an equal share."

"Give me my penny," sobbed the victim. "It's mine. My daddy gave it to me. I'll tell the Rector."

"Come on," said Rodgers to Stirling. "They've spoiled the game. Let's go and buy those chocolate-boats. He's talking a lot of balderdash." But he spoke the last word with a frown and a worried shake of his head. It was his own father's favourite word, used to condemn Western films, the Rover and Adventure story-papers, and complaints about loneliness.

"My dad's a cripple," said Tull calmly.

They looked at one another, not sure what to do with this information, whether to laugh at it or be sorry.

"Can he not walk?" one asked, with ambiguous grin.

Tull shook his head. "He can't walk. I've never seen him walk."

"Did somebody steal his legs?" Awkwardness rather than vindictiveness caused this shrill question.

Tull turned and smiled at the boy who had asked.

"Nobody stole them," he said. "He's still got them. It's just he can't use them. They're paralysed."

They looked away in their constraint. One whistled at the sky, one noticed the green moss on the wall, another scraped the ground with his shoe.

"Oh, come on," said Rodgers to Stirling. "This is balderdash."

"Wait a minute," murmured Stirling, on the point of confessing he did not have enough money to buy a chocolate-boat. Surely if Tull had the courage to make such dreadful confessions, he himself ought to be able, with a rueful laugh, to say he had come away that morning without his money.

"The chocolate-boats will be all finished if we don't hurry," complained Rodgers. "I'll stand you one, Stirling." He put his arm round John's neck. "I'd like us to be friends," he said. "What's your first name?"

"John."

"Mine's David. Come on, John."

Smiling Tull watched them go.

"Here's your penny," he said, and unclenched his fist.

Its owner snatched at it and raced off, accompanied by his chum who kept crying out his indignation and sympathy.

The rest moved away, leaving Tull alone. He leant with his back against the wall and gazed up over the school buildings at the blue sky.

Meanwhile Stirling had discovered to his relief that the skinny green-jerseyed boy helping the ice-cream man at the gate was not Gourlay.

Chapter Five

GOURLAY was back at school over a week before he decided to carry out his promise to visit Stirling at the Academy gate. In the morning during the division and multiplication of decimals he had infuriated Mr. Martin by his persevering stupidity, had been strapped six times, and finally had been ordered to stay in during playtime to finish his sums.

For a minute or two after his classmates had gone he lounged at his desk, scowling and grinning by turns, and drawing wee fat men on his jotter. Sunshine glittered on all the other jotters open on the desks, ready for correction after the interval. With blue pencil in one hand and belt in the other, Martin would creep round correcting them. Those with less than six sums right were to be strapped. Some would bawl.

Suddenly Gourlay jumped up. From Jackie McKenzie's desk he grabbed the jotter and tore out of it the page containing the sums done that morning. The class always got a good laugh when Jackie got the belt. He was so nervous he would hide his hands anywhere, up his jersey, in his pockets, down his stockings, and even inside the front of his trousers. All the time he was swearing at the teacher, or pleading with him. Martin often lost patience and gave it to him on the legs.

As he crumpled the page and threw it into a corner, Gourlay had another idea. There was another coward in the class, another comic at the belting; his name was Tommy Harris. Over Harris's very neatly set down sums Gourlay drew with the point of his pencil dipped in ink a fat man with a long nose. Hinneying at his own audacity and at the shock in store for Harris, Gourlay wrote the teacher's name at the foot and to increase the resemblance added large spectacles.

Boldly, knowing the teachers would be busy taking their tea, he swaggered out of the room down the corridor. Near the outside door was the wall tablet with the names of former pupils who had been killed in the war. Some last year's poppies were still pinned to it, black with dust. Gourlay leapt up and plucked one out. Where he stood, there in the open corridor under the memorial, not very far from the men teachers' staff-room, he waited till he had stuck the wire stalk through his jersey and had arranged the red cloth petals neatly on his breast. The dust displeased him, and he blew some of it off.

Out in the playground some of his playmates came running up to him, in awe at his poppied freedom.

"Did he let you oot, Sam?"

"Where did you get the poppy, Sam?"

Most of them were more than a year younger than Gourlay, and now as he looked at them he felt more disgusted than ever with their timid and cringing juvenility.

"He never let me go," he cried. "I never asked him."

"Did you just walk oot, Sam?"

"Sure, I just opened the door and walked oot."

He caught sight of Jackie McKenzie slinking anxiously among them.

"How many sums have you got right, Jackie?" he asked.

Jackie, who had been consulting classmates as to answers, groaned as he replied. "Five, I think," he muttered, groaning and licking his dry lips.

"Five?" grinned Gourlay. "It's the belt if you're under six."

"Oh, I ken," moaned Jackie.

"Maybe you'll not even hae five," said Gourlay. "I wouldn't be surprised if you had nane at all."

"I've got five," muttered Jackie.

"That's right, Sam," said one. "He's got five."

"Has he?" chuckled Gourlay. "Glad to hear it. Where's Tommy Harris?"

Harris was in another part of the playground.

107

"He's all right," muttered Jackie McKenzie. "He's got eight or nine right."

Gourlay laughed and clapped Jackie on the shoulder.

"Take it like a man, Jackie," he said. "Look at my hand, and I've already had six this morning."

Jackie gazed at that tough palm; then he glanced at his own.

"I get nervous," he whimpered. "That's the trouble, I get nervous."

"Bah!" cried Gourlay. "Martin's belt's made of shammy-leather."

"Armstrong's isn't," said one. "He takes it hame and heats it at the fire to make it hard."

Even Gourlay had to admit the terribleness of Armstrong's belt. There was a moment's shuddering silence.

"To hell with them all," cried Gourlay.

"Even Armstrong?"

"Aye, even Armstrong. Have you ever seen me greeting when I got the strap from Armstrong?"

"No greeting, Sam, exactly. Just tears in your eyes."

"Liar!" Gourlay punched his accuser in the chest. "I never had tears in my eyes. That was the time he hit me on the wrist and it all swelled up black and blue? But I never had tears in my eyes. If they see tears in your eyes, it makes them worse; they gie you mair, just to finish it, just to make you greet properly. I know them."

They nodded: it was true, he knew them; no boy in the school had had half the strappings he had had.

"They can all go to hell," he cried again, and made for the wall separating the playground from the railway track. It would have been easier to escape over the locked gate, but scaling the spiked wall was more spectacular.

They followed him.

"Where are you going, Sam?"

He didn't answer, for at that moment he didn't know.

"Keep back," he shouted, waving them aside.

Dozens had gathered to watch as he made a race at the wall

and sprang. He did not spring high enough and his fingers could not grip the short spikes.

"Hard lines, Sam," muttered a sycophant.

"Your poppy's fell out," said another, picking it up and handing it to him.

"Put it back in," ordered Gourlay, and stood with his chest thrust out while the boy nervously obeyed.

Again Gourlay sprang, again failed. He glared round at his silent watchers. None was grinning at the failure.

"My legs are cramped with sitting at that bloody desk," he said.

Nobody smirked, nobody by as much as a scratch at his nose scoffed at that excuse. Everybody was aware that in a minute or two the bell would ring, big Armstrong would be out to bring in the lines, and Gourlay like them all would have to rush to be in his line in time. To try to escape over the wall while Armstrong was watching demanded a recklessness even Gourlay would not risk.

"Help me up," he ordered, and strode to the wall where half a dozen of them heaved him up and let him stand on them, until they had him at last sitting astride the wall between two spikes.

For a minute there, hands lightly on the spiky mane, he was the daring horseman, the cowboy about to ride through Indian country with the news, the Cavalier escaping from the Roundheads.

"They'll never catch me," he said.

"Where are you going, Sam?" asked one.

"Going?" cried Gourlay, patting his steed. "I'll tell you where I'm going." It was then that the idea struck him. "I'm going to the Academy gate to shout hello to Stirling."

"John Stirling that went to Muirton?"

"Aye, wee mammy's pet. I want to ask him," and again inspiration came, "I want to ask him if his neck's still burning."

They did not understand.

"Muirton's more than seven miles away, Sam."

"What are seven miles?" jeered Gourlay, high on his great horse.

One of them came closer, smiling up with excessive servility, for the question he was going to ask was intended to turn the horse into a spiked wall again.

"Supposing you reach the Academy gate, Sam, what will you do there? What good will it do you?"

The bell saved Gourlay the perplexity of answering. At the first dong he rose to his feet, carefully because of the spikes, and leapt daringly, down like an eagle, with his arms outstretched like wings. So exhilarating was that leap, especially with the tolling danger behind, that Gourlay when he landed amidst the rusty tins and broken bottles and the other rubbish in the grass there, crouched fingering his soft nose and staring at his familiar fingers with a slow reluctant sense of relief that he was not an eagle after all, was just Sam Gourlay in his old green jersey and with not even a ha'penny in his pockets.

On the other side of the wall the bell stopped ringing. He heard the scuffle of hundreds of boys lining up in classes in front of the door. He could picture in his imagination the panic of those suddenly deserted by their partners and left solitary in the midst: being without a neighbour in the lines was in Armstrong's eyes the second worst crime, the worst being to talk, and the third worst was to glance to the side maybe or to move your feet.

Then there was silence, such perfect silence that Gourlay heard as if it was an eagle flying the whirr of a jenny-long-legs climbing the mountains of the grass. He knew Armstrong had appeared on the steps and was surveying the lines. As he crouched there, plucking the jenny-long-legs limb from limb, Gourlay grinned: he did not know if there were any being taken out for the belt. Armstrong seldom roared to a boy to come out, he merely pointed with his forefinger, then jerked backward with his thumb. Sometimes the wrong boy crept out. Sometimes in their uncertainty and fear half a dozen from the fatal area faltered towards the steps, looking at one another in anguished

110

hatred and at Armstrong in entreaty like prayer. He would say nothing, but like a great black spider would welcome them all up the steps and make them stand in his shadow to be dealt with later.

Gourlay waited, letting the debris of the insect fall from his fingers. Suddenly, startling him though he was waiting for it, the command "Attention!" was bellowed. A bird flew out of a bramble bush. Beyond the wall the hundreds of boys straightened themselves to the tips of their fingers, missed one or two or even three breaths according to their degree of intrepidity, and tried to make with the clicking of their heels together a thunderous martial noise pleasing to Armstrong. But this was still summer, it was a dry day with the sun shining, and many of the boys, like Gourlay himself, wore rubber-soled sandshoes which could not be clashed together even if ankle bones were splintered in the attempt. The soft resultant scuffling always annoyed Armstrong; he was aware it was unintentional, but he could not forgive it. Gourlay knew therefore that the nicotined forefinger and the hairy thumb were busy. Soon the marching began, and Armstrong with his loud sonorous voice kept roaring "Left-right, left-right, left-right," as if it was a song. Those lucky enough to be wearing leather-soled tacketed boots made a smug thunder on the pavement, while the padders in sandshoes tried to atone by a corpse-like stiffness of neck, body, and arms.

Free himself, Gourlay felt a desire to see who were the victims trapped in Armstrong's black shadow this time. Placing an old biscuit tin on top of a large stone, he was able from that shaky eminence to peep over. Yonder was the doomed squad, some blowing on their hands, some rubbing them against the rough stone of the school, and others just standing still, too demoralised even to risk those legitimate preparations. Among these frozen ones Gourlay saw, to his astonishment and giggling joy, Jackie McKenzie who had no sums in his jotter for Martin to correct. After getting his allowance from Armstrong Jackie would go moaning along the corridor for another dose from Martin.

Then the last two boys of the last line disappeared into the school. The doomed squad tidily in twos followed. Only Armstrong himself was left. He stretched his arms high above his head and seemed to yawn; Gourlay thought he heard him. It could be of course he was loosening his muscles in readiness to belt the misbehavers in the lines. Soon he too went in, and suddenly, as if by magic, by the action of some invisible devil, far huger and far more terrible than Armstrong, the playground was empty. Gourlay, gazing over the wall, was left alone. Frantically he stared about him: at that particular moment, so cunning was the invisible devil, there was no human being, no bird, no insect even to be seen. Far away was a noise like laughter. Gourlay, gasping, listened; and the noise became a train passing Drumsagart junction on its way to Glasgow. Listening, he heard too a class in the school begin to sing 'The Road to the Isles.' He thought it was likely Armstrong's class, for Armstrong was fond of singing.

Gourlay was chuckling as he climbed down and began to walk along by the side of the wall. It was not the contradiction between Armstrong's love of discipline and his fondness for singing songs like 'The Road to the Isles' that made him chuckle. No, it was the realisation that, despite the great invisible fiend, the world was not empty, in the school over the wall were hundreds of boys and girls; up in Drumsagart main street were dozens of people, everywhere were innumerable human beings. Gourlay began to whistle 'The Road to the Isles' as he crossed the railway line and made up the road towards Drumsagart. Although among those human beings were many he did not like, indeed although he hated most of those he knew, all his teachers, his sister Jeanie, her sweetheart Donoghue, his mother, Farmer Gilchrist, and Stirling, still it was comforting and reassuring to know they were there.

He found Charlie Dean watching a quoiting match between two unemployed miners. Luckily his father wasn't there; he had already been at court for Sam's truanting and had promised next time to drag him by the hair back to school for big Armstrong to punish.

He tried to sneak up to Charlie's side without being noticed by the men, some of whom might clype to his father. Old Muldoon was among them, squatting, with a stalk of grass in his mouth.

Charlie, as he often did, as he did too with intention and malice, gave him away. Instead of responding to the appeal of finger on lip and right eye closed, he cried out loudly, "Where the hell have you come from, Gourlay? Have you plunked it again?"

Some of the men looked round, prepared to be amused by this boyish escapade. But Muldoon, still crouching on his heels in practised miner's fashion, was at once antagonistic.

"I'll give you exactly one minute, Gourlay," he said. "If you're not away out of this by that time I'll break my toes on your backside."

Some of the men winked at one another, remembering the feud.

"This is not private," muttered Gourlay. "I've a right to be here."

"One minute," repeated Muldoon.

One or two laughed to sweeten Muldoon's bitterness.

"Now, Pat," one said, "just leave him to—what's his name? —big Armstrong. He'll gie him what-for for plunking."

"Ach, he's only a laddie," said another.

"The trouble with young Gourlay," said a third, "is he's too damned stupid to be a successful villain. You ought to behave yourself, Gourlay; for sure as Christ you get away with nothing."

"Come on, Charlie," muttered Gourlay, "I've got a plan."

Muldoon rose up. "I warned you," he said, and got ready to swing his boot.

Gourlay showed his teeth; but he knew that if he attacked the old man in return for the kick, the rest would join in against him. He had to walk away therefore with Muldoon after him in bow-legged remorselessness.

Soon they were apart from the others.

"You auld mucker," muttered Gourlay, "you auld Irish mucker. Go and kick the man that bairned your Nancy."

Muldoon said nothing, still chewed the grass and still pursued.

"Why don't you leave me alone? Dirty auld pape. It was the priest bairned your Nancy."

Even that lump of filth picked up by Gourlay from an adult conversation failed to stop Muldoon or make him show hurt. His face, all wrinkles and short white hairs and tiny blue coal-flecks, seemed intent on chewing the grass. It was the kind of face Gourlay had seen on sheep grazing, except that in spite of its lack of horns and teeth it seemed a dangerous face: seventy years of humanity concentrated now in inexplicable disapproval and contempt made it dangerous.

"What have you got such a spite against me for?" muttered Gourlay. "I never did you any harm." He noticed that the quoiting match was suspended whilst players and spectators looked on amused at his retreat. He heard Charlie's treacherous laughter.

At last Muldoon spoke.

"You're rotten," he said, "you're rotten to the core."

He took the chewed grass out of his mouth and flung it away.

Gourlay grinned at the grass with its spittle on it. He was reminded of the many spittles on the grass where he had dismembered the jenny-long-legs. Small insects made those spittles.

"You'll roast in hell," said Muldoon, and then turned and went rolling bandily back to his companions.

Gourlay pounced on a stone. It was heavy with sharp edges, and if it landed on Muldoon's bald head would split it open. He dared not throw so large a stone, however much Muldoon had provoked him. Yet he raised it to his shoulder as if to throw it.

As he stood thus Muldoon turned round.

"I kent it," the old man muttered, with a queer laugh. "As soon as my back was turned." Shaking his head and again uttering that queer laugh, he walked on.

Dropping the stone, Gourlay watched as Muldoon rejoined the other men. He heard their laughter and their cheerful chaffings. He saw one of them catch Muldoon's bonnet by the skip and playfully pull it down over his eyes. Even Muldoon himself laughed good-humouredly as he tugged his cap to rights and crouched down again to pluck another stalk of grass and watch the quoiting.

Gourlay felt, without understanding it, the same threatening loneliness as when the playground emptied.

He slunk behind some wash-houses to sulk. He had to dodge under clothes hanging out to dry, and as he passed a wash-house door a woman clumped out steamy and angry, with her fat arms dappled with white suds. She wore her husband's boots and walked heavily and stiffly as if she'd wet herself. Over her big pregnant belly gleamed an oilskin apron. By the wash-house door stood a pram with an infant asleep in it.

"I thought it was you, swine," she shrieked in a tired querulous voice. "Look what you've done to my sheets." With her big boiled hand she pointed and at the same time menaced.

Startled, he glanced towards the sheets; he hardly remembered coming past them.

"I never touched them, Mrs. Jamieson," he muttered.

"You did!" she screamed. "You did! I saw you. I watched you through the window."

He knew she was telling a lie; the window was opaque with steam.

"I don't think I touched them," he said, smiling.

"You did. Are you calling me a liar to my face? I'll let your mither ken. Me that's not fit to be washing at all, am I to hae to do it all over again just to gie you satisfaction?"

Her screaming awoke the child in the pram; it began to fret.

"Now see what you've done," she cried. "God," clumping towards the pram with her hands clutching her wet hair, "would a body's heart not break?"

Gourlay escaped round the wash-house to the midden. There

he sat out of everybody's sight on top of a dustbin, hoping Charlie would come to hear the plan, hoping even a cat would come to break the loneliness.

It was an old woman called Granny Howden who came, dressed in her customary black dress that glittered with black beads. She carried an ashpan, and the ashes in it were not so white as her hair. As always, she talked to herself in a scolding voice. Over eighty, she still did her own housework and was insulted when any neighbour offered to help.

There were three dustbins in the midden, but she always emptied her ashes into a certain one. For years she had done so, no matter how full it was and how empty the other two. It was the one Gourlay was sitting on.

She emptied them on to him. Peching under their weight she tottered round the corner of the midden, with the pan already tilted.

He was too late in trying to spring aside; in any case there was no room. With her ashes all over his trousers he stumbled and fell over the other dustbins. Howling he got up and desperately tried to slap the ashes off him, but succeeded only in driving the white dust deeper in. He seemed to have on white shorts; he looked like a toff going to play tennis.

While he howled, she screeched.

"You auld idiot," he howled, "just look what you've done to my trousers."

She had let the pan clatter to the ground, and stood in a white cloud, screeching and gripping her dress near her stomach, though she thought it was her heart.

"Michty me!" she kept screeching. "Michty me!"

"Daft auld bitch," he cried, hurrying away, still slapping uselessly at his trousers.

Beyond the midden he met Charlie sauntering up from the quoiting.

"Look at this mess, Charlie," he said. "That stupid auld bitch Granny Howden couped her ashes over me."

Charlie began to yell and slap his own trousers in great merriment.

116

"Were you hiding in a dustbin," he cried, "in case Muldoon came after you again?"

Gourlay, at great cost, afforded a smirk. "Do you think I'm frightened of Muldoon?" he asked, and then added, more eagerly, "Come on doon to the daisy park, Charlie, and we'll sit in the sun behind the dyke and I'll tell you the plan I've got. And maybe I'll be able to rub some of this ash off with bunches of grass."

He hurried, with Charlie strolling and chuckling behind him, to the daisy park. There while Charlie sat with legs outstretched on the grass and his back against the dyke, Gourlay tore up bunches of grass with daisies and bees amongst them, and rubbed at his trousers. All he did was to give the white ash a greenish smear.

In the warm sunshine the clink of the quoits and the buzz of bees were sleepy peaceful sounds, so that soon Charlie was lying on his back with his eyes closed.

"What's this plan you're talking aboot?" he asked, already contemptuous of it.

"Oh aye." Gourlay came and squatted beside him. At first he could not tell what the plan was for giggling. "It's a great plan," he said, and chewed at a daisy.

"I've heard your great plans before."

"Aye, but this is a good one, Charlie. What do you say if we go to Muirton and stand at the Academy gate and shout in to Stirling?"

After a long pause, during which a cow at the far end of the park mooed, Charlie opened one eye. "Is that the great plan?" he asked.

"That's it, Charlie. Just think of the things we could shout in the gate at him. You should be good at thinking up things to shout. I'll shout, 'Mammy's pet,' and 'Is your neck still burning?' and 'Does your mither scrub floors?' What will you shout, Charlie?"

He waited for Charlie's answer. It took a long time in coming. Again the cow mooed.

"That one wants the bull," said Charlie.

Gourlay nodded, and waited for him to say more.

"What do you say, Charlie?" he urged.

"What about?"

"About the plan."

"Oh, the plan." And again Charlie fell silent, his eyes closed, his hands stretched out on the grass. A bee hummed near one, taking it for a flower perhaps, and Gourlay chased it away. Even then Charlie did not open his eyes.

"A bee nearly stung you, Charlie," said Gourlay. "I chased it."

"I've been wondering," said Charlie at last.

"What, Charlie? What hae you been wondering?"

Again there was a long delay. Gourlay kept chewing and spitting out daisies. The cow mooed.

"Wanting the bull," murmured Charlie sleepily.

"Are you in favour of the plan?" demanded Gourlay. "You said you were wondering. What was it aboot?"

"I was just wondering how we were to get to Muirton. It's nearly seven miles."

Gourlay smiled flatteringly, though Charlie's eyes were shut. He giggled before he spoke.

"I thought, Charlie," he said, "you'd maybe hae enough for our bus fares there, and we could walk back. You've always got plenty of money. Your auntie's always slipping you tanners."

"Don't talk about her," said Charlie harshly. "You ken what I said."

"I forgot, Charlie. But have you got enough? Count it and see."

After another long minute's delay Charlie's right hand crept along the grass into his trousers pocket where it counted the money. The little clinks could be heard against the greater clinks of the quoits.

"How much, Charlie?"

The hand crept out again and began to behead daisies.

"If daisies were shillings," chuckled Gourlay, with a glance across the millions in the field, "we'd be rich."

"I've not got enough," said Charlie.

Gourlay did not think it safe to call him a liar. "It sounded a lot," he chuckled, "the way it clinked."

"Ha'pennies clink the same as shillings."

"Well, we could walk it. If we started noo we could walk it."

"We'd miss dinner."

"Hell, that's nothing. All I get's a piece spread with margarine and a bit of corn beef on it; and the corn beef's black."

"Is that what you get for it?" asked Charlie softly.

"That's what I get. Maybe it'll be cheese instead of corn beef: blue-mouldy cheese."

"Will I tell you what I've to get?" asked Charlie, with that same tantalising softness.

"What is it, Charlie? Pea soup? I like pea soup, if it's hot."

"Chicken soup."

"I've never tasted chicken soup. Maybe I wouldn't like it."

"You'd like it all right. Two platefuls. Then roasted tatties, and fresh green peas, and a big lump of pink chicken."

"Peas make you fart." It was an observation, not a jeer.

"Then apple sponge with custard."

"What's apple sponge?"

"Sponge baked in the oven with apples. It's great. I could eat a ton of it."

Gourlay nodded. "Look at all the cows' turds," he said, and in the remark was his envy of Charlie's feast. "Do you get tea?" he asked.

"Sometimes."

"I always get tea." But his triumph was spoiled by the knowledge that the tea was too weak or stewed or cold or hadn't enough milk and sugar.

"Tea?" repeated Charlie disgustedly. "Who wants tea? I could get it if I wanted. Who wants tea after chicken soup, and chicken, and roasted tatties, and apple sponge?"

"I heard it all the first time," said Gourlay bitterly.

Charlie laughed softly in satisfaction at that bitterness.

Gourlay gazed over the field of beautiful but inedible daisies. He gnawed at his knee-cap.

119

"You're lucky," he said. "I wish my mither and faither had died when I was a baby, and I had been brought up by an auntie." He laughed wistfully. "I don't want to talk about your auntie, Charlie, for I ken you don't like it. But I ken one thing she would never allow."

For an instant Charlie opened his eyes and saw white clouds above; his aunt's face was always white.

"What?" he asked.

"She'd never allow me to go and hae dinner with you."

Charlie laughed scornfully.

"I know," said Gourlay quickly, with a grin. "I said she wouldn't."

"She thinks you're an evil boy, Gourlay. That's what she said. She says you lead me into trouble. She gives me money if I promise to keep away from you."

"You don't keep the promise, Charlie."

"Some day I will, Gourlay."

Gourlay pulled up a daisy and rubbed it against his nose.

"She's got a spite against me," he muttered. "Everybody's got a spite against me."

He remembered them all that morning: first, his mother who wouldn't let him have a third slice of bread dipped in the frying-pan; then Martin with his fankling decimals; then the empty playground; then Muldoon and Mrs. Jamieson and Granny Howden.

"I don't care," he muttered. "They can all go to hell."

"Your sister Jeanie's not got a spite against you," said Charlie.

"She has."

"When you go to stay with her when she's married she'll make you good dinners. Maybe she'll make you apple sponge."

"Do you think I would go to stay with her?"

"You would if wee Donoghue let you."

Gourlay said nothing, but gnawed again at his knee-cap.

"Have you got your ain back yet?" asked Charlie. "Mind Jeanie gave you away to auld Gilchrist."

"I mind. I'll get my ain back."

"No, you'll not. You'd be daft to fall oot with Jeanie."

"I'll get my ain back."

"When?"

"I'm waiting for a chance, that's all."

"She'll be married and away before you get your chance. You'll hae to hurry up, because if she keeps cuddling Donoghue on yon seat under the cherry-tree in the public park, she'll need to get married. Has she got a lump under her apron yet?"

Obscurely Gourlay resented this talk, but he did not know how to express his resentment without seeming to take Jeanie's part.

"If she has a wean," said Charlie, "there'll be no room for you."

"I said I wouldn't go."

"A chance is a good thing."

"My mither wouldn't let me anyway. She says I've to work for her, not for Jeanie." He laughed. "I ken who I'll work for. Me. I thought you were starting work in the steelwork."

"Sure. So I am. There's no hurry. You can't start an apprenticeship till you're sixteen."

"Are you going to be an engineer?"

"Maybe." Dean rose up, and began to sniff. "What is it I've been smelling?"

Gourlay sniffed too. "It's something," he agreed. "Cowdung? Daisies?"

"Some daisies!" Dean's nose questing like a bee hovered over Gourlay's shorts. "I thought so. It's cats. It's on your trousers."

Gourlay bent down to smell; his nose couldn't deny what was there: the strong rank smell of cats.

"Hell," he muttered.

Charlie was bawling with laughter. "Auld Granny Howden's got two cats," he cried. "She must hae emptied the ashes from their box into the ashpan, and you ken what she did with the ashpan."

Gourlay still sniffed as if he hoped by perseverance to change the odour into that of daisies, say.

"I rubbed them with grass," he muttered. "Maybe it's just the smell of grass."

Charlie had got up, and was walking away across the grass and daisies. He turned in the sunshine and held up his nose, fairly snorting.

"Do you ken whit I'm smelling now?" he cried.

Gourlay scowled, thinking it was still cats.

"Chicken soup," cried Charlie, "and chicken, and roasted tatties, and apple sponge."

At those delectable words Gourlay himself risked a sniff: cats again, and, just as bad, stale bread and margarine and black corn beef.

Charlie was walking away again in the sunshine.

"I'll meet you outside Curly's pub," cried Gourlay.

Charlie paid no heed.

"At one o'clock," cried Gourlay.

Still without heeding, Charlie reached the fence, clanged over it, and disappeared up the road towards home.

Gourlay raced to the fence, and standing on the bottom wire leaned over.

"What do you say, Charlie?" he cried.

Charlie did not even turn to wave.

Gourlay remained perched on the fence, grinning. After a minute or two, watching Charlie go away, watching daisies with bees and wasps buzzing over them, watching the blue sky and white clouds, listening to the clinks of quoits and a shout or two of applause for a good shot, thinking of the bread and marge and black corn beef, smelling his ridiculous trousers, remembering Muldoon and Mrs. Jamieson and Granny Howden, remembering he was playing truant and tomorrow would suffer severely for it, he became aware that his grin was quite unjustified and indeed was a kind of treachery against himself. He stopped grinning therefore and scowled instead. There seemed no way of getting revenge. He thought of throwing a stone from a distance at old Muldoon, of dirtying Mrs. Jamieson's

122

sheets, of couping Granny Howden's dustbin or kicking her cats. He even thought of not turning up at one o'clock outside Curly's pub, to teach Charlie a lesson.

He felt through his pockets in the hope a threepenny bit or even a ha'penny might be lurking there. He found only the cloth poppy he had stolen from the school war memorial, and this he flung into a pancake of cow-dung.

Then there was nothing to do but go and sit behind the dyke till it was time to go home for the black corn beef and stewed tea.

When he arrived outside Curly's pub at ten to one he realised it was a silly place for a tryst. It was on the main street, and he might be seen by an attendance officer or policeman or even his father. Yet if he went away to hide he would miss Charlie. Across the road, half-hidden amidst trees, stood a dark-green iron urinal with no roof and perforated walls. Without considering whether it would be a pleasant place to wait, he darted over to it and found, to his initial delight, he could get a spy's view of Curly's pub by standing on tiptoe and peeping through the perforations. True, he had to stand in wet, and he had sandshoes on; but at first this discomfort added authenticity to the thrill of spying.

About half-past one however, after forty minutes' incarceration, he had become too constantly aware of the smell. Shaking his head, covering his nose with his arm, thinking of corn-fields, none of these won him relief. His eyes too were gone skelly with keeking through such small holes, and his legs ached with stretching. He kept wishing aloud Charlie would hurry.

When Charlie did come, after two o'clock, he was sauntering. Sam slipped out and raced to him.

"You're late, Charlie," he said.

"Is that so?"

Gourlay nodded. "It's after one. Did you hae chicken? And the apple sponge?"

Charlie's tongue ran along his lips. "Did you hae your black corn beef?" he asked.

"No. It was cheese, blue-mouldy."

Charlie sniffed. "You're still stinking."

It was true, as Gourlay had to admit; his hour's vigil in the urinal had added odours.

"Every cat I see," he muttered, "I'll kill it."

Charlie lounged against the pub wall.

"What about this trip to Muirton?" he asked. "Are you still game?"

"I've been waiting for you, Charlie. We'd better hurry now if we've to be there in time. It's late."

Dean looked at him, up from the soaked sandshoes, past the ashy shorts and snotted green jersey, to the thin wild freckled face.

"If you turn up at the gate like that," he said, "Stirling will die of fright."

"And I'm going to shout his mither scrubs floors. He said he wasn't going to tell the toffs that."

"He'd hardly tell them that."

Gourlay jumped in impatience. "Will we start, Charlie?"

"Sure. What's keeping us?"

They set off, Dean strolling, Gourlay wishing to sprint.

"You can run if you like," said Dean. "I'm taking it easy. My belly's full."

Gourlay rubbed his; it felt empty. Indeed he felt rather sick. But he shook the sickness off.

"It would be great if we could bus it," he said.

Dean grinned but said nothing.

"We'd get there a lot quicker if we bussed it," went on Gourlay.

Dean jingled the coins in his pocket.

"Are you sure, Charlie, you've not got enough?"

"Not for us both."

Gourlay nodded, and then laughed. "It's a good day any-way," he said. "The walk will be good for us." As he spoke another spasm of sickness seized him; he thought he was going to vomit.

"What's up?" asked Dean.

"Nothing, Charlie. Maybe it was the cheese, it was blue-mouldy."

"You should hae cut the blue-mouldy bits off."

"If I'd done that there would hae been no cheese left."

They had walked rather less than a mile and were on the lonely stretch of road between Drumsagart and the next village Kirkton when Dean began to limp and groan as if in agony every time his right foot touched the ground.

"What's up?" asked Gourlay.

"My ankle. I think it's sprained, Sam."

Immediately Gourlay squatted down beside the hurt ankle and offered to massage it.

"No, leave it alone," cried Dean, hopping back rather agilely for one lame. "I'll just try to bear it."

Bravely for a few yards, as far as the next bus-stop indeed, he struggled on, supported by the sympathetic Gourlay.

At the bus-stop Dean had to give up the effort. Groaning he sat down on a grassy bank there, and caressed his ankle. "I'll never make it, Sam," he said.

Gourlay looked down at him, credulous and worried.

"That's hellish," he muttered. "You've never had a sprained ankle before, Charlie. How did it happen? I never saw you fall."

"It happened at dinner-time, Sam. I had to bring in a pail of coal for my auntie. I fell over a big lump in the cellar."

Gourlay grinned wistfully. "Did the chicken and the apple sponge not make it better?" he asked.

"How could they?" Dean pretended to be angry, because of the pain he was enduring. "How could they? Hae some sense, Sam."

Gourlay laughed. "If I had broken my leg," he said, "I bet you chicken and apple sponge would hae made it better."

Dean's face was all screwed up with the agony. "You talk a lot of nonsense, Sam," he gasped. "What's bothering me is that we'll hae to give up your plan. And it was a good plan."

"Wasn't it, Charlie? What would Stirling's face hae looked like when I cried in, 'Does your mither scrub floors?'"

Dean tried to smile. "It would hae been fun watching his face, Sam, when you cried that in. I could still try to go, if you are willing."

"Oh, I'm willing all right, Charlie. It's you, it's your ankle. Is it swollen?"

"I think so. It feels swollen. No, no, don't you touch it. What I was thinking, Sam, was that I could take the bus to Kirkton and wait for you there. I could be resting, you see, and maybe the swelling would go doon."

Disappointment mingled with the credulousness on Gourlay's face. "Could we not both bus it to Kirkton?"

"It's the money, Sam," pointed out his friend gently. "I've only got enough for myself. Have you got any?"

"I've never got any."

"Except when Jeanie slips you a tanner."

"I don't want her tanners."

"But you take them when you can get them. If you don't want to walk yourself, Sam, if you're frightened to walk yourself to Kirkton, then we'll just go back."

"I'm not frightened. But it's a long walk."

"It's longer to Muirton, Sam."

"It's all right if you hae company."

Dean sighed and apparently gave up his persuading. He fondled his ankle. "Stirling's the one who'll get the laugh," he said.

Gourlay trembled. "No, he'll not," he said. "He'll not get the laugh. I'm the one that's going to get the laugh. All right, Charlie, I'll walk to Kirkton myself. You wait for me there."

Dean had to bend low over his ankle to hide his grin. "Sure I'll wait," he said. "I'll keep rubbing it all the time to get it better. Lucky, here's a bus. Will you stop it for me, Sam?"

Gourlay leaped almost into the middle of the road and held up his hand.

"It's a good job we're near a bus-stop, Charlie," he cried. Then he laughed. "I stopped the bus for Stirling."

He helped his friend on to the bus, and kept waving to it as it went swiftly away. He did not notice Charlie waving back.

Then he began the two and a half lonely miles to Kirkton.

He was limping himself when over an hour later he arrived in the main street. Waiting for him outside an ice-cream shop was Charlie, with a big double-nougat wafer conspicuously at his mouth. He made no attempt to hide it as Gourlay hirpled up to him; rather he licked at it with sweeter ostentation.

Gourlay was hot-mouthed as well as sore-footed. At first, in his desire for a share of the wafer, it didn't occur to him that the sixpence it must have cost could have paid his bus fare three times over.

Charlie let him beg. "It's no hygiene to lick somebody else's wafer. Mind what Miss Douglas used to say? It could bring your mouth out in scabs."

Gourlay snarled that Miss Douglas had scabs in a delicate place. "I deserve a bit. It's a long walk. I'm thirsty."

"There's a water tap along at the garage," said Charlie, with a helpful jerk of his head.

"A double-nougat," said Gourlay bitterly. "It must have cost a tanner. Did you get raspberry on it?"

Dean shook his head. "Raspberry always makes me think my nose is bleeding. Are you not going to ask me how my ankle is?"

"My ankles are sore, both of them; and the soles of my feet. Sandshoes aren't good for walking long distances." It was then that he remembered Charlie's claim not to have enough money. "I thought you said you couldn't pay my bus fare."

"That's right." Charlie, as befitted one licking so big a wafer, spoke very coolly.

"How could you buy a double-nougat then?"

"Don't forget, Gourlay, that it's my own money and I can buy what I like with it."

Gourlay sneered. "I don't believe your auntie gies you all that money. Do you ken what I think?"

"Nobody cares about what you think, Gourlay. Not even Stirling."

"I think you pinch the money out of your auntie's purse when she's not looking."

"Is that what you think, Sam?"

"Aye, that's what I think."

"Well, surely you wouldn't want share of a wafer that's been bought with money that was stolen?"

Gourlay could not help grinning. "I never said that." But his grin soon vanished; the wafer was steadily growing less. "If I got the chance I would do the same. My mither's purse is always in her pocket. She kens my faither might steal tuppence for a packet of Woodbine."

"What about Jeanie's purse. Don't tell me you've not taken a tanner or two from it."

Gourlay grinned. "Sometimes," he admitted. "Come on, Charlie, don't be mean. I'm your pal. Look, Charlie, at my heel." Bending, and pulling down his stocking, he showed his right heel, skinned and bleeding. "The other one's just as bad. Should I not get a lick, Charlie?"

"Do you know what time it is?" asked Dean.

"No."

"There's a clock along there. Can you tell the time, Gourlay?"

"Sure I can tell the time."

"Somebody told me you couldn't."

Gourlay's fists clenched. "Who was he? I'll batter his face in."

"Maybe he was bigger than you, Sam. What time is it then?"

Gourlay glared along at the clock. "It's too far away," he muttered.

"I can see it easily."

"You've not been walking for miles."

Dean laughed. He looked at the small portion of wafer left. "I tell you what, Sam. This'll be your prize if you can tell me the time."

Gourlay, glaring at the clock, concentrated. His lips moved as he counted. "It's past ten," he muttered at last, doubtfully.

Dean took another lick. "How the hell could it be past ten?" he asked. "Do you mean ten at night?"

128

"Keep your bloody wafer," muttered Gourlay, turning away, ashamed and hurt.

"I said I got no raspberry on it. How can it be bloody? I'll tell you what the time is."

"I don't want to ken."

"You should. It's ten to four. That means Stirling will soon be on his way hame. He'll pass here in the bus in about half an hour if you like to wait for him. You could shout his mither scrubs floors."

"He wouldn't hear it."

"No, Sam, he wouldn't hear it. Folk would think you were daft." The wafer now being finished Dean wiped his fingers on his handkerchief. "Well, I'll be getting the bus back. You know, Sam, I'd just bought that wafer when I minded I should hae kept the money to let you bus it hame. I knew your feet would be sore. You could hae got the same bus as Stirling too. Maybe some toffs from the Academy would be in it with him. You could hae shouted about his mither."

Gourlay became eager for that compensation. "Go on, Charlie," he urged. "Gie me the tuppence. I'll sit beside him and shout as hard as I can."

"The conductress would put you off." But Dean was undecided. Financing Gourlay to bait Stirling was tempting; but to keep on baiting Gourlay was perhaps even more appealing. He shook his head. "I'm sorry, Sam," he said. "I've not got enough money."

"Are you going to walk back yourself?"

"How can I, Sam, with my ankle swollen?"

"Maybe," suggested Gourlay cunningly, "your ankle's not swollen. Maybe you're just taking a rise oot of me."

Dean looked surprised. "I thought nobody could take a rise oot of you."

"Nobody can. And don't you try it; not even you, Charlie."

"But we're pals, Sam."

"It didn't look like it the way you guzzled all that wafer. I give you share every time."

Dean touched his friend. "Never mind that, Sam," he said. "The important thing noo is to find some way you can bus it hame. With a heel like that every step would be torture."

"Two heels like that; and I think I've got a blister on my wee toe."

"That's right. You don't want to walk hame. I've got a plan."

In spite of his scowl Gourlay was impressed; he knew Charlie was clever.

"You could beg," said Dean.

"Beg? Do you mean, here in the street?"

"No. Chap at some doors. You did it before, mind."

"Aye, and I got nothing."

"It wasn't exactly nothing, Sam."

Gourlay swore and rubbed his behind. A man, disturbed from his snooze at the fireside by Gourlay's knock at the door, had dashed out and kicked him fiercely as he fled.

"But you might be luckier this time, Sam. It might be a soft-hearted old woman that'll open the door."

Gourlay remembered Granny Howden. "Auld women are just as bad," he muttered.

"If you try hard, Sam, you can surely get the price of your bus fare. All you need's tuppence. Of course, it's up to you. Maybe you want to walk hame."

"You ken fine I don't."

"You look like a beggar, Sam. I mean, your clothes are ragged-looking and dirty. Anybody smelling you would think you slept in middens."

Gourlay frowned. The adventure with its risks, its uncertainties, and its possible rewards, might have appealed to him if his feet hadn't been so painful and if that sickness hadn't kept surging back. Moreover Charlie's greediness over the wafer still rankled.

"I don't know," he muttered.

"Suit yourself," chuckled Charlie. "It's nothing to me. It's you that'll hae to walk it."

"Could we not bus it halfway?" asked Gourlay. "Then we could get off and walk. Maybe the conductress wouldn't notice and we could just sit on."

Dean was amused by that uncharacteristic shrewdness; but it was easily countered. "You're forgetting my sprained ankle," he said.

Gourlay didn't mention his own skinned heels, but gazed along the alien street. He knew none of these shops or people; even the big policeman approaching was unfamiliar.

"If somebody was to chase me," he muttered, "I wouldn't be able to run."

"Suit yourself. I'll just cross the road and get the next bus. I'm thinking of going to the pictures tonight. Will you be coming?"

"No." Then he looked round challengingly. "How can you go if you've no money?"

"I'll get more."

"You'll pinch it from your auntie's purse."

"I'll get more."

They were quiet to let the policeman pass. In spite of their assumed innocence, he stopped.

"Where are you twa from?" he demanded.

"Drumsagart," replied Dean coolly, ignoring Gourlay's frantic winks.

"And what's brought you to Kirkton? Should you not be at school?"

"I'm left."

After a long professional blank stare at Dean, the policeman turned to Gourlay. He sniffed.

"Don't tell me you've left," he said. "From the stink of you it would seem you're not even started school."

Dean laughed pleasantly but treacherously.

"I'm fourteen," growled Gourlay.

"Is that so, now?" Thinking bluff would work, would produce some salutary terror, the policeman took out notebook and pencil. "I'll have your names anyway."

"What for?" snapped Gourlay. "We're doing nothing. You can't take our names just for standing in the street."

131

"I can take your name for breathing, see. Policemen hae an instinct, that tells them wha look honest and wha don't. Have you ever had your name taken before?"

Gourlay shook his head.

"Well, there's always a first time. You must hae been lucky to escape before. Now, without impudence, your name."

"Stirling," said Gourlay, "John Stirling."

"Sure it's not Perth? or maybe Hamilton?"

"No, Stirling."

"H'm. And your address."

"11 Brookbank Terrace, Drumsagart. I think it's 11."

Of course that was a mistake as even Gourlay a moment after understood. The policeman laughed at having successfully trapped the suspect into a blunder.

"So you think it's 11?" he asked. "Well, well. Of course," and he sniffed again, "a boy who's not passed the wetting stage is hardly likely to be sure of his ain address."

Dean laughed. "Please," he said nicely, "please, John's not very bright." To emphasise it he touched his brow.

Gourlay grinned. For a moment he had wondered who this John was; he had even turned round to look for him.

"I could believe that," said the policeman. "Are you at some special school?"

Dean nodded. "That's right."

The policeman gladly turned from the green-jerseyed smelly loonie to the well-dressed pleasantly spoken boy with the red tie.

"And what's your name, sonny?" he asked.

"Robert McDonald, sir," said Charlie promptly. "I live at 61 Main Street, Drumsagart."

Feet wide apart, solemnly nodding approval of this sane co-operation with the law, the policeman wrote down the name and address. He was a brawny slow-witted man who took a pride in his handwriting, even with a pencil an inch long. At school, when the same age as these two boys, he had often been complimented for his neatness. He had had a teacher, a lady who dyed her hair, and she had gummed silver stars to pages

132

that had earned more than eight out of ten. Nearly every page in his copy-book had been silver-starred. Now as he painstakingly wrote in his notebook in the sunny street, after nearly thirty years, he almost saw the star in the usual top right hand corner.

It occurred to him the names might be false, but he hid the suspicion away in a corner of his mind. These two, so physically small and inferior, would never dare to deceive his celebrated muscularity.

He made the small notebook snap authoritatively shut.

"Drumsagart lies that way," he said. "Get going."

"I'm up to visit my auntie, sir," said Dean sweetly, with smile to suit.

"Oh." The policeman rubbed his chin and considered this claim. If it was a lie, a crafty question or two could easily uncover it; but if it was the truth and the boys had a lawful reason for being there in Kirkton, then this investigation and name-taking might be condemned in a certain quarter as too officious. There was in Kirkton a Communist county councillor voted in by the many disgruntled unemployed: this was the sort of ridiculous case Cropper used to make trouble. There might too be significance in the boy's red tie. Like a typical agitator Cropper forgot police were workers too, and damned poorly paid.

He put his notebook away, slowly so as not to put his dignity away with it.

"If you take my advice," he said reasonably, "you'll get home to Drumsagart as quick as you can."

Then, with a tap on his unseen truncheon and an easy laugh, he resumed his patrol.

They leant against the wall, winking at each other. When he was too far away to hear they laughed. Though Gourlay laughed almost hysterically, trying to clasp the wall and kissing it, he was the first to grow serious again. He happened to remember the nougat wafer. The way Charlie wiped his lips made him remember.

"I never knew," he sneered, "you had an auntie in Kirkton."

Dean at first could not believe that was a sincere remark; he laughed all the louder when he did.

"You think you're lucky with aunties," jeered Gourlay.

Dean just went on laughing.

"Do you ken what my mither said at dinner-time?" asked Gourlay.

Dean nodded, to Gourlay's astonishment. "Sure I ken," he cried.

"What was it then?"

"She said, 'Sammy my darling, here's your piece with blue-mouldy cheese'."

Gourlay almost crashed his fist into that merry taunting mouth; he had it uplifted. But he could not strike Charlie, who was his only friend. He dropped his fist and tried to join in Charlie's laughter. For a moment he even forgot what it was his mother had said besides that about the piece and blue-mouldy cheese.

"It was about your auntie," he said, when he remembered it.

Dean stopped laughing. His face became bleak and dangerous. He looked at Gourlay very closely, and then looked far away. Gourlay touched his sleeve in fear, to bring him back.

"I didn't believe her, Charlie," he said. "She's always telling lies."

"She's a big fat dirty bastard, your mither."

Gourlay nodded. "So she is. She said your auntie was dying with consumption. I didn't believe her, Charlie. She said she'd not live long. She said it would be a pity for you when she died. She said you wouldn't get any chicken or apple sponge then. She said your uncle wasn't such a mug as your auntie. She said he kept quiet now because he didn't want to worry her. She said he knew she was dying. That's what she said, Charlie, but I didn't believe her."

Dean kept staring into that bleak distance.

Gourlay laughed to recall him. "Come on, Charlie," he said. "Come on and watch me begging."

To his surprise and joy, Charlie immediately agreed. "All right," he said.

134

"I'll not say anything about your auntie again," promised Gourlay.

"It doesn't matter."

They set off down a side-road that led away from the main street with its shops into the country with its fields and coalbings. Gourlay was the one who limped. He didn't notice that, so eager was he to placate Charlie and bring him close.

"I'd better wait till we see a hoose by itself," he said.

"Are you feart?"

"No, I'm not feart, Charlie. But that big cop's got our names."

"Sometimes I think, Gourlay, right enough you are daft. He's not got our names."

Gourlay remembered. "Oh, that's right," he laughed. "He's got Stirling's name. Who did you say you were?"

"Robert McDonald."

"Who's he, Charlie?"

"Christ, he doesn't exist. There's no such person. It's just a made-up name."

"I see."

"61 Main Street in Drumsagart is Logie's pawnshop."

Gourlay frowned. "But nobody lives there, Charlie."

"Are you trying to be daft, Gourlay? Are you doing it to annoy me?"

"No, Charlie. You see, I've got a sore head. I've been feeling a wee bit sick. I should never hae eaten that cheese. I hope I can manage to cadge enough for my bus fare hame. I don't feel like walking. My heels are getting sore again."

They came at last to a small lonely whitewashed house standing in a large wilderness of a garden. A burn with a wagtail flicking from stone to stone flowed by. At the burnside on a hawthorn bush above some brambles a black cat slept in the sunshine. It did not waken when two big grey rats suddenly sneaked out of the shaggy grass and splashed across the burn.

Gourlay, seeing the rats, jumped about looking for a stone to throw. By the time he found a suitable one the rats were gone. He swore and then, calling the cat a lazy sleeping stinking beast, he hurled the stone furiously at it. Usually he was a poor shot, but this time he was very lucky. With a thud that they heard clearly the heavy stone struck the cat, which squeaked, faintly but with an even more terrible audibility, and feebly protesting with its paws toppled over down into the brambles where after a few more faint squeaks and struggles it lay still.

"Talk about lazy," yelled Gourlay. "Look, it's gone to sleep again."

"Is it?" grinned Dean. "Do you think that's sleep?"

Fascinated, Gourlay gazed down at the cat and noticed now how uncomfortable and twisted it looked. Before, sleeping in the hawthorn, it had looked so snug and peaceful. Because it lay black and sinisterly still among them the green leaves and white flowers suddenly blazed and seemed themselves to be alive. At any moment the whole bush might fly up and away. The wagtail came down the burn again, dipping its long elegant tail.

"It's deid," whispered Gourlay.

"Sure. Do you ken what I should call you, Gourlay? I should call you the cat murderer. That's the third you've killed."

"It deserved it. It was up that tree trying to catch sparrows. Cats are stinking brutes; they deserve to be killed."

"The cat murderer," laughed Dean.

Gourlay too laughed, but a little uneasily. "It must hae been deid before I hit it."

"You heard it squeak, you saw its paws move."

"Well, do you think I care?"

"No, Sam, you don't care. You wouldn't care if it was a human being. Donoghue's got black hair. Now if that was Donoghue lying there deid would you care?"

"Not if it was Donoghue."

"Well, Sam, I'll give you a bit of advice. When you chap at that door and ask for your bus fare don't tell them you've killed their cat."

"Do you think I'm daft?" Then in a sudden passion he looked crazy. "There are millions of cats, all over the world. My faither says rich folk spend pounds every week on their cats.

I'm glad I killed it. And do you ken what I'm going to do? I'm going to kill every cat I see from now on."

"You'll be busy killing them."

"I'll be busy killing them all right."

Dean whistled and shoved both hands into his pockets. "Well, if you're going to stand here all day boasting about the cats you're going to kill, I think I'll just get away up to the main street and take the bus."

"I'll get the bus too," said Gourlay grimly, and marched off towards the cottage door.

Dean in delight followed to watch the fun.

Nothing happened after the first, the second, even the third knock, except that Gourlay's anger grew worse. Kicking did no good, as his sandshoes were too soft and his feet too tender. He picked up a chuckie from the weed-grown path and cracked it like a machine-gun against the door.

This time it opened. He snarled with disgust. It was an old woman, white-haired like Granny Howden but not dressed in black. She wore spectacles and the skin on her face was so loose it seemed that if she sneezed she would blow it all away. After blinking at him for a few moments she let out a small shrill cry and began to stroke his face. Grinning, he endured her fondlings. Old folk were crazy: maybe she took him for her cat; maybe she would give him a sixpence.

She began to weep, as if she already knew her cat was dead. But in a moment he realised with a change of grin that she'd hardly be caressing him if she knew he'd killed her cat.

"I thought for a minute, son," she squeaked, in her little cat's voice, "you were somebody else. He's been away in America noo these past twenty years and mair, and never a scrape of the pen."

"Crazy," he thought, "auld and crazy."

"Could you gie me threepence, Mrs.," he muttered. "I'm hungry."

"I would never hae expected him to send me money," she squeaked, "if he was having a hard time of it himself yonder. But never a scrape of the pen."

137

"Just threepence, Mrs.," he muttered again. "I've miles to walk hame, and I'm hungry."

She sighed. "I've nae siller to spare, son, me living my lane now, except for poor auld Malky. Hae you seen auld Malky aboot?" She began to sniff, with a bright expectant smile amidst her tears. "He seems to be aboot," she said. "We've been company to one anither for so many years, do you ken, he can smell me oot and I can smell him. Malky, ch-ch-ch-ch." She snapped her fingers as she called, but it was a snapping so soft it wouldn't even have annoyed a teacher.

"There's no cat here," muttered Gourlay.

"Oh, he's aboot somewhere, son. I can smell him. What is it you're selling?"

"I'm selling nothing, Mrs. I'm hungry. My faither's not working. Could you gie me threepence?"

She caught only one word. "Hungry, did you say, son? I'll tell you what I'll do. I'll gie you a rare big chit with my ain bramble jeely on it. I hae my ain brambles doon by the burn; it's handy for me, you ken. When I was a lassie your age I could walk miles gathering them in my wee tin. I aye liked gathering the brambles. Just you wait here, son."

Grinding his teeth in rage at her doted persistence in ignoring his request for money, and calling her a mean auld bitch, he watched her in the dusky room trotting from one place to another, finding the bread, then the jam, and then the breadknife. With the breadknife in her hand she rushed to the door as if to stab him; but it was to assure him she wouldn't be long.

When she tottered in again he took a step after her and saw on the edge of a dresser near the door, her large fat black purse. As he grabbed it and stuck it up his jersey, and retreated back outside with it, he was thinking of the cat among the brambles as much as of the purse. On the doorstep he hesitated, doubtful whether to rush away at once with his booty, or to wait and see if her boasts about her fine jam were lies or not. He felt that if he had something tasty to eat he might stop feeling sick.

138

At last, staggering in her gladness, she came with the bread wrapped in newspaper. The excitement and energy of preparing the sandwiches, and the joy of giving them to him, exhausted her, so that she had to hold on to the side of the doorway with one hand and to Gourlay with the other. She clutched him by the jersey not far from the bulge her purse made. His heart thumped not so much because she was close to discovering his theft, as because he thought her purse must surely contain a lot of money, pounds maybe, enough to take him to the pictures for weeks and buy him unlimited chocolate and chips and lemonade and fags.

"Twenty years is a long time, son, withoot a scrape of the pen," she gasped, beginning to sob again. "This is my hoose. I bide here alone now, with auld Malky, and he's gey deaf and blind getting. Is he not aboot?"

He shook his head. "I'll need to go, Mrs."

"He's fourteen years auld," she sobbed, "and I can mind the winter's day he came here as a kitten in a man's pocket. Bob Hendry that was, and he's deid since."

Gourlay gave an impatient shake. "I'll need to go."

He was surprised and alarmed to find she was holding him tightly, almost as if she knew he had her purse up his jersey and was keeping him there till a cop arrived.

Roughly he pulled himself free. She staggered forward and nearly fell.

"Go to hell," he cried, startled, running down the path and out of the gate. "Oh go to hell, you and your Malky." His last glimpse showed her at the door, leaning against it, weeping, her face hidden in her withered hands. "Christ," he laughed, as he raced along the road, the sandwiches in one hand, the purse kept in place by the other, "she'll hae something to greet aboot when she looks in the bramble bushes."

Dean came running alongside him. "What's the big hurry for?" he asked, smiling as if he knew.

"Nothing," said Gourlay, not decided yet whether to tell Charlie about the purse and share its contents with him.

"I thought you had two skinned heels."

Gourlay laughed. Pressing the purse against him, he thought that never again would he feel pain.

"You took something," gasped Dean. "I saw you. What was it?"

"This piece, Charlie." He held it up. "She bummed about her bramble jeely. She said her brambles were the best brambles. Do you ken what her cat was called?"

"Was it her cat, the one you killed? The one in the bramble bushes?"

"It was called Malky. It was fourteen years auld. Didn't I tell you it was time it was deid?"

"What was it you took?" insisted Dean.

Suddenly, so wonderful was the flow of delight through him, Gourlay stopped running and flung his hand holding the sandwiches round Charlie and gave him a squeeze.

"I'll tell you, Charlie," he said, "for you're my pal. It was her purse." He could hardly whisper it for chuckles. "Oh, it was her purse." And the delight kept flowing through him, more wonderfully than the water flowed past its green banks: his flashes of anticipation were like the wagtail's darts, only far more swift and brilliant.

Dean flung off the embrace. "Her purse?" he repeated, and whistled. "That's serious stealing, Gourlay."

"Pounds," gasped Gourlay, "pounds and ten shilling notes. She said her son in America never sent her any money, but she was an auld liar."

"She looked poor to me. The house was tumbling down. Look at the garden; it was all weeds. For stealing a purse, Gourlay, they wouldn't let you off with a ten-bob fine."

Gourlay shook his head, unable to express that delight which flowed through him more wonderfully than the light flowed out of the blue sky. He was free now from his mother's meanness and from Jeanie's pennyworths of generosity. Tomorrow if he went back to school Martin would likely take him to old Richards and Armstrong would be there, and together they would try to thrash him into saying he was sorry and would never do it again; but he would be able now more than ever to

140

defy them, because that night, and every night after, he could go to the warm cosy exciting pictures and suck sweeties and forget them all.

He began to run again, forgetting his skinned heels, his sickness, his headache, and his smarting feet.

"We'd better," he panted, "find a secret place before we look in the purse." He laughed. "You wouldn't pay my bus fare, Charlie, but I'll pay yours."

"Maybe I'll not let you," said Dean. "If I take share of it, even just a ha'penny, they'll say I'm your accomplice. That's the name they use: accomplice."

"You're my pal," laughed Gourlay.

"That's not to say I'm anxious to go to the reformatory with you."

"When your auntie's deid, Charlie, and it's just your uncle left in the hoose, maybe you'll prefer then to go to the reformatory."

"I thought you gave a promise never to talk about her."

"I forgot, Charlie. It just slipped oot. Do you think we're far enough away now? Over the hedge there would be a good place, doon beside the burn." He burst out laughing. "I'm carrying this piece," he cried, "and I'm not eating it, and yet I'm starving with hunger."

Halfway through the hedge, in some difficulty because of its denseness and because both his hands were not available to help, he laughed again, in the same astonished glee. "Do you ken what I think I'll do? I think I'll gie Stirling a shilling. I would say to him, here's a present for you, Stirling. Auld Richards said everybody in the school should be proud of you, so here's a shilling."

His cheek was bleeding from a scratch when he at last shoved through the hedge and jumped down into a little hollow by the burnside. There he unwrapped the sandwiches and began to munch at one. His right hand still guarded the purse up his jersey.

"It's good," he said, nodding. "She was right. I like bramble jeely. Do you want a bit, Charlie?"

141

At a much more leisurely pace Dean came down into the hollow. Like old Muldoon he was chewing a stalk of grass.

"It's tastier than grass, Charlie," grinned Gourlay.

Dean shook his head. "When are you going to open it?" he asked.

"You mean the purse? Will I do it now, right away?"

"Suit yourself."

"I meant to finish my piece. I was hungry; that's why I was feeling sick. But I'll do it right away if you want, Charlie."

"It's all the same to me," said Dean.

Gourlay's hand trembled as he laid the bread on the ground beside him, but when he began to pull the purse down the trembling increased so much as to be a nuisance, causing the purse to become stuck in a hole in his jersey. He cursed as he tore it free, making the hole larger. At last the purse was in his hands between his knees, his to open whenever he wished; or so, gloating, he thought; but when, after a triumphant glance across at Charlie, he proceeded to unfasten the clasp he found he could not, either because it was broken in some way or because it was locked. He pressed with his thumb till he yelled with pain as much as with fury; then he gnawed at the clasp with his teeth; then, after another glance at Charlie, a different glance this time, he scraped in the grass for a stone, found one embedded, almost broke his nails digging it up, and hammered at the clasp with it. All the time he was calling the purse and the old woman and even her cat Malky all the obscenest names he knew.

Dean sat chewing the grass, offering no advice or help or taunts.

At last, in desperation, snarling like a dog threatened with the loss of its bone, Gourlay took the purse and straining it across his chest ripped it apart, so that for a moment he seemed to be playing a concertina. Next moment he was delving into its numerous empty compartments with demented betrayed fingers. He pulled out a key wound round with red thread, and threw it over him into the field. He took out without meaning to, for it clung to his fingers, a lock of brown hair, and worked it madly off into the stream where it hesitated and then floated calmly away. Then finally he took out and held up between finger and thumb, for the whole treacherous world to see, the only coin in the purse, a ha'penny with a hole in it. Long after he had seen what it was, and Charlie had seen, he kept holding it up. Once he tried to speak, to express his devastated hopes, but had to stop, for it was evident he would have wept. He could not prevent tears, more traitors, from gathering in his eyes.

"She must have kept her money in another purse," said Dean in a flat cautious voice.

Gourlay did not speak.

"Women are like that, they have two purses."

Then Dean in readiness dropped the stalk of grass.

"Well," he said, with the first faint mockery creeping into his voice, "half of that wouldn't amount to very much."

Still Gourlay did not answer, and he tried again, more wary, ready to strike back.

"Likely that's her lucky ha'penny," he murmured, and then laughed. "It's certainly not yours. You'll have a hard job gieing Stirling a shilling out of that."

This time Gourlay responded by taking his eyes off the ha'penny and looking at his friend.

Dean rose up, laughing.

"No ha'penny tickets," he said, "on the bus. Even if there were, no conductress would take one with a hole in it."

He scrambled backwards out of the hollow, like a keeper leaving a tiger's cage. When he was safely out he grinned down.

"You'll have to walk it after all," he jeered. "You'll miss your tea. Of course you've got those pieces with bramble jeely."

Had Gourlay flung the bread at him, or the purse, or a stone, or had he even flung himself in a suicidal madness into the burn, he would not have been astonished. But what Gourlay did do, amazed him so much that his final gibe faltered on his lips and almost was never spoken. Seated there in the hollow, with the purse and the ha'penny in his hands, Gourlay turned his face away and sobbed.

Dean watched him for a long minute in delicious silence. Listening to the strange sobs and to the familiar murmurs of the burn, he remembered what he had intended to say as his farewell.

"I'd better hurry," he said. "After my tea I'm going to the pictures."

Then, with laughter that started quietly but grew louder and more and more derisive, he climbed through the hedge and went up the road.

Chapter Six

THE RAINCOAT, bought for one and sixpence from a second-hand clothes' barrow in Glasgow, proved surprisingly acceptable: it fitted; had no smell; was dark blue which allowed discreet darning and sewing; and still bore, a little scummy from the rub of time, the gold and crimson trademark of an expensive maker. His mother lovingly sponged and pressed it, and put mothballs in its pockets as disinfectants. He stood for a long time in front of a mirror, with her standing anxiously by, and at last smiled wanly and nodded: it would do. She had been for her demonstratively joyful, clapping her hands and even stroking him in the lucky coat with them. Before she moved away from the mirror she gazed in it at herself, amazed at her own visible joyfulness, which made her young again, not so much in the irredeemable face as in hope.

"You see," she said to him, now back at his studies at the table, and also to herself, "things are never as bad as they seem."

Memorising the declension of *mensa: a table* he nodded.

She said no more to him then but let him study undisturbed. Yet there seemed many things, many hopeful things, she could have said then. Instead, as she hung the coat up on a hanger and carefully put by his suit which as always he had taken off as soon as he came home, she sang quietly, not any known song, not even her favourite Land of the Leal, but simply the mild outflowings of her gratitude and hope.

"I'm not disturbing you, am I?" she asked.

He shook his head. "I'm nearly finished this."

She peeped over his shoulder. "Is it French?"

"No, it's Latin."

"Do you think——" fear made her pause, fear that could so quickly and so completely drive out hope—"do you think you'll be able to manage a thing like Latin? Other boys will hae faithers and mithers to help them that had Latin themselves at school. But I never saw a Latin word in my life, and neither did your faither."

"That makes no difference," he murmured. "It's easy."

She shook her head, unconvinced. That fear grew sharper, for what caused it could never be remedied. It had not been her fault she had never had Latin and French and Science at school. Perhaps, given the chance, she might have been good at those subjects, for she had been clear-witted then. Now she was ignorant and dull, fit only to scrub and wash. She looked at her charwoman's hands. In the iciest weather for his sake she would gladly work them till they felt not like human hands at all, but grotesque lumps of pain. But that sacrifice was useless if her coarse manners and speech, her ignorance, and her inability to read a book right through, were to handicap him owing to some inexorable trick of heredity.

He turned to her with a smile beautiful in its confidence.

"Don't worry, mother," he murmured. "I can do it."

"But will you always be able to do it? Maybe it's easy now at the beginning. When it gets harder, will you still be able to do it?"

He nodded.

"I hope so." Foolishly, knowing it was the worst example she could show him, she allowed her foreboding to grow and darken. "But if you were to become the dux of the school even——" She turned away, sighing. If he were to become dux in five years' time, as he had said he might, she would have to keep away from the prize-giving when the gold medal was presented to him. There would be important people there, and she would not know how to speak to them. They would wonder how so talented a boy could have such an uneducated mother.

"If I get a chance to study, that is," he was saying. "If Mary doesn't play her violin every night."

She became thrawn and took Mary's part. "She's got to practise," she muttered, "or she'll forget the little she kens. You ken as weel as me why she'd to stop her lessons. And she's working too."

"I know. I just said I hoped she wouldn't practise every night."

"She's hardly likely to do that."

"Maybe she will, for spite."

The last two words were very quietly uttered, but she caught them; and though she knew they were largely justified, she bitterly attacked him.

"Don't dare say that," she cried. "Don't you dare. I ken, mind you, that I hae been unfair to her making too much of you. Getting high marks in examinations isn't everything; remember that. If it's a comfort to Mary to play her violin, then she'll play it, aye, even if it means you don't open a single book. It's downright wicked of you to hint it's spite makes her play. She plays for her ain pleasure, and sometimes for mine."

He knew that if he kept silent and looked unhappy she would soon begin to pity him and blame his sister; but he could not refrain from murmuring, "She can't play."

Thus provoked, his mother kept haranguing him. Soon however, with his Latin grammar open in front of him, he scarcely heard her as he repeated inwardly those magically consoling words: mensa, mensam, mensae, mensae, mensa; mensae, mensae, mensarum, mensis, mensis. . . .

Some weeks later, as he was in the middle of his French exercise in ink, Mary, who had been standing under the gas-light manicuring her nails, suddenly marched to the corner where her violin-case stood like a little coffin against the wall. She took out her violin, chose some music, propped it against a jug on the dresser, and began to play.

At first he persevered, but the music, badly played though it was with many shrieking mistakes, lured away his attention. He could not concentrate on translating into French the sentence 'I close the door of the classroom,' while in the small yellow-lit shadowy kitchen the melancholy Highland song 'Turn Ye to Me' reverberated, however shrilly, conjuring up seagulls and waves and far-off sad rocks. He kept waiting, his pen arrested, until she stopped; then in the violent silence that fell his pen neatly and accurately wrote the French words: 'Je ferme la porte de la salle.' He murmured them, and they sounded somehow as sad as the song. Before he could begin the next sentence: 'I have my uncle's pen,' Mary had started again, the same song, the same mistakes, the same petrifying melancholy.

She paused in the middle of the tune; he turned to protest politely, to ask for just five minutes to finish his exercise, and found her staring at him vindictively, but with tears glinting down her cheeks.

"Put cotton-wool in your ears," she screamed, before he could speak. "I've got a right to play, and I'm going to play."

"I just want to finish this exercise," he said, smiling appeasingly. "It's my French one."

"I don't care what one it is. My music is as important to me as your French is to you."

This seemed to him so absurdly untrue that his smile, though still appeasing, was affected. She became immediately furious.

"It is," she yelled, stamping her foot. "It is. I tell you it is." And turning away from him she began to play again, worse this time, faltering, with more and screechier errors; and like an accompaniment she wept harshly.

He sighed, and with an effort of concentration that brought a cramp into his belly wrote slowly, with incomparable neatness: 'J'ai la plume de mon oncle.'

She stopped so abruptly he shrank as if from a blow.

"I'll tell you something," she cried, "that'll take the smugness out of you."

He did not turn round but waited, gazing down at his immaculate page.

She took a step nearer. "Your coat that you're so proud of," she said, "it was bought from a barrow that sold second-hand clothes."

"It was a shop."

"No, it wasn't; it was a barrow. It would be lying among other old clothes that came off people who were dirty and had skin diseases, likely, and fleas. Maybe your coat belonged to somebody like that."

He smiled: that gold and crimson trademark easily exorcised the bogey she tried to raise.

"You think it cost ten shillings," she said.

His smile vanished. Although he had not moved, she divined that he was now waiting anxiously.

"It cost one and sixpence," she sneered, "just one and sixpence."

After what seemed to both of them a long time he murmured, "Well," and she knew she had failed to terrify him.

Surprised and ashamed, she turned back to her playing. This time she could not bear sadness and tried the jaunty tune: A Highland Lad. But she could not play it long, and soon was putting the violin away. In the corner, as she stood in the shadows, with her back to her brother, she said, eyes closed and hand on top of her violin case, "I'm sorry. I'm sorry I said that about your coat. I promised my mother I wouldn't tell you the price. I shouldn't have. I'm sorry."

"It's all right, Mary." He could be magnanimous in this matter, for the coat had by now been accepted at the Academy; it had been appearing there for weeks, sometimes in sunshine, sometimes in rain, and nobody had as much as looked at it, so safely similar was it to many others. It had even one afternoon, in quite heavy rain, walked from the school to the bus stop alongside Tull's jacket that had the collar turned up.

"How are you getting on with your French?" she asked.

"All right, Mary, thanks."

"It had better be more than all right, for my mother dreams you'll be dux of the school some day."

He smiled, remembering Mr. Malvern's praise, since repeated several times, and remembering Stinker's surprise only yesterday when after rejecting John's suggestion as to how a geometrical problem might be done he had had to admit that it could be done that way.

149

"Of course," she said, "it's a long time till the fifth year. Anything could happen before then. You could be dead."

He shivered, knowing she could have made a more dreadful prophecy, because one far likelier to come about. She could have said that long before he reached the fifth year one of those twelve hundred spies would have found out about his mother being a scrubberwoman.

During those first few weeks at school he had had another reason besides the fascination of knowledge for preferring the periods of lessons to the intervals and lunch-times. No one was likely to ask him during English, say, or Maths or Science, questions that might probe out his secret. In the cloakroom though or in the playground or the refectory room where cups of tea were sold for three ha'pence each, anyone might blurt out, not meaning any harm, "What does your father work at, Stirling?"

Often, drinking his hot weak milky tea from the chipped cup, he pictured some companion's munching mouth suddenly fire that question and crumbs with it, while all the others waited, teeth halted, for the interesting reply. It would not be difficult to answer his father was dead; indeed, that might even be congenial to murmur, for there was a sad distinction in being an orphan. The danger was, someone, such as Henderson, might see there was another question still to be asked. How then, if his father was dead, did he live? Who bought his clothes? Who paid for his jotters? Who fed him? Who worked for him? He could hardly say, Mary my sister; her job was respectable enough to be spoken about, but she was only fifteen, and earned about that number of shillings per week. What could he say then? He knew that if, like Tull, he kept his head up and his eyes smiling and did not blush or stammer, he could tell them the truth and make them in their hearts feel his mother ought to be honoured and not despised. Some might sneak away and mock her behind his back, as some mocked Tull's crippled father; they might even go down on their knees on the stone steps of the school and pretend to be washing them, just as they hopped about on one leg or walked

150

crooked. But if others laughed at that imitation it would be conscience-stricken laughter; while far more would not laugh at all, but rather would rebuke the mockers.

Therefore, although he knew instinctively that his mother's patient low-paid work was as honourable and as beyond contumely as Rodgers' father's high Daimlered post in the Iron-works, he stole away from conversations as soon as these turned on parents and the money they earned. At that particular moment he would need to go to the lavatory, or would hear somebody call him, or would decide to wash his hands in the cloakroom washbasins. What surprised him was that nobody seemed to notice his peculiar shyness. They kept on shouting their monied boasts and laughing at one another's discomfiture when a boast, too huge to be tolerated, was operated on by the whole company and cut down to a healthy size.

The suspense, the constant defensiveness, and the frequent isolations, of course, did him harm. Often he had headaches; his heart would suddenly race and become audible; he felt sick; but worst of all, and most regularly, he suffered from depressions. He never believed he would do badly in the approaching examinations. Even in his blackest self-pityings he could not think Henderson would beat him. Indeed the certainty that he would be first, probably in every subject, was the chief ingredient in his pessimism. To fail like Tull because one was a dunce was expected, nothing to weep about; but to fail when one was brilliant, was the best among hundreds and those hundreds containing as Mr. Richards had said 'the cream of the county', this was a great tragedy, this was good cause for weeping, although weeping would not mend it.

Therefore he walked in this private terror, knowing every minute what would dispel it; but not even the irremediable tragedy that happened to Tull in his sight almost, gave him the necessary anger against himself.

The bell to end the interval had just been rung, and they were all streaming into school, when a long black car with an aerial stopped outside the main gate, and a policeman came out. Stirling was in the vestibule when the policeman came in and asked some boys where the Rector's room was. When they showed him, he went straight to it, removing his helmet. He turned out to be almost bald, although to Stirling he had seemed young.

Stirling had forgotten him and was doing his nineteenth example of the profit-and-loss sums Miss Naismith had been teaching 1A, when the Rector entered in his flowing black gown. He had his mortar board in his hand and his baldness reminded Stirling of the policeman. Like a good pupil, however, he gave only the briefest glance and went on with his sum.

The Rector whispered to Miss Naismith who let out an 'Oh!' which even Stirling heard at his back desk. She began to stroke her big bosom in perturbation, and nod as the Rector still whispered. He held up his mortar board as a screen. She began to tidy away some papers on her desk; then she took off her gown and hung it on its hook behind her cupboard door. The Rector, while she did so, glanced at the jotter of a boy in the front seat. He did not say whether the sums were correct or not.

Miss Naismith was ready. She tapped on the desk for attention.

"Listen, please," she said solemnly.

They all looked up.

"Put your pencils down for a moment."

They did so, some reluctantly but most with sighs of relief.

"The Rector wishes me to do something for him," she said. "And I want you to do something for me. It is simply this: work on quietly, and when the period bell rings, which it will do in about ten minutes, leave the room without any fuss or noise. I shall correct your sums next day. Now this is 1A, and ought to be trusted. Can you be trusted?"

They nodded virtuously. Some called out, "Yes, miss."

The Rector coughed, tapped his teeth with his mortar board, considered underlining her appeal, but shook his head instead.

"Now pick up your pencils again and go on with your work," said Miss Naismith.

Henderson put up his hand. "Please, miss," he said, "if we finish the twenty in this exercise, will we just go on to the next exercise?"

"Yes. Yes, just do that. What number are you at now, Henderson?"

"Please miss, the fifteenth."

She glanced at Stirling. "What about you, Stirling?"

"I'm finished, miss."

"You mean the whole exercise?"

"Yes, miss."

Again that miracle of unassumingness. She could not help smiling in approval. This boy Stirling never showed off. He seemed so confident of his own ability that he did not need to. Poor Henderson on the other hand was always boasting, making himself vulnerable. She knew the others teased him.

Then she remembered the news the Rector had brought and the errand she was about to set out on.

"Work steadily," she said, at the door. "Check every answer."

Henderson who hadn't time to check every answer looked across in dismay at Stirling who would have time.

Then Miss Naismith and the Rector went out.

Immediately the class relaxed, in sprawls, in whispers, in shouts, in arm-stretchings, in yawns, in nose-picks, in cribbings, and in mere vacancies.

"Did you hear that?" called the boy at the front desk, the one next to the teacher's. He turned and shouted his question to McGregor his friend in the second-back row.

"Hear what?" shouted McGregor, who was sharpening his pencil.

"Tull's father's dead."

McGregor kept on sharpening his pencil, although the news interested him.

"How do you know?" he asked.

"That's what the Rector said. He asked Miss Naismith if she

153

would go home with Tull. A bobby came with the news. He fell down the stairs in his wheel-chair. He was a cripple, you know."

"Who? The bobby?"

"No, you chump. Tull's father."

"I saw the bobby," said somebody. "He went to the Rector's door."

"Poor Tull," said another, a boy called Dawson.

Stirling, whose pencil had stopped in the middle of a figure, looked at Dawson and loved him for his two words of pity. Before, he had hardly noticed Dawson, who was average and ordinary: he lived a mile or two outside Drumsagart in one of the big houses at Dechmont, but he travelled to school by train and he and Stirling met only in the classrooms. But from that moment Stirling felt he would, even if they never spoke to each other or spoke only about lessons, love Dawson and wish him well.

Henderson, noticing Stirling was idle, worked even harder and reached the nineteenth sum.

"I wonder if they'll go in the police car," said Rodgers. "I've always wanted to travel in a police-car."

"They're fast," said somebody. "Eighty miles an hour."

"Our Daimler can touch eighty," said Rodgers.

"Your Daimler. A police-car would overtake your Daimler. Stands to reason. After all, Rodgers, criminals could buy Daimlers."

"Thanks," said Rodgers.

Another boy called Eastman had ventured over among the girls and was looking out of the window.

"The police-car's gone," he said. "So they can't go in that. I'm not touching your jotter." This was to the girl whose desk he was leaning on. Suddenly he became excited. "Jings, there they are!"

"Who?"

"Miss Naismith and Tull. She's got her arm round his neck. So she has."

There was a rush over to the windows. More girls protested

their jotters were being interfered with; but some girls stood up and peeped out.

Stirling sat at his desk. Some of the bold ones at the windows, glancing back into the room, thought he was either scared to go over and look out or else grudged the time away from the profit-and-loss. But Stirling did not have to go over and look out of the window to see Tull, with Miss Naismith's arm round his neck, walk past the lawns and the bare flagpole, through the gate and along the street towards the bus, which would take them to his altered home.

"Tull had no mother," said Dawson, coming back to his seat. "At least I've never heard him speaking about her. It was always about his father."

Then the period bell rang, and there was a stampede to reach desks, put books away, and be the first out of the door.

Tull did not return to school that day. Miss Naismith came back alone, and Stirling saw her, again with her black gown on, talking in the corridor to Mr. Bradley, who had Tull for maths. He could not tell from her face, or from her quick schoolmistressy hands, whether it was true that Tull's father was dead. Mr. Bradley just kept nodding and moving away, but then most of the men teachers just kept nodding and moving away when Miss Naismith was talking to them.

He did not know anybody in Tull's class to ask, and even if he had known someone perhaps he would not have asked. The answer might have spoiled his sad and solitary walkings under the trees in the playground. As he walked on the leaves that just a few weeks ago had fluttered high above his head, and now lay in mud, he seemed to see Tull's hopes and his own come drifting down from the sky to be similarly trampled on. From Tull's disaster in the present to his own inevitable ruin in the future the way was short and somehow led through a great wood full of such leafless trees.

As he paced there in the playground a ball would be kicked towards him, and pausing in his melancholy he would kick it back to the shouting footballers.

Days passed, and Tull did not return to school. Even his own classmates in 1E did not know whether he had left for good. Although he had been popular among them, they had already shed their memories of him with the same instinct of conservation as the trees did their leaves. Once Stirling, in his unobtrusive investigation, saw the small boy, even smaller than himself, whose penny Tull had pretended to steal on the first day. He was squirting barley through a glass pea-shooter at another boy, who was squirting it back. Both had their heads protected by the lapels of their jackets held out. Stirling, as he watched, recollected how Tull never seemed to protect himself against anything. Whether it was friendly barley being shot at him, or spiteful laughter, he had made no attempt to hide his face. But now, wherever he was, did he still stare boldly, smiling, with unexpected winks and cheerful tugs of his hair, so disconcerting to his teasers? Apparently he had lived alone with his father, and certainly he had loved his father very deeply: well now, with his father dead and by this time buried and gone forever, did he still smile and tug his hair and wink? And to whom? Stirling did not know, and nobody could ever tell him.

One day, however, about a fortnight after Tull had been escorted home, Stirling to his own later weeping vexation asked Miss Naismith about him.

She had given the class a number of sums to do, and Stirling as usual had been finished first. She had called him out to her desk and with blue pencil was marking sum after neat sum correct.

"You're like a little machine," she said, laughing. "Don' you ever make mistakes?"

"Sometimes, miss." He took his jotter and was about to return to his seat when this impulse seized him and he suddenl asked in a murmur she had to lean forward to hear: "Please miss, is Robert Tull not coming back to school?"

She stared down at him. Already he was blushing at his ow stupid temerity.

"Did you know him?" she asked.

"I sometimes talked to him."

She was puzzled: there seemed to her no connection between this small neatly dressed infinitely responsible brilliant boy and Tull.

"Did you know him before you both came to the Academy?" she asked.

"No, miss."

She had to rattle on the desk with her pencil. Some in the class were more intent on eavesdropping than on calculating. Henderson had his hand up.

"Well, what is it, Henderson?"

"Please, miss, I'm finished."

"All right. I'll look at them in a minute." She turned again to Stirling. "No, he's not coming back. He's gone to another school. You know of course his father died?"

"Yes, miss."

What he did not know, and what she certainly would never tell him, was that Tull's mother, when her son was an infant, had run off to live with other men.

Casually she asked, "What does your own father do, Stirling?" She ought to have known he was dead, for it appeared on the school records, and indeed she had already remarked on it to another teacher. She had forgotten.

"He's dead," whispered Stirling, and his very reluctance gave to the whisper a penetration that made it reach even Henderson in his back seat.

Miss Naismith could of course say nothing. As she gazed down at the blushing rather sweet-faced little boy, she pitied him and indeed loved him with her fallow maternal heart. A recollection was born there: she remembered how when she had read Stirling's name out on the first day of the session Tull had patted his shoulder in congratulation. She remembered too how she had admired the gesture.

"No, he's not coming back," she said. "He was a nice boy really."

"Yes, miss," murmured Stirling. Then, the conversation over, his fortress breached, he walked back to his seat.

Henderson hurried out with his jotter; he had three wrong. That his father was alive, and able to buy him the *Children's Eycyclopaedia*, was at that moment no consolation. Miss Naismith scolded him for his carelessness, and warned him in the examination it might have cost him thirty marks.

Chapter Seven

THREE weeks from Christmas, about the time of Stirling's examinations, came Gourlay's chance of revenge on Jeanie. She did not know he had been waiting all those weeks. Often during them she had given him money, had mended his clothes, had taken him to the pictures, had protected him from their mother's brutality and their father's contempt, had embraced him, wept over him, and even prayed for him. Accepting those services, he had nevertheless managed many little preliminary revenges.

Always, no matter whether she coaxed with words or coins, he refused to praise Donoghue: it was always easy to hurt her by calling the little labourer names, even apparently joking names like short-legs or big-ears or pape. Every such name seemed like a blow on the face to her. Tears would spring into her eyes under the spectacles; red blotches would appear on her brow; her pimples would seem to grow glossier and more numerous. She would cover her face with her large hands and deny the aspersions, but it was obvious even to her puzzled delighted brother that she hated them: this was not because she was afraid they might be true, but for a reason so deep and obscure she could hardly have explained it herself.

The truth was, towards Donoghue she felt a constant darkening guilt. Although she had let him speak to her of marriage, and she had agreed, she had not yet been brave enough to tell him about her and Geordie Lucas. Any criticism of him therefore accentuated her own enormous sinfulness towards him. About this matter too she prayed, every night on her knees; but her prayers seemed to her only to complicate and worsen her guilt, and make more inevitable the coming disaster, for he did not go to church, lived in a house and worked in a

159

laundry where God's name and Christ's name were used as swears only, never read the Bible, knew no hymns to sing, listened daily to filthy talk, and thus steeped in the general irreverence and foulness was utterly and insultingly unfit to pray. She would realise, as she knelt in the darkness, as she tried to find pardonable words amidst her tears, that God would be justified in using his power not to save her but to destroy her without pity.

During that first week of December it looked as if God had at last decided to strike. That he chose Sam as his instrument shocked and convinced her.

From Charlie Dean, now working as can-boy in the steel-work beside Donoghue, Sam learned about Jeanie and Geordie Lucas. Charlie had described the thing that had happened with as obscene gestures and expressions as Gourlay's scowl indicated were safe. He had patiently explained that no man, not even the simple stupid Donoghue, liked to marry a woman who had done that thing with another man. Every man liked to be the first to do it with his wife. He had said that the men in the steelwork thought Jeanie ought to hurry up and get Donoghue to marry her before he found out. Once they were married, it was said, he was bound to find out; there were signs he'd see; but all he could do then would be to blacken her eyes or else the favourite punishment, give her a wean every year for ten years, make her carry round the big drum perpetually. At the end of the conversation Charlie had walked away laughing with the remark that one thing was certain, Jeanie would do anything, pay anything, to keep Donoghue from knowing.

They were alone in the kitchen, their parents having gone out to a spiritualist meeting. Jeanie had been washing her hair, and now with a towel on like a turban was ironing her underclothes at the table. Delicately she had her back turned to her brother and kept between him and the chemise and knickers and underslips spread out on the table. He sat at the fire chewing caramels he had bought with a penny she had given him, and looking at a comic sent to him, so she had lied, by Donoghue; she had of course bought it herself.

160

She liked when they were alone in the house by themselves. Sometimes she would send him out for two penny pokes of chips, and when he came back she would have tea ready, hot fresh tea, and pieces spread with real butter if there was any in the house. Always when their mother returned and saw them so friendly she would call Jeanie an easily deluded fool, and then would rage at her for throwing away money and kindness on somebody without as much as—so her mother coarsely put it—a fleashit of gratitude. Jeanie never heeded; she thought it was those cosy evenings and those penny pokes of chips which were helping to reclaim her brother, or at least helping to prevent him from being the vicious criminal everybody prophesied he would become.

She was about, that evening, to suggest he should run along for the chips when he spoke first.

"Does Donoghue ken," he asked, "what you and Geordie Lucas used to do together at the back of Drumsagart hill?"

Shocked to the depths of her simplicity, she remained where she stood bent over her ironing. She smelled the cloth burning as she held the iron motionless on it. The underslip of artificial silk was her best: it was being ruined and she did not have the strength or the ambition, for one long hellish minute, to lift the iron on to the asbestos pad less than a foot away.

"Does Donoghue ken that yet?" It was the same question, the same well-known well-loved chewing voice. "Your clothes are burning," it added.

Released for a moment she placed the iron on its stand. Still she kept her back to him. In the mirror at the sink, where her father shaved, she saw herself, ridiculously and loosely turbaned, with the even more ridiculous happiness falling from her face.

"He doesn't ken," said the voice. "Don't try to kid me. If he kent he would never say he was going to marry you."

She made a great effort. With trembling fingers she fastened the towel. It was not possible though to restore the happiness to her face. She could not clearly think. In the kitchen, a minute ago so snug and good, all kinds of evil swarmed: the very furniture seemed alien and hostile.

"Don't try to kid on you don't ken what I mean," said the voice. "You ken what I mean all right. Geordie Lucas and you, behind Drumsagart hill."

Still with her back to him, she pressed her cheeks hard with her hands: cheeks, hands, head, body, legs all shook. Horror smothered her power to think. Here into her own wickedness had walked her young brother who she had, against their mother, against all the world, maintained was innocent, was adventurous rather than vicious, inexperienced rather than evil, thoughtless rather than cruel; here he was now amidst her own sin, toying with it, and hinting at sins she had never dreamed existed at all in the whole depraved world, far less in him.

"Oh Sammy," she sighed at last.

"Don't try to get round me," he sneered. "You said auld Gilchrist was gone; you said everything had been settled."

She began to weep, not at her own forsaken plight but at his.

"Greeting will not save you," he said.

"What's going to save you, Sammy?"

"Me?" He was genuinely amazed and indignant. "It's not me that's to be saved, it's you. I'm going to tell Donoghue."

For a moment, as she saw the burnt mark on her underslip, and as she saw the still hot iron on its stand, the handle towards her, she felt a burning temptation to seize it, whirl round, and brand his face, deal out to him in this consummation more dreadful hurt than all his enemies together had done to him since his cradle days. He would carry the mark till he died. She pressed her cheeks harder and still harder, making herself like a horrid Hallowe'en mask, until that temptation cooled.

"Keeping your back turned makes no difference," he said, obviously grinning, obviously still enjoying the caramels as well as the words. "I ken you don't want Donoghue to find out. Everybody kens but Donoghue. Everybody says he's daft for not kenning. I'm going to tell him."

162

"You don't know what you're saying."

Her voice was so low and so squeezed because of her pressed cheeks that he didn't hear.

"What did you say?" he cried.

"I said, you don't know what you're saying." She thought he was too young to know, too innocent, too much in the protection of the Jesus to whom she had so ineffectually appealed.

He was indignant. "Oh, I ken all right. I've seen dogs do it."

"Sammy!"

Her shriek of horror startled and even frightened him. He waited for an attack with the iron, with a knife from the table drawer, with her nails. He had his own hand stretched out for the long poker on the hob. But after the shriek she did not move, only burst into a passion of weeping so absolute in its sorrow that even he might have been shaken by it into compassion or at least remorse had it not been for her turban and her bare skinny legs, which made him grin at their incongruity. At the pictures he had often watched heroines weep, but they were always lovely, never comical like this.

"I ken what I'm talking about," he said. "I'm not a wean. I'm not a mammy's pet. If you don't want me to let Donoghue ken you'll have to pay me to keep quiet. You ken I don't like him. A penny poke of chips will not be enough this time. This is serious. A half-crown will not be enough even." He paused, remembering the disappointment the old woman's purse had contained: he must take care now not to be disappointed. "I don't like Donoghue," he added.

Leaving the iron on its stand, and the smudged garment spread out on the table, she rushed from the kitchen through to the room.

He glowered over his comic, angry at her bad manners in running out while he was talking to her. He got up and went to the room door. She had locked it. He heard her weeping.

"Jeanie," he called, "Jeanie," and knocked on the door.

163

The weeping, after a second or two, altered slightly. He noticed the change but did not wonder what had caused it.

Inside the room in the darkness she was staring towards the door, thinking perhaps he had come, calling her name, to say he was sorry, that he had just been repeating what he had heard others say.

"Give me ten shillings," he cried, "and I'll not tell him."

Again he noticed the change in the weeping, but again didn't bother to wonder. He banged on the door.

"Ten shillings or I'll tell him."

"I'll tell him myself," she wept.

The weeping distorted her voice so much Sam didn't catch what she said.

"Do you agree?" he cried.

She made an effort apparent even to him outside the door. She controlled her weeping. For an instant she was quiet. "I'll tell him myself," she said.

Her brother laughed sarcastically. "Who are you kidding?" he cried. "You ken better. He wouldn't want you to be his wife if he kent." Again he laughed. "He'll want to be the first to do it to you."

But she was again weeping, and although he stood there by the door, jeering in insults, bringing his price down to five shillings, she did not speak again. Cold drove him back to the kitchen fire.

About an hour later, just before their parents returned, she came through, shivering from cold and from the aftermath of weeping, removed the ironing material from the table, and went out again. She still wore her turban.

She was still through in the room when their parents came in. They were arguing about the reliability of the medium's messages from the dead, but they soon stopped to ally themselves in an attack on Sam and Jeanie for not having the table set for supper.

"A cauld welcome," grumbled Mr. Gourlay, "for folk straight in from paradise."

"Where's Jeanie?" shouted Mrs. Gourlay.

"I think she's gone to bed," muttered Sam.

"Why? Is there anything the matter with her?"

"Maybe she's got a sore head."

"I never hae anything else but," cried his mother, barging out of the kitchen and banging on the room door. "What's this, Jeanie? Why's the supper not ready? Are you in bed?"

"Aye, I'm in bed."

"What's up? Hae you been greeting?"

There was no answer.

"He says you've got a sore head. Is that right?"

After a long pause came a sighing, "Aye."

"That's what he said, but you ken what a liar he is. But I forgot, you're the one, the only one, that doesn't ken. You'll never believe a word against him. Some day you'll get your een opened."

Mrs. Gourlay thumped into the kitchen again to find her husband, still with cap and muffler on and fag-nip in his mouth, wandering from press to table with a cup in one hand and margarine in paper in the other.

"She says she's got a sore head right enough," she said. "She seems to hae been greeting. You," the bark was to Sam, "could hae had the table set. She's guid to you, too bloody guid. Can you not do anything to pay her back? What hae you stopped for?"

The last question was to her husband who, now carrying sugar-bowl and another cup, had stopped midway between press and table.

"It just struck me," he said, "they must be a gey miserable crew up by. Do you ken what I think, Nelly? I think if you could hae a peep at them, you'd find them all sitting in a temperance hall up there, on hard narrow benches, just like us: them waiting to send messages, and us waiting to receive them."

She never liked his scepticism regarding the spirits.

"Get on with setting the table," she grunted. "You're talking tripe."

He began to move again, set down cup and sugar-bowl, and prowled back to the press.

"I wonder though," he said, "if they go hame to a supper of bread and marge with a scart of jam."

His wife laughed fiercely. "I don't ken where you're going to get the jam," she cried. "That one scraped the pot at tea-time."

Sam, pointed to as culprit, frowned.

"It was nearly empty," he said. "I'd to scrape it for five minutes to get enough for half a slice."

His father snickered. "Manna," he said. "And what else was it?" He picked up a sauce bottle, almost empty, with the cork missing and the top thick and black with a dubious coagulation. He sniffed at it and set it down in the press again. "What else besides manna?" he asked. "You're at school. You should ken. What is it the gods eat? Manna. But what else?"

"I don't know. We never got that."

"There was something else, besides manna; something they drank, I think. It'll come back to me. I'll mind it before the night's out."

"Mind what?" growled his wife.

Looking at her, so overwhelmingly earthy, he decided not to explain.

"Nothing. I was talking tripe."

"As usual."

"Sure, Nelly, as usual." Then as he was pouring the hot water into the teapot he cried out, "Nectar. That was it, nectar. I knew I'd mind it. Manna they ate, and nectar they drank." He repeated the word as if the celestial liquor itself was in his mouth. "Nectar." Then he suddenly laughed and bent down to sniff the tea in the pot. "Maybe after all we're better off wi guid hot human tea. I bet you that crew sitting up by on the hard seats would gie their right wings for just one cup."

"They hae nae wings," cried his wife angrily. "How many times hae I told you that? They're just like yourself."

"Just like myself," he repeated, nodding. "I suspect that's true. The only difference is they're waiting to get oot, and we're waiting to get in. It's a thought that, that fairly puts the tin lid on theology."

166

Pouring out the tea he hovered over the handleless cup he'd slipped out for Sam. "Is he to get some?"

His wife glowered at their son, who stared with thirsty innocence into the fire.

"He doesn't deserve it," she snapped. "Too damned lazy to set the table."

Her husband laughed. "I set the table, Nelly," he said, "and I made the tea. I bear him no grudge."

"Half a cup then."

He made it three-quarters of a cup. "And what about Jeanie? Will she want a cup poured out for her?"

"Hardly if she's gone to bed with a sore head."

"A cup of tea is often the best cure for that; aye, and for a sore heart. Better than nectar." With teapot in hand, and bonnet still on head, he went over to the door, opened it, and called through to the room. "Could you go a cup of tea, Jeanie?"

He had to shout again before an answer came, a long tremulous heart-broken no.

"What's up?" he asked, turning to his wife. "Is she greeting?"

Mrs. Gourlay was seated at table, enjoying her supper. What butter was left was already thick on her bread.

"How do I ken?" she asked, with mouth full. "Ask him. He's been in all night."

"I think it's Donoghue," said Sam meekly, daring to reach out for a scrap of the stalest bread.

His father took the teapot to the hob.

"What do you mean, it's Donoghue?" asked Mrs. Gourlay eagerly. "Do you mean they've had a cast-oot?"

He nodded, making it sad. "I think so."

"Let's pray to God it's true," said his mother. "If she marries him, we flit. Do you ken where to, Gourlay?"

Her husband, mufflered and bonneted, sat down. His knife went out to the butter plate, reacted sensitively to the insult of emptiness, and curved sadly aside to margarine paper.

"Where to?" he repeated. "Make it China, Nelly. I've always had a hankering to visit China."

"The poorhoose!" she roared. "That's where."

"The Chinese," he said, "had a civilisation of silks and lacquer when we were running aboot dressed in deid cats. When we left this evening I thought Jeanie looked happy enough; she was singing. Of course, here or in China, love's a strange thing; up in the clouds one minute, doon in hell the next. Eh, Nelly?"

His wife ignored his smile and wink. "I hope Donoghue does gie her the heave," she said, "if she's not got the sense to gie it to him. Once a pape, always a pape. Let Donoghue say what he likes, they wouldn't be married a week but the priest would be up chapping their door. What are you grinning at?"

"I wasn't grinning," said Sam.

"It looked damned like it. Hurry up with that tea and get to your scratcher."

Mr. Gourlay, munching his bread and marge as if it was manna, debated in the cathedral of his mind whether, as a broad-minded atheist, he would object to having a Catholic, supposedly renegade, as his son-in-law. It occurred to him it was the kind of question one might pose to the waiters on the benches up above. The intermediary, fat Mrs. Peele the medium, would snort, sway, gargle, foam, and look badly costive; then in that loud lamenting sing-song voice she would announce the awful earth-shaking wisdom of the dead: You are not to worry; everything will come out all right in the end.

"What are *you* grinning at?" asked his wife sourly.

He shook his head. "To answer that, Nelly," he said with a bitterness transcending margarine or shrew, "I would have to gie you the story of my life."

"God forbid," she said, almost piously.

A few minutes later Sam slipped out into the little closet in the lobby where his bed was. As he undressed in the darkness there he wondered between yawns what would be his best way of telling Donoghue about Jeanie and Geordie Lucas. To tell him to his face might be dangerous. Maybe it would be safer to write him a letter. But who would write it? No, not Charlie Dean, who might just laugh. Stirling perhaps. Yes, he could ask Stirling to write it; he could make Stirling write it. Stirling

168

was great at writing compositions. He had once written one about a journey to the North Pole that Mr. Richards had read to nearly every class in the school; he had given Stirling a shilling.

About ten minutes after leaving the kitchen Gourlay was asleep.

Next morning, sleepy and shivering, he was surprised when Jeanie did not give him her usual smiling, "Hello, Sammy." In a yawning minute of course he remembered last night, and knew why she was in such a swollen-eyed huff; but he still remained surprised, and even annoyed. Donoghue wasn't as important as all that?

Their mother noticed the strangeness between them. It compensated her for the lack of ham for breakfast; she loved ham, especially if it was fat. She would lie awake for an hour savouring it in advance. That morning breakfast had been bread dipped in the frying-pan.

"Will you be seeing Donoghue the night as usual?" she asked, trying to make it sound casual.

Jeanie was most unnaturally sharp. "Of course," she snapped. "Have you any objections?"

"None at all, in this bleary-eyed world as your faither would say, if he was awake to say it."

"I'm awake," came from the set-in bed.

"This is your picture night," remarked Mrs. Gourlay.

"What if it is?"

"Somebody seems to hae stolen your scone, Jeanie." But it was at Sam Mrs. Gourlay looked. When Jeanie was gone, she decided, she'd soon screw out of him what had really happened last night.

"Nobody's stolen my scone," said Jeanie. "I'll thank you all to mind your own business."

Then she went out, without even a word. Sam was disgusted, for he had been hoping she would slip him a penny at least just to make up for last night. As the door slammed behind her he called her inwardly a greedy bitch, and renewed his intention to tell Donoghue.

His mother rapped his knuckles hard with the blunt edge of a knife. He had not been expecting the blow, and he let out a howl.

"Tell me," she said amicably, "what happened last night?"

A voice came from the bed, "Last night we had a communication from the deid."

"You shut your trap," she said, still pleasantly. "Well, what happened?"

Sam licked his knuckles. "Where?" he muttered.

"Here. Between you and your beloved sister."

"Some beloved."

"You fell oot. What was it over?"

For some reason he did not want to tell her the truth. Certainly it was not loyalty towards Jeanie or affection for her made him reluctant. Nor was it because his mother, in spite of her apparent good-humour, might roar into a rage and thrash him.

"I'm waiting," she grunted, and, with what was intended as a mindful prelude, cuffed his head, almost overturning his chair and making his ear ring.

"For God's sake," came a muffled protest from the bed, "even the Spanish Inquisition waited till a decent time of the day. Before eight in the morning's not trade-union hours for torture."

"You shut your trap," she said aside. Her fist again was raised, still not wholly in earnest, still a little playful.

Sam had an inspiration. "It was because she wanted me to go and stay with her and Donoghue, after they were married."

The great jocular hammer poised over him dropped down, became a fat heavy hand that slid under her blouse and fondled her left breast. Years ago he had sucked it. Idly she let the recollection slip in and out of her mind.

"So they're still talking about getting married?" she asked.

Sam couldn't help grinning. He tried to temper it with an energetic nodding.

"Did she say anything about a date being fixed?"

"No."

She grinned. "So she still wants to take you away with her to nurse?"

"I said I wouldn't go. That was what made her angry."

"So you're too fond of us here to leave us?"

"I don't like Donoghue."

"Is there anybody you do like?"

Charlie Dean, he thought, just Charlie Dean.

"Auld Pat Muldoon's a favourite of yours, isn't he?" she cried. "I hear every time he meets you he wants to kiss you. Or is it kick you?"

He muttered Muldoon was an old bastard.

She laughed. "He's not," she said, "but his grandwean is."

"This is bonny talk," came bitterly from under the blankets. "For God's sake send him to the Co. for his messages."

"Your faither's sensitive," she said, taking her purse and counting the coins in it. "So they're thinking about getting coupled? I wish them no harm, but if he's walking in the steel-work and a lump of iron the size of a hoose falls on him, I don't think I'd grieve very much. I wouldn't want the poor wee man killed clean oot, just paralysed, say from the waist doon." She bellowed with bawdy laughter and stamped across to the bed where with both fists, her purse in one of them, she rolled her husband back and forward. "From the waist doon, Gourlay," she repeated.

Sam grinned; he understood.

His father's head, minus the cap of course, heaved up out of the blankets. The long grey hair straggled over his eyes; the sad lips were pursed for the missing fag.

"When he's at the Co. for the messages, Nelly," he said, "could he not get a packet of Woodbine. I'll pay you back on broo day."

"Away to China," she cried, laughing.

He scratched his head. "China?"

"Aye, where you were for flitting to last night, where they were civilised long before us."

He remembered. "Confucius," he muttered.

"A packet of Woodbine?" she cried. "Would that do instead of the trip to China?"

171

"Nelly, it would do instead of a trip to heaven."

"I think you were for going there too last night. You were far travelled, Gourlay, with the teapot in your hand. Here," she cried to Sam, "go and get twa pound of tatties, a quarter of corn beef, an ingan, a loaf, twa ounces of butter and a quarter of margarine; and ask if they've any old boxes for firewood."

"Is that all?" asked Sam, taking the money and the basket.

"That's all," she said, with a finality that drew from the squatting Bhudda in the bed a groan. He sank down under the blankets again.

"Your faither's away to China," she said, and merrily went to clean out the grate. . . .

That evening Jeanie spent longer than usual in making herself up in front of the mirror. Rouge and lipstick she dabbed on with customary lack of finesse; hair she arranged after the fashion of a film actress famous for her siren parts; legs she covered with artificial-silk stockings that hid the tawdry varicosed skin in a bronze lustre; eyebrows she pencilled in two dark sophisticated curves. When she was finished she looked rather like a cheap and ingenuous whore, an apprentice still finding the trade attractive. But she thought, and knew Donoghue would think, that she looked wonderfully smart and modern for a laundry girl with spectacles and a bad skin.

Her father watched the metamorphosis and philosophised.

"It's a funny thing," he remarked, "that in the human species it's the female that's braw, or to be mair exact that tries to make herself braw. Now in nature it's the precise opposite. There it's always the male that's braw. Consider the peacock; consider the blackbird; consider the lion with its mane."

"When you were young, Gourlay," laughed his wife, glancing up from the newspaper she was reading word by word, "you had no mane; but you had always such a polish on your heid wi brilliantine that I could see to powder my nose in it."

Pleased, and at the same time saddened, he put up his hand to feel his hair, now grey and inglorious.

"You were a masher then, Gourlay," she went on. "Do you mind the scarves you used to wear? Silk they were; you had a green one and a blue one; and you had one that was a kind of pink with wee yellow hearts all over it."

"Was there ever such a scarf?" he asked, in wonder.

"There was. Often I was minded to strangle you with it."

He looked at her across the devastation of the years. "You mind those old days well, Nelly."

"You were a dapper wee chap then, Gourlay. Do you ken this, Jeanie, your faither there that's sitting in ruins was once as smart a dancer as was ever seen in Drumsagart?"

"True," he smiled, nodding. "I liked dancing, though I often wondered if it was against my principles. I was like a feather on my feet, a peacock's feather. They said I had grace, I could waltz." He sighed: there did not seem to be any need for him to describe how beautifully he could waltz then, twenty years ago and more. It was just enough to say he could waltz. Tears came into his eyes. "You're young, Jeanie, you and Donoghue, cherish your youth; don't waste it in stupid misunderstandings."

"As we did, Gourlay?" cried his wife.

He hung his head and looked at the hole in the rug his toe always caught in, especially when he was pouring out tea.

"You were jealous, Nelly," he murmured.

"Jealous!" she roared, and then laughed while her bosom and her belly and her fat neck all wobbled. "Me jealous about you?"

"You were jealous. Why shouldn't you have been? I could waltz. I could dress. I knew the arguments. Once in Drumsagart hall I talked with Keir Hardie." He felt then in his waistcoat pockets for the fag he'd smoked half an hour ago. "I knew poetry," he added.

"I'll grant you that. I was your Helen of Troy."

"You were." He sighed. "I used to sit then with a book in my lap and thoughts in my head, and I would greet."

"You're greeting now," she jeered.

"Will I deny it? There's much need for tears, Nelly, for honest tears."

173

Jeanie was now ready. She stood at the door. The kitchen reeked with the scent she'd dabbed on her brow and behind her ears as finishing touches. She wore her best hat and coat.

"I'll be back about my usual time," she said, "if not earlier." Then she was gone before they could question that bitter addition.

"Do you know what I'm thinking?" asked her mother, with satisfaction. "I'm thinking there's something wrong there, and I'm glad to see it."

He nodded, and then was aware how vast a treachery was that little nod, especially with his eyes still moist.

"If she marries him," said his wife, "one thing's certain, you'll give up smoking."

Fingers in waistcoat pockets he pondered that horrid consequence.

"Meat comes before fags," she said, for all her bloated stupidity representing the keen cruel sword of logic.

"I could waltz," he muttered, and picked up a page of the newspaper. There, smug foot on smug ball, with smirking face above, was pictured a famous footballer, called in the caption 'Scotland's pride.' All his life Mr. Gourlay had been a heretic, expressing contempt of football and its devotees. Several times he had been persecuted. Now for five shocked minutes he stared at the beefy smirker in the wee white trousers. Scotland's pride, he murmured. Every Saturday at the tremendous shrines thousands gathered to worship and bawl their adoration. Here was he now, at this fireside with the feeble fire, a man witty, intelligent, perceptive and knowledgeable, with tears in his eyes for the pathos of human destiny; and there was no one to praise what he was within, and no one to lament what he was without, no one, not one single solitary get.

"I see there's a fellow been saying," remarked his wife, "that all this depression's caused by spots on the sun. What the hell's he raving about?"

At first he was about to shrug off irritably that unpolitical, uneconomic, and unscientific explanation; then he paused; then he muttered, "Maybe he's right," for there was a consolation

174

in believing that the ruin of one's short and only life was caused, not by the greed and incompetence of fellow-men, but by majestic disturbances at the source of all life, the great sun itself. He had read that those eruptions of fire shot up many thousands of miles into space; one lick of those flames and the globe would shrivel up stinking like a wean's balloon blown into the kitchen fire. It was possible to accept, with a bitter dignity, defeat from so cosmic a cause.

"When that fire goes oot," said his wife, jerking her thumb towards the grate, "it stays oot. It's the last the night."

"It's early, Nelly," he protested, with a glance at the clock. "It's just seven. We'll freeze."

"You were never anything else but frozen all your days," she sneered. "Maybe you could waltz, Gourlay, but one faculty you never had."

"Keep to the point, Nelly. I thought you said you were going to send Sam to the bing for a bag of gum."

"As a consequence, Gourlay, it's me that's been allowed to freeze, to freeze and go sour. You were bragging."

Bitterly he laughed and showed her his hands, powerless and fagless. "I could hardly brag, Nelly."

"You were bragging. Freeze? It's been a pitiful flame I've had all my married days to warm myself at. I needed to be kept warm, Gourlay. I always knew that if I was allowed to get cauld I'd get sour."

He thought of the sun-spots, of the thousands of miles of streaming scarlet flames, and tears again came into his eyes.

"You should have married the strong man in a circus," he said, trying to laugh at his joke but weeping instead. "I was a reader. I could have studied philosophy. I never had muscle."

"Don't brag, that's all," she said from behind her newspaper.

"I don't see what's to hinder *you* from going to the bing for a bag of gum," she added, after a minute's silence. "You say I'm hard on the boy. What's your sympathy worth? Jeanie maybe has a right to talk, but you have none, absolutely none." She shouted the last two words, but next moment subsided into

175

a growling behind her newspaper. "Give me peace, for God's sake," she growled.

He knew, though she did not and in her cormorant's obtuseness could not, that this request for peace had been man's prayer since the evolution of the soul. He got up and wearing his cap walked about the little kitchen in quest of peace. It was not in the sink where the tap dripped and could not be stopped dripping; he stood watching it and saw it as a symbol of life, minute by minute, coming from the sky and disappearing down the drain. Nor was peace to be found in the set-in bed behind the curtains; no, no, wherever else, not there. Nor was it under the table, nor in the table drawer; nor did it lurk in the lobby; nor was it hanging to the pulley overhead; nor was it lying in the dust on the mantelpiece, shoved to the back and forgotten like an old fag-nip.

"What's the matter with you?" asked his wife, in annoyance. "What are you looking for?"

"Peace."

"Do you think you're funny?"

He was by this time searching, still without success, in the small mirror by the sink. But if he did not see peace there, neither did he see anything funny.

"No, Nelly," he murmured, "I don't think I'm funny."

Again she relinquished the argument with growls, and went on reading.

He turned and looked at the clock. The thought of the long cold eternity till bedtime distracted him. Little diversions such as putting on his jacket, winding his green muffler closer round his neck, blowing his nose into the sink, investigating in the coal bunker, keeking out of the window at winter, rifting in the middle of the floor, turning up the gas and having to lower it again because of its snakelike hiss and his wife's she-bear's snarl, pokering the last few embers, searching four times through all his pockets: all these passed a terrifyingly short time. When he glanced at the clock again it was just half-past seven. Thirty drips only had fallen from the tap. Likely Nelly had read no more than thirty words.

He sat down by the fire, and himself underwent a slow extinguishing. . . .

Sam too found it a difficult evening to pass. After tea, without waiting to gloat over Jeanie's preparations for doom, he had rushed out and raced all the way to the gardened council houses where Charlie Dean lived, arriving there breathless but happy. Last night Charlie had promised to pay him into the pictures; he had to be under the lamp-post at the corner of the avenue by six o'clock, and wait there; on no account was he to go up to the house and bang the knocker or shout, for Dean's aunt was ill in bed.

It was before six when Gourlay arrived, and for a little while he was glad to wait, resting and recovering his breath; but after a quarter of an hour he began to feel cold, doubtful, and lonely. It was not raining, but black sullen clouds kept crawling across the sky, hiding the stars; and in all the withered gardens a wind sighed chillily.

Loyalty kept Gourlay close to the lamp-post. At first he leant against it, until the ridged iron froze his back through the thin jersey. Then he played at jumping on and off its thick base without using his hands: using his hands was cheating; and two or three times he cheated. Once he pressed his brow against it, shut his eyes, and counted up to a hundred, as if playing at hide-and-seek. At one hundred he looked up eagerly, expecting to see Charlie in his long thick overcoat come strolling along; but there was no Charlie. Another time he had to slink away from the post when a man passing asked him roughly why he was skulking there. Soon, with the man gone, he returned and clasped the post, rubbed his head against it, nudged it with his cheek, and once even licked it, as if showing it affection was like showing affection to Charlie, who was the only person he liked and who would soon come with money enough for them both.

At seven o'clock he had not yet come. Gourlay, with anxious glances back at the lamp-post, crept along the avenue till he stood outside Charlie's house. Two windows were lighted, one upstairs and one down. A bush just inside the gate persisted in

177

looking like a man. Gourlay even sneaked in and boldly touched it to make it become a bush only, full of dark rustling leaves; but as soon as he returned outside the gate, it again talked and nodded and threatened to come running.

By now his teeth chattered from cold; he had to keep rubbing his body for warmth; once or twice in his vexation his rubs became punches. The lamp-post at the corner when he glanced at it every moment seemed very far away, becoming more and more unattainable as if it too was a star amidst the black clouds. Bush and lamp-post and Gourlay himself cold and Charlie not coming were for a long time the only things in the world. Windows up and down the avenue and in other avenues, were lit; roofs showed against the dark sky; buses roared below in the main street; occasionally a man or woman hurried by: but everything, except that bush and lamp-post and Gourlay cold waiting and Charlie never coming, seemed very far-off and illusionary. Even Jeanie and Donoghue quarrelling and breaking apart somewhere in the darkness, seemed trivial to Gourlay forlorn between bush and lamp-post.

About eight o'clock he gave up, and set off into the night, with no destination or purpose, except that, feeling lonely, he might find some boys and play with them.

In a street lower down he found some boys playing at moshie under a lamp-post. They knew him and at once snatching up their marbles fled up closes.

He thought of pursuing them to their very doors: there would be time for one kick at least, one punch in a back. Instead, regretting their flight for he would have liked to play with them, he took out of his pocket his prized glassie, the only one he had, and down on his haunches began to plunk it from one moshie-hole to another.

He was smiling as he plunked, for the lamp-post reminded him again of Charlie, who was a good moshie-player, able to plunk straight and hard. He himself usually plunked crooked; but that night he found that rather than the three shots he often needed to go from one hole to another, he was managing it sometimes in one. The very best players couldn't do it in less.

178

He was concentrating on the plunk, back of his hand on the cold ground, glassie gripped in the right position between thumb and forefinger, when he was startled by a quick padding up to him and the sudden seizure of his head as if it was being taken for a marble. He was not lifted up so much as plunked up to his feet. A man in slippers and shirt sleeves had captured him. He was the father of one of the dispossessed moshie-players, who all crept behind him.

"Listen, you," cried the man, belting Gourlay's ears with one hand while he held him with the other. "If ever you come here again interfering with the weans playing, I'll skite the head off you."

"That's what you're doing," howled Gourlay.

"So it is. Right. So it is. Look, I'm skiting the head off you."

The moshie-players tittered.

"I was just wanting to play with them," cried Gourlay. "They ran away."

The man laughed. "A friendly visit, like?" he asked.

Gourlay tried to nod.

"We ken about you, Gourlay," roared the man, in an access of anger. "You're notorious."

Gourlay did not know what it meant, but he denied it. "No, I'm not," he muttered.

"You're the kind that steals marbles off laddies smaller than yourselves. Let's see what you have in your pockets."

The search did not take long. Gourlay didn't resist, for to struggle to protect nothing seemed to him foolish. Indeed, he co-operated. He held out his hand. "I've only got this glassie," he said.

The man grabbed it. "Who'd you steal this from?"

"It's mine, mister. I never stole it."

"Thief and liar both. Look, Georgie," turning to his son, "is this yours, son?"

Georgie, bold chubby smirker, stepped forward: he was approaching the captured tiger while his comrades still hung back. His two fists were crammed with marbles.

179

"It's mine, daddy," he piped, before he had taken a close look at the glassie. He had to empty one hand into his pocket first. As he held up the glassie to examine it in the lamplight, he giggled with greed and pleasure: it was a beauty, with red, white, and blue curves through it. "It's mine all right, daddy," he said. "I left it lying on the ground."

"He's a liar," shouted Gourlay. He tried to snatch it back, but the man held him.

"Wolf!" he cried, banging Gourlay's head again and kicking him. "Wolf!"

"I'll tell the cops," yelled Gourlay in fury, but he knew what a stupid threat it was.

The man enjoyed it as a great joke. "So you're going to tell the cops?" he cried. "Of course, I should have minded you and them were great friends. Off you go then, and tell them. I'll give you a good start-off." He manhandled Gourlay for about twenty yards along the footpath and then released him with a last enthusiastic kick. "Now be sure and tell your pals the cops."

Gourlay halted a yard or so away, rubbing his kicked buttocks and waggling his jerked neck.

"What are you waiting for?" cried the man. "I thought you were for telling the cops?"

"I want my glassie. It's mine."

"Listen, you. I'm getting cold. I wouldn't be surprised if I caught a cold out of this."

Gourlay interrupted him. "I hope to Christ," he said passionately, "you catch the flu and die." Then he ran away down towards the main street while the man brandished a white-shirted arm and shouted, "In the auld days they'd hae burnt the likes of you as a witch."

Near the main street Gourlay met another group of boys. They were playing 'Run, Sheep, Run,' but he did not ask them for a game. He did not even answer when one of them, in his class at school, cried, "Hello, Sam." Though he still felt lonely he no longer wanted company.

As he crossed the main street he saw a number of boys and

men outside the door of Freddy's chip shop. They congregated there for the smell of the chips and vinegar, and for the heat. He hesitated, swithering whether to go and join them or to continue on his way to one of the little caves or holes dug out of the bing at Gateside and lined with jagged bits of corrugated iron. He could sit there and wait in the dark till it was time to go home and spy on Jeanie and Donoghue stepping out of the bus.

Two policemen came pacing in their dark uniforms and their rubber-soled boots along the pavement towards him. In the darkness they walked in pairs.

He stood his ground. "What's the time?" he asked as they passed.

They suspected he was trying to defy and mock them.

"Time you were in bed," grunted one.

"There's a clock in Freddy's over there," said the other.

They walked on, feeling they had saved their dignity and at the same time snubbed evil. He heard them laughing.

Leaving the brightly lit main street he trotted off into the darkness towards the caves. Sometimes boys lit fires and roasted potatoes. He hoped he would find some there tonight: the fires would be cheerful and the hot potatoes would be good to hold and eat. But when he arrived, stumbling in the dark over heaps of broken sharp-edged bricks, he found the place like a desert, cold, foodless, and full of lonely noises. With difficulty he groped into one of the holes, felt for a stone or can to sit on, and sat down facing the entrance.

For over an hour he remained there, chilled, numbed, listening to the creaks of the corrugated iron and to sighs that after a while he discovered were his own. Continually he dropped asleep. Once when he started into wakefulness he found he had his arms folded in that attitude of classroom submission he hated and feared; and during one of his short sleeps he dreamt that Jeanie and Donoghue that night in the back seat of the cinema were doing the thing Charlie had spoken about, while Charlie, leaning over to watch, spat pellets of caramel papers at them.

When he crawled out of the hole, stiff, cramped, and confused, and emerged into the cold chilly night, he gazed about in alarmed bewilderment. Somehow it seemed late, too late. A star or two glittered in the black sky. The radiance above the houses on the main street showed that the lamps still shone. Buses whizzed along towards the great dark city of Glasgow, or whizzed home from it. A far-off train whistled. Likely outside Freddy's shop boys still smelled the chips. If he hurried home, he would be in time yet to see Jeanie and Donoghue come off the bus. But, despite all these reassurances, he felt there at the mouth of the hole in the bing, something of great importance to him had happened and he had missed it. He could not think what it was. His glassie was gone; but that was not it. Charlie had not turned up at the lamp-post; but that did not seem to be it either. Yawning and grinning, he shook his head hard and tried unsuccessfully to remember.

He raced home and had been standing in the closemouth less than half an hour when a bus halted at the stop beside the church and several people alighted. Jeanie and Donoghue were amongst them; they came walking slowly along towards the close. There was something different about them that night. At first he could not tell what it was. They were almost upon him before he realised it was because they were not walking close together, with Donoghue's arm round her waist, but were walking apart as if they had been married long ago.

As in silence they arrived at the closemouth he slunk down towards the lavatory. The door was open, fixed with a piece of string as the lock was broken. He slipped inside, but kept standing with his ear to the door. Unfortunately the cistern above kept up a gurgling song, and if the two at the closemouth had talked in low voices he wouldn't have been able to make out what they said. They did not talk at all, however, and he would have thought they had gone if Donoghue hadn't coughed once and Jeanie sighed.

For over five minutes that cough and sigh were all he heard, except of course for the cistern's song, which was almost hypnotising him to sleep. Then he heard Jeanie in a low clear

182

despairing voice cry out, "What difference does it make?" He did not catch Donoghue's answer, which was muttered; but he did catch, as sensitively as a seismograph, Jeanie's weeping that followed.

In a minute she had come rushing down the close, fumbled in the lock with her key, and went into the house.

Donoghue, after a pause during which Gourlay in the lavatory rubbed his hands and sang the cistern's song, walked down the close and stood in front of the house door. "Jeanie," he kept moaning, "Jeanie," and he too seemed to be weeping.

Somebody, old Mr. Timpson it was, came out with a candle in his hand. His braces trailed behind him on the stone floor; he was shuffling towards the lavatory.

"God Almighty," he squeaked when he caught sight of Donoghue suddenly run up the close. "Murderers."

Sam quickly slipped out, blinking in the candle-light.

"Is that you, Mr. Timpson?" he whispered.

The old man, who was nearly eighty and no friend, peered at him.

"Did you see that fellow sprint alang the close?" he asked.

"No."

"Aye, as I came forrit he bolted. He had a knife in his fist, I'm sure. Hae you made a mess in there? I never heard you pull the plug. Seventy-nine, and nae rest yet." He went in, still grumbling in his thin squeaky voice. "Make you take syrup of figs and then scarce the life oot of you." A draught blew out his candle, and he had to strike a match to relight it.

Sam knocked at his own door. His father opened it.

"So you've found your way hame at last?" he grumbled. "What pleasure do you get stravaiging the dark streets? Do you want pleurisy for the pity of it?" He made to push past Sam, heading out into the close.

"Auld Timpson's in there," advised Sam.

"Is that so?" Mr. Gourlay was bitter. He stepped out, rapped sharply on the door, and stepped in again. "Otherwise he'd sit there till midnight. They say the aulder you get the wiser and the mair tolerant. I've never found that to be the case." As they went down the lobby towards the kitchen he gripped his son's shoulder. "Jeanie's just in," he muttered. "She rushed straight into the room. Did you see her at the closemouth? Was Donoghue with her?"

"I don't know."

They went into the kitchen. Mrs. Gourlay sat reading by the fire. She seemed, to Sam's amazement and relief, in an indulgent mood.

"You're late," she observed. "Supper's past."

"I ken. Can I get a piece?"

"Take one."

He went to the bread-bin and was taking out the loaf when his father objected.

"Are you not going to wash your hands?"

Mrs. Gourlay laughed. "Your faither's frightened you've brought in some germs to murder him."

Mr. Gourlay seized his son's hands and looked at them.

"Filthy," he muttered. "Germs? Millions of them. Wash your hands."

Lounging by the sink, with many impatient glances towards the door, he watched the ablutions.

"I thought you were for out-bye," said his wife.

"Auld Timpson's in."

"With his candle?"

"I think so."

"He's got his candle," said Sam.

"He falls asleep in there," remarked Mrs. Gourlay. "One of these nights he'll be cremating himself alive."

"Will that do?" asked Sam, holding out his hands.

His father, as if disgusted with the smallness of that cleansing in so putrescent a world, surlily nodded.

"You said you never saw Jeanie in the close?" he muttered.

Sam was cutting himself a thick slice; he knew his father wouldn't find fault with that.

"I never saw her," he said, laughing because in a way it wasn't a lie.

"There's nothing to laugh about," snapped his father. "She came in greeting."

184

"Music it was," said his wife, "music in my ears."

Sam thought of the gurgling cistern. He spread the piece with margarine. "Can I get some sugar on it?" he asked.

"There's a fresh pot of jam, if you'd look," said his mother.

"Can I get some?"

"That's what it's for," she said, quite coolly, as if she never at the same request threatened to break the pot over his head.

Astonished but alert, he spread the jam on with daring thickness.

"The ancient Romans," said Mr. Gourlay bitterly, "were famous for their sanitation."

"Auld Timpson's an ancient Roman, and no mistake," remarked his wife.

"He said they'd given him syrup of figs," put in Sam.

"Are we human beings, or are we beasts?" cried his father.

"What's the difference?" asked Mrs. Gourlay.

"You think you're being sarcastic, Nelly? Maybe you're not; maybe you're telling the naked truth."

"There's a wean present," warned his wife, grinning.

"What is it puts us above the beasts? Is it dignity? Hardly that, for I noticed yonder in Edinburgh that the lions in their cages were a damned sight more dignified than the idiots grinning in at them. Is it intelligence then that gies us our superiority? Do beasts slaughter their ain kind in millions, and then blame it on spots on the sun? It must be beauty then."

"Beauty!" she repeated, laughing heartily.

"Weel may you laugh, Nelly. Is the hairy gamekeeper brawer than the deer he shoots?"

"You'd better gie the door another bang," she advised, "if you're that impatient."

"It must be kindness then," he muttered, as he went out.

"Kindness?" she repeated, puzzled. "What the hell's he talking about?"

Sam sat by the sink on a low stool munching the sweet bread happily.

"I don't know," he said.

"Nobody was talking to you. Did you see Jeanie come in?"

185

"No."

"I think it's finished between her and Donoghue. Judging by the way she came in, I should say it's finished. And thank God."

The jam tasted sweeter. He nodded.

"You'll be pleased?"

He nodded again.

"It's the best thing that could hae happened. She's no beauty, nothing like what I was at her age, but if she waits surely she can get better than Donoghue."

The door opened and Mr. Gourlay came slowly in.

"No luck?" asked his wife.

He shook his head. Suddenly he laughed. "Kindness." He sat down on the edge of a chair and tapped on the table with his fingers.

"I wonder what caused it," said his wife.

"Caused what?"

"The cast-oot."

He laughed. "Something trivial of course. We break our hearts over trifles. We look for perfection in them we love." He glanced up at his wife, saw her there, dour and massive, as smelly, hefty, and dangerous as a she-bear. "I used to be irritated out of all proportion by a habit you had, Nelly."

"And what was that?"

"You snored."

"I still snore."

"That's true." But now it was in keeping with her other she-bear qualities. Then, when she had been young and lovable, it had been an apocalyptic bitterness to lie in the dark listening to the honks and the gurrs and the hocks, and sometimes in desperation to sit up and see in the flickers of the fire flames her young red kissable mouth ganting.

"You're used to it now, Gourlay?" she asked, grinning.

"That's right, Nelly."

"I used to be disgusted by your conceit," she remarked.

"My conceit?" He was genuinely shocked.

"Now I can laugh at it. You were always such a speug of a man, Gourlay, even when you were on your tip-toes."

"When did you ever see a speug on its tip-toes?" he asked, contemptuous of her ornithological knowledge.

"Every time I saw you, Gourlay, I saw it; and your wee wings were always in a flutter."

"I could have flown high," he muttered.

"God, when I think of the guid walks you spoiled with your twitters. The whole world was wrang in those days, Gourlay."

"It still is."

"And nobody but you had the solution."

He shook his head. "I've lost it," he muttered. "I had it then."

"That's him oot now," she remarked.

Sighing he got up and went out.

"You get to bed," said Mrs. Gourlay to Sam.

Sam, the piece finished, jumped up immediately. "All right."

As he went into the lobby leaving the kitchen door a little ajar to give him light, Jeanie came out of the room. He was startled for she still had on her hat and coat.

She clutched him. "You'll be pleased," she whispered, in a voice he didn't recognise: hate made it strange. "I told him. You know what I told him."

He nodded, and next moment she struck him on his upturned unsuspecting face. It was a fierce blow, and her hand was large and hard. Blood streamed down from his nose. As he dabbed at it with his sleeve, she struck him again, and then rushed back into the room.

He stood in the lobby holding his head back to keep the blood from running into his mouth. From the kitchen he heard his mother's hearty reassured laughter; she had jaloused what had happened.

It was the first time Jeanie had ever struck him, but as he felt his way into his box of a bedroom, his head still tilted back, he vowed she would pay for it. Even if he had to wait for weeks again for another chance, he would take his revenge.

He did not have to wait so long this time. On Saturday as he was standing outside his close wee red-haired Creepie Overtown the postman came along at his customary grudging pace.

"Ony letters for Gourlay?" asked Sam with a grin. It was the usual teasing query boys put to Creepie, and the usual answer was a snarled asthmatic 'Beh!' like a goat's. Creepie never got tips at Christmas.

Creepie stopped and chose a letter from the bundle he held in his hand.

"One for your sister," he snapped, and held it out.

Perhaps Sam grabbed at it too eagerly, perhaps Creepie's anæmic trust expired; at any rate he snatched the letter back.

"I was forgetting," he said. "There are folk wha wouldn't trust you to feed tattie-peelings to pigs. Do you ken why?" He thrust his little face forward, wrinkled with malevolence. "Because you'd eat them yourself."

Sam was mystified by this rubbish, but he followed the postman into the close and watched the letter being pushed through the letter-box.

"Even if you were to eat it now, or burn it," said Creepie, as he went out of the close again, "it's nane of my business."

Sam was immediately aflame with that desire: to get to the letter, and burn it. That would be his revenge for the two blows. The letter was certain to be from Donoghue. Yesterday morning Jeanie had purposely made herself late for work waiting for the postman; and when she had come home in the evening she had asked in a trembling voice if there was a letter for her. When her father had said no sadly, she had smiled, shrugged her shoulders and even hummed a bit of a song; but afterwards she had gone through to the room to weep. Her mother had shouted in a warning that weeping wouldn't improve her appearance any.

Now the letter had come, was lying in the lobby, and could be easily burned by Sam if only he could get to it. Unfortunately no one was in and he had no key. His father this dry winter morning was off on one of his unaccountable solitary strolls round Drumsagart hill, 'soul-savers' he called them. His mother was along in the Co. If he went there to ask her for the key, she would be suspicious; perhaps she might make him stand in her place waiting to be served.

He peeped through the letter-box, but could not see the letter. He tried to thrust in his hand, although he knew how impossible it would be to stretch down to the floor and pick up the letter; even if he had an arm as long, hairy, and clever as a monkey's he could not do that.

It did not occur to him to wonder what Donoghue had written in the letter. If he had wondered, he could have offered no conjecture. For him the romance was ended. Jeanie had told Donoghue about her and Geordie Lucas, and Donoghue as everybody had foretold had decided he couldn't marry her now, seeing he wouldn't be the first. The situation was simple and complete. What Sam wanted, and wanted more excitedly with every minute that passed, was just to reach the letter, hold it in his hand, and then throw it into the fire. He did not think of reading it.

He hurried along to the Co. His mother luckily was talking to a group of women. It wasn't likely she would tell him he couldn't have the key in front of them. Everybody knew she treated him harshly, but sometimes in public, as if to disappoint them all, she would laugh at him and shake her huge head maternally, indicating that his rascality was boyish and in any case would bring retribution on his own young head and on nobody else's.

She gave him the key without question, waving away his lie about wanting his comic to exchange it for another.

"See there's a guid fire on," was all she said.

As he hurried away with the key he overheard a whisper of their resumed conversation. It was about Mrs. Slaven a little pink-faced woman who lived in his tenement. In some way her husband, a big fat man with tight trousers, treated her badly. If he had got drunk and punched her, marking her face, or kicked her, marking her body, the women could have spoken openly about it; shrilly and publicly they would have condemned him; but his cruelty was of a different kind, and had to be whispered about.

At the door Sam met Stirling coming in. He carried a basket and wore an ordinary jersey and patched shorts.

Sam went back into the shop with him. He held up the key
of the house and remembered like a pain the letter waiting to
be picked up and burned. Yet Stirling fascinated him and
somehow he wished to talk to him.

"Hello, Stirling," he said, grinning.

"Hello." Stirling walked over and put his book in the box
on the counter.

Gourlay watching the book disappear into the slot remembered the letter disappearing into the letter-box. His impatience
grew more painful; yet he could not go till he had spoken to
Stirling, and he still did not know what to say to him.

He had to go up to Stirling, who had not returned to him by
the door but had taken up his stand by the biscuit display
cabinet.

"How are you getting on, Stirling?" he asked.

"All right."

"I mean, at your new school? At the Academy?"

"All right."

"Do the toffs laugh at you?"

Stirling did not answer.

"I've never been to the gate yet," laughed Gourlay.

"No."

Gourlay decided not to tell about the unsuccessful attempt.

"Are you first there as well?" he sneered. "In the examinations, I mean."

"They start on Monday."

"What is it you get? Sums?"

"French. Latin. Science." Stirling spoke each wonderful word
slowly, and feasted on the ignorance on Gourlay's face.

"French?" grinned Gourlay, who had been admiring the
cream and chocolate biscuits in the glass cabinet. "Can you talk
French? Say 'I like biscuits' in French."

Stirling shook his head. He would not confess it, but he did
not know the French word for biscuits.

Gourlay noticed the key in his own hand and remembered
the letter.

"You can keep your French," he whispered, with his mouth

190

close to Stirling's face. "Do you know what I would like? I would like if this was the key of the Co. I'd come back here when it was dark and I would sit on the counter and eat butter and biscuits and sweeties and raw ham." He stared all round as he named these delicacies. "You can keep your French. But I'll need to go, Stirling. I've got something to do quick, something mair important than French. Cheerio, Stirling."

He ran laughing out of the shop. Reaching the house door, he could hardly put the key in the lock for eagerness. As he rushed in he stepped on the letter, and had to clean it against his jersey. Somehow to throw it dirtied into the fire would detract from his joy as he watched it burn.

Certainly it was from Donoghue. The little labourer was no better at writing than Sam himself. As he gazed at the big shaky painstaking characters, Gourlay could not help feeling a pang of sympathy: how easy it was for him to imagine Donoghue gripping the pen tightly, putting out his tongue, crossing his legs under the table, and wondering in agony how the next word should be spelled. Indeed, it was this sympathy which first caused him to be curious as to what was written inside. As soon as the desire struck him, he began to laugh and feel even more sympathetic towards the writer; he felt almost friendly towards Donoghue who was like himself such a poor scholar and who, besides, was helping him to get his revenge on Jeanie.

The three sheets of the letter had more blots than the envelope, and the writing being longer was much harder to make out, especially at the end where it was a scribble. Sam had to sit down on a chair and study it with a scowl as he had to study a sentence he'd to analyse and divide into clauses. During the first reading he was so engrossed in making out the individual words that the general sense escaped him. Even the second and third readings left him only vaguely aware that he had been betrayed. In the middle of the fourth attempt the revelation burst on him brighter and more searing than any actual flames the letter in burning would have made.

The letter said: Jeanie my Darling, I new all the time you should never have toled me. I new all the time but do you not

191

see you should never have toled me. I didnt like Jeanie to hear
you talk about it that was why I said we would better be finished
But surely you new I never meant that, I think maybe I said
things to you you'll not forget Jeanie that I never meant them
Do you no I stood outside your door crying? Maybe I would
have chapped on it if an old man with a candle hadnt come out
I walked home Jeanie and I struck my fist against nearly every
lamp-post my knuckles are all skint. I didnt hit the lamp-posts
because I thought they were him you no who but it was because
I had said we were finished and I called you you no what. If
you are finished with me Jeanie I cant blame you but o Jeanie
it would be a terrible pity. I cant say here what I want to say
I'm not good at writing but if I can see you again maybe I'll
not be able to say it either for I'm not good at talking either
Jeanie as you well no. You said before it happened we should
go to the pictures on Tuesday night to see that picture you
wanted to see. At half past seven outside the Regal. I'll be
there Jeanie wet or dry rain or shine. If you come we'll say
nothing about it or anything else, we'll just go into the pictures
together together for always Jeanie other folk get married on
£2 13s. 4½d. and so could we.

Till Tuesday night
Your Loving Sweetheart,
Tom Donoghue.

As Gourlay, trapped, glanced quickly from one sheet to
another, he knew there must be many mistakes in spelling and
punctuation. Chapped was wrong for instance, it should have
only one p, and anyway it wasn't the kind of word to use in a
letter. Sam himself had been given a row for writing 'ben the
room'. Mr. Martin had said it was Scots and should never be
used in ink writing. Oh yes, on these three sheets there were
bound to be dozens of such mistakes, for Donoghue was only a
labourer and must have been a dunce at school; but Sam, not
able to tell for certain what those mistakes were, could not
therefore by an accumulation of separate little triumphs over
come the defeat that the whole letter represented. He felt

tempted to rush back to the Co. and get Stirling to ring with a pencil all the places wrong, but of course his mother was still there and she would see.

He had already capitulated, and was about as a mere condition of surrender to throw the letter into the fire when suddenly, in a blaze, he realised that Jeanie had not yet read the letter and therefore did not know Donoghue wanted to meet her outside the Regal on Tuesday night. If Sam burnt the letter, or kept it alive in his pocket, she would never know and on Tuesday night she would be weeping on her bed in the room, while Donoghue would be waiting uselessly outside the Regal.

So elated was he by this unexpected reversal that he kissed the letter and pressed it against his heart, just as Jeanie herself would have done. On Tuesday he would not know what to do: whether to stay in and, with his hand on the letter in his pocket, listen to Jeanie's weeping; or walk the mile and a half to the Regal and from a close opposite gloat over Donoghue at his long stupid useless waiting.

But on Tuesday night it turned out he didn't have a choice after all. Jeanie came home from work, not cheerful right enough, but also not as mournful as she had been all week-end. She asked if a letter had come from her, and Sam, slipping his hand into his pocket, answered no, so quickly that he forestalled his mother who had had the sweet negative melting in her mouth all day.

"You speak when you're spoken to," snarled his mother then, making as if to clout him. "There might have been a letter for all you kent. There might be one lying in the drawer there this very minute."

Sam in alarm, Jeanie in tortured wonder, glanced towards the drawer.

"There's nane," cried Mr. Gourlay. "That's cruel, Nelly."

Jeanie rushed out of the kitchen, as if going to weep after all. Sam watched her in relief, stroking the letter in his pocket. All that day it had rained, and it was still pouring. To the Regal, where Donoghue was to wait, it was over a mile.

"Cruel?" Mrs. Gourlay was shouting to her husband. "Did I say there was a letter?"

"You hinted at it."

"Shut your trap." She banged the table with her fist, making the delf dance. "I tell you, Gourlay, she's got to be scunnered oot of the very thought of love."

"This is the place then," he muttered, recklessly. "This is the place."

"See, I'll rub her face in it as I would a kitten in its ain mess to cure it. I'll make her grue at the very whisper of the word."

"Love, you mean?"

"Love, I mean, Gourlay."

He nodded. "I thought so." He felt through his pockets, found a nip, couldn't believe it was real, stared and sniffed at it, and then panting with belief like a fervent convert put it tenderly between his lips. He did not immediately light it, for, transitory as love or smoke, it would not last long lighted.

His wife stood scowling down at him, grudging him his oasis. "Did you pick that one oot of the sheuch?"

He took it from his lips to squint at it again, most fondly.

"Somebody with scabs on his lips tossed it away," she jeered.

He returned it to his lips which called for it with little impatient smacks.

"He had cancer of the tongue likely."

Deliberately he tore a strip from a newspaper, folded it neatly, poked the end between the ribs of the grate, and withdrew it lighted. He put it to his fag-end as delicately as a princess come of age might have put taper to the first of her eighteen candles.

"Did you wipe the snotters off it?" persisted his wife.

Up through the first blue fragrance of smoke he smiled at her, and shook his head.

"Nelly," he murmured, "you can't scunner love."

She burst out laughing. "What keeps me from strangling you?" she asked.

"Love," he murmured, with a wink. "It's imperishable."

194

She pointed from her great bosom to his well-snubbed nose. "You mean," she cried, "you and me, still?"

"Imperishable, Nelly. Why is it when a man's in the dock for half-murdering his wife, she's in the witness box shedding tears on his behalf?"

"Because she's daft."

"Daft, if you like, Nelly. But love is imperishable. Beyond the grave even, on the hard benches up bye. Abuse it as we may, we can't destroy it."

"We abuse it all right," she muttered.

"Mony a tear spilled at a graveside, Nelly, is caused through regret, not just for a man or woman deid, but for injuries done to love. We hae one another such a short time, why waste it in spites and angers?"

"It's weel seen you've a fag between your lips," she said. "When it's done, we'll hear a different tune."

Before he could deny that cynicism, Jeanie came back in. She was not weeping, nor were there marks of tears on her face.

"I'm going out," she said, as she sat down at table, "after tea."

"Are you for running after him then?" sneered her mother. "Hae you nae pride? He's the one that should be running after you."

"What are you talking about? Maggie Anstruthers asked me to come down and visit her. Don't worry. I have as much pride as you, mither; maybe more."

"Nane of your impertinence," snapped her mother.

"Pride's dangerous," said Mr. Gourlay, also sitting at table. He had nipped the nip and replaced it in his pocket; its presence there gave him courage for philosophy. "I often wonder why folk make such a song aboot their pride. Countries go to war for national pride: men hae their guts winkled oot of them by bayonets, just because of a kind of pride. It's one of the seven deidly sins, or it should be. Am I supposed to eat this banana, Nelly?"

"It's for your tea. Whether you eat it or not, is your business."

195

He held it like a yellow pistol. "You ken bananas make me costive."

"With auld Timpson getting syrup of figs that's a guid thing to be these days."

He shot her through the heart.

She laughed. "What are you sniggering at?"

At your corpse, he almost said; but it was a corpse making free with the butter dish.

"Pass the butter, Nelly," he said urgently.

"There's a dish beside you."

He picked it up and sniffed at it. "Butter? Which dish is he to use?" indicating their son.

"That one."

"This one?" jabbing at it with sceptical nose.

She nodded.

He banged it down with decision and disdain: it was not butter.

"Pass it, faither," asked Sam, humbly; he had been waiting with knife poised.

Instead of skiting it along the table his father, wearing his bonnet, walked the step or two with the dish in his hand, and presented it with a salaam.

Sam took it earnestly and began to spread his piece. He kept glancing from clock on mantelpiece to rain on window.

His father returned to his chair.

"Can I get my faither's banana," asked Sam, "if he doesn't want it?"

"Why ask her?" cried his father. "I'm the one you should ask."

"Can I get it then?"

His father however with grandee's scorn began to peel the banana. "Food for the monkeys," he muttered.

"Well," chuckled his wife, "you've often said we're all descended from them."

He nodded with sinister cunning. "Maybe I was wrong. Maybe Darwin was wrong. Maybe it was the other way round. Maybe the monkeys hae descended from us. Who's to be judge? Are we at the top of creation? We say we are, but maybe we're a bit prejudiced." He noticed his son, his own descendant, gobbling down his food. "You," he cried angrily, "for God's sake eat like a human being. Keep up the pretence."

"He's a pig," said Jeanie, pronouncing the word with no affection in it to soften it.

Sam just grinned, and wriggling on his seat made the letter crackle.

"We're coming on," remarked his mother. "First monkeys and now pigs. What next?"

She-bears, thought her husband, but he did not say it aloud. He kept watching his son. Christ himself was once a boy, he remembered, and gobbled his food.

"I'm in a hurry," said Sam. "I'm going oot."

"Oot? On a night like this? It's lashing, you damned fool, you scunnersome glutton; just listen to it."

Sam listened, with a frown. The rain hissed against the window so coldly that for a moment of bareness, of shivering dereliction, he thought maybe he wouldn't go at all; but only for a moment. He had to go.

"Is it this Dean fellow you're going to meet?" asked his mother.

He nodded.

"I was hearing his auntie's gey bad. She's not expected to see the year oot."

Mr. Gourlay gazed at mortality in the margarine dish; he shook his head. "I wonder," he muttered.

"What d'you wonder?" asked his wife.

"I don't know," he said, and he didn't know. He just wondered.

"The whole family's rotten with it," said his wife. "His mither died with it. He's full of it himself. He'll never scart a grey heid."

Still wondering, Mr. Gourlay put up his shy hand and scratched.

Sam jumped to his feet; he had a lump of bread in his hand.

"Can I go?" he asked. "I'm in a hurry." Suddenly he was

197

afraid that Donoghue had already arrived outside the Regal; maybe he was there now, with nobody to watch.

"Sit down," said his father sternly. "This is no night to be running out into."

"Let him go," growled Mrs. Gourlay.

"It's pouring," said Jeanie, but she turned her head away as she spoke, as if it had been merely an observation on the weather and not an involuntary concern for him. She knew he had no raincoat or cap even, and still, in December, wore canvas sandshoes.

"Get," said his mother. "You're safe from pneumonia. It's the guid, they say, that die young."

He ran out then and they detected his excitement in the slamming of the door.

"The guid die young," repeated Mr. Gourlay, almost in tears, with the margarined bread insipid as living in his mouth. "It's true."

"What about auld Timpson?" grinned his wife. "He must have been a rascal in his day. He's over eighty."

"He's deid. You're deid. Jeanie's deid. I'm deid myself."

"I'll not deny that last one," she said, glowering at him over a cookie thick with butter.

"The guid that was in us all at the beginning is deid," he explained. "When we were young we were guid."

"I'm glad you think so," said Jeanie, rising up with a glance at the clock. "He that's just gone oot is young enough."

"No, no, no," he cried. "Hae you ever watched the wee toddlers?" His joy was sudden and spontaneous. He put out his hand to point to innocent and delightful infancy. He could hardly speak for joyful laughter. "They're pure, God kens. It's like watching green leaves growing in the depths of winter. It's a miracle. It's the springtime of the human soul. Everything's sweet and pure."

"Pure?" snorted his wife. "Pure tigers, some of them."

Jeanie went out laughing.

"I'm referring to the very young," he said, and lowered his hand a little till it was the height of undeniable purity, two feet high.

198

"How young is wee Mysie Scoullar?"

"How should I ken that? Am I auld Moore? Do I ken the ages of all the neighbours' weans?"

"She's three. Is that young enough?"

He nodded uneasily. His hand dropped down another half inch.

"Well, do you ken what she did yesterday? She lifted a stick and took a scud at Mrs. Dunsmore's wean sleeping in its pram."

"She missed."

"Damn the miss. She hit him on the brow. There's a lump the size of an egg. Them that saw it happen said it was as deliberate as murder. She's a bad wee bitch, yon one."

"Three, did you say?"

"That's all she is."

"Evidently then," he admitted, with consummate bitterness, "three's too auld for purity."

"It is," she agreed.

Though Sam had slammed the door eagerly he had nevertheless hesitated at the closemouth. Wetness, and cold, and dark, besieged him there like cruel but humorous enemies. When he thrust out his hand, instantly it was soaked and chilled as with a kind of blood. Thousands of huge round drops stotted in a jolly way on the lamplit pavement, each one seeming to want to jump higher than all the rest. He felt it was going to be easy and a good joke, for the night to keep on soaking and chilling him with that kind of blood. Not only his hands, but his hair, his body, his thighs, his feet, would all be soaked; in his belly-button and in his ears would lie pools of it.

For nearly five minutes he shivered there at the closemouth, shrinking back, pummelling himself already for warmth, and sneezing.

A bus whishing past, with folk dry and cosy inside and cold spray flying from its wheels, reminded him of his tryst at the Regal. On so wet a night Donoghue wouldn't wait long, and might be gone by the time Sam arrived. Surely too the wetter the night, the stupider the disappointment. If it had been a fine dry night with stars shining Donoghue might not mind his useless walk to the Regal nor his useless wait outside.

As Sam left the closemouth he was trying to laugh with the night in its wet gusty jokings, and to pretend that the rain and the cold and the wind were his friends and allies, rather than his tormentors.

That pretence could not last long. Quickly icy trickles zig-zagged down his back and down his warmer belly; but even while he gasped and rubbed, his whole jersey and shirt under his hand became soaked and clung to him like a cold poultice. From his saturated hair a second rain kept dripping into his eyes, along his nose, on to his lips, and down his chin; he kept trying in anger to puff it off his nose. More frequently now he sneezed, which exasperated him, for surely everything was wet enough already. Under him unseen his feet slapped against the pavement; even between his toes the rain seemed to be flowing.

When he reached Freddy's chip shop he found it lit but deserted. The night was so wild people wouldn't leave their firesides even for hot chips. He stood in the doorway and tried like a dog to shake some of the wetness off him. This involuntary attempt annoyed him, not just because of its futility, but also because it didn't take into consideration the pouring mile he had still to walk.

As he rested there, shivering and sneezing, a boy he knew came running to the shop under a man's raincoat which he held up over him like a tent. He peeped out at Gourlay.

"It's an awful night, Sam," he said, laughing as if he didn't really think it was awful, and of course he shouldn't have, for he had a raincoat to shelter him, his boots were thick and water-tight, and he was there to buy chips.

"There's nothing wrong with the night," muttered Gourlay, putting his hands into his pockets and leaning back as if he was quite dry and comfortable, and was just passing the time there until he could be bothered going in to the shop to buy a two-penny pokeful.

"It's pelting," laughed the boy, whose name was McIntosh, and he went into the shop.

Through the glass in the door Gourlay watched the transaction. He saw the penny planked down on the counter, and sneered because it was only a penny, whereas in his dream he had had twopence. He saw McIntosh, who still had his raincoat over him, collect the vinegar bottle and salt cellar in readiness. Freddy, fat and grumpy, took a poke and poured some chips into it. Steam rose up out of the shining fryer, but especially out of that little poke. He added two or three chips, not because he was generous, for he wasn't, but maybe because it was such a filthy night and he was pleased to have a customer even if one buying only a penny poke. McIntosh, with glee in his fingers, shook vinegar and salt into his poke. Freddy stared at him but didn't that night object; usually he wouldn't allow penny-pokers to help themselves.

Then McIntosh, already eating a chip, crossed the sawdust and came out. Gourlay pretended to have been looking, not into the shop, but out at the interesting rain.

"Would you like a chip?" asked McIntosh.

Gourlay turned at bay, provoked by the kindness. McIntosh though seemed in earnest; he was grinning under his coat and was holding out the poke.

"Just one," he warned. "You can make it a big one."

With his mouth filled with saliva, Gourlay chose a long succulent golden chip. It was so hot he had to shift it from one hand to the other, chuckling and even hinneying a little hysterically in his amazement and impromptu gratitude.

"Och, you can take another," said McIntosh, and bravely held out the poke again.

Gourlay took another.

"That's a big one," said McIntosh, needing all his bravery to laugh.

"Thanks," gasped Gourlay, who was wishing he could transmit this wonderful heat from his hands through his whole body.

"My mither gave me the penny," said McIntosh. "She's making tablet."

201

"Tablet?"

"Sure." He nodded under the coat. "She makes it great, better than the shops, sweeter. It's a knack."

"Do you take it hot?"

"Hot?" McIntosh laughed. "You've to wait till it's cold and then you cut it into squares. You would need to take it with a spoon if you took it hot."

"I would take it hot," gasped Gourlay.

McIntosh went away laughing. "You'd just waste it that way," he said.

Gourlay gazed after him and nibbled at the chips. He could not understand why McIntosh had given them to him. At school they never played together; in fact he had always thought McIntosh one of the cissies, like Stirling. Now he envied him, not just because he was going home with chips to watch his mother make tablet in the warm kitchen, but also because of some other luckiness he had, which was far more difficult to name.

The very scent of the chips was washed out of him by the time he turned the corner at Dechmont and saw in the first glance a Glasgow tramcar bright and desolate at the terminus, and the crimson neon lights of the Regal which turned all the rain there, stotting on the pavement, gurgling down the gutters, streaming down the tramlines, into blood.

People hurrying up the cinema steps were steeped in that blood, not only their faces and their hands ready with the ticket money, but their very clothes. Donoghue wasn't among them; nor was he to be seen at all there, neither waiting on the steps, nor in the doorway of the sweet-shop nearby.

Slinking past the tramcar, Gourlay saw the driver and conductor seated inside, leisurely smoking, their peaked caps pushed back from their dry brows. Immediately he became freshly aware of his own sodden miserable coldness. Every lighted window shone like an oasis of dryness and warmth. The rain, with its various voices now familiar, hissed and spat and slobbered at him unrelentingly: Donoghue wouldn't come, this long wet walk would be for nothing but sneezes, even to stay in and look at a comic on the stool by the dripping sink would have been better than this.

He stood for a few minutes in a tiled close opposite the picture house. A cold draught blew through all the time, and he kept telling himself, in a queer drowsy angry indecision, that he ought to find a warmer place to wait in. When he did move however, it was because he was ordered to go by a big woman in a red oilskin who came down the stairs and surprised him. As she was putting up her umbrella she noticed him, and at once began to poke him with it as if he was a bit of dirt stuck on her close, crying in a harelipped snuffly voice that he didn't understand. But he understood the poking and had to rouse himself and leave the close, though he now shrank from the rain which, relentless as ever, was as painful as fire in spite of its chilliness.

He found another close, this time not tiled: it had the same sour dank plastery smell as his own, and he thought the people who lived in it would be too poor to chase him. But it wasn't as good a vantage-point, and this worried him, but vaguely; indeed, his anticipation of Donoghue's arrival and waiting was itself vague now. He kept shivering so violently that when a tramcar thundered past, swaying and striking out sparks, he felt for a silly moment he was it. As he tried to understand and stop that foolishness, he began involuntarily to remember warm days in the summer, fishing for minnows in the pond behind Drumsagart hill, walking along the cool sunny top of a bing, hiding amidst the rhododendrons in the park with the leaves cool and the scarlet flowers blazing.

Often he found his eyes closed, and once, when he opened them with an angry shake of his head, he saw coming along the street, not Donoghue, but Stirling and his mother hurrying along from the bus-stop. They seemed bound for the pictures. At the sweet-shop they halted, gazed at the window, and then Mrs. Stirling went in.

Gourlay hurried across the street.

Stirling, dressed snugly in dark-blue raincoat and cap, gazed at the bedraggled sniffing figure.

203

"Are you going to the pictures, Stirling?" asked Gourlay hoarsely.

Stirling nodded: still he gazed without pity, even without interest.

"Is your mither in to buy sweeties?"

Again Stirling nodded, and suddenly he found sweeter than any caramel or jujube every detail of wet misfortune about Gourlay: the green jersey black, the hair in long streaks, the squelchy feet, the soaked blackened sleeve across the raw sniffing nose.

"I thought you didn't go to the pictures," said Gourlay. "I thought you were too poor. I thought you had to stay in every night to study. You never came oot on Hallowe'en even."

"I've just finished my examinations," murmured Stirling.

Gourlay grinned as he remembered the fun on Hallowe'en: it it had been dry too that night. "I was dressed up as an auld woman," he said. Jeanie had lent him some old clothes. "I got lots of apples and nuts. It must hae been a guid disguise, eh, Stirling? If they'd kent it was me they'd hae gi'en me nothing. Did you do your examinations weel?"

Stirling nodded.

Before Gourlay could say anything further, if indeed he had been going to speak again, for he seemed as he gaped along the gleaming street to slip into a shuddering dwam, Mrs. Stirling came out of the shop. She had a bag of sweets in her hand, but her face turned sour and angry when she saw who was talking to her son.

"Come on, John," she said sharply, and as they went up the cinema steps in the crimson light she went on, loudly enough for Gourlay to hear, "Hae I not warned you never to hae anything to do with him and his likes? You're far above such rubbish now, remember that."

Without rancour, with only a yearning human envy, Gourlay watched them as they got their tickets and disappeared through the door that the usher in the green uniform held open for them. In imagination he followed into the warm cosy dry scented darkness, down the carpeted aisle with a girl in a green uniform

204

lighting the way to his plush seat. Then he sat down, put a caramel in his mouth, and looked at the screen where cowboys chased one another on swift horses across wide sunny prairies.

As he reluctantly awoke from those prairies so rainless that the dust rose up from them and hid the flying horses, he saw hurrying towards the picture-house the small raincoated figure of Donoghue. Stupidly in his fading dream, he wondered why Donoghue didn't come on a horse and why no dust rose up; then, awake on the streaming red street, he realised that if he didn't flee he would be discovered by Donoghue and perhaps spoken to by him. Donoghue might even ask him about Jeanie and the letter.

He ran across the street back to the close, but there was a couple in it kissing. He had to run along to the tiled forbidden one. He was in a panic lest while he was running Donoghue might—he didn't know what Donoghue might do—but it could be something to spoil the delight for which Gourlay had waited so long and endured such a soaking.

However, when in the tiled close he looked across anxiously, there was Donoghue doing nothing deceitful after all: he was just standing on the bottom step of the picture house, red from the lights above.

As Gourlay watched, Donoghue pulled one hand out of his pocket and taking off his cap hit it against the wall to knock the rain off it. As he tugged it on again he had to take the other hand out of his pocket, and there he was on the red bottom step of the picture-house, tugging on his red cap with his red hands, waiting, and every half-minute glancing along the street in the direction from which Jeanie would have come had she got the letter.

In the close Gourlay sighed: he told himself he was now enjoying his revenge, that this was worth all the sneezes, all the drips down the back of his neck, all the shivers, and the sore throat and tomorrow's stiffness; but he found, to his alarm, he was not convinced. Anxiously, appealingly, he looked over, hoping Donoghue would do something that would convince him: pray on his knees on the red stone step, weep, wave his arms and shout in his disappointment, break a window, curse the commissionaire, trip up one of the people going into the cinema. But Donoghue, after he had his cap on, lit a cigarette and kept glancing along the street.

After one of those glances he seemed to grow stiff and snatched the cigarette out of his mouth and forgot to put it back in again. He kept staring along the street, and Sam without much interest, certainly without expectation, gazed there too; and saw Jeanie in her green raincoat and with her small green umbrella come hurrying along.

They met in front of the picture-house. All that happened was that Donoghue put out his hand to catch her arm and hold it for a minute while they looked at each other. Then he rushed into the sweet-shop and after a minute or so, during which Jeanie stood motionless and private, he rushed out again and handed her a box of chocolates. She took it, and then up the steps they went, he helping her as if, the fool, he thought she was a cripple and couldn't climb the steps without his help. She waited for him as he bought the tickets, and then she made for the stalls door but he caught her again, he seemed to take every opportunity to catch her, and directed her towards the balcony stairs. He helped her up these stairs too; and thus they disappeared, he holding her, she holding the box of chocolates and her umbrella.

Gourlay came out of the close and stood in the street. He tilted his face so that the rain streaming down his cheeks and into his eyes, diluted the tears there. But he could not deny the tears, nor stop them; nor could he say why thus treacherously they were flowing. It was not just because Jeanie and Donoghue after all had met, were re-united, were holding hands in the warm cinema, and later would get married. Towards them indeed he felt only a numb sodden wonder, which was no source of tears. He wept for a greater reason: again he felt, but much more poignantly, that something important, something indispensable, something without which he must always fail as he had failed tonight, had come close to him but had passed him by. What it was of course he did not know.

Before starting on his journey home he took the soaked letter from his pocket and dropped it gently into the gutter. Immediately it was carried away as the lock of hair from the old woman's purse had been carried away by the burn. There had been nothing in the purse; there had been nothing tonight; there would be nothing always.

Grinning, but still with warm tears amidst the cold rain on his cheeks, he set off for home, walking for a little while, as a kind of joke, with one foot on the kerbstones, and the other ankle-deep in the racing gutter.

Chapter Eight

EVEN BEFORE the results of the examination came out Mrs. Stirling's pride in her son, for all her simpleness, contained in it some spite and even a little arrogance. She had never forgiven a world that had sacrificed her own ambitious childhood, forcing her to leave school at twelve and work from dawn till dusk in a carpet factory. The death of her husband, and the ingratitude of a country that refused her an honourable pension, had confirmed and reinforced her embitterment. She had struck back through her independence. As soon as she could, far sooner than most, she had renounced the parish's assistance in bringing up her children, even though it meant scrubbing houses by day and offices by night, and resulted in rheumaticky fingers and an aching back. Towards others without the same inspiration of resentment, who surrendered readily and took what they could, she had always shown a contempt, amusing to the tolerant but vexatious to realists like Mrs. Gourlay for instance, who considered cheating the parish as the best and most praiseworthy sign of spunk and gumption.

Her daughter's bonniness and her son's brains she put forward not as her contributions to society, but challenges rather like her steady payment of the rent. From her, so small, so swollen-handed, dressed in the same drab coat for the past ten years, had been born these wonders which other women, taller, with delicate ringed fingers and many coats, tweed or fur, could never equal, far less surpass. One of the women for whom she worked had a daughter who would have been astonished and aggrieved had she been told how much satisfaction her straight-haired plainness, so unsatisfactory to herself, gave to the small quiet rather sulky-faced woman she sometimes noticed scrubbing the floors of her house.

But bonniness faded; Mrs. Stirling's own mirror told her that: it faded, and even while it bloomed it had no power or wealth. Brains though did not fade: they grew, developed from class to class, from boyhood to manhood, from school to University, and afterwards out in the world claimed and achieved respect, position, and money. She knew her son John had brains; she knew, not because she earliest of all had seen the signs of high intelligence, but because every teacher he had had right up from the penny-buff had reported him to be a brilliant pupil. Perhaps what helped to cause this spitefulness in her pride in him was a doubt which she hid but always felt: she had never herself noticed this particular cleverness of his. He read many books, he was quiet, he was sensitive; yes, but in many practical matters about the house he was stupid and not nearly so helpful as Mary. Now he was at the Academy, and according to the marks he got for his exercises was doing well. But that doubt persisted, the feeling that all these outsiders, these strangers, these teachers, were deceived and she, who had given birth to him at a bitter, but clear time, judged him more truly. It was a tiny doubt, privately and jealously suffered like a disease; but its presence made her pride dangerous, liable to explode.

She kept her head high these days, and her lips very tight.

One of her employers had recommended her to a Mrs. Dawson, who lived in the same avenue of ivied villas. On the afternoon fixed for the interview Mrs. Stirling walked along to Sunnybank, Mrs. Dawson's house. She did not mind that the gardens on either side were obscured by rails and thick bushes or in some cases by high walls. Nor did she notice that winter with its harsh patience so akin to her own lay waiting in the roots of flowers and trees and grass.

Her appointment was at two o'clock. Ignoring her own irrelevant tiredness, she proceeded so as not to be late or too early, and kept considering with tight mouth what duties she would agree to and what terms.

Mrs. Dawson turned out to be a big soft-bodied, goldhaired, green-ringed, lipsticked, well-spoken blatherskite. She brought

Mrs. Stirling into the kitchen, insisted on giving her a cup of tea, and all the time smoked and blethered. Mrs. Stirling, suspicious of such hospitality to a menial, kept waiting at the edge of the chair, cup in hand, for the shrewdness sure to be at the back of all this amiable well-bred prattle: a sharp announcement of terms, threepence per hour less than usual, and outside steps to be pipe-clayed as well as scrubbed. But the shock that did emerge from the soft ceaseless good-natured chatter was there, flowing out with the other inanities, for a minute or two before Mrs. Stirling noticed it. Then she sat straighter in her chair, the cup lingered longer at her lips, and something beginning to glimmer from her small canny face, not friendliness exactly, nor trust, suddenly withdrew. Mrs. Dawson had begun to speak about her son Gerald, her only child, her darling, who was at Muirton Academy where he was one of the brightest pupils and likely to be dux of the school.

Tempted, Mrs. Stirling watched and listened to the green-ringed boasts. She knew that with a few modest words she could make that hand stop its plump proud waving and take the very glitter from the emeralds. After she had quietly spoken the whole house would have to give up its grandeur. If afterwards she washed its floor or its outside stone steps, she would never, even on her knees, even wringing out the cloth in cold weather with chilblained fingers, appear its pitiable drudge: this house, for all its seven rooms, its fine furniture, and its jewelled mistress, would be her inferior always.

She did not however speak the words. Two reasons restrained her: she did not wish to risk losing the job, and she dared not, having spoken herself, trust the Dawson boy to keep quiet. If he were to blurt out at school about his mother's charwoman, and his mother in jealousy might put him up to that, then indeed his mother's charwoman would become just that and nothing else, the magic would go out of her pail, scrubber, and swollen hands for ever: John, laughed at, would leave. Therefore, although she did not respond to Mrs. Dawson's maternal boasts, she did not on that occasion silence them.

After resisting the larger temptation she yielded in relief to the smaller one of confiding in Mary. They had to go through to the room for their secret conversation; John, as always, sat at the kitchen table with his books spread out before him.

It was cheerless in the room where the only furnishings were the lace curtains, John's bed, and a chair. There were no carpets. They stood by the window, as if from the lamp-post outside shone heat as well as light.

"What is it?" asked Mary, impatiently. The secrecy had already told her the matter concerned John, and she refused to be interested.

"Don't speak so loud. I've got a new job."

"New?" Though Mary in the snobbish office never hid her mother's occupation, still she was not proud of it.

Her mother understood the hope in her voice, and was peeved. "Oh, it's just the same kind of work," she muttered. "That's all I'm fit for."

Mary let that bitterness dissolve into the cold air slowly like their breath.

"Aye, it's all I'm fit for," repeated her mother, seeking sympathy. "I know that fine."

"What's this new job?"

"I don't think you really care."

"I'm cold."

"Well, I've got another house to go to."

Mary turned and glanced round the bare room; she laughed.

"It belongs to a Mrs. Dawson. I must admit," said Mrs. Stirling grudgingly, "she seems nice enough. She offered me a cup of tea, and she's not stingy with the money. But she's a big fat lazy show-off. Guess how many rings she has on her one hand? Just her one hand, mind you. Four. That's as true as I'm standing here. All with green gems in them."

"Surely you didn't ask me to come through here to the cold to tell me that?"

"No." Mrs. Stirling lowered her voice. "You see, Mrs. Dawson's got a son at the Academy. That's it."

"Is that it? What do you mean by it?" Mary laughed. "There are hundreds of boys at the Academy." But it was obvious from her laughter that she understood and enjoyed the implications.

"I know that," said her mother. "She's a great big fat boaster. You should have heard her. To hear yon you'd have thought her boy was the cleverest in the whole world."

"You think that about him, mother," said Mary, with a nod towards the kitchen.

"That's not true, and you know it. He has his limitations, and you've heard me say it. But I'm sure for all that he's far above this Dawson boy. Is he not in the top class, and is he not the best of them in it?"

"That's what he says."

"It's what all his teachers have said. What are you trying to do, for God's sake, Mary? Are you trying to destroy my faith in him?"

"He's clever enough; at lessons anyway."

"What do you mean, at lessons anyway? That's the only way to be clever in this world. It's what will some day give him a position and a good wage, and that's the main thing, the only thing worth getting."

"All right. Forget what I said. Only I've heard you say it yourself."

"Say what?"

But Mary was silent, and her mother's sullen heavy sigh was all the admission she needed or wanted. For a minute or so they were both silent. Mrs. Stirling thought perhaps after all he would fail. Mary thought that next summer she might be able to afford to buy a tennis racquet.

"Is this boy Dawson in his class?" she asked at last, but evidently not interested.

"I don't know that. I never asked. You forget I'm just a skivvy yonder. It's not for me to ask."

"Does she know you've got a son at the Academy too?"

"No, she doesn't. Didn't I say it's not for me to ask or say."

"She told you, why shouldn't you have told her?"

Her mother didn't reply, but smiled with the shadows of the

curtains obscuring her face. It seemed a strange cold barren smile.

"Why?" persisted Mary. "You're as good as she is."

"Better," murmured her mother proudly.

"All right. Why didn't you tell her then? If she was boasting, why didn't you boast back?"

"You know why. You know fine."

"Yes, I know," said Mary, after a pause. "You were frightened he got to know. Well, he'll get to know all right, for I'm going to tell him." She made a step or two towards the kitchen, whether really intending to go there and tell her brother, or whether just pretending, her mother couldn't say. With a cry of fury like an animal's, shrill and hardly intelligible, Mrs. Stirling seized her daughter and dragged her back. "No," she kept crying, "no, no, no."

"Let me go," muttered Mary. "You're tearing my jumper."

Her mother let go. "I'm sorry," she gasped. "I hardly knew what I was doing. But you mustn't tell him."

Mary stood with her face in darkness. Tears of pity for her mother, for her brother so faithfully studying, and for herself, ran down her cheeks. She could not speak at first lest she revealed them.

"You know what will happen if you tell him," said her mother, clutching her own hair with one frantic hand. "For God's sake, Mary, don't."

"What difference could it make?"

"It should make nane."

"Is he so ashamed of you? Is that it?"

"Mary, please." The hand in the hair clutched even more cruelly, with keener penitential pain; yet it was not possible to do penance for someone else's wrong, even if that someone was your own prized child.

"The Dawson boy might not be in his class even," said Mary. "Maybe he's not in the first year."

"He is. She said he was in the first year. I think he's in the same class."

There was another silence. Mary could hear the creaking of

her mother's hair, and thought too she could hear through in the kitchen the ceaseless pencil move over the paper.

"Why did you take the job then?" she asked.

"We need the money."

Mary heard then a great heart-heavy sigh, and was astonished to realise it was her own. Yes, they needed the money: not next summer, nor next, nor the next again, would she be able to get her tennis racquet. Standing there in the bare room, she saw their poverty menacing them, creeping into their very minds; and again she felt an involuntary pity for her brother, and admiration. It could not be easy to study so intently with poverty, the most insistent of all distractors, at his elbow always.

"All right," she muttered. "I'll not tell him."

Her mother sighed. "Will we, Mary, ever be out the bit?"

"Don't ask me. I'm only fifteen, remember."

After a long pause, Mrs. Stirling murmured, "That's true. I ken I'm not being fair to you. I ken. But I hae been alane for such a long time; I need company."

"It's all the same to me," said Mary, pretending to laugh. "Only don't expect me to give you any advice. I was a dunce at school, remember."

"You were never a dunce."

"Compared to him I was."

No reply meant agreement. Mary laughed.

"I hope you're remembering, all the same," she said, "that when he grows up, if he does manage to become a teacher or a doctor or somebody grand, he might just go away and leave you without any gratitude. That happens."

For such a long time her mother delayed answering that in impatience she turned round to look at her. Covered with the lace shadows like a kind of small-pox, her mother's face actually wore a smile.

"It does happen," repeated Mary angrily. "I've heard you say it yourself. It could happen with him."

Slowly her mother nodded. "It could," she agreed, and yet she continued to smile. If he went through the University and

214

became, as Mary said, somebody grand, then any subsequent ingratitude was irrelevant: he would have given her a personal triumph nothing could spoil.

"I don't see what there is to smile at," said Mary. "If I thought he would do that after all you've done for him, I'd —I'd go straight through and tell him about Dawson."

Immediately her mother returned from the future glory to the present tribulation. "You promised," she muttered. "Leave him alone. Give him a chance."

"He's bound to find out. Mrs. Dawson is sure to learn you've got a son at Muirton too, and naturally she'll tell hers. He'll spread it about."

"So he would too, if he's onything like his mither for gabbing. Her tongue, and yon fingers with the green rings, never halted. But how can she find oot if I don't tell her?"

"You will though. You'll let it slip. Sometimes you get bad-tempered, mother, and say things you don't want to."

"When my back's sore."

"Well, some day when it's especially sore and this Mrs. Dawson irritates you you might blurt it out, just for spite."

Mrs. Stirling put her hand round to touch her back, as if pleading with the pain in it never to goad her into that fatal disclosure.

"If she finds oot," she muttered, "it'll not be through me."

And she set her lips even tighter.

The day John brought back the examination results she came home to find him brooding in the darkness in front of the fire, pokering at the ribs. Even from the rattle of the poker she sensed he was in one of his black defeatist moods inherited from her. Always she felt afraid when she saw her own weakness in him. She could not then conquer it and punish it as she could in herself. Coaxing was useless, bullying worse; nor did she think force would succeed, although she had never tried it.

That evening she sank down silently on the sofa in the darkness. Her back ached, yet sitting in the bus she had been singing to herself, sad songs because in the midst of many troubles she felt happy and safe. She had plenty of work while her strength lasted, and John at school was doing well. Any night now, perhaps that very night, he would bring home the results of his first examination: that would be her best payment, her medicine, her rest, her liniment, her anodyne.

Now on the sofa she thought he had been told the results and he had not done well after all. For nearly five minutes she sat there afraid to ask, and he volunteered nothing except some sighs.

At last she spoke. "Why did you not light the gas?" she asked, far more angrily than she felt.

"I didn't want to."

"Did you just want to be sorry for yourself in the dark? Have you no lessons to do?"

"Yes."

"Then what's wrong? Usually you're started on them by the time I come in. What's different tonight? Don't tell me you've had your examination results?"

He drew the poker along the ribs. "Yes," he muttered at last.

She waited. She still had her bus ticket in her hand, and began to tear it into pieces. She felt she might be tearing up all their lives, certainly her own destructible hopes.

"Well?" she asked, and tried to laugh, as if light-hearted. "Don't tell me you were last."

He did not answer.

"How did you get on?" she cried, blunt at last. At the same time she began to weep. In the darkness she gestured bitterly against this futility of weeping, but she could not stop it. "If you've not done as well as you thought," she sobbed, "don't be frightened to tell me. I'm your mither, and I understand weel enough this must be a gey miserable place to do your lessons in, with a poor light and me always greeting because we lack so much that we need. I ken other boys hae big dictionaries and encyclopedias, and maist of them hae faithers and mithers that can advise them. Me, I'm useless, except at greeting; though at school I was clever enough."

He listened for a little while to her weeping.

"I was first," he said.

"First?"

"In every subject."

It was true. In the darkness where she could not see he smiled as he remembered Henderson's shocked face. Somebody had said he'd seen Henderson sneaking into the lavatory to weep. Henderson hadn't even been second in English and Latin.

She was weeping now with gladness and relief. It astonished her how easy the transfer was. "In every subject?" she asked. "In them all?"

"Yes."

"What did your teachers say?"

"Nothing."

"Surely they must hae said something? I'm sure it's not a common thing for somebody to be first in every subject."

He did not answer, but again he smiled in the darkness. Miss Naismith had asked him how he'd got on in other subjects. When he had told her, she had touched him very briefly on the head. "Good for you, Stirling," she had murmured, and she had blushed.

"How did Henderson get on?" asked his mother, whom he had told of course about his chief rival. "Was he second? Was he next to you?"

"Not in English and Latin."

"Who was second in English and Latin?"

He frowned: she was talking just to please him, or what was worse, just to please herself.

"You don't know them," he muttered.

"Not a boy called Dawson?" It was out before she could withhold it. But even after it was out, and she was waiting in horror for his answer, she could not help being thrilled. In the darkness somewhere Mrs. Dawson too waited for the answer, all the green rings still, the lipsticked mouth wide open.

"Dawson?" he repeated, puzzled. "What are you talking about? I've never said anything about Dawson. How did you know there was a Dawson?"

217

She almost screamed then in fury against her own stupidity. No subterfuge occurred to her. She felt any moment the whole secret would burst out, shouted by herself madly. She pressed her hands against her mouth.

"Maybe I did mention him," he muttered. "But it wasn't because he's good at lessons."

"Aye, you mentioned him." She tried to laugh. "The name must have stuck in my mind."

"He was sorry for Tull," he murmured, and warm tears trickled down his cheeks. Where was Tull now? Was he still smiling and winking at people who mocked? Of course now that his cripple father was dead, would anybody mock?

"How did Tull do?" she asked, trying to change the subject. But she had found that Dawson was not good enough at lessons to be worth mentioning.

"Tull's left," muttered her son. He had not told her about Tull's father dying and Tull's sudden leaving.

Cheerfully now she rose and lit the gas. She avoided looking at him as she took off her coat and hat, and set about preparing the tea.

"Good for you, being first," she said. "Mr. Richards will be proud to hear it. Funny how a name sticks in your mind. Of course Dawson's a common enough name. Is he much of a scholar?"

"He's not very good," muttered John, rising and getting his books out of his case. "But he's quite kind."

"Kind?" She turned, startled by the praise; then she laughed. "Well, that's a fine thing to be; maybe better than being clever."

"Aye," he muttered, and sitting down at a corner of the table began to do his French translation.

At Sunnybank next day it happened simply.

Mrs. Stirling, sick with holding back the information and with the fear of releasing it, worked less speedily than usual and kept glancing up every few moments, not knowing what she expected or wanted to see. Finally when she glanced up she found Mrs. Dawson gazing down at her solicitously.

"Are you feeling all right, Mrs. Stirling?" she asked. "You look tired today."

"Oh, I'm fine," said Mrs. Stirling tried hard to scrub vigorously and joyfully, but she could not. This strange paralysis bound her muscles. She stared at the soap-suds and the linoleum patterns, and it was as if she'd never seen them or their like in her life before. Suddenly she found herself glancing up again and saying, "How is your boy getting on at school now, Mrs. Dawson?"

Mrs. Dawson, touched, was also surprised. She had often noticed Mrs. Stirlng's deliberate indifference whenever she spoke about Gerald; she had put it down to the small charwoman's own childlessness.

"He's getting on fine, Mrs. Stirling, thanks."

Mrs. Stirling still scrubbed weakly and gazed in fascination at the soap-suds.

"Has he had an exam yet?" she asked.

"Yes, he has." Mrs. Dawson sighed, and then laughed. "As a matter of fact he got his marks yesterday."

"How did he get on? Did he do well? Was he among the best?"

"No, I'm afraid he wasn't. I must admit I was a bit disappointed, and annoyed too. He wouldn't talk about it; he didn't seem to think it was very important."

"But it is."

"Of course it is. But you know what boys are. They never realise that what is a bore to them is of great interest to us." Then, as she sighed again, a remark of her son's recurred to Mrs. Dawson. Dismissing his own performance as mediocre, he had remarked, with his mouth full of chocolate cake, that Stirling had done very well, was first in everything. Yes, Stirling had been the name. Mrs. Dawson, too busy chewing over her own tart disappointment, had paid little heed to this tiny titbit of a coincidence. Now, paying such keen heed that she forgot the cigarette burning away between her fingers, she gazed down at the small dour woman kneeling in front of her. Then in a minute she relaxed and smoked again. It was

219

hardly fair to poor Mrs. Stirling to gape at her just because of a coincidence in names.

"It seems," she said, "a boy with the same name as yourself was first in every subject. It seems he's very brilliant. The same name as yourself; Stirling. It's fairly common, I suppose."

Mrs. Stirling scrubbed away for about a minute, and then looked up, with either tears or jaups from the pail on her cheeks. "He's my son," she said, and lowering her head went on with the scrubbing.

Mrs. Dawson smoked, but could not taste the cigarette. She felt like giggling. Everything, even the soap-suds, struck her as very funny. She struggled hard to control herself.

"I didn't know you had any children, Mrs. Stirling," she said.

"I don't talk aboot them, but I've got two, a girl and a boy."

"You certainly don't talk about them. I didn't know. No, I didn't suspect it. Why didn't you tell me?"

"I ken my place. I'm here to work, Mrs. Dawson, not to bother you with stories aboot my weans."

"No. But still, I'd liked to have heard. You wouldn't have been bothering me. Mind you," she added, laughing, "I might have been a wee bit jealous." Then she laughed again, louder this time, proudly as she remembered that Gerald had many fine qualities, some of them more valuable than cleverness. "No, I don't think I would have been jealous, Mrs. Stirling." As she laughed, compassion and liking and congratulation suddenly all together gushed through her heart. Ignoring the sour-smelling pail and the danger of soiling her lilac-coloured frock on the soppy floor, she bent down beside the other woman.

"I'm very pleased, Mrs. Stirling," she said, and since shaking hands wasn't practicable she touched Mrs. Stirling's shoulder. "Now I come to think of it, I believe Gerald's mentioned your boy once or twice. He's very clever, isn't he?"

"He seems to be."

"I never connected him with you."

"No blame to you, ma'am."

Mrs. Dawson noticed the bitterness; the sobbing that immediately followed was of course impossible not to notice. "What's the matter?" she asked gently.

"Nothing. I must finish this. I'm behind my time."

"There is something the matter, Mrs. Stirling. What is it? I'd like to help you, if I can."

"I should never hae told you, that's what it is."

"Told me what? About your boy, you mean?"

"Aye. You'll tell yours, and he'll tell the whole school. You ken as weel as I do that weans hae no mercy on one anither."

Mrs. Dawson was surprised and hurt by that observation. Judging from her Gerald, she had always thought children were very fair-minded and often more considerate than grown-ups.

"Would you rather I didn't mention it to Gerald?" she asked.

"I'd be much obliged, ma'am, if you gave me your word."

"Gerald's a scout, you know; he's got a sense of honour. If I asked him not to, he'd never breathe a word about it at the school. He'd be pleased, I think."

Mrs. Stirling said nothing; her silence was dour.

"Would you rather I didn't tell him?"

"I'd much rather you didn't tell him."

Mrs. Dawson reflected; she decided she could ignore the implied insult to Gerald. "All right then," she murmured. "I'll not tell him. I'll keep your secret, although I hope you'll let me say it's a shame it should have to be a secret. Your son should be very proud of you, Mrs. Stirling."

"So he is."

"He should be. His cleverness might be wasted if you weren't sacrificing to give him a good education. It won't be easy."

"No, it's not easy; and it's not easy for him either. He's very sensitive."

"He will be, I'm sure."

"It seems whiles it's no advantage to be too intelligent. You imagine what's not there."

221

Mrs. Dawson didn't quite understand. She rose, stiff already from her little stooping. She felt then she had the better bargain: a luxurious house, a husband with a good income, and an average cheerful son.

"Don't worry, Mrs. Stirling," she said. "I'll not tell. I can keep a secret."

Mrs. Stirling did not believe her. "I'll be much obliged to you, ma'am," she muttered.

Chapter Nine

DURING the week following the announcement of the examination results Stirling was able, in his own reticent rationed way, to enjoy his triumph. All his teachers congratulated him. Even the remote Rector, visiting the English classroom for some other purpose, had him pointed out by Mr. Malvern as a future medallist.

The Rector had asked him if he intended to take Greek, and then had gone on to rhapsodise to the whole class on the beauty and academic usefulness of that language. He had even, turning to Mr. Malvern and laughing apologetically, quoted two lines from Homer about the great Achilles at the siege of Troy. Stirling, on his feet, pre-eminent in the class, had felt the strange sonorous words like a personal benediction, and when he had sat down, thrilled, he was resolved to take Greek in the third year. To take it, Mr. Malvern explained as soon as the headmaster went out, a pupil would have to drop Science; which was a pity in that it divorced the modern from the ancient, and helped in the acceleration of the world towards scientific doom.

Nobody in the class had understood, although everybody showed a practised polite interest; and Mr. Malvern in revenge had dashed on to the blackboard a long complex sentence containing two adverbial clauses, one noun clause, and an adjective clause beginning not with the usual relative pronoun but with a treacherous where. He had commanded them to go ahead and analyse it. In dismay they had done so, while he, wrapping his gown about him with machiavellian twitches, had sneered at all the young brains engrossed in the prescribed but useless numbo-jumbo. Stirling though had mastered it in less than five minutes, and was correct down to the last detail. Mr. Malvern paradoxically was displeased: he thought that any boy so smart at the traditional and reverenced rubbish was to be pitied.

Gerald Dawson too, though he could not himself analyse the sentence, thought Stirling was to be pitied. His mother, after holding out for two tortured days had told him her secret, making him promise very solemnly not to whisper it even to his best friend at school. Rodgers was his best friend, and would have kept the secret without in any way blackmailing Stirling; but he had not told Rodgers, and never would. During the history lesson he pictured himself at the stake, like Patrick Hamilton, being burnt, but never telling. Purposely, as part of the plot, he kept back from Stirling. Once when Stirling's pencil was broken he refrained from offering his pen-knife to sharpen it, although he was proud of his knife with its six sharp blades. He waited till somebody else offered his, not half so good. Every act of Stirling's, even the sharpening of his pencil, seemed to happen in a strange clarity and had a curious sad echo. Alone in the school, Dawson noticed the careful darns in Stirling's blue raincoat.

At home Stirling could not help being aware that his mother suddenly had become more sulky and bad-tempered. Once, not deeply interested, he asked her why, and was satisfied with the snapped explanation that she was tired and had, besides, just lost a job. Sympathetically nodding, he had gone on with his studies: the duty of finding the money to run the house and provide him with his needs was hers. Certainly, if she failed, he would share in the disaster; but he had lived so long now in the shadow of that black risk that his terror, though always present and always at its incalculable subterranean work, had become endurable. His mother had lost a job, she was worried and bad-tempered over it, he sighed, and went on with his Latin grammar.

She watched him at his silent conjugating, with spite, with pity, with fear, and even with a little hate. She could not tell him that she had had to give up the job because of his cowardice. She could not say to him, smiling, with her hand on his shoulder: John, son, I was working for a Mrs. Dawson. She lives in a big oose called Sunnybank, doon in Dechmont. She's got a boy Gerald in your class at the Academy. She kens aboot you. I houldn't have told her, but it burst oot because I was so pleased ou were first in the examinations, and she was always bragging boot her Gerald. She promised not to tell him, but she's a big-mooth and she's broken her word and she's told him. He kens. He kens, John, that you hae a mither wha, because her man's leid, has to work at scrubbing floors and steps to earn her ain ivelihood and her family's. That's all he kens, nothing mair. He's promised his mither not to tell anybody at school, and she wears he'll keep his promise. You said yourself he was kind. But what if, like his mither, he breaks his word and tells? What s there for him to tell? Nothing to be ashamed of surely. I hae heard many famous men in oor country were very poor when hey went to school. David Livingstone, for one. You've seen he hoose at Blantyre where he was born. Oors is nae palace, God kens, but better than yon, and he grew up to be a great man respected all ower the world. If at school they laugh at you, in God's name why? But if they should, you can gie them a straight answer, honest and prood.

No, she could not say all that to him, although inwardly she rehearsed it often; nor, supposing she had said it, could she ever expect him to look up from his books and reply: Aye, mother, I'll give them their answer all right. Let them laugh, if they're fools enough to want to. I have the last laugh. I was first in the examinations. As long as I have peace at home here to study, why should I worry about them and their jeering? If you're worried because you've had to give up your job at the Dawsons' for my sake, go and ask for it back. I know we need the money. Gerald Dawson won't say anything; he's not cruel. But in any case, don't worry about me. You've got enough to worry about as it is.

She knew that was all fantasy, that the problem was not so simple. If John found out that the boy Dawson knew, the danger was not simply of an exhibition of childish rage and petulance and self-pity. His nature was deep and complicated, darkened by a pessimism inherited from her but more involved than hers

because of his much subtler intelligence. He might, feeding
that pessimism, refuse to go back to the Academy and thus
throw away his career. Of course he would weep and be in
despair; but deep down within him would be an evil satisfaction
at his own wilful destruction. She divined this, helped by her
love for him and by a knowledge of her own nature; but nothing,
neither love nor self-knowledge, could help her to protect him
against himself.

Mary kept threatening to rebel. She thought, or said she
thought, that her brother ought to be told the truth brutally
and forced into shame at his cowardice. For too long he had
been humoured and pampered. If he was clever, then let him
understand. Even if telling him failed to make him brave, even
if he did like a coward leave school, the lesson learned might
be the most valuable of his life, far more important than any
amount of French or Latin or Science. She kept saying she
would tell him, and her mother kept begging her, in God's
name, not to do it.

He did not notice the particular tension in the house. During
that week, after his lessons were done, he read *Wuthering
Heights* till bed-time; and the lonely house on the moor, outside
and in, and its wild unhappy inmates, were more vivid than his
own with his mother so infinitely more prosaic in her misery
and his sister through in the cold dark room playing her violin
angrily.

On Saturday afternoon he went to the Co. for potatoes which
his mother had forgotten to bring in. The procedure was to
have the ordinary money exchanged by the girl at the cash-
desk for a Co-operative token of the same value, a note of the
transaction being made in the Co. book for dividend purposes.
He had handed up his book and half-crown and was waiting,
when he overheard a conversation between the two girls in the
little office. One of them, the older, had a bad cold. She spoke
with a continuous huffy sniff, and kept dabbing tenderly at her
nose. Bitterly she blamed the draught from the window in the
office for her cold. Its snib apparently was faulty, so that it
didn't shut properly: eight times she had mentioned it to the

anager; one of these nights, she had told him, the place would
e burgled and she wouldn't be to blame.

Then she had viciously made the entry in Stirling's book and
ad almost thrown the half-crown token at him; it had fallen
mong the sawdust on the floor. He had waited his turn at the
ne-message counter, enjoying the smells and sights of all the
xtra treats in for Christmas, such as silver-wrapped buns and
artan-covered shortbread. When he got his potatoes and
hange he went home, and on the way met Gourlay.

Instantly he smiled, not because he had information likely
o interest Gourlay very much, but also because Gourlay that
aturday afternoon was curiously alone, seated with his hands
n his pockets in a silly little corner full of old wet bus-tickets.

Often he had seen Gourlay by himself, but never had thought
f him as alone. Gourlay's bold assurance no matter what he
vas doing, even if it was just standing still, had always given
im the appearance of having as much company as he wanted.
Now in this damp corner it was different; he had no assurance,
e looked lonely.

Most boys were away watching Drumsagart Rangers
laying, or else were at the penny matinee at the Regal. But it
ould not altogether be the lack of money that kept Gourlay
ere in this deserted corner, because it was not necessary to
ay anything to get into the football match. Any obliging man
ist had to take you in front of him as if you were his son or
ephew, and you were allowed in free. Of course maybe it
vould be difficult for Gourlay to find a man willing to do him
ven so small a kindness. Even then, Gourlay could still get in,
r there was a daring route up over some wash-houses and
arbed wire.

Stirling stopped, but pretended it was to change his bag of
otatoes from one hand to the other.

"Hello, Sam," he said.

"Hello," muttered Gourlay. "Hae you been for messages?"

Stirling nodded: had it been safe he would have laughed, so
lly somehow, because so tame, did Gourlay's question seem
o him. He could hardly believe this was the same Gourlay

who months ago had rubbed his neck with nettles. There seemed however opportunity for a little revenge.

"Are you not at the pictures, Sam?" he asked.

"No." Gourlay shook his head.

"Have you no money?" Stirling laughed to disguise the cruelty in the question.

"Nane," smiled Gourlay. "Not a ha'penny."

Like everybody else Stirling knew Gourlay often was given money by his sister. But it was rumoured she was to be married after the New Year, and likely was saving up.

"Are the Rangers playing at home today?" he asked.

Gourlay shook his head. "I don't know."

"Where's Charlie Dean? Do you see him as often, Sam, now he's working?"

"He's at the hospital."

"To see his auntie, isn't it?"

"Aye. He goes every Saturday."

"She's very bad, isn't she?"

"I wish she would dee."

Stirling inwardly chuckled at that flash of the old bitterness. "Maybe it would be better for her," he said lightly. "Likely she's in pain all the time."

"If she dee'd there would be nae need for Charlie to waste every Saturday going to see her. When he comes hame——" but he did not finish the sentence.

"Does he go to the pictures then, Sam?"

"Aye."

"And they're dear at night." It occurred to Stirling now was a suitable time to dangle the temptation about the Co. window. Of course he didn't; but, virtuously refraining, he felt as superior to the other boy as good is to evil. He even, in his great confidence, added, "You've never been to the Academy gate yet, Sam."

Gourlay just shook his head, and Stirling in delight realised that he had no place at all to go to, never mind the Academy gate. That was why he was sitting here, in this corner full of old bus-tickets and withered grass.

228

"Well, I'll need to be getting home," he murmured, and picked up the potatoes. "I've got a book I want to read." He remembered reading was another refuge from which Gourlay was shut out, and thought how like young Heathcliff he was in his loneliness and wickedness. "How are you getting on at school these days, Sam?" he asked.

Gourlay grinned. "Same as usual. I got eight yesterday."

"Eight of the belt?"

"Sure. Three from Martin, four from Armstrong, and one from auld Richards."

"Four from Armstrong?" repeated Stirling, awed. "Was it sore?"

Gourlay held out his left hand, palm uppermost.

"Your left?"

"Aye, he said my right was too tough; he said I never felt it sore enough on my right."

"Was it sore, Sam?"

Gourlay nodded.

"I was lucky in the examinations," murmured Stirling, and in the remark there was some pity for Gourlay. "I came out first."

"You were always first."

"But it's different at Muirton, Sam."

"You get French there."

"And other subjects. But the competition's greater than it was at Drumsagart school. You see, they come from all over the county to the Academy."

Gourlay nodded, but it was clear he wasn't interested. Stirling was more astonished than peeved. Usually Gourlay's interest, shown often as animosity or opposition, was fierce even if stupid. Now he just sat there and nodded. He looked thinner too, and Stirling saw hollows in his neck he couldn't remember having noticed before. There was a big scratch across his left cheek. His voice too was a bit hoarse as if even yet he hadn't recovered from his terrible soaking outside the Regal a week ago.

"Cheerio, Sam," he muttered.

"Cheerio."

As Stirling went down by the burnside he looked back an saw that Gourlay who formerly had prowled the world, wa still sitting in his obscure corner. The tiger was tamed at las As he went into the house he was laughing at this demon stration of the ultimate defeat of evil and the victory of goo The likes of Gourlay were always crushed, whereas boys lik Stirling himself, clever and deserving, always succeeded in th end: that was surely how the world went, that was how Go arranged it.

He could not have said who arranged it, though it happene next day on the Sunday, that Mary should come home fror church embittered, envious, and quarrelsome. She came int the quiet lamp-lit kitchen, and pulling off her gloves tossed ther contemptuously into a corner. Her Bible was still tucked unde her arm. When she noticed it there she flung it down on th sofa carelessly, so that it bounced to the floor, the many-coloure little texts scattered from between its pages.

John was studying at the table. His mother by the fire wa reading in a twopenny paper a story she knew was trash bu which comforted her because in it in the end, after man disappointments and dangers, goodness won.

She watched her daughter in alarm. "What's the matter? she asked mildly.

"Nothing," yelled Mary. "Nothing's ever the matter wit me. I'm supposed to have no feelings. It's only him anything ever allowed to be the matter with."

Her mother's alarm increased. She dropped the paper and a the same time the facile optimism it encouraged.

She tried to smile. "This is not the kind of mood a body expected to be in coming hame from kirk," she said. "It mus hae been an awful dreich sermon surely."

"I never heard it. They all are, but I never heard it."

"I've heard Mr. Dougary's a terrible mumbler getting. He too auld for the job; he must be over seventy."

"I never heard it because I wasn't listening. Likely anywa it was a lot of drivel."

"These are not respectful words, Mary, and there's no need to shout."

"I'm trying to concentrate," murmured John, before his mother could stop him. She knew any remark from him, no matter how innocent or justified, might make Mary shout out words that would destroy them all. To silence him she had to pretend she was furiously angry with him for interfering.

"You be quiet," she cried. "Nobody's talking to you."

He gaped at her in hurt astonishment.

"If you've got to study," she went on, not relenting, "then study, but don't expect everybody else to talk in whispers just so that you'll not be disturbed." But she knew she could go too far in thus unfairly rebuking him. He might be provoked into an outburst of self-pity that would set Mary talking to bitter purpose. Yet Mary must be appeased by a sufficient show of anger. It was a difficult proportion, and in her agitation she could not trust herself to judge rightly.

He dropped his pencil, and with elbows on table pressed his face against his hands.

"You've done plenty for today as it is," she said. "You've been at it all day. You'll study yourself blind, and then where will it hae got you?"

He took his hands away to stare again at her in amazement. Just before Mary had come in his mother had been praising him for his persistence.

She tried to ignore him, and humour Mary.

"Was there a good turn-oot?" she asked.

Mary had taken off her hat and was swinging it in her hand. "It was half-empty," she said.

Her mother nodded. "Not many folk gang to kirk these days," she murmured. "And them that do seem to get little benefit from it."

"Meaning me for one, I suppose?" sneered Mary.

"You ken fine I don't mean you, Mary. Don't be so touchy. How could I hae meant you? Take your hat and coat off, and come over to the fire. It's chilly the night."

For about a minute Mary said nothing but stood swinging

231

her hat, with a sneer that was all the more hateful because of her bonniness. She kept staring at her brother who still covered his face with his hands.

"I walked home with Chrissie Anderson," she said.

Her mother laughed, "Did you indeed? She's one of the kind I meant. If you want an example, then she's one. Who was she miscalling tonight?"

"Me, I think."

"You?"

"Me, and my clothes. She had on a new coat and hat, and she had a new pair of gloves."

At last Mrs. Stirling understood. She trembled, for she saw now how very dangerous the situation was. She did not know what to say next, whether calmly to inquire after the new clothes and belittle them, or whether to continue her aspersion of their malicious owner.

"She very kindly reminded me," said Mary, "that it was the second new outfit she's had since I got this one." And with a cool viciousness, menacing in its very restraint, she threw the hat after the gloves.

"Her faither's alive," muttered her mother, "and in a guid job."

"I suppose it's my fault that mine's dead, and never had a good job while he was alive?"

"Mary, for God's sake, don't speak ill of your ain deid faither." Mrs. Stirling, betrayed by this unexpected sadness, began to weep. She strove to stop, to contain herself, to smile to speak in a matter-of-fact voice, to dispel the atmosphere of storm that was gathering. She could not, however, and her own weeping in the quiet room was a considerable contribution.

"I spoke no ill," said Mary, apparently calm herself. "I spoke the truth."

"It was not the truth then. You've nae right to speak in that way. The little time he kent you he doted on you. If he was here this day I'm sure you'd hae a new outfit for every one Chrissie Anderson got. He was generous, too generous for his ain guid, and nothing was ever guid enough for his family."

Mary, in no way responding to that praise of her father, gazed coolly at his portrait on the wall.

"Last week," she said, "you promised I would get new gloves. That pair's done, and you know it."

"I know that last week I had six shillings coming in that are stopped now."

"And whose fault's that?" screamed Mary. "Whose fault is it you had to leave the job at Mrs. Dawson's?"

"Mary!" cried her mother.

But the name was mentioned, and had been heard. John took his hands away and showed his face not frightened yet, but startled and puzzled.

"Dawson?" he repeated.

"Yes, Dawson," cried Mary, shouting the name into his face. "She's got a boy at the Academy. Is he in your class?"

"Gerald Dawson?"

"If Gerald's his name. Is it Gerald?"

The question was to her mother, and the answer to it was another scream from Mrs. Stirling and a wild blow from her on Mary's face. Mary, jerking away, pulled some of John's books and jotters off the table. Her mother, shocked by her own violence, stood with mouth open, staring at her hand as if Mary's blood was on it. She kept moaning, "Oh God."

For over a minute no one spoke except for Mrs. Stirling's moan. John was on his knees picking up his books and at the same time praying against the vague terrors in his mind. Mary stood with her back to her mother, stroking her cheek as if to show fondness and gratitude for the blow, which released her from all her pledges.

"Mary," moaned her mother at last.

Mary did not speak or turn.

"Mary, before God I swear I'm sorry. I had no right to strike you. I'm beholden to you. I have no right to strike anybody, but you least of all."

Still Mary did not answer, and Mrs. Stirling, suddenly afraid she had forfeited her daughter's sympathy and love, shrieked at John as the real culprit.

"You're the one I should hae struck," she cried, and lifting up a book, his French grammar it was, she flung it to the floor. "It's you I should hae struck."

He began to whimper. "What hae I done?"

"If you weren't such a coward," she cried, "there would hae been no need for this."

"There's something," he said. "What is it? You and Mary know something. What is it? What were you saying about Gerald Dawson?"

"I'll tell you," cried his mother, looking towards Mary to see what effect telling would have on her; none, it seemed. "I'll tell you."

The three of them waited.

"I had a job," muttered Mrs. Stirling, "at Mrs. Dawson's of Sunnybank in Dechmont."

His voice was lower even than hers, and had shudders in it. "Were you cleaning her house?"

"That's right. With these hands." But as she held them up she remembered they had just struck Mary, and in horror she lowered them quickly and thrust them behind her.

"Does she know about me?"

His mother heard, hoarse and timid though it was; but she pretended not to.

"If you've anything to say," she cried, "for God's sake, speak it oot. Must you be a coward in everything?"

"Does Mrs. Dawson know about me?"

"What are you talking aboot? What is there to ken aboot you?"

"Does she ken——?" but even as he tried to find reassuring words to express his meaning, the implications began to crowd like fiends into his mind. "Does she ken about me?"

His mother, sorry for him, wishing to protect him, hesitated. She looked at Mary as if she hoped from her a reprieve, a relaxing of the condition of pardon; but Mary still stood with her back turned, unappeased.

"Does she, mither?" he appealed.

She could not speak it, and had to nod, though Mary of course would not see the nod. "I gave up the job," she muttered, and knew the words were like repetitions of that blow on Mary's face. She began to weep afresh, feeling she had betrayed them both, and not knowing where to turn for advice and comfort. She glanced up at her husband's picture, and shook her head.

John stood considering what effect her giving up of the job could have.

At last he asked, "Does she know about me?"

"For God's sake," she cried, "hae I to tell you a thousand times? How is it you're said to be smart at school? You never prove it here. You don't seem to hae the brains to ken what's for your ain guid. Aye, she kent aboot you. Will I tell you how she kent? She bragged aboot her son, and I bragged aboot mine. Did I commit a sin?"

Again he tried to consider. He felt confused and terrified. Mary's silence troubled him, and his mother's weeping suggested there was still more to be known. Then the crucial question occurred to him: did Gerald Dawson know it was his, Stirling's mother, who had worked in his house, scrubbing the floors? Licking his lips, he looked from his mother to Mary and back again. He dared not ask that question. A picture of Dawson flashed into his memory, and yes, surely Dawson had these past two or three days been gazing at him suspiciously. But, even though the fears grew monstrous in his mind, and his legs began to tremble so that he had to hold on to the table for support, he still couldn't bring himself to ask the question.

"Her boy kens nothing," muttered his mother. "She promised me that."

Mary laughed.

"He does ken," shrieked John to his mother. "You're telling lies. He does ken."

She hid her face in her hands: it was an act of surrender, and when she spoke it was in a resigned voice. "Likely he does. His mither promised not to tell him, but what faith is there in folk? Likely he kens, but what of it? You said yourself he was kind."

"Did I?" he cried, glancing about him as the bars of the cage came nearer. "Did I say he was kind?"

"You did. Nobody asked you to praise him, but you did."

Suddenly he saw what was in the narrowing cage with him: his own most savage shame. "He'll tell," he screamed. "Oh mither, he'll tell the whole school."

"He hasn't yet," she said wearily. "He's kept his word so far, hasn't he? Why should he ever break it?"

"No, no, no, no," he cried, throwing out his hands as to ward something off. "I can never go back. Surely you see I can never go back. Never."

"I see nothing to hinder you. But if you cannae, you cannae. It's up to you."

He clutched at his hair; he clawed his cheeks. He thought of the knives in the table drawer, especially the long bread knife, and remembered how in Julius Caesar Brutus had escaped capture. Knowing he lacked courage for that, he knew also he must stay in his cage snarled at and torn every moment by his insatiable shame. Only by leaving the Academy could he escape, and to leave would break his heart, would leave him still in the narrow cage with defeat this time, irremediable defeat that would keep him pressed against the bars in agony and sorrow all his life. Therefore there was no escape at all.

Wildly he glared at his mother who, with face hidden, wept softly; it was as if she was enjoying her quiet weep. Then he looked at Mary who stood with her back turned but with her head erect as if she was proud of having helped to destroy him. With a shriek of hatred and despair he seized her hat and threw it towards the fire, and on his way to the door he trampled on her texts and kicked her Bible.

As he went out of the house he heard his mother calling his name.

Chapter Ten

On Sunday evening Dean, bored with grief, felt a desire to seek out Gourlay, who never grieved and who never had anybody grieving over him.

Though it was a cold night he walked slowly, hunched into his long thick overcoat. For hours that day in the warm house he had watched his uncle go round touching every familiar object, until it was no longer familiar and the whole house was strange. Now in the dark raw street he found to his amazement and sullen anger that this strangeness continued; even the lamp-posts and the pavements were different, as if his uncle, weeping but pretending not to be, had touched them with his long fingers shy as spiders.

Carefully, as he strove by an effort of will to make everything as it had once been long ago, Dean thought only of his uncle as the cause of the transformation. His aunt, whose hand, skinny as a hen's, he had held yesterday, lay in hospital, many dark miles away: she could not be to blame. Her hand had been skinny and yellow like a hen's.

Under one lamp-post he stopped, took his own hand from his pocket, gazed at it, all thought suspended, and then walked on again. He pretended his hand had felt cramped and he had had to examine it to see what was wrong.

As he came into the area where Gourlay lived he met some boys.

"Have you seen Sam Gourlay anywhere?" he called.

Far worse than anything else, they seemed transformed. They stood round him, staring and giggling strangely.

"No, we've not seen him," they said.

He thought they were going to attack him. Among them were some whose trousers he and Gourlay had once pulled off

237

and thrown up into the branches of a tree. Perhaps now, catching him alone, they plotted revenge.

"What's up?" he snarled. "I can't be bothered with you. What are you all grinning at? Have I said something funny? What's the matter with you all?"

"Nothing. There's nothing the matter with us, Charlie."

"What are you staring at?"

"We're not staring, Charlie."

Then as he drew his hands out in readiness, they suddenly turned and ran away, laughing. They did not laugh in an ordinary fashion, nor did they run ordinarily, but shrieked and jumped and waved their arms. A safe distance off, they turned and shouted.

"Tell Gourlay to go and boil his heid."

"Gourlay's hanged to a lamp-post."

"Gourlay's a bastard."

"Who's frightened of Gourlay?"

"Gourlay got a dozen from Armstrong."

He listened, grinning involuntarily. He did not mind this abuse of Gourlay, although the discourtesy to himself annoyed him. He was about to shout a threat after them, but refrained: he, left school and working, ought not to heed such small fry. Perhaps though he would tell Gourlay what they had yelled about him, and Gourlay, of course, like the brainless fool he was, would wallop them all in turn, and have their parents and their teachers and the police after him again. Gourlay would never learn to be cunning in getting his own back: he struck one blow out in the open, and got a hundred in return.

But it was this vulnerability of Gourlay's that he had come this evening to comfort himself with. He wanted to see Gourlay's face with maybe his mother's punch-marks fresh on it; he wanted to feel with his fingers the thinness on this chilly night of Gourlay's jersey, and the sharp nearness of the bones under it; he wanted to gaze for minutes on the belt-weals sure to be on Gourlay's palms, if Armstrong had given him a dozen recently; he wanted to hear Gourlay's grumbles about having no money for pictures and only mouldy cheese and black corn beef to eat.

As part of this desire to feast on Gourlay's misfortunes he did what he had hitherto contemptuously refused to do: he went into Gourlay's close and rapped on the door.

It was Mrs. Gourlay who came, cursing at being roused from the fire.

"Wha is it?" she grunted. "If it's any collection for church funds, mind, charity begins at hame." Then she laughed, as if relenting. "Wha is it? I'm sorry it's dark. There's a feud in this close: naebody will pay for a new gas-mantle."

"It's me, Mrs. Gourlay, Charlie Dean, Sam's pal. Is he in?"

"Oh, it's you." She seemed to be trying to study him in the darkness. He put his fingers to his nose at her.

"How's your auntie?" she asked.

Astonished and insulted, he could not reply.

"You'll miss her," she said. "No, he's not in. God kens where he is. Aye, you'll miss her. They say she was a guid woman." Again she laughed.

This time he did not understand her laughter, and perhaps neither did she; but he felt he understood why Sam hated her.

"You'll ken his haunts better than me," she said. "Maybe he's doon in the cellar. One thing's certain," and she laughed, differently now, "you'll not need to look in the kirk. There's naething there to steal, not even religion. I'm sorry, son."

Then she went in again, closing the door quite quietly.

He stood for a minute or two at the closemouth, cursing her silently and monotonously with every obscene name he knew, but taking great care not even to think why he was doing it.

Below in the backcourt was a row of cellars intended for storing coal, but through dilapidation, damage, and neighbourly dishonesty, they had for years not been used for that purpose. Most of them lacked doors, and any door that still remained was usually kept unlocked, otherwise thieves might be enticed. In any case everybody thought it was more sensible to keep the coal in the kitchen bunker and have the coalman carry it up the stairs.

Gourlay's cellar was his lair. He had furnished it with junk flung out on the nearby midden: a striped flock mattress darkened with dubious stains and once a continent of fleas; a chair with three legs and a seat of green scabby velvet plush; a chamber-pot with a big hole in it, used facetiously as helmet or earnestly as seat; and even a picture with broken frame, showing some crimson tulips that smelled of sauce, for the lady who had jettisoned it had once tried to sober her husband with a flung sauce bottle.

There was a door with only one hinge; string kept it closed, and a section in the top corner had been mended with the lid of a biscuit tin. Dean saw as he stumbled towards it that Gourlay must be inside, for a light was showing. He approached as softly as he could, hoping to be able to peep secretly in at Gourlay. Perhaps he might catch him weeping.

There were many peep-holes to choose from. He tried to keep his nose back from the wood, for he had often seen dogs wetting against it. As he had guessed, the light was from a candle; it was about an inch long, and stood in a hole in the brick wall near the picture of the tulips. The floor therefore was partially shadowed, and there, stretched on the mattress, lay Gourlay as if asleep.

Dean grinned. He thought how funny it would be if one of the rats that lurked there was suddenly to loup on to Gourlay's face and chew at it. One had done that to Mrs. Hampseed's baby as it sat in its pram with its cheeks jammy. Gourlay would pretty soon waken up if a rat's teeth sank into his nose; he would stop pretending he was asleep.

For minutes Dean watched, seeing the wished-for rat several times as the shadows moved, and seeing Gourlay jump up as often in comical alarm. Yet in reality Gourlay did not move, lay all the time stretched out, lying on his left side, with his arms awkwardly protecting his face.

It slowly occurred to Dean that Gourlay was really asleep, in spite of the cold, in spite of his many misfortunes, in spite of the waste of the candle. He had then in anger and retaliation to waken him as quickly and roughly as he could. He shouted and kicked on the door, dragged it open, and hacked at the mattress, careless whether he hurt Gourlay's feet.

"Wake up," he shouted. "Wake up, Gourlay. What are you sleeping for? Are you just a wean, Gourlay, or an auld man, to fall asleep not in your bed?"

Gourlay awoke in confusion. "What is it?" he gasped, and held his arms in front of his face. "What time is it, mither? Hae I slept in?"

"Aye, that's right," cried Dean. "You've slept in. You've been sleeping in all your life, Gourlay."

Gourlay recognised him and beyond him the dark winter Sunday night. Immediately he shivered and grinned.

"It's you, Charlie," he said, yawning. "That's guid."

Dean, stooping eagerly, saw the scratch on the left cheek. He took the candle down to hold it closer to his friend's face.

"Who scratched your face?" he asked.

Gourlay's finger tenderly followed the curve of the scratch. "This?"

"It's new. Who did it? Was it your mither?"

Gourlay hesitated, and then nodded cheerfully. "You ken her," he said.

"No." Dean shook his head. "No. It wasn't your mither. Who was it?"

Gourlay grinned. "Don't worry. It's just a scratch. It makes no difference. I was doon at your gate today, Charlie. It's quite a while since I saw you. You never came. I waited for a long time, but you never came. I thought you must hae gone to the hospital."

"Don't change the subject. Who scratched you? Don't tell me it was an accident. Don't tell me you were playing with a kitten and it put out its paw. When that was done there must have been a lot of blood."

That was true. Yesterday evening Gourlay had gone staggering round the kitchen, asking for a bit of cloth to wipe off the blood, some of which was flooding his eye. He had grabbed the towel from the brass-rod across the mantelpiece, but his mother had snatched it from him, crying he wasn't going to waste a good towel: blood was hard to wash off. Jeanie had stood laughing like a madwoman with blood on her nails. It had been his father who had led him to the sink and washed his face.

Nevertheless he shook his head. "There wasn't any blood," he muttered. "I don't bleed easy."

"Half an inch to the side," whispered Dean, "and your ee would hae been oot. It was Jeanie."

Gourlay said nothing.

"It was Jeanie. Don't deny it. She used to gie you pennies, is it scratches now?"

"Don't you talk, Charlie," said Gourlay, laughing good-humouredly. "What about your auntie? What about her, eh?"

Dean was puzzled. "What d'you mean?" he muttered. "You ken she never scratched me."

"Oh, I ken that; but she's going to die."

"Listen," said Dean bitterly and urgently, "all I'm asking you is who scratched your face. Is that asking too much? Are we not supposed to be pals?"

"Sure we're pals, Charlie."

"How can we be pals if you tell me lies? Look, Sam, we can't be pals if you tell me lies."

In his pretended great earnestness he seized Gourlay's arm.

Gourlay pulled it quickly back, with a gasp.

"I've got a boil on my elbow," he explained, and as if sight of it would act as propitiation he rolled up his jersey sleeve and revealed the boil, swollen enough, sore enough, and ill-tended enough, almost to satisfy Dean, who gloated over it.

"But who was it scratched your face, Sam?" he asked quietly.

"It was Jeanie," admitted Gourlay. He tried to laugh. "I pinched a letter Donoghue sent her."

"Tell me about it, Sam. Is it very sore?" He meant the boil, and to test its tenderness he flicked it with his forefinger.

Gourlay yelped, and drawing back his arm cracked it against the brick wall. Tears burst into his eyes. "Christ," he murmured, and tried with his other hand to soothe the agony.

"Are you praying, Sam?" chuckled Dean. "Your mither said I wouldn't find you in the kirk. Is this the kirk? Are you

242

greeting, Sam? I thought you boasted nothing ever made you greet."

"I'm not greeting," said Gourlay. To try and prove it he laughed. "It's sore, you ken. I think I'm anither one coming."

"Anither boil? Where?"

Gourlay pulled down his left stocking and showed another boil, younger this time, but showing promise of a quick and fiery maturity. "And one on my back, maybe," he added, fingering there. "It could be just a pimple."

"That's all right, Sam," whispered Dean. "You've got boils. But what I want to ken aboot is this letter you said you pinched. Tell me, Sam."

He replaced the candle, which had become too small to be held with safety. Then he sat on the green plush chair; an upturned pail substituted for the missing leg.

"I'm sure it's a good story," he said.

"You'll laugh," muttered Gourlay ruefully.

"Me, Sam? Do you think I'll laugh? Am I not your pal? Did you not say yourself my auntie was going to dee?"

"Is she, Charlie?" Gourlay was very eager as if he took it for granted his friend wished for the death. "Did the professor say it? When 's it to be?"

For a moment as he stared at Gourlay's scratched grinning face the reality behind all pretence came too close for Dean. He had to look away: in Gourlay's misfortunes there was at that moment no solace. Seeing a cobweb in a corner of the low ceiling, he wished he was a cobweb. But next moment he was pretending again, laughing and urging Gourlay to hurry on with the story about the stolen letter.

Soothing his boil while he spoke, like a mother her fretful baby, Gourlay told how he'd kept the letter, how he'd gone to laugh at Donoghue outside the Regal, how Jeanie had turned up after all, and how, after Donoghue had questioned the post-man, she had flown at Sam in that nailed madness.

He told it in a laughing voice, as if seen backward it had become a joke, but he kept glancing up to investigate the chuckles Dean let out nearly all the time.

At the end Dean broke out into a great aggressive feigned laughter, and banged his own knees and slapped Gourlay on the legs, on the shoulder, and on the sore elbow.

Gourlay, trying to laugh in defence, guarded his elbow; but a more vulnerable part of him could not be guarded. In spite of his laughter he looked worried.

"You should hae seen wee Donoghue," he muttered, "banging his bonnet against the wa' to knock off the rain."

Before Dean could think of his next gibe, both of them were startled by a sudden clatter just outside and then a long queer horrified whimpering.

"What's that?" muttered Dean, wetting his lips.

Gourlay shook his head, grinning. "Maybe it's your auntie's ghost, Charlie."

"Shut your mouth, Gourlay."

"It sounded like a ghost. There it's again."

Dean jumped up and almost frantically tugged open the door. He glared out as if indeed he expected to find his aunt's unpardonable ghost.

Behind him Gourlay grumbled at the draught.

The candlelight flickered and nearly went out.

"Who's there?" shouted Dean. "For Christ's sake."

Then the answer came, miserable, feeble, but natural.

"It's just me, John Stirling."

Dean yelled in a sudden wild delight. He turned to Gourlay. "Guess who it is?" he cried.

"It's Stirling," muttered Gourlay. "I heard. Whit 's he doing oot at this time. I thocht he stayed in every night and did his lessons."

"Come in, Stirling," cried Dean, laughing very loudly. "Gourlay wants to see you. He thocht you were a ghost."

"I don't believe in ghosts," grumbled Gourlay. "And I wish you'd shut the door; it's cauld."

Stirling came to the door and looked in.

Even Gourlay, shivering with cold, could not help being impressed by the extraordinary misery and despair on that face in the candlelight. Tears, still active, begrimed it in zigzag streaks; but strangest of all, green smears of cow-dung daubed it, as if somewhere in a field he had been lying on his face, weeping. As they stared at him, amazed and concerned, the candle went out. Dean let out a cry. It was as if the desperate face at the door had itself gone out, as if indeed it had been a ghost's face, come from some region where dead people suffered. Only the smell of tallow was left, and a great chilliness.

From the door came a little weird noise of passionate but wearied suffering.

"Is your mither deid?" asked Gourlay harshly, with a laugh. "I wish mine was."

Dean chuckled and stuttered in his glee. Another barrier had come between him and reality. "Did you see his face? Do you smell it? He's been rubbing it wi' cow-dung. Try it, Sam. Maybe it's a cure for scratches and boils."

"The snib's broken," sobbed Stirling.

"Snib?" Dean laughed. "In your heid there's a snib broken."

"That's it," agreed Gourlay. "His brain's turned. My mither said to my faither that reading had turned his brains. And he thocht he was going to be a teacher."

"Maybe he's failed in his examinations?" suggested Dean.

"No, that's not it. He was first. He told me yesterday. He was all right yesterday. I knew he would be first."

"Stirling," asked Dean softly, "what snib's broken?"

"The Co. window," moaned Stirling.

"What!" Gourlay sprang up and tried to seize Stirling. "Are you saying the snib in the Co. window's broken?"

"Sure, that's what he's saying, Sam," murmured Dean.

"But, Charlie, if it's broken we could easily climb up the pipe and get in."

"You've got boils."

"Aye, but they've got lots o' medicines on the shelves yonder; maybe there's a cure for boils. And there's currant bun and shortbread and chocolate biscuits in tins wi' tartan wrappers. Come on, Charlie. This is oor big chance at last."

Dean did not at once answer.

"Come on, Charlie," cried Gourlay, impatiently wheedling.

Dean's voice was very quiet. "Is Stirling coming?"

"Don't be daft, Charlie. You ken fine he would never come. He's a mammy's pet."

"But he told you aboot the snib, Sam. Whit did he tell you aboot the snib for? Maybe he wants to come."

Gourlay snarled his derision.

"Ask him, Sam," murmured Dean.

"I'll ask him," yelled Gourlay. "Are you coming wi' us, Stirling?"

"Tell the world," murmured Dean.

Gourlay, now on his feet, had hold of Stirling. In the darkness their faces touched. He grinned as he thought some of the cow-dung had come on to his from Stirling's. Again he bellowed his question.

"Hit him," advised Dean.

"Sure." Gourlay punched but not very heartily.

"Harder," said Dean.

Gourlay laughed. "Whit's the use? He'd never come. He just wants to go back to his mammy."

"I'll hit him," said Dean, and putting out his hand touched Stirling's face. It drew back but the door stopped it.

Dean at first kept stroking that cold wet face. As he touched the cow-dung he smelled it strongly, and he remembered pleasant summer days in the fields.

"What's up, Charlie?" asked Gourlay, with a chuckle.

Dean suddenly decided. He withdrew his hand to bring it back again in a slap more loud than painful against that cold unhappy face in the darkness. Then he heard a queer stuttering sound of sobs, and seconds later realised it came from him.

Gourlay laughed in curiosity and amazement. "Did he hit you, Charlie? Did you let him? Whit are you greeting for?"

"Go to hell, Gourlay," screamed Dean.

"But, Charlie——"

Dean viciously threw off the hand seeking him in the dark. "Go to hell, I told you. I hate you, Gourlay. I've always hated you."

Gourlay's mind was far too clumsy to follow these swift changes of mood. He wished there was somebody he could appeal to for an explanation.

"I ken your auntie didnae like me," he agreed reasonably.

Dean let out scream after scream of obscenity. Then he pulled open the door and rushed away.

They heard him clatter over a tin-can on the ground. Gourlay couldn't help grinning, despite his perplexity. "Did you fall, Charlie?" he shouted. "Did you hurt yourself?"

There was no answer, and Dean was gone.

Gourlay peered out. "Poor old Charlie," he chuckled. "It's his uncle that's worrying him. I see through it a' right. When his auntie dees, his uncle will be efter him for his revenge." Gourlay laughed. "That's it. There'll be nae picture money or fag money then. Poor old Charlie."

He became aware Stirling was still with him. When he turned towards him, it was as towards a comrade, in friendliness, without rancour.

"Do you ken whit my mither said I should do for my boils?" he asked. "Spit on them. That's whit she said."

Stirling spoke, so quietly Gourlay didn't catch it.

"Whit did you say, Stirling?"

Stirling was silent.

Gourlay gave him a good-humoured nudge. "You said something, Stirling. Are you frightened I'm going to hit you because you hit Charlie my pal? No, Stirling, I'm not. Will I tell you something? That's whit you should do all the time: hit back."

Stirling spoke at last. "I'm going hame."

Gourlay nodded. "That's right." This going home was in the meantime inevitable, like cold in winter or strap in school. Later, when he grew up to be a man, there would no longer be any need to go home.

"Will you get supper?" he asked.

Stirling thought of the supper his for the taking: a cup of hot cocoa made half with milk, a slice of bread with jam, and a biscuit.

247

"I'll get nane," said Gourlay. "Maybe I'll not go hame. Maybe I'll just sleep here in the cellar. But there's school tomorrow."

He felt his companion shudder.

Gourlay grunted. "It's all right for you, Stirling. You can do vulgar fractions."

Again Stirling muttered something too low for Gourlay to hear it.

Gourlay this time was cross. "Whit did you say?" he cried. "I'm fed up wi' your mumbling."

Stirling repeated it, but not for Gourlay's benefit. He had been saying it to himself dozens of times. "Dawson'll not tell."

"Dawson? Who's he? I don't ken onybody called Dawson."

Stirling said nothing.

"Is he one of the toffs at your new school?"

"Yes."

Something in that yes, a sort of groan, impressed Gourlay.

"I bet you he wears swanky claithes," he said. "And he'll hae lots of money, mair than Charlie even. Has his faither got a car?"

Stirling didn't know; and he realised, with a fresh shock of foreboding, that he knew very little about Dawson.

"He's bound to hae a car," said Gourlay, "if he's a toff. Whit's his first name?"

"Gerald."

"Aye, that's a toff's name. He'll live in a big mansion. Where does he come from?"

"I don't know," lied Stirling, and realised again how many and unexpected were the dangers surrounding him. Gourlay might find out where Dawson lived, just three miles away, and visit him.

"He's lucky," admitted Gourlay, though he had been bred to hate people better off than himself. "I wish I was Dawson."

Stirling was startled by that idea, Gourlay being Dawson, and next moment hope lit up in him. Gerald Dawson was so utterly unlike Gourlay that he would never be cruel. Had he not been sorry for Robert Tull, while others were laughing?

"I'm going hame," said Stirling, and went abruptly.

Gourlay was taken by surprise. He had been enjoying this chat about the well-off boy Dawson.

"Hey, Stirling," he called. "Come back."

Stirling kept hurrying away, carrying that light of hope. By the cellars, where Gourlay called, was dreadful darkness.

"Stirling, I just want to talk to you."

There was no answer, and soon the sounds of the quick feet died away.

"I wish——" muttered Gourlay, his fingers on his boil, "I wish——" but he couldn't name it.

Nor could he say where he wanted to go. Not home, to bed with curses and a drink of cold water; not to the lighted street where cops would grab him and demand why he was wandering about so late; not down to Charlie's gate, where no one ever came; and not up the drain pipe into the store, for in spite of his eager boasts to Charlie he knew it would be agony to climb with his boils so inflamed.

There seemed no place except back into the cellar, and thither after two or three minutes he crept with baffled grin. It was a pity though the candle was done.

Chapter Eleven

"I'm going home," said Stirling, and went abruptly.
Gourlay was taken by surprise. He had been enjoying this
chat about the world . . .
"Hey, Stirling," he called. "Come back."
Stirling . . . . boys. By
the cellar, where Gourlay called, was dreadful darkness.
"Stirling, I just want to talk to you."

MONDAY began like any other ordinary day at school. It was
raining, and the cloakroom was jammed with boys hanging up
their raincoats. Stirling felt, as he unbuttoned his and took it
off, that he was surrendering a defence against Dawson and the
others. He hung it up carefully, tab round the peg, and the darns
hidden over which his mother had spent hours. The coat represented her, who loved him, protected him, and sacrificed herself
for him. He wanted to keep telling himself all that. He wanted
not to forget that it was his own cowardice which was threatening to ruin him.

He stood smiling against the tiled wall, his case at his feet.
Boys in his class passed with a friendly "Hello, Stirling."
Others in his year but in lower classes, who knew him as the
wonderful scholar, gave him curious but not hostile looks.
Everything was as before. In one corner there was a tremendous
laughter; and over at the wash-hand basins a tall boy with a
reputation as a comic was combing his long fair hair, while
his cronies stood by and joked.

Then Dawson hurried in, almost late. He was with his close
friend Rodgers. They saw Stirling and gave him a wave. He
noticed it was Rodgers who waved first. He waved back as
calmly as if, his mother a lady with jewels, he'd been driven up
to school in a gleaming car. He knew his outward calm was
well done, and would deceive anybody, except his mother, and
Mary, and Gourlay. But with them he wouldn't need this mask
of calmness, preserving which caused him so much strain; with
them he could let his weakness be seen, in a release of weeping.

He tried to picture Gourlay there, beside Dawson and
Rodgers: like a monkey grinning and fingering their expensive
clothes.

Dawson, after several quick glances, swaggered along with a jolliness genuine enough but a little nervous. His mother had urged him not to ignore Stirling but to seek him out and be his friend.

"Done your maths eccy for Stinker?" he asked.

Stirling nodded. Without seeming to, he watched Dawson with great closeness and thought he detected in the midst of that merry grin a shyness and slight uneasiness, but not any malice; no, not a trace of that.

"So have I," said Dawson cheerfully, "but they tell me my answer's all foozled."

Stirling smiled.

"Likely it is," added Dawson, laughing, as he went away. "Dad helped me. If it dries up," he cried from the door, "what about a game of football at playtime? Rodgers' got a ball."

Stirling nodded. Then, holding back his terrors, he considered the position. If there was any change, it was for the better. Dawson, whether by order of his parents or from his own decency, was going out of his way to be friendly. He would not reveal the secret from cruelty or envy or malice; but of course it was possible for even friendliness to blurt it out without meaning to.

After prayers the first period for 1A was history. Mr. Arbuckle the teacher was late in coming into his room, and when he arrived three boys happened to be out of their seats. They scrambled back but not soon enough.

"Out," he snapped.

They went out to the floor in dismay. One of them was Dawson.

Mr. Arbuckle opened the drawer, laid his hand on the coiled strap within, and then hesitated. It was Monday morning, and their offence was not heinous. Besides, they were boys not often in trouble. Could he risk pardoning them? No, he decided, no he couldn't: pardon was dangerous, it could become a lazy paralysing habit, and indiscipline would soon run riot in the room.

He took out the strap.

Clarkson, a timid boy, faltered the excuse he'd been trying to borrow a knife to sharpen his pencil.

"You'd no right coming in here with a blunt pencil. You're making it worse, Clarkson, instead of better. Out with your hand."

Clarkson, whimpering, held it out, but snatched it back tenderly just as the strap descended. Had Mr. Arbuckle been less expert, his own thigh might have been strapped.

"Double," he said, "if you try that again."

Stirling was watching with pity for Clarkson but far more solicitude for Dawson. The latter, strangely enough, though a cheerful football-playing boy, cried rather easily when hurt. Once he'd skinned his knee in the playground and hadn't been able to keep the tears out of his eyes. If he was hurt now, unfairly, might he not find his revenge where he could?

Clarkson, eyes shut, kept his hand out. He yelped as the strap struck it. Some of his classmates tittered, and Mr. Arbuckle grinned too. He could relent now: justice was being done. But in fairness to Clarkson the other two must be strapped.

Stewart in his kilt was tough. He thrust out his hand, took his whack, and swaggered back to his seat.

Dawson, putting out his hand, involuntarily put out his tongue too.

Mr. Arbuckle in his new good-humour pretended it was a gesture of mockery. He let out a bellow. "Do you dare to put your tongue out at me, Dawson?"

More tittered, and Dawson with a gulp withdrew his tongue. "Sorry, sir. I couldn't help it."

"All right."

The strap purposely just grazed Dawson's fingers, so much so he wasn't sure whether that would do as adequate punishment or whether a second stroke would be necessary.

"Sit down," grunted Mr. Arbuckle. "We're here to do history. If there are to be any more executions, let's read about them in our book."

The class laughed at the joke, and the lesson began. Dawson

sat licking his fingers. His blush took minutes to go away. It was obvious he had been humiliated.

Mr. Arbuckle, when he became keen during a lesson, was liked and trusted. This morning, on the theme of the battle of Flodden, he turned from the bleak mention in the text-book and told them how twenty thousand Scotsmen had been killed, a man from almost every family in lowland Scotland; how the king himself, James IV, the centre of a ring of nobles, had been slain; how when the news reached Edinburgh by a weeping messenger everybody there had been stunned with horror; and how later the king's bloodstained jacket had been sent to Henry VIII in France, as a gift from his wife Katharine of Aragon.

Class 1A, most of them with names represented at the battle, sat thrilled and full of pity.

"For the English who won it," said Mr. Arbuckle, "Flodden was just another border fight with the Scots; for the Scots who lost it has remained one of the greatest days in their history. I wonder why?"

That was a teacher's question, and he looked about for hands up with answers. They were slow to rise. Some, belonging to boys, were dead and bloodied, with swords still gripped by them; others, of the girls, were squirming in the ancient sorrow.

"Why?" repeated the teacher.

Henderson, first to be released by imagination, put up his hand.

"Well, Henderson?"

"Because, sir, the Scots likely killed more Englishmen. I mean, maybe there were more Englishmen to begin with, and if the Scots killed more of them, then the Scots really won."

Mr. Arbuckle wasn't quite sure of the respective sizes of the armies, but he was sure this answer, so matter-of-fact, insulted the glory. Henderson, however, was just a boy.

"I hardly think so, Henderson," he said. "I don't think nations remain for hundreds of years proud of the number of men they've slaughtered. Surely they're more likely to become ashamed of that."

Henderson still standing, shook his head.

"Sit down, Henderson. Well, Rodgers, what's your opinion?"

Rodgers stood up. He spoke out clearly with his English voice. "I think, sir, the Scots are proud of the courage their ancestors showed, and the endurance too."

"Exactly." Mr. Arbuckle found himself thrilling, which was very unusual on a wet Monday morning. "It was superb courage: the modern word is guts. And it's something that's handed down through the generations. In the World War the Scots regiments were second to none for courage."

Stirling noticed that Dawson was frowning, and knew it was because he was ashamed of his timidity while getting the strap.

Mr. Arbuckle clapped his hands: the class was whispering. No doubt it was legitimate talk, they were exchanging examples of courage, perhaps drawn from their own family history. But the rule must always be observed, if anyone had anything to say then let him or her put up a hand.

"Our history is full of such displays of courage," he said. "Can you give me some examples?"

One or two hands went up.

"Well, Georgina?"

"Bruce and the spider, sir."

Some laughed. Mr. Arbuckle smiled. "Courage, Georgina? Was that not an example of perseverance?"

"It's the same thing, sir. My last teacher told me that. She said it was very brave to persevere if things went against you."

"Did she, Georgina?" Mr. Arbuckle smiled: Georgina was a solemn little girl. "And do you take her advice?"

"Yes, sir." Georgina's voice trembled. She had done poorly in the examination, disappointing her parents; but she had vowed to do better next time.

"That's fine, Georgina. Well, Rodgers?"

"Captain Oates was courageous, sir. He walked out of his tent into a blizzard because he was keeping the others back. He was with Captain Scott's expedition to the South Pole."

"True, Rodgers, but he was an Englishman."

"He was brave, all the same, sir."

"Undoubtedly, but I asked for examples from our history."

"Yes, sir. I thought 'our' meant British."

Then the period bell went, ending the argument. Mr. Arbuckle grinned and turned back to his desk, while the class collected its books together and clattered out of the room to go downstairs to mathematics.

Stirling was accompanied by Stewart.

"All right for Arbuckle to talk about courage," said Stewart dourly. "It's not him that gets the strap."

"No," agreed Stirling.

"All the same," admitted Stewart, "it was a good lesson."

Stirling didn't agree, but he did not say so. During the lesson he had kept thinking how easy it was to be brave if people knew you were being brave and gave you credit for it: they forgot everything else except that you were brave. But what about Robert Tull? Had he not been very brave, as brave as any killed at Flodden, coming here to this grand school, the most poorly dressed boy in it, the one with the least money, not very clever either, and openly proclaiming his love for his father who'd been a cripple in a wheel chair? Yet Tull had been laughed at, his bravery had never been recognised, and now he was left nobody remembered him.

Gourlay too was brave: strapped at school, starved at home, detested everywhere, he never yielded and never let anybody see him weep. Better for him surely if he was a coward and always gave in; he would receive far fewer blows and some people would like him.

Yet as he entered the maths room Stirling felt a great yearning for Tull. He knew that if Tull was still at school he would never have confided to him about his own terrors; but it would have been a comfort just to watch Tull's smile and hear his rough dauntless voice.

He did particularly well at geometry that morning. He found it a far safer shelter than history, and solved the three given deductions so fast that Stinker was amazed. Nobody else in the class could solve the third one, and Stirling was invited to stand up and explain how it should be done. He had not wanted that, everybody looking at him, and some trying enviously to find something against him, which could bring him down. There was something too. But he went through the exposition coolly and lucidly.

"Very good, Stirling," said Stinker, "very good indeed."

Afterwards during playtime, under a dripping tree, Henderson maintained to his little court that Stirling must have been shown how to do the deduction at home. When asked who had shown him, as they all knew his father was dead, Henderson suggested perhaps his mother had been a maths teacher, or else he had an uncle who was one. If so, it wasn't fair.

Dawson, playing football, happened to be within hearing. He approached angrily.

"You talk a lot of jealous rot, Henderson," he said. "Can't you just admit it, Stirling's better at maths than you are, much better?"

"If he gets special help," said Henderson doggedly, "that could explain it. How do you know he doesn't?"

"I know."

"How? Do you know everything about Stirling?"

"I know he doesn't get any special help. I know you likely get more than he does. And I wish you'd give Stirling the credit he deserves. He'll be dux, and I'm one that'll cheer when he is."

"There's Stirling," said one. "Go and ask him."

"But would he tell the truth?" asked Henderson.

"He'd be a fool if he was to answer all your questions," said Dawson, and ran across to meet Stirling, take his arm, and pull him towards the school.

"What is it?" asked Stirling faintly.

"Nothing really, Stirling. It's just that jealous fathead Henderson."

Stirling was very pale. "What was he saying?"

"Just that somebody had shown you how to do that deduction."

256

"Somebody? Who?"

Dawson did not say his mother had been mentioned. "I just said you didn't need anybody to show you; it was as easy as pie to you. You'll have to keep beating him, Stirling, or it would be terrible. Can't you just imagine him going about showing all his teeth in glee?"

They went into the school.

Under the tree Henderson was insisting he had been proved right. To weaken Dawson's testimony he had reminded them of how he had behaved in the history class when getting the strap.

Dinner-time came and passed. Dawson took lunch in a restaurant in the town, while Stirling ate his sandwiches in the school. Afterwards he went for a walk in the rain.

It seemed as if that long first day would pass safely; but of course there would be tomorrow with the same sickening dread, and the same smiling dependence on Dawson's faithfulness and on luck. After tomorrow would come the next day, and so on for five years. He saw it could be gone through, but at great cost.

There were times that first day when Stirling, so outwardly composed, felt his very bowels quaking under the stress within him. During the English periods in the afternoon he felt at one time he would have to ask leave to go to the lavatory.

The classroom was quiet, with everybody looking up the meanings of words in their dictionaries, and Mr. Malvern, hoarse with acting Bottom during the first period, was taking a rest at his desk. The door opened and in came the janitor with a note. Many of the scholars glanced up, as they did at every diversion. Stirling, seeking the meaning of reprehensible, kept turning the pages.

Mr. Malvern took the note, nodded his thanks, and the janitor left. Still several watched. They saw the teacher's brows shoot up in exaggerated surprise. Everybody heard his long whistle.

"Dawson," he called.

"Yes, sir?" Dawson stood up.

"And you, Stirling."

Stirling too stood up, very pale.

"The Rector would like to see you both now in his study."

Dawson looked at Stirling in wonder. Stirling seemed to see no one. He tried to put his pencil into the groove on his desk; his fingers trembled so much the pencil fell. The boy in front immediately swooped down and retrieved it. He set it in the groove with a reassuring wink.

"And what have you two desperadoes been up to?" laughed Mr. Malvern.

"Nothing, sir," replied Dawson, "as far as I know."

"And I know our friend Stirling's been up to no other mischief than having all his exercises correct, and breaking all his rivals' hearts. Off you go then. This note says immediately."

They went out into the corridor.

Dawson tried to joke. "Did you see old Hendy's face? I bet he's praying we've been caught cheating in the exams." He laughed nervously when he saw his joke hadn't been noticed. "All the same, I wonder what he wants us for."

"I don't know."

They went downstairs. Stirling touched every green railing in the banister. Dawson didn't notice that, but he couldn't help being aware how slow they were and how pale Stirling's face was.

"Is there anything the matter, Stirling?" he asked.

Stirling shook his head.

"You're terribly white."

They were about to enter the great empty hall, across which was the Rector's study. Dawson paused at a radiator.

"Let's warm our hands," he said, smiling, "just in case. Mine are frozen. What are yours like?" He reached out and touched his companion's hand. But the glimpse of sick terror, so patiently suffered, in Stirling's eyes shocked him into not noticing whether the hand he was holding was cold or not. "Are you feeling ill, Stirling?" he asked. Then the words

258

gushed out in warm friendliness and sympathy. "Listen, Stirling, please. I know about your mother. My mother told me. She shouldn't have, for she broke a promise. But she told me, and I know; and Stirling, it's nothing, nothing at all to be ashamed of. But I'll tell nobody. If I was to be cut in pieces I'd tell nobody."

Stirling gazed into the earnest face with the tears in the eyes, and shook his head.

"It doesn't matter," he murmured.

And indeed it made no difference after all whether Dawson told or not. The secret would leak out in some other way, sooner or later. Nor would it make any difference whether people mocked or like Dawson pretended politely there was nothing to be ashamed of. The whole burden would be too much.

"We'll have to go," whispered Dawson. He kept hold of Stirling's hand as they crossed the hall. "Don't you worry, Stirling." He nodded towards the dux-board. "Your name'll be up there some day."

Stirling did not look up.

Dawson knocked.

"Come in," called the Rector.

He was seated at his desk in the middle of the large comfortable room, and looked so small that, but for his long meek nose, white hair, and black gown, he might have been taken for some joker of a boy playing a prank. Indeed, he was smiling in that character.

Dawson couldn't help grinning at the thought he was as tall as the Rector. It was however a cheerful respectful grin.

Stirling saw nothing funny; he remained pale and serious.

The Rector had his hands clasped on his open copy of the *Iliad*. He peeped through his shrivelled skin and pale blue veins at the Greek, and could not keep from chuckling at the contrast between this little contemporary problem he was about to settle, and the dreadful tribulation of Priam watching Hector's desecrated body dragged along the plain by Achilles. Still, the inspiration of those heroic ancient days afforded not only courage, but wisdom too.

He gazed at the two boys with confidence. He smiled at Dawson who wore most becomingly the Academy uniform, blazer, tie, and stockings. At Stirling, who wore none of these, he refrained from frowning.

"Gerald Dawson and John Stirling of 1A?" he asked.

"Yes, sir," said Dawson promptly.

Stirling nodded.

"Sit down, boys."

They sat on chairs at the edge of the green carpet.

There followed a silence in which could be heard only the ticking of the clock on the wall and the crackling of the fire. It was hard to remember they were in a school with over a thousand boys and girls; that in less than an hour there would be heard outside the happy cries of those boys and girls liberated to go home.

The Rector, hunched in his black gown, smiled too amiably to seem an enchanter.

He turned with especial mildness to Stirling.

"I hear wonderful reports from all your teachers, John."

Stirling waited.

But the Rector turned to Dawson. He lifted one hand from the book to wag a long finger.

"You, Harold, don't seem to be meeting with as much success."

"Gerald, sir. No, I'm afraid not, sir."

The report on Dawson had been: eager, good-natured, happy, trustworthy, well-mannered boy, somewhat deficient in academic attainment, but intelligent enough.

Stroking his chin, the Rector stared at him. Failure in scholarship was a pity, always; but there could be compensations sometimes; and it had to be remembered that in all probability the great Achilles had not shone at school.

"I'll do better next time, sir," volunteered Dawson.

The Rector was relieved. He smiled. Here surely was the authentic heroic spirit, however humbly shown.

"Very well spoken, Harold."

"Gerald, sir." Dawson's voice had laughter in it.

"Gerald is it?" The Rector nodded, but without repentance. Modern names seemed to him cacophonous, compared with such magnificent sonorities as Aeschylus, Demosthenes, Xenophon.

He turned to Stirling. "Your mother was here to see me this afternoon, John."

"My mother, sir?"

After the shock, Stirling felt, next second, he'd scream, fall down on his face, and weep into this green carpet as he'd wept last night into the cold grass. Outwardly he remained composed, only a little paler. His mother would have on her old coat and hat. Had she sat on this chair or on Dawson's or on that empty one nearer the desk? Likely that one. Her hands would be clasped, and in gloves: their scrubberwife's rawness would not be seen. She'd try to speak as genteelly as she could, and her voice luckily was low and respectable. But, oh Christ, what had she to come here for? Who else had seen her?

"An admirable woman, your mother, John," said the Rector. Then he laughed. "Though she did seem in a way to regard me as an ogre, a Cyclops with one eye."

Almost crazy with despair, Stirling waited, face as emotionless as a doll's.

"She particularly begged me not to inform you she had been here." Again the Rector laughed, and glanced up at the clock. "She seemed to think it would upset you. I told her that was nonsense. I told her boys were made of sterner stuff. I'm glad to see she was wrong, and I was right. You should, of course, be very proud of your mother, John. I hope you appreciate the great sacrifice she is making on your behalf."

"Yes, sir." His appreciation of that was like a red-hot bar laid across his brain.

"You have a sacred duty to your mother," went on the Rector, more solemnly. "And, if I may add, to myself too. For do you know what I did? I took your mother out into the hall and showed her the dux-board. Now you must understand that I, as Rector, must be impartial towards all you scholars. I must have no favourites."

"No, sir," agreed Dawson.

Stirling waited.

"Nevertheless, John," continued the Rector, warmly, with authority, "I showed your mother the dux-board and suggested to her she might some day see your name upon it. She went away, therefore, with tears; tears, I need hardly add, of happiness." He kept nodding firmly. It was to reassure himself, for he hadn't been at all convinced Mrs. Stirling's tears were of unadulterated joy. She had seemed to be, in spite of her obvious worthiness, rather a moody, pessimistic little person. Naturally he had made every allowance.

He did not think it necessary to add it was his custom while showing parents out, to indicate the dux-board to them with its golden promise.

"Mind you, John," he added, "you will have to strive very hard if you are to remain on the peak. Keen winds of competition blow here in Muirton. It is not easy to remain supreme. Not only scholarship of the highest class is required; character too is essential. But you must strive, John, for your mother's sake."

Yes, he must: for his own sake too. Supposing it was discovered she was a cleaner, that sometimes she'd to get money from the parish, he might be protected by his brilliance, but only if he stayed at the very top. If he slipped, next year or the next again, as he might, for the work would become harder and circumstances at home would worsen as his needs grew greater, if he slipped then to even second or third place there would be no protection and no consolation.

The Rector, catching a glimpse of Achilles between his fingers, regretted there was no opportunity here for heroic decision. He felt a little peeved that he was compelled to smile now like some simple-minded benevolent uncle.

"Your mother and I had quite a confidential little chat," he said, and inappropriately frowned. He could not help it. Had there been in Mrs. Stirling's attitude a perverseness, a defiance, hardly complimentary to him? "Yes," he went on, smiling again, "we had a nice little chat. She was telling me she used to do a little—housework for Mrs. Dawson." He nodded approval of his choice of word. Tact and courtesy were as necessary in dealing with children as with adults; and very often children were tactful and courteous in return, whereas adults were curt and brusque. "I understand, of course, John, you are not—shall we say keen?—that this should be shouted around the school. It's a little matter best kept private, eh?"

"Yes, sir."

The Rector noticed nothing peculiar about that quiet affirmative. He sharpened his own voice a little. "Now I want you to understand this, and I am speaking with the utmost sincerity." He clenched one fist and rapped on the page of Greek. "There is nothing, absolutely nothing, to be ashamed of in being poor. You must understand that. It is——" and here it occurred to him that Homer had been only a blind minstrel—"a shining universal truth."

This time Stirling did not murmur yes. Being poor meant to the Rector not having as much money as somebody else. It did not mean being terrified his suit would wear out, for it couldn't be replaced. It did not mean having a raincoat bought off a second-hand clothes barrow. It did not mean an oil-lamp at home because the gas had been cut off. It did not mean his mother at court for arrears of rent. It did not mean his sister hating him because he'd prevented her getting new gloves.

The Rector relaxed: it was obvious this was a clever boy, he listened so intelligently; and his confidence was being won.

"Indeed," added the Rector, smiling, "in our country being poor has often been a mark of honour. Many famous Scotsmen as boys were very poor. There was David Livingstone for instance, and Thomas Carlyle, and even Robert Burns, our national bard. What names are more honoured now?"

Yes, now. Stirling's mother had used this argument, and he had tried to let it deceive him. But he knew that if afterwards he was ever to become famous he would look back on these years of poverty, shame, and despair, not with amusement or pride, but with fear and sorrow.

The Rector glanced at the clock. Then, confident he'd reassured Stirling, he hurried to deal with Dawson.

"I'm sure, Harold, you'll understand why I wanted you to hear what I had to say to John."

"Oh yes, sir."

"You and I and John here are the only ones who know our little secret."

Dawson grinned uncomfortably. He wished to please the Rector, who was trying his best; but he was aware Stirling must be suffering and he didn't want to add to it.

"We can depend on you, Harold?"

"Yes, sir," murmured Dawson.

The Rector was delighted. He liked the Hellenic frankness of this smiling lad, and thought him, in his Academy uniform, a credit to the school.

"Very good," he said. "Very good indeed." With a gracious gesture he closed his Homer; he had not, he felt, disgraced the mighty and beautiful lines. "Well, boys, as you see it's nearly four o'clock. You'll want to get back to your room to collect your books."

"Yes, sir."

The Rector noticed it was the alert Dawson who answered. Stirling, in appearance so like his mother, seemed also to have inherited a little of her pessimism.

"Fine then. Perhaps we'll have another little chat some other day."

"Yes, sir." Dawson rose smartly. "Thank you, sir."

The Rector beamed. "Thank you, Harold." He even jumped up and hurried over to open the door for them, as if they were his guests.

Dawson went out first. "Good-night, sir."

"Good-night, Harold."

The Rector, chuckling, on an impulse touched Stirling's brow. It was drenched in sweat. At first he thought the room had been too warm, but quickly realised the inadequacy of such an explanation. He was shaken in his confidence. For a moment he sensed tragic suffering in this little boy; then he dismissed that, as too exaggerated. He watched them cross the hall, Dawson's hand on Stirling's shoulder.

Dawson did not know what to say. He kept glancing anxiously at Stirling.

"Did you hear him keep on calling me Harold?" he asked. "All the same, he's a decent old ass, though I'll admit he does talk at times like an old wife. I heard Mr. Forbes call him that to Arbuckle. But he tries to be fair."

They went upstairs. Noises customary at three minutes to four were heard: desks being banged up, classes being marshalled at doors, teachers bawling last orders.

It would come out, thought Stirling, till the whole school knew. Dawson would not tell, but the Rector would. He was an old wife, true enough, and he would blether it to some teacher. Pupils would overhear, and so it would spread.

"Do you think," asked Dawson anxiously, "he was talking a lot of rot?"

Stirling lied. "No," he murmured. The truth would have stirred up many terrors. For the same reason he postponed thinking about his mother's visit.

Dawson was relieved. "I'm glad," he said, smiling, with a firmer squeeze of Stirling's arm.

Stirling could not help responding to that smile and squeeze. He smiled himself, faintly and briefly. When it did come out, the best of them, like Dawson and Rodgers and Stewart would be on his side always; they would rush to his rescue against sneerers like Henderson. But five years of pity and sneers, humiliation, rescue and vigilance, would be a long time. He felt now he would be able to endure it, but it would be full of suffering, with himself always his worst and most cunning persecutor; and of course it might not end in success.

They found their class lined up at the door. Georgina Meikle was at the front. She gave Stirling a smile as he passed. She often prattled about him at home, praising his ability and modesty, to the amusement of her parents. Stirling smiled back at her, and murmured "Excuse me, please," as he pushed past.

Henderson grabbed Dawson by the blazer; his face was tormented with curiosity.

265

"What was it, Gerald?" he asked. "What did he want you for?"

"Didn't I tell you?" asked Dawson. "We were cheating a the exams."

"Yah," said Henderson, unwillingly incredulous. "Wha was it for really?"

Dawson and Stirling hurried to their desks for their cases Mr. Malvern had already gone.

The bell shrilled and the class marched off.

"Some hopes, cheating!" shouted Henderson, as he left "But I'll find out tomorrow, Dawson."

Dawson and Stirling went out when the rest had gone.

"Don't worry about old Hendy," said Dawson. "If he had smaller teeth he'd be a decent chap. It's his father really, he wants Hendy to be dux and keeps worrying him. Did you hear him call me Gerald? I'll jolly soon shut him up tomorrow if he has the cheek to ask."

Stirling smiled. Of course Henderson would ask tomorrow and somebody else would ask something else the next day There would be questions. He knew he would have to answer them or at least face them; and he knew the cost. But hope, which had lit up outside Gourlay's cellar last night, was not quite out.

"It doesn't matter," he murmured. "I'll be all right."

Dawson was delighted. "Of course you'll be all right. You'll be dux. Good for you, Stirling."

Then they entered the turmoil of the cloakroom and were separated.

Chapter Twelve

ON THE bus going home, Stirling was able to relax. Other Academy pupils were there, some of them obstreperous enough to have the conductress rebuke them two or three times; but crouched in his seat next to the window, with a fat woman shutting him off, he felt temporarily safe and gazed out at the lamplit streets, the skip of his cap touching the glass, and all his worries lying in his mind quiet and gathered.

Not even when the bus stopped to set someone down at the stop where Robert Tull used to get off, did any of those worries rise and snarl. Stirling smiled faintly. He did not expect to see Tull, nor did he see him. He thought he would never again all his life see him; and he knew he would remember him always, with wonder and a strange envy. No, Tull wasn't there; but under a lamp-post were two girls about his age. One shoved a pram to and fro with one hand, while with the other she held something, bread or apple or lollipop to her mouth. The other girl was bouncing a ball. Stirling saw them for less than a minute, but, associated with Tull, they would remain memorable. The baby in the pram seemed to be crying.

It was dark when he got off the bus and hurried down the road beside the burn to his house. Not even yet had he decided how he would greet his mother, whether with gratitude for her brave journey to the Academy on his behalf, or with a passion of resentment against her stupid interference, or even, most cruelly, with a long silent calculated sulk, which would torment her all evening.

He entered the close, still undecided. He put his hand on the door handle and made to turn it, still not knowing what he should do when his mother, after pretending to be busy with

267

preparations for tea, would turn to him with the appeal in her eyes.

The handle turned, but the door wouldn't open: it was locked. He was so astonished he tried again and again, although he knew it was useless. So confident had he been his mother would be in, ready to endure his anger or be delighted by his forgiveness, that he couldn't bring himself to believe she was out. Yet the door was locked, and when he bent to lift the mat there lay the key.

Trembling, his composure shattered, he opened the door and entered the dark house.

"Mother," he called from the lobby, "mother, are you there?"

There was no answer. From the door still open he heard footsteps hurry down the road. He closed the door, and his heart began to race as if, by that simple and necessary act, he'd committed himself to some ordeal.

Stumbling into the kitchen, he could see no glow from the fire: it seemed to be out. From the scullery came sighings of air in pipes.

"Mother," he called again, "please, mother. It's all right. I'm not angry you went to the Academy. It's all right. Gerald Dawson's my friend. The Rector said——" He stopped, for he felt if he continued to talk thus to himself in the empty house he would rush into an uncontrollable panic.

He groped along the mantelpiece for the matches. Striking one, he looked resolutely for the oil lamp and paid no heed to the shadows leaping monstrously up the walls. That match went out as he wondered, with the panic again threatening, if he would have the courage and resourcefulness to light the lamp. In the darkness he forced himself to smile.

He lit it safely, at the expense of eight matches. Afraid of fire, of cracking the globe, he kept the wick low, so that the light given was feeble, with the great shadows permanent. Pride in the achievement gave him resolution to achieve more. He set to work rekindling the fire, finding sticks in the oven, paper under the cushion, and coal in the dark mouse-haunted cellar. The job was done, and he was standing, brow against the cold tiles of the fireplace, watching the little flames like hopes flicker, grow, die away, and reappear, when he remembered he still had his Academy clothes on and perhaps had dirtied them.

He changed into his old shorts and jersey.

Lifting the clock, he was bewildered and alarmed to find the time twenty-five minutes to two. It couldn't be: he was home from school; outside it was dark; it must be at least five o'clock. Then, noticing the tremendous increase of silence, he realised the clock was stopped. He shook it and after several hiccups it restarted. He turned the hands to indicate five o'clock. His mother, he thought, after the visit to the Academy, must have gone straight on to some new job. Involuntarily then, indeed almost against his will, a rush of understanding and gratitude filled him. The Rector had praised his mother, but it had been out of politeness and a desire to relieve John's own snobbish fears. Now the boy saw, perhaps for the first time in his life, saw vividly and nakedly the real nature of his mother's love for him. He saw it as in an inspiration, which inevitably faded. Ten minutes later, as he set the table for tea and worried about his Latin and French exercises waiting to be done, he was pitying himself again and blaming her for taking so long to come home.

Lamp lit, fire rekindled, kettle filled, table set, himself changed, he felt free to begin his homework. It would be the best way to postpone his anxiety until Mary came home. She would know what to do. At any rate she would relieve him of most of the burden of worrying about their mother.

But he found he could not concentrate on his Latin. Simple words like *ambulo* and *nuntio* which he had used dozens of times seemed strange as if he was seeing them for the first time. An easy sentence like 'The soldiers and sailors of the king love their native land' suddenly had become too difficult. It was as if the part of his brain for doing Latin was paralysed. He could not understand what was wrong and painstakingly looked up the lost meanings or searched through his Grammar for conjugations he had learnt by heart. Even when he found the meaning: *ambulo; I walk*, it still seemed strange to him, and he could not make up his mind what tense to use.

He had to put down his pencil and cover his face with his hands. His eyes were tired: perhaps that was the reason, perhaps the light was too poor. He could improve it by rising and turning the wick up only a quarter of an inch, but he sat still, face covered by his cold hands. He remembered dully and stupidly the events of the day. Like the Latin they were incomprehensible.

The rattling of the door handle, the opening of the door, and the entry of either Mary or his mother, had him jumping to his feet with a cry of relief and hurrying to welcome whoever it was. He hoped it was his mother. He would not complain to her about her visit to the school, not then at any rate, but he would tell her he might have to leave all the same as he was unaccountably finding the Latin too difficult, he seemed for some reason to have lost his ability.

It was Mary. She pushed past him into the kitchen.

"What a poorhouse light!" she cried, and turned up the wick dangerously high.

The kitchen became very bright and alien.

Mary drew off her gloves. She did it ostentatiously, with fastidious sneer, so that he was reminded how last night these gloves had caused all the trouble.

"Where's mother?" she asked.

"I don't know."

She smiled, took off her hat, rumpled her hair, and then went out into the lobby to hang up her coat.

"So you don't know?" she asked, as she came in again.

"No, Mary."

"Did she leave a note?"

"No."

"I suppose she's landed another job. Well, if there's anything for eating I'm going to take my tea. I'm hungry."

He realised he was hungry too. "There's a wee bit cheese."

"Mouldy, I suppose. But it'll have to do. Is the kettle near the boil?"

"I think so. It's been singing."

"Has it?" She laughed. "Well, it doesn't look as if it's been a duet." Vigorously she pokered the fire and set the kettle more firmly on the flames. Her back was to him. "Well, and did the dragon Dawson bite you?"

"Bite me?"

"You know what I mean. Did he roar your disgrace all over the school?"

"No."

"He didn't even look at you. One thing you've got to learn: people are too busy thinking about themselves to worry about you or anybody else. This is a selfish world. You should know."

Yes, he knew: in his own case she was right. But she was wrong in Gerald Dawson's case. Gerald was not selfish.

"I'll make some toast," said Mary, "as an added delicacy. You can get on with your homework."

Obediently he sat down at the Latin, but found the paralysis still afflicted him.

Mary sat at the fire, holding the bread close to the ribs. She forgot her brother and smiled into the flames at her own dreams. That day, coming down in the lift, she'd spoken again to the boy who worked in Thomson and Sourby's office. He was about eighteen and had fair hair. His voice was always laughing and he had dimples, though nobody could say his face was effeminate. She was sure she had impressed him.

Turning her head casually she noticed her brother wasn't working. His hands were clasped on his knees, and his eyes were closed.

"What's the matter?" she asked.

He didn't seem to hear.

"I asked, what's up?" she shouted.

He turned to her with a weary smile. "Nothing, Mary."

"You're sitting there as if it was beyond you. What is it?"

"Latin."

"I thought you were a genius at Latin."

He sighed. "It's mother."

271

"Don't expect me to believe you're worrying about her Anyhow, she's often been as late as this."

He said nothing.

"I'm glad all the same you are worrying about her. It's taken you a long time. I hope you realise what you owe to her."

"Yes."

"Then please show it occasionally. Sometimes it seems as if instead of being grateful to her, you had a grudge against her. When a word from you would make her happy, and make her feel her sacrifices were worth it, you won't give her that word, you give her its opposite, and then she's in misery. I've seen it often."

He could say nothing. He was amazed by her percipience.

"I know you're young," said Mary, turning the toast with a frown for she'd let it burn during her eloquence. Then she laughed. "Three years younger than me," she added. "Just three years, and here I'm talking to you like a granny."

"I'm grateful to my mother," he murmured.

"Then show it, once in a while. And let me remind you that the best way to show isn't by letting her see you're utterly ashamed of her. I'll admit," she added, coolly, "it's nothing to rejoice about that she's to scrub out offices and other people's houses, but it's nothing to be ashamed of either."

He had not yet said what several times he'd been on the point of saying: that his mother had been at the Academy that day.

"Well, that should be enough," said Mary. She came over to the table, where she spread margarine on the toast. "It must be marvellous to be able to afford butter," she said. "You read in magazines of hot buttered toast. 'The heroine came in from walking over the moors to tea with hot buttered toast.' " She laughed as she returned to the fireplace for the teapot. " 'The heroine came in from addressing envelopes all afternoon to tea with margarined toast.' It's a good job we have a sense of humour and can laugh at ourselves." She laughed again, still more defiantly; and the boy with the fair hair and the dimples laughed with her.

The other boy, her brother, with the black hair and serious

eyes, gazed at her in surprise. He could not understand how she could be so merry when their mother had still not returned.

"That's the trouble with you, of course," she said, as she sat down at table. "You don't laugh at yourself enough. Look at your doing Latin. Great emperors spoke it thousands of years ago, and here you, with your darned jersey and your margarined toast, are trying to learn to speak it. I think that's very funny."

He smiled: it was funny enough. That would have been a good moment for his mother to arrive, he thought: Mary and he laughing together, the tea hot in the cups, the fire burning cheerfully, the house warm and bright. If she had returned then he would have assured her not to worry about him any more; that, whatever anybody said, he was determined to do his best and recompense her.

She did not return then. They ate their meal in silence, except that Mary hummed snatches of song as she read a magazine propped against the milk jug. Nibbling at bread and cheese, he thought she sang to torment him. Once she remarked, as if to nobody in particular, still keeping her eyes on her magazine: "Still worried?" She had noticed his quick glance towards the clock on the mantelpiece. He nodded, although worried was too vague a description of his feelings. Not only did he yearn to see his mother, to know she was safe and well, he also wanted to weep to her, not hostilely, not against her, weep away his anxieties on her lap, tell her of all his fears and forebodings, and of his hopes and resolutions. He felt that somehow, in the long war against his own weakness, he could that night win an important battle: if only his mother were there, if only she would come soon!

Tea over, Mary, whistling a tune he'd heard her play on her violin, jumped to her feet, walked or rather danced across to the mantelpiece, jauntily picked up the clock, glanced at it, and danced back, still whistling, to the table.

He thought her cheerfulness was false.

"Finished?" she asked.

He nodded.

"I'll clear away," she said.

"Are you———" the words were like dry crusts in his mouth—"are you going to leave my mother's place?"

"Of course. She'll be in soon, and she'll want her tea, won't she?"

Again he nodded. Then with a sigh he drew back his chair to give Mary room to clear away.

"You can get on with your emperor Latin," she said, and went into the scullery where she set about washing the dishes.

He put out his books again and struggled to concentrate on them, but he kept glancing towards the clock and towards Mary singing in the scullery.

Soon she appeared with the washed dishes.

"I'd better wash my stockings while I'm at it," she said. "I got them splashed today. A fool in a big car did it." She quickly stripped them off. "I wonder what it's like having a dozen pairs." Smiling with more anticipation than envy she opened the drawer reserved for her belongings, and tenderly looked in it for her other pair of stockings, her best pair, those she wore on Sundays, those she'd wear if ever the fair-haired boy asked her out.

She couldn't find them. Her search became anxious, irascible, in the end frantic. She threw things out on the floor.

"She can't have pawned them," she cried. "Surely they don't take stockings in the pawn? Yet where are they?" Another fear struck her. She dashed to a cupboard, dragged it open, and with a cry of relief turning quickly to rage brought out a white box. It was empty and she flung it furiously on the floor. "My shoes too!" she cried. "She's gone and pawned my shoes and stockings!" She began to weep in anger but also in genuine distress. "My poor shoes and stockings. I'd to save up for weeks and weeks to help to get them." She caught sight of her brother gazing at her in unhappy sympathy. She rushed at him. "You know what she's done with them," she shrieked. "Now I see what's been worrying you. You've been frightened I would find out before she came home to protect you. What has she done with them?" She enforced that question with a smart blow on his head. "I owe you that anyway for last night.

274

Last night it was me who was struck, if you remember, but it ought to have been you. What is it you need now, that she's gone and pawned my shoes and stockings?"

The shrieks terrified him more than the fear of further blows. Amidst them insisted the quiet questions: where is my mother? is she safe?

"I don't know, Mary," he said. "I never asked for anything."

But she'd caught sight of something that snatched her attention away from him. Under the sofa were shoes that astonished her by their simple presence there. She picked them up and both she and her brother gazed in silence at them, old, creased, with circles of ruin on their soles and with the heels chewed by much anxious hurrying.

They were their mother's shoes, her only pair.

"She must have mine on," cried Mary, in indignation hardly alleviated by relief that after all they hadn't been pawned.

John understood: his mother must have borrowed them for her visit to the Academy. Then, with a resurrection of his qualms and terrors, he realised how shabby and poor she must have been, despite the new shoes. Her coat was old, worn, drab, even dirty; she could not wear Mary's Sunday one, which was too small for her round the waist; nor Mary's best hat, which she'd tried on once, saying it reminded her of what she'd been like twenty years ago.

"And my stockings too," cried Mary. "She'll be wearing them. Good God," she shrieked in despair, "she'll ruin them, she'll make them all baggy. They'll be no use to me again. Is that not maddening?"

He knew if he explained Mary wouldn't be mollified but rather would be more exasperated.

"It's a good job," said Mary vindictively, "she's dumpy and shapeless. Otherwise she'd have my coat on as well. Where has she got to go to, that she's to go all dressed up?"

Not much dressed up, he thought.

"Wait till she comes home," cried Mary. "She'll hear me. It's about high time I stuck up for myself here. I can see I'm being victimised."

For the next hour or so she continued in this selfpitying rebellious strain, with an occasional jab of a finger in her brother's back for emphasis.

He struggled through his lessons and at last finished them, with no confidence they were free from mistakes. As he put his books into his case, he imagined his French and Latin teachers, after they'd corrected these exercises, talking to each other in the staffroom and saying that Stirling was slipping. Soon that dreadful discovery would be known to the whole school. He wished his mother was in, not to look over his work for of course she could not, but just to listen to his explanations and believe his assurances that, given peace, he would still be as good as ever.

He sat by the fire and tried to read.

Mary pushed past him, knocking the book off his knees. She grabbed up the clock. "Stopped," she snapped, and gave it some irritable shakes.

"Does it need wound up?" he asked.

"No, it doesn't. It needs flung into the dustbin."

He choked back a yawn. "What time is it?"

"How do I know? Didn't you hear me say it's stopped?"

"What time did it stop at?"

"Quarter to nine."

"Do you think it's much after that?"

"How should I know? You're the genius of the family."

But he saw her anger was not directed against him but against their mother's lateness.

"She was at the Academy today," he murmured.

She only partly heard. "What? What did you say? Who was at the Academy?"

"My mother."

Her reponse astonished him. She burst out laughing. "What in heaven's name was she doing there?"

"She went to see the Rector."

"Did she? What a nerve she had! Was it about Dawson the dragon? Was it to get his teeth pulled out?"

That mocking way of looking at it disconcerted him. "I didn't

276

see her," he muttered. "The Rector sent for me and told me she'd been."

"So that's why she put on my shoes and stockings! I was right after all. It was for you. Everything's for you. I don't see what you're worried about just now. If she's late, you can be sure in some way it's for your sake."

Not for the first time he wondered if that were true. Had his mother, by some miracle, gone to get a blazer, say, or an over-coat? Then, in a moment, he realised how foolish it was to give way to such hope, and also how selfish. He strove to think of his mother's lateness as it concerned her only. Had she been knocked down by a car? Was she, so late as this, still working on her knees, for him?

Mary unexpectedly answered that last question. "She can't be working," she said. "At least I hope she isn't. She's got on my good shoes and stockings. Of course," she added sarcasti-cally, "she could take them off and scrub away in her bare feet."

He nodded, and drowsily missed the sarcasm. It was quite likely his mother, if offered a job suddenly with no time to come home and change, would work in her bare feet. He smiled, still without sarcasm or bitterness, as he saw how inevitably in her efforts to help him his mother must humiliate him. There was no escape for either of them. That morning he had been terrified people at school would find out his mother was an ordinary scrubberwoman, with shoes and stockings on; now he had to face their discovery of her working, like a slave or peasant, in her bare feet. Hundreds of people, many of them with Academy caps and blazers crowded round him and his bare-footed mother. He had his case in his hand, she carried a pail full of dirty water. The people crowding round jeered and shouted.

Mary gave him a push. "You're falling asleep."

He was confused. For a minute, as his eyes opened, he thought everything had been a dream, the people jeering, his mother in her bare feet, his mother at the Academy with Mary's shoes and stockings on, the green carpet in the Rector's room, Dawson taking his hand by the radiator in the hall.

"If you're going to sleep," said Mary, "you'd better go to bed."

He shook his head.

"What good do you think your staying up will do? Are your brains not supposed to be fresh in the morning?"

"I couldn't sleep," he muttered.

She laughed. "Why, you were sound when I gave you that push."

"No."

"Oh, you were. I spoke to you and you didn't answer."

"I didn't know."

"Of course you didn't: you were asleep. I asked you if you thought she's gone to Aunt Bessie's."

He shook his head. Surely his mother hadn't gone to Aunt Bessie's. She lived in a Glasgow slum. She had six children and her husband, it seemed, was seldom working but was often drunk. John remembered seeing her twice only. She was older than his mother. He could think of no reason why his mother should want to go there, especially after visiting the Academy. Surely she should want to let the distance between her and Aunt Bessie grow wider and wider.

He yawned.

"Oh, go to bed," said Mary.

"No."

"I don't understand it," said Mary crossly. "Why couldn't she leave a note as she usually does? You said the fire was out when you came home?"

"Yes."

"So she's not been home since she left the Academy?"

"No."

Mary frowned. "Did anything happen there to upset her? Did you make a scene?"

"No. I didn't see her."

"Maybe the Rector said something that frightened her?"

That suggestion frightened John. "No, no. He said I should be proud of her."

"Did it take him to tell you that?"

278

"He said he told her I had a good chance some day of being dux."

"How nice of him."

"He's nice, but he's——" He could not, in his weariness, find a word to describe the Rector's strange childish ignorance.

"So she should have come away delighted?"

He nodded.

Mary sneered. "Maybe."

Then, in the silence that fell, they heard the outer door handle turning, and, as they gazed at each other, they heard their mother enter.

"Thank goodness," muttered Mary, with a long sigh.

John's eyes filled with tears.

Mary walked briskly across to the kitchen door and flung it open. "Well, you're a fine one," she cried cheerfully. "Don't you think you deserve a smacking, coming home as late as this?"

John, in tears, loved his sister for her cheerfulness. He waited for his mother to come in.

She came in quietly, dressed in the familiar drab coat and subdued hat. She carried a small parcel wrapped in brown paper.

They had seen her enter thus many times. Yet this time there was a terrifying difference. There was a remoteness about her small face, a fatal bitter resignation about the tightness of her lips, and a repudiation of everything previously dear and important to her as she glanced at Mary by the door, at John at the fire, and at the table set with her place for tea.

She threw the parcel on to the sofa.

"Why are you no' in bed?" she asked harshly.

John dared not reply.

Mary, who had glanced at her shoes, replied with some indignation. "We were waiting up for you," she said. "It's pretty late, you know. We were anxious."

Their mother laughed. "Anxious aboot me? Do you expect me to believe that?"

"Yes," cried Mary, "I do."

Her mother laughed again and gazed away. She muttered something.

"What did you say?" asked Mary.

"Nothing. When did I ever say onything that was ever listened to?"

Mary turned and glanced at her brother. She noticed his tears.

"Is there anything the matter, mother?" she asked crisply. "I don't think it's at all fair, coming home so late and then being mysterious about it."

"Fair?" repeated her mother. "Fair? When was onybody ever fair to me?"

"Never mind past occasions, mother. I'm referring to the present. Something seems to be the matter. What is it?"

"Nothing's the maitter, nothing at a', except that I'm finished."

"Finished?"

"Aye, finished wi' the whole bluidy effort." The sudden screamed swear, the first she'd ever used, shocked them. "For years I've struggled, and a' my sacrifices hae been flung back in my face, like mud; aye, like mud. Did ye think I never had ony pride?"

Mary frowned at this attack. "What have I done?" she cried.

"It's not you. You ken it's not you."

Mary again glanced round at her brother. Her first impulse was to step aside and let him suffer their mother's spite, as he deserved; but she decided to take his part, from thrawnness and pity.

"And it shouldn't be him either," she said. "I don't see what harm he's doing."

"Last night," muttered her mother.

"Last night's past."

"I struck you."

"I said it's past."

"Never for me." Mrs. Stirling kept shaking her head in a fashion Mary thought silly and weak.

"What's the good of saying that, mother?" she asked. "You

know fine you'll have forgotten it by next week. I think you'd better sit down and take some tea. The kettle's boiling. It's been boiling for hours. You haven't told us yet where you've been."

Mrs. Stirling held up her head: she thought she was looking dignified, but Mary thought her huffy.

"Am I answerable to my weans?" she asked.

Mary shrugged. "Please yourself," she said. "I don't think I really want to know."

Mrs. Stirling at last began to take off her hat and coat. As she threw them on the sofa she picked up the small parcel. She handed it to Mary.

Mary, making the tea, found it inconvenient at that moment to take the parcel; besides, she needed the small delay for her pride's sake.

"Just a minute, mother," she said coolly. "What is it?"

"Open it and see."

John was reminded of that summer's evening, a long time ago, when his mother had returned with his parcels.

Mary, without hurry, poured the water into the teapot. Calmly she took the parcel and unwrapped the paper. A pair of gloves was disclosed.

Neither pride nor surprise could stifle her delight. She cried out and pressed them to her lips. They were the kind she'd wanted, the very pair she'd pointed out to her mother in the shop window.

"Thanks," she cried, drawing them on.

"It was the least I could do."

John, watching as closely as he could for tiredness, felt excluded.

Mary held up her hands, fingers outspread.

"But how could you afford them?" she cried. "Where did you get the money?"

Mrs. Stirling sat down at the table, as if patiently waiting for her tea to be poured. She did not immediately answer.

Mary was inclined not to repeat her question. It might reveal unpleasantness, and she preferred to enjoy her new gloves.

Carefully, lovingly, she drew them off. "They're lovely," she said. Then she gaily poured out her mother's tea.

Mrs. Stirling stirred it. "You're no' asking me again," she muttered.

Mary's gaiety went. "No. To tell you the truth I was afraid. I can see I was right. Well, where did you get the money? Don't tell me you stole it?"

Mrs. Stirling smiled bitterly at her daughter's laughter. "I did," she muttered. "In a way, I did."

Mary, glancing at the gloves on the table, saw them turn ugly and hateful. It was a transformation customary in that house. Her face hardened.

"Tell us," she said. "Don't be mysterious."

Her mother spoke with eyes closed; she still stirred her tea. "I used the rent money."

Mary's fists clenched. "Did you?" she asked, quietly.

"I did."

"You were warned, weren't you, that if you missed another week, we might be turned out of the house?"

"That's so. It micht be the streets for us."

"For God's sake," cried Mary, "what's the matter with you?"

"I've told you: I'm finished. It's been a long struggle, and I've gi'en in. That's all." Suddenly she opened her eyes and at the same time stopped stirring her tea. With the spoon she pointed to John. It was a quiet but dreadful gesture. "Ask him," she said.

Mary glanced at him so mute, pale, and exhausted.

"All right," she said. "I know you were at the Academy. He told me. But he said nothing happened there to upset you."

"Did he tell you that?"

"Yes, he did."

"Little he kens me."

"I can't say, mother, I know you very well myself in this mood."

Mrs. Stirling smiled. "Do you ken where I've been a' night?"

282

"I don't."

"I've been at the pictures."

"The pictures!"

"Aye. I had a shilling left, and I thocht I would go in for a est. It was dark. A body cannae greet in public. It's no' decent."

Again Mary glanced at her brother, as if to ask him what he nade of all this. She was so struck by the resemblance between iim and their mother that she smiled. He saw her smile, but lid not resent it though he felt ruin rushing upon them all.

"Don't think I gret though," said Mrs. Stirling, "and don't hink I'm going to greet here." Yet her voice was familiarly lose to weeping. "I hae gret too often."

Mary put her hand on her mother's head. "What's wrong?" he asked.

Her mother tried, but not insistently, to shake off Mary's iand. "Nothing's wrang that wasnae wrang before," she said, nd after a pause began to weep. It was to be a dreadful weeping, hough it began so quietly. It was like a storm beginning with few drops of rain on high trees. John felt it coming; it was the uin he had foreseen; and though he sat amidst it pale, silent, nd not understanding, it disturbed and terrified his inmost soul.

"I'm going to put up wi' it nae longer, Mary," wept their nother.

Mary's voice was gentle. "Is it some new debt?" she asked.

"Debt? You can ca' it that if you like. I brought him into the vorld, and they say that's a kind o' debt a mither owes her vean. But I hae been paying it back as much as I was capable. You're a witness to that yourself. You ken how I've fended for iim; you ken how you've been neglected for his advantage."

"No."

"Aye, you hae. Last night I struck you. All night I never lept for thinking o' it."

"You know I forgave you."

"If you did, Mary, you never showed it."

Mary was silent. That charge was true. Last night she'd lept beside her mother unreconciled, and this very morning he'd gone off to work still in a huff.

"But don't think I blame you. You're right in this worl' never to forget blows. If you forget them, you get mair. I wer' to the Academy today, Mary."

"I know, mother. That's nothing to worry about."

"I swithered aboot going. I kent it would be a great risk, bu' I thocht, if it could be kept secret, it might do some good. Bu' the Rector yonder for a' his black gown and his education' nothing but a silly auld man wha thinks a' things can be mende' wi' a smile and twa or three nice words. He wouldnae agree no' to tell. He kept saying it would be a mistake to keep it secre' He said shame's a thing must be brought oot into the open' otherwise it will eat the hert away. He seemed to think he ken' my ain son better than I did. And I couldnae argue wi' him; hadnae the words, and I hadnae the claithes. Yon was na' place for me, and I kent I had made a mistake to go. I put o' your new shoes and stockings, Mary."

"Yes, I know. That's all right. But you're wrong to worry about this. John's not angry with you. Ask him."

Mrs. Stirling would not; nor would she face him. Instead she wept more sorely than ever. It was as if, though suffering greatly, she still in a way was enjoying this release from the torments shut up all that day, and many other days, in her mind.

"Sitting in the pictures," she sobbed, "I made a vow, and I prayed to God to gie me strength to keep it."

Mary and John waited.

"I vowed that if ever he spoke to me again aboot leaving his school I'd take him at his word. If he was twenty times as clever, is it worth the poisoning of a' oor lives? Whiles I thin' it's been a punishment to me for being sae proud. Ither women I passed in my rags, I smiled doon at them. Their sons were ordinary boys, no' brilliant like mine. On my knees wi' my hands in dirty water, I have had contempt for Mrs. Dawson, whose son's a dunce. But it seems he's a kind-herted boy, trusted by everybody; and that's mair important than being clever."

"I've always said so." Mary couldn't resist those words,

284

lthough, a moment after, she looked at her brother with pity
nd contrition, for she knew she'd betrayed him.

"Aye, that's true, Mary," wept her mother. "You've always
aid so. God forgie me, I thocht it was jealousy speaking in
ou."

John rose then to go through to his bed. Never before had
e felt so exhausted, so utterly at everybody's mercy. His eyes
vould hardly stay open even to watch his mother, who loved
im and who was his enemy. Her weeping had become merely
nother disturbing sound like the clock's unsteady ticking, the
ettle's whimpers, the fall of coals in the grate. As for what she
vas saying, despite its dreadful menace to him, his brain could
carcely understand it now, far less devise answers and evasions.

Once, making an agonising effort, he thought: Is this all?
s it just the same old story all over again, my mother in misery
ecause of our poverty and my shame of it and her? Did she
eally stay away all evening just because she was afraid I'd be
ngry with her for going to the Academy? Is this all the reason?
Yes, he thought, it does seem so.

Then, as if outside his control, his thought changed and
there now seemed to be behind his mother's weeping some far
leeper, some fatal reason, hidden from him, hidden perhaps
rom his mother herself. But what it was, he could not in his
great weariness seek out, any more than he could tell why the
lock for a minute or two would tick regularly, and then for
the next few seconds would gasp and hiccup.

"John," called Mary, urgently.

He halted at the door.

"Usual time in the morning, remember."

He nodded. Tomorrow was a school day: he supposed it
would be the usual time for getting up.

His sister looked long at him, at first with a strange stern
impartiality, but soon with a smile of complete surrender. She
left her mother's side and going over put her arms round him
and pressed him close, with her face against his black hair. It
was not the first time she had embraced him; often, as two
lonely children with their mother out at work, she'd comforted

him and tried to soothe away his fears. Since then, however, she had grown up and made the discovery that fortune and their mother favoured him. From that time she had never as much as nudged him in affection.

"Don't worry," she whispered. "It's been a great strain on her."

He sighed.

Their mother still wept.

"I'll talk to her," went on Mary, still in a whisper. "But of course it'll really depend on you."

He tried to nod, though he wasn't sure what depended on him.

"No more complaints, mind. We're poor, John, and you've just got to face it. Of course people will be nasty, but that's no reason why you should cringe before them or run away. If Dawson sneers at you, laugh at him."

Dawson would never sneer at him, and not many people would be nasty. He tried, but could not tell her that. Instead he yawned and shivered.

"Good night," she said. "Everything will seem brighter in the morning."

He nodded.

Five minutes later he was sound asleep.